Bear

Rebel Wayfarers MC
Book #3

MariaLisa deMora

Kristiann, xoxo MariaLisa deMora

Edited by Hot Tree Editing

Melissa Gill @ MGBookcovers and Designs

First Printing 2014

ISBN 13: 978-0990447344

DEDICATION

To love is to risk not being loved in return. To hope is to risk pain. To try is to risk failure, but risk must be taken, because the greatest hazard in life is to risk nothing. –Leo Buscaglia

To my fracas-causing bestie, Hollie. Boom.

CONTENTS

ACKNOWLEDGMENTS

While the idea for this book was percolating before I did a solo hike on a section of the Appalachian Trail in Georgia, spring of 2014, it was vague. There was no clear character study, nor even a complete concept for the story itself. I was still actively working on *Slate* at the time, not *Bear*, so it certainly wasn't top of mind. That all changed the moment I met a man on-trail who had recently separated from the Navy. I spoke with him for what seemed like forever, and his open, comfortable personality shone like a bright beacon for me. I went to sleep that night in the hostel at Neel's Gap and dreamed, then woke myself at 3 a.m. to jot desperate notes on my phone. Because from that conversation, I knew exactly what Bear (the man) needed. I knew who he was as a person.

Combine that encounter with my first glimpse of Mandy Hollis' brilliant photography that now graces Bear's cover, and I also knew the central theme of the story. One single additional image from the same shoot gave me even more insight into the man and his history, about his pain and triumph. And so the story was born.

Over the past year, since beginning this writing gig, I've been blessed to both strengthen existing relationships, and develop new friendships with a wide variety of people. Each of these people have made my life better in so many ways. I am blessed.

Hollie, my best friend, you should hear yourself in the voices in this book because much of what they say could have been taken directly from our conversations. Lub joo, woman!

Brenda, thank you for reminding me every day that life is good, and gifts such as this experience should not be taken for granted.

Andrea, thank you for putting up with me and treating me like I'm normal, even when I'm editing. Remember, keep the tequila coming and no one gets hurt!

I have two of the world's best critique partners in my friends LeeAnn and Kristen. Thanks for helping keep me on track with your honest emotional responses and attention to detail. You've made this story better, never doubt that.

To the Fort Wayne motorcycle riders and club members who tolerated my persistent questions with grace and amusement, becoming alpha readers (Small leap, because they're already alpha bikers!) and letting me know when I got it right—thankee kindly. We'll have a couple rounds on me, yeah?

Kayla the Bibliophile, here's hoping I continue to provide you goose bumps and tears for many books to come. Muuuwah!

Melissa Gill, your enthusiasm for my vision is contagious and girl, I wanna catch what you have!

Miranda, I meant what I said. Because you are generous with your time, expertise, reassurances, and laughter, you deserve more.

You there, yeah you, reading this. *Thank you.* You readers have all voted with your wallets, and it's because of each and every one of you we'll see more of our favorite Rebels, yeah?

Finally, last but certainly not least, to Rob Kula, inspiration for Bear, thank you for your service to our blessed nation. You are a good man and one I am honored to have met. Hike your own hike, and live well, yeah?

~ML

BEAR

Prologue

Rob smiled up at Ashley from his prone position on the sandy beach. "Sweetness, did you know you are the most important woman in my life? I love you, Ash," he said thoughtfully. She nodded, brown eyes twinkling as she grinned down at him. "I love you so much," he told her, reaching his arms up and gathering her to him as she fell into them.

"I love you, too," she whispered in his ear. Laughing, she kissed his cheek and then with a grin, she rubbed wet sand into his hair, pulling away and hopping up from the sand.

"Oh, I'm gonna get you for that," he yelled at her as she stopped, barely out of reach, holding her stomach and laughing.

Rolling to his feet, tearing down the beach after her as she sprinted away, he called, "Last one to the blanket buys lunch." She glanced over her shoulder at him and put her head down, arms pumping as she ran hard towards the section of beach they'd claimed as their own with a blanket and lounge chairs.

Rob slowed down with a smile, letting her pull ahead of him, watching as her long, blonde ponytail swung back and forth with her efforts, brilliant in the sunshine. She was so beautiful, and he was astonished every time he realized she was his.

Looking ahead, he saw they had a visitor and knew the moment she saw the person sitting in one of the lounge chairs, because she angled her trajectory towards the chair, leaping over it at the last moment and scattering sand all over her target.

"Aahhh, not on my dress," came a yell from the chair, tempered with laughter. Ashley danced on the blanket, stomping her feet and waving her arms in the air with a wide grin on her face. "I won! I won! I beat you, Daddy!"

Jerking awake, Rob jackknifed up off the couch to his feet, walking stiffly across the room. It was no use; he could never go anywhere to get away, but he just had to move. Breathing hard, he leaned his back against the wall, looking down at his hands, curling them into fists over and over in an effort to control the shaking.

He saw drops of something on his chest and stomach, and lifting a hand to his face, he found it wet. He hadn't even realized he was crying. Scrubbing the tears away with his palms, he held his hands out again, seeing the tremors were beginning to subside. He hated these fucking dreams; they destroyed him for days. He would much rather not dream at all, not think, not remember.

Twenty-five years ago, life was simple and easy. When he was thirteen, his parents had moved the family from Painted Post, New York to Bayonne, New Jersey for his dad's job. He went to school, saw his friends, hung out, and went home...rinse and repeat.

Hell, even just eleven years ago, life had still been easy and good, predictable. Go home and love on his two angels, deploy and sink below the sea, visit ports of call so he could buy things for his family...rinse and repeat.

Now, his life consisted of a new name in a new city; he'd gotten as far away as he could from where he'd lived with his wife and daughter, from his family. He was Bear, badass enforcer for a Chicago MC, had hundreds of brothers, and lived a loveless life. Wake up, fuck somebody up, come home alone...rinse and repeat. Life was fucking easy.

Pulling in a deep breath, he counted to ten and then slowly released it, looking down at his hands. Steady and rock-solid now, it seemed the moment had passed. He grabbed a bottle of water from the refrigerator, intending to head over to the corner of the apartment that held his desk. He spent hours working on the computer. It was engrossing, and the required preciseness of his work soothed him.

Pausing, he stopped and turned, going to the couch and sitting down instead. He reached behind the table next to the couch, pulling out a battered acoustic guitar. Settling the PRS across his knee, he hunched over the instrument, aptly named Angelus, and set his fingers to the frets and strings. Bear closed his eyes, hearing the music in his head. Slowly, his hands began to move, and he softly played the intro to a classical piece.

1 - Beginnings

"You'll see, Robby. The house is wonderful, and Bayonne has so many things to do." His mother twisted around in the front seat of the car to talk to him. "You're going to love it here." Her gaze swept to his father, who was driving. "Isn't he going to love it, Douglas?"

"Maggie," his father scolded, "leave him alone. It's okay to be sad to say goodbye. Painted Post is all he's known. Let's give him a couple of days to adjust before you start the selling spiel." Robby was silently grateful and caught his dad's eyes in the rearview mirror. With a nod, his dad acknowledged him, turning his eyes back to the road in front of them.

Looking out the windows at the buildings and traffic surrounding them, Rob didn't know about loving it, but there sure was a lot more to look at here than in the little town where he'd grown up in upstate New York. He'd always enjoyed watching people, paying close attention to their puzzles, how they fit into roles and surroundings. There'd be more people to watch here, that was for sure.

He smirked at a memory. He'd been the only one to figure out their math teacher was nailing the art teacher last year. When he casually mentioned the relationship to Mr. Rasmussen, the math teacher, the man had about gone ballistic. *Who knew it was against policy for teachers to see each other?* He'd gotten good math grades out of the deal, and for his silence, Ms. Pettigrew tutored him for free, letting him use her computer programs to enhance some of his drawings.

When asked how he'd put it together, he wasn't able to articulate it, because most of the knowing was tied up in the differences of how they acted when they were together. He'd seen small, casual touches in the hallway, and then watched them head into the teacher's lounge a strict three minutes apart, never together. In all honesty, it was as much about what they didn't do as what they did.

Bayonne had so many people out and on the streets; he couldn't wait to start exploring. His dad pulled the car up in front of a two-story house with a porch running the width of the structure. There was a cement walk splitting what looked like five whole blades of grass heading to the front, but the best thing of all were piles of bikes in the yards of the houses to either side, which meant kids lived there.

"The movers will be here this afternoon with the van, boys, and I want to get everything swept and mopped before they show up," Mom told them. He and his dad groaned, their eyes catching in the mirror again as they grinned nearly identical grins. "Might as well get started, Robby," Dad said, opening his door.

Hours later, Robby fell face first onto the couch, letting his body bounce on the cushions. "No more, Mom. Please." His voice was muffled into the fabric. "I beg of you. No more. Mercy. Have mercy." Something swatted his butt and he jerked, rolling off the couch onto the floor. "Hey!" he yelled, looking up at his mom with a scowl.

"Just making sure you could still move." She laughed, twirling the dishtowel again. "I'll get sheets on your bed so you can go to sleep when you are ready. Why don't you go outside and sit for a bit? Your dad bought some soda; you can have one if you want."

Scrambling to his feet, he headed into the kitchen, seeing the brown bottles on the counter. Taking an opener out of the drawer, he popped the lid off the bottle of root beer and went out the front door. Sitting on the brick wall surrounding the porch, he leaned back against the pillar, shifting and adjusting to get comfortable on the hard surfaces as he drank the soda.

He'd only been outside a few minutes when there was a yell from the street, and he looked up to see a mixed-age group of about eight kids walking slowly towards his house. "Hey there, what's your name?" That was a girl's voice, but he couldn't see which of the kids had spoken.

"Robby," he yelled back, setting down the empty bottle. "What's yours?"

The leader of the group looked to be a boy who had to be sixteen. There was movement behind him, and a blonde girl about Robby's age stepped into view. "I'm Andrea Graham, and this is my brother Joel," she said, pointing to the boy, who was huge in comparison to her petite frame. The rest of the kids introduced themselves, but he only had eyes for Andrea; with her blonde hair and gamine features, he thought she looked like an angel.

"Want to go walking with us?" she asked Robby, and her brother frowned. She punched him in the shoulder and he made a show of wincing and rubbing it with a grin on his face.

"I better not tonight. We just moved in and there're still boxes to unpack," he said and she looked disappointed.

"Go ahead, Robby," his mom's voice came from the doorway. "You are released into the wild, young man. Just be home before it gets too dark."

"Yay," Andrea said, holding out her hand. Robby jumped off the porch, walking out to where Andrea and Joel stood. Taking her hand in his, he followed as she pulled him up the street, giving him a tour of the neighborhood as the other kids dispersed to their homes. Her and Joel's house was right next to his, and she told him Joel was her oldest brother, but she had two more who were younger.

Robby was an only child and couldn't imagine sharing space with so many people. "Is it hard to find time to be by yourself with three brothers?" he asked curiously.

She blushed and ducked her head. “I have a place I go when I want to be alone. Well, I used to go there.”

“Why can’t you go there now?” he asked, tilting his head.

Joel laughed. “Because her ‘alone place’ is the treehouse in your backyard. Now you’ve moved in, Dad told Drea she can’t use it anymore.”

Robby smiled, asking incredulously, “There’s a treehouse in my backyard? I *have* a backyard?”

Acting silly in an effort to put Andrea at ease, he jumped around for a minute. “I have a backyard! Yay! With a treehouse! Whoop!”

She slapped his shoulder, but not hard. “Stop making fun of me,” she said, and he sobered, looking at her.

“I would never make fun of you,” he said and paused, “and if you want to, you can still use the treehouse to be alone. We’ll have to work out a signal or something, so I know not to bother you.”

Rewarded with a brilliant smile, he was stunned. As she walked down the street towards their houses, Robby tried to gather his scattered thoughts and vowed he’d do anything as long as she’d smile at him like that again.

***

Four years later

“Mom,” he argued with a sigh, “I don’t want to go back to the hospital. Dad’ll be home tomorrow, so why do I have to go tonight?” Rob stood in the doorway to the kitchen, hands hanging onto the top doorframe, biceps bunching, and his lean frame stretching as he watched his mom drape the wet dishcloth across the handle of the stove. He saw her bite her lips, dragging them in-between her teeth and pressing down hard. She stood still for a second, then blew out a breath and looked up at him.

"Because I want you to go with me, Rob. I'd like some company on the drive," she said softly, "and your dad would be happy to see you, I know. Plus, he expects you to eat the nasty Jell-O so the nurses will leave him alone."

Rob shook his head. "Nuh uh, I hate squishy food. Plus, I wanted to ask Drea to come over and help me with intro calculus. I'm having trouble with the homework. Or...maybe she can come to the hospital with us? She and I can work in the car, and that way, if the Jell-O is *lime*, she can eat it." He grinned. Everyone knew she had a penchant for citrus things, and he was pretty sure even gross Jell-O wasn't excluded from that.

"Sounds like a good compromise." She nodded, turning to take the dishcloth back in her hands, wiping across an already clean countertop.

"Mom," he said softly, coming up behind her and putting his hands on her shoulders, "he's going to be okay. He's too stubborn for anything else."

She laughed, her voice breaking as she covered her mouth with one hand. "I know, Rob. It's gonna be okay. Go ahead and call Andrea; see if she can go." She reached her hand up and covered his, patting softly. "Thank you," she said as he turned away.

"No prob, Mom," he threw back at her. "No prob."

It was hard to believe they'd lived here four years already. The time had flown past. Drea had become his best friend right away, and now two years into high school, they still did almost everything together. Rob walked through the house, grabbed the phone to call her, and fell back onto the couch, waiting for her to answer. A little startled when a masculine voice came on the line, Rob sat up, grinning. "Holy crap, Joel, is that you? Man, when did you get home? God, it's good to hear your voice."

"Just walked through the fucking door, kid. You want Drea?" her brother asked.

"Hold on. How was boot camp?" Rob wasn't ready for Joel to hand the phone off. He'd joined the military after graduation, had been gone for weeks, and Rob wanted to hear all about it. "Is the Navy treating you well, Joel?"

"Eight weeks of hell, but worth it," Joel said. "The Navy is the best thing to ever happen to me. We'll catch up soon, Rob. Here's Drea."

"Rob?" Her voice came over the phone, laughing. "Calc, right? What time do you want me to come over?"

"How do you know that's what I called for?" He made a face and grumbled into the phone. "Shoot, I'm not even calling about homework. Mom wondered if you wanted go to the hospital with us to see Dad." He paused a beat. "You know, in case he has lime Jell-O." He waited for her laughter to die away, and continued, "Plus, yeah...maybe I thought you could help explain the homework on the way."

Andrea laughed again, and he heard Joel's voice rumbling in the background. "When are you leaving?" she asked Rob.

"Soon," he said, "but that was before I knew J-Boss was home. If you want to stay and visit with him, I totally get it. He said he'd barely walked in, and I know he's only got a couple days before he has to report to Virginia, right?"

"Pffftt. He's going to be swallowed alive for hours by the terrors. I'll get my time with him in the morning before they wake up," she said, referring to their younger brothers. "I'll head over now. Meet you outside?" she asked, and then hung up when he gave assent.

At the hospital, he and Andrea sat on the floor of his dad's room, leaning up against the wall at the foot of the bed. They were looking over his work, the textbook and handwritten papers spread out on the floor around them. She was sitting close against his side so she could coach him through his mistakes. Every time her arm brushed against him, his breath caught in his throat. This was slow torture, because he'd liked her as long as he'd known her. But as much as he wanted her to view him differently, he knew she looked at him as a fourth brother, not as boyfriend material.

"This is wrong, too. Everything on this problem from here forward needs to be reworked, Rob," she said, tilting her head up to look at him. "I know you can do this. What's the problem? Are you off because of your dad?" she asked softly. He looked out the door and across the hallway to where his mom and dad were sitting in a waiting room, their heads close together as they talked.

"He's not getting any better, you know?" He ran a hand nervously through his hair, looking down at her. "Working in the shipyards ruined his lungs, and he's just not gonna get better." Closing his eyes, he leaned his head back against the wall.

Something soft brushed his cheek and he jerked as he turned his head, finding Andrea's lips nearly touching his, her eyes wide. They froze and stared at each other, a fraction of an inch between them until he leaned in and pressed his lips to hers gently, then pulled back. "Thanks," he said softly, leaning his head back again. He couldn't believe he'd kissed Andrea. *Oh, God, she'll hate me now. It's gonna be weird. Everything is gonna be weird.*

He felt her head settle on his shoulder and cracked one eye open, stealthily looking down at her. There was a smile on her lips and she lifted her hand, running it up his arm and circling his bicep. He held still, closing his eye again. Slowly relaxing, he bit his lip when her other hand stroked tenderly across the backs of his knuckles. Holding his breath, he turned his hand over, and when she threaded her fingers with his, he blew his breath out in a relieved sigh.

Holy crap. Drea is holding my hand. He grinned and tilted his chin up a little more, tightening his hand around hers. He'd kissed her, and now she had her head on his shoulder and was holding his hand. *Holy crap. Best day ever.*

***

Two years later

"It's warm enough. Let's go to Wolf's Pond, out on Staten Island," Rob suggested, throwing a towel and a couple of water bottles into his bag. Looking over at Andrea, his heart swelled. God, she was so beautiful, and she was his. She loved him. He took the two steps to where she was seated on the edge of his bed, pulling her up and into his arms. "Kiss me, sugar," he whispered, gazing down into her deep brown eyes.

"Insatiable, that's what you are," she groused, going up on her tiptoes to brush her lips across his.

"A real kiss," he growled, pursuing her mouth as she went to pull away.

She smiled, reaching up with both hands to cup his jaw. "Rob, I love you," she whispered and pulled his face down to meet hers, her tongue questing along his lips, seeking entrance.

Rob groaned, opening to her, relishing this rare instance of boldness from his girl as she stroked her tongue against his. Her fingers caressed his face, one hand sliding up to cup his neck as she tipped her head for better access to his mouth.

Knowing she could feel his erection where it was pressed between them, Rob broke the kiss, placing his forehead against hers as he shifted away. Andrea's breath came as harshly as his own. They'd been treading a fine line for weeks and were both frustrated, but neither wanted to take that final step yet. They had graduation and the upcoming summer to get through.

She was taking an intern job in her uncle's law firm in Manhattan, and would be staying with him and her aunt in their home on Long Island over the summer. Rob had joined the Navy, following in Joel's footsteps, and he would be headed to Chicago and boot camp not long after school was over.

After his dad's death two years ago, he and his mom had been going through papers when they found a letter addressed to Rob. It was from his dad, written right after he'd gotten the diagnosis. In it, his dad urged him to follow his dreams and not remain in Bayonne simply because that was home and known. It had encouraged him to travel too, and that's one of the things he was hoping to get out of the Navy.

"Rob—" she started in a husky tone, and he stopped her words with a kiss.

"I know, Andrea. God, I know." His voice was breathy and he took another step back, running his hands up and down her arms.

She pulled in a shaky breath, saying softly, "So...Wolf's Pond?"

As the sun headed down to the western horizon, they were lying on towels positioned on the narrow strip of sand that separated the trees from Raritan Bay. It had been a good day; they'd played in the water until exhausted, and then eaten the lunch Andrea had packed, feeding each other bites between kisses. Rob realized he wanted to spend every day just like this—not on the water, not playing, but with Andrea. Never away, always with her.

He reached his hand out and clasped one of hers, tugging lightly. Lying on her stomach, she raised her head from where it was pillowed on her other arm, arching her back as she lifted her shoulders. "What?" she asked, blinking against the slanting sunshine.

Rob sat up, the idea gaining focus in his head. "Marry me."

"What?" she exclaimed, tilting her head to look at him.

"Marry me," he repeated, tugging her hand again.

She sat up, folding her legs and sitting back on her heels, their joined hands stretching between them. "You want to get married?"

"Yeah. I don't want to spend another day without you being mine. I know what our folks will say, but I love you. We're not too young to know what we want, and I want you for always, Drea." He reached out and touched her cheek with the back of his fingers. "I love you," he repeated in a softer tone, "for always."

"When?" She was a little short of breath, looking at him with wide eyes as the idea took shape.

"As soon as we can." Grinning, he pulled a strand of her hair forward and ran it between his fingers. "Then we can be together. I want to spend the rest of my life with you. I know you've got the intern thing, but I'll be gone to boot camp most of that time anyway. This way, you'll be my dependent too. I've been worried about how we'd be able to stay in touch, but if you are my wife, it will make it easier when I'm in port and stuff. Kinda like how you can check up on Joel, since he's your brother. You'll be my family."

"Okay," she said softly and squeaked when he gathered her up in his arms.

"I'm so happy right now, Andrea. Love you," he said. "So much."

2 - Made for me

Standing at the front of the church two months later, Rob was waiting impatiently for Andrea. "Take it easy, Rob. She's coming; I promise," came from beside him, and he looked at his best man.

"It's taking so long. What's taking so long?" he whispered. "You sure you've got the ring, Joel?"

Andrea's brother patted the front of his dress whites. "Right here, got it right here. Easy."

Kelly, Andrea's best friend and the maid of honor, finished walking up the aisle, stepping into her place on the other side of the altar and the music changed tempo. Everyone in the church turned to look at the entryway, and Andrea appeared in her white gown, standing there with her hand wrapped tightly around her dad's arm. He drank in the sight of her; he'd been kept away for two whole days while both their moms had worked through all the final details of his wedding with Andrea.

"Breathe, Rob, or you are gonna pass out. Suck some air, man." He heard Joel's whisper and realized he was seeing dark spots because his lungs had stopped working. Taking in a slow, deep breath, he watched her pacing towards him, moving confidently into their new life together. She was beautiful beyond belief, and he was so very in love with her.

Her dad stopped next to him, and it wasn't until the priest cleared his throat that he realized he was still staring at Andrea, honing in on her like a compass. Taking a breath and turning, he faced the front, listening as her father recited his part of the ceremony, and then placed her hand in his with a stern look, shaking his finger reprovingly at Rob.

He grinned his one-sided smile at Mr. Graham and sidled closer to Andrea, pulling her hand to his chest. Her eyes were squeezed shut and she was shaking her head. "Baby? Sugar, what's wrong?" he whispered, leaning close to her.

"Daddy cracks me up," she whispered with a laugh in her voice, opening her eyes to smile up at him. "Nothing's wrong, Rob. Everything is right."

"If you are finished, may we continue?" The priest spoke with a humorous tone and Rob whipped his head back to the front again as tittering laughter came from the pews behind them. He tried to pay attention to the rest of the ceremony and instructions, but his sole focus was Andrea standing beside him. In another few minutes, she'd be his wife, and his thoughts were jumbled. They would be married. Mrs. Robert Crew. Andrea Elaine Crew. Drea Crew. Mr. and Mrs. Rob Crew. This was happening right now. His wife. Her husband.

He felt a tugging on his arm and looked down to see her smiling up at him. She mouthed, *rings*, at him, and he blushed, holding out his hand to Joel without looking while she retrieved his ring from Kelly. With the ring in his hand, he faced her. All he could see were her eyes looking up at him with so much love and trust that he thought he might burst.

The priest grasped their hands in his, praying over the rings as he blessed their marriage vows. Rob slid the ring halfway onto her finger, holding her hand gently in his shaking ones as he said, "I give you this ring as a token of my love, trust, respect, and faithfulness to you. I love you, and this ring symbolizes the endless nature of that love."

Seating the ring on her finger, he stooped and kissed her hand softly. She giggled and slid his ring on his finger, looking into his eyes and saying, "I give you this ring as a symbol of our vows, with all that I am and all that I have, I give you me. With love and affection, respect and honor, trust and faithfulness. I love you, Rob, for always."

The rest of the ceremony went by quickly, and soon, he was granted the opportunity to kiss his bride. Carefully cupping her face in his hands, he lifted her lips to his, kissing her softly and reverently as she placed her hands on his biceps. Pulling his lips away, he rested his forehead against hers. "I love you, Andrea Crew."

She smiled and responded, "And I love you, Robert Crew."

At the end of the night, after what seemed like millions of pictures, the cake cutting, first dance, and toasts galore, Rob held Andrea in his arms for one last dance. Swaying together on the dance floor, he laced his fingers around her waist, pulling her tightly to him. "My wife," he whispered against the side of her head. "Are you about ready to go, sugar?"

Humming softly along with the song, she tipped her head back to look at him. "Yes, I'm ready to be alone with you, husband." The heat in her eyes created an urgency in him, and he grabbed her hand, dragging her off the dance floor and towards the door. "Rob," she laughed, "we have to let people know we're leaving."

Tilting his head, he looked at the ceiling in frustration. "Why? Why do we have to let people know?"

She laughed at him again. "So they can throw rice and bird seeds at us and make lewd comments about our upcoming nocturnal activities. We've waited our whole lives for this, Rob; we can wait another five minutes."

He pulled her to him, folding himself around her and kissing her fiercely. "Andrea, we need to go," he growled in her ear, nipping at her earlobe. "Let's get this moving. If we have to amuse our friends, then let's get going. But the first guy to mention our 'nocturnal activities' is gonna earn a beatdown, so warn those brothers of yours."

"Mom," she called loudly, "we're leaving in three minutes. Rally the troops." Reaching up, she cupped a hand around the back of his neck, pulling him down to meet her lips to kiss him again. Breathing hard as she broke the kiss, she called again, "Mom, we're leaving in one minute." He grinned against her lips and wrapped his arms around her, lifting her against him to twirl around, pressing his erection into her soft belly.

"Mom," she whispered, "time's up."

Driving away from the reception in his pickup, cans and noisemakers dragging behind them, he looked over at her. She was shaking seeds and rice out of her hair, laughing. "Uuugggh. Some of it went down my gown." Pushing one hand down into the bodice of her dress, she complained, "It itches, Rob." She looked over at him and he caught his breath at her smile as he'd done every day since he first met her.

Reaching, he grabbed her hand, pulling it over to rest on his thigh. "I love you," he told her for the hundredth time that day. "Do you remember the first day we met?" Tilting his head, he watched her face as it softened.

"Yeah. You looked lost and tired sitting on the porch. Joel had just finished with baseball practice and we were on the way home. But I wanted to talk to you, so I made up a story that we were walking through the neighborhood." She grinned. "Joel was pissed until he got a chance to talk to you and found out you'd played on a travel team in New York. You became his best and most secret weapon in pickup games that summer."

"You wanna know what I remember most about that day?" he asked her.

She nodded. "Yeah, we've never talked about it."

"Your smile…and how Joel called you Drea. I was glad you weren't an Andy, because you seemed special to me. Drea was unique, more singular, and seemed to fit you." He lifted her hand, kissing her fingers. "But your smile was what sealed the deal. It was so bright, and when you smiled at *me*—when we were talking about the treehouse, and you smiled at me—I remember taking a step back, because it was so powerful. I'd do anything to keep that smile on your face, sugar."

Pulling up at the hotel, where they'd spend the next two nights, he looked over at her, smiling his one-sided grin. "Are you ready, Mrs. Crew?" She nodded, and he shook his head. "Stay right where you are. Don't move." Opening his door, he ran around the back of the truck to her, handing the keys to the valet. Lifting her into his arms, he walked towards the entrance.

"What are you doing, crazy man?" she asked, wrapping an arm around his neck.

"Well, it's gonna be a while before we have our own place, so I'm just gonna carry you over every threshold I see for the next two days," he said, leaning down to kiss her. They were already checked in; Joel had taken care of the hotel earlier in the day, and had brought the key to the wedding with him.

"Oh, no, Rob. What about my bag? We were in such a rush I forgot to grab it," she gulped, biting her bottom lip nervously. "I need it. It's got my present to you in it."

"No worries, sugar. Your bag's upstairs waiting on us," he said. Moving his hand, he flipped her dress out of the way to push the button for the elevator. Turning around with her in his arms, he faced the hotel lobby, taking in the amused and approving looks they were receiving from the hotel clients and residents. "This is my wife," he called loudly. "This is Mrs. Robert Crew."

There was a smattering of applause and calls of well wishes. The elevator dinged behind him, doors sliding open, and he backed up into the car as she buried her face in his shoulder, sighing in embarrassment. "God, Rob, why would you do that?"

“Because I’m so proud to be your husband.” He tightened his arms and kissed her again. “I love you and want everyone to know how lucky I am you love me back.”

Once in the room, there was just enough light to see the fruit and snacks arrayed on a table, water and soft drinks with a bucket of ice nearby. He was still carrying her and he stopped to lean in and press his lips against hers. “Andrea, you made me so happy today. My wife. Mine.” He exhaled against her lips, gently kissing her.

Relaxing his arms, he let her slide down, holding her close even after her feet were on the ground. “I want to get out of this suit,” he said. “Come on. Let’s get changed.”

Waiting on her to come out of the bathroom, Rob sat on the bed in only his boxers, leaning against the headboard. He’d brought over some water, and in his brief exploration of the suite, he had found where Joel had left condoms in the drawer of the nightstand.

He snorted and shook his head at the idea of Andrea’s brother leaving protection so he could have sex with the man’s little sister. As far as he was concerned, that protection would go unused. He couldn’t wait to start their lives together, with all the mess and love that came with it.

***

There was a slight noise as the door opened, and he looked up to see his wife padding gracefully towards him. She was dressed in a short, sheer nightgown that did nothing to hide her stunning body. Her breasts lifted the material out, showing her hardened nipples in the center of rosy areolas. From there, the gown fell in transparent folds that swayed halfway to her knees. Her movements had caused the see-through fabric to slide between her thighs as she walked, becoming taut and outlining the blonde curls nestled between her legs.

He couldn't believe she was finally his wife, and that they were together. They'd be together forever, because now he had her, there was no way he'd ever let her go. He didn't have to wait to hold her any longer; she was his and he could love her like he'd wanted to for so long.

"Sugar," he said, not recognizing his own voice as it growled out of him thick with desire, "you are so fucking beautiful. I am so lucky. I don't know why you would ever settle for me, but I thank God you did." He held out his hand and gave an impatient gesture to hurry her. "Come here. Come lay with me."

Andrea smiled at him and put her hand in his as she sat on the edge of the bed. He tugged gently, and she swung her legs up, turning onto her side next to him. She slid in close, putting her head on his shoulder. "Hey, husband, do you like your present?" she whispered the question, running one hand up the side of his face and into his hair, cupping the back of his head. "I love you."

His breath whooshed out of him and he shifted, bracing himself on either side of her head with his forearms, leaning over her and smiling down. "I love it. God, I love you, too, baby." He held her for minutes, looking at her, breathing in the subtle scent that meant Andrea to him. He needed her to understand how important she was to him, what being her husband meant to him. "Baby, look at you. You are so beautiful. I love all the parts of you. All of you.

"You have such pretty eyes, Drea. Stunning, like the rest of you. Some days, they are brown like liquid chocolate, with light, shifting colors in the sunlight. Then at other times, like now, they are so dark and intense." He stroked her hair back from her face with his palm. "I've wanted to make love to you for a long, long time. Now, it's hard to believe you're actually mine. It's finally our time. Our first time."

He lowered his face, covering her lips with his own, nibbling at her bottom lip and sucking it into his mouth. Releasing it gradually, he slanted his mouth over hers, questing and probing, asking her to open for him. Stroking her tongue with his, he took her mouth again and again, the kiss growing deep and demanding, giving her a glimpse of the passion he held brutally in check so they could go slow. It was hard, because he wanted her so badly.

He broke off, breathing hard, and pressed his cheek against hers until he regained some control. It would be their first time together, their first ever; he hoped he'd be able to make it good for her. Over the years, they'd done a lot of petting, and some of it had gotten intense, but they'd held back from crossing the line and making love.

When he could breathe near-normally again, he pulled back, looking into her eyes. "I love you, sugar. Oh, baby, your hair, so pretty." He leaned down, kissing the tip of her nose. "Gorgeous. Such a unique color, it looks like pale, white gold. The sun bleaches the color even whiter in the summer, but during the winter, that gold comes back, rich and beautiful, matchless."

"But, God, your mouth," he murmured against her lips, "I could kiss you all day, baby. Your lips call me, even from across a crowded room. They are so soft and inviting, and I could lick and nibble them all day. Your tongue slides along mine, making me want something more, something rougher, making me want to be inside you. You taste intoxicating, like the sweetest champagne, and I want to eat you up. I want to get love drunk on you."

She shifted under him and he froze, worriedly asking, "Am I too heavy?"

"No," she reassured him with a slow smile. "I didn't expect you to start inventorying the things you like about me. Babe, you know I'm a sure thing, right? You don't have to try to win me. Limited wooing required."

"Sugar, I don't think of you as a sure thing. I don't want to ever take you for granted. Just gimme a minute and see how this looks from my perspective," he responded leisurely, his hands framing her face, stroking her hair back as he stared down at her. "You're beautiful, poised, and so smart. God, you're perfect."

He gave her a small smile, "Now, take a gander at me. I'm average, nothing special, not wealthy, not handsome—just ordinary. You could have anyone; absolutely anyone would grovel at your feet. So, why would you ever want to be with me? I need to remind you every day that you've made the right choice. I adore you and wanna show you how much I love you. You are so important to me. My angel. Can't live without you."

"You are not ordinary," she argued, reaching up to stroke her fingertips down his cheek. "Exceptional, beyond the pale, yes. Never average. Not to me. To me, Rob Crew, you are everything."

Rob stroked the backs of his knuckles down the side of her face and along the line of her jaw. Cupping her chin, he tilted her mouth up to his again; he couldn't get enough of her. The soft kiss quickly became hard and demanding, his tongue thrusting into her mouth and sliding along her own again and again, bruising and rough. When her breathing grew ragged and her mouth greedy on his, he slowed, pulling back to drop kisses along her jaw.

Nibbling her earlobe gently, he moved along her neck to her shoulders, tugging at the neckline of the nightgown to expose her beautiful breasts. Rolling slightly to the side, he cupped them in his hands, his fingers tweaking and teasing her nipples until they were rouged and peaked. She was moving her legs slowly, restlessly pressing and arching up against him. That was good. He wanted her aroused and wet for him.

Kissing across her collarbone, he drew his tongue deliberately down her sternum and she moaned in frustration. "Do you need something?" he inquired softly, his fingers still kneading and teasing her breasts. Her eyes remained closed, but she nodded and ran her fingers through his hair. "What, sugar? Tell me what you want," he whispered, his lips moving back up her chest to her throat.

"Kiss me, Rob," she said, eyes still closed. "Love me." He smiled and laved one nipple with the flat of his tongue, continuing to caress her other breast with his hand. She moaned again, arching up into him, and he sucked her breast into his mouth, licking and nipping at the hard nipple until she cried out.

Skating one hand down her body to the outside of her thigh, he gathered the fabric of her nightgown in his fingers, tugging and dragging it up along her body until he could take it off over her head. He followed the path the hem took along her body, trailing soft kisses along her belly, over her breasts, up her throat, and across her lips.

Impatient with the barrier still between them, he quickly shoved down his underwear and kicked them off the bed. He gathered her up, sliding one hard arm under her back and one around her shoulders, bringing her up alongside him in the bed until he could reach her lips again.

Kissing her deeply once more, his touch roaming across her body, he slipped between her thighs with his hand, groaning into her mouth when his fingers found her wet and slippery. "God, you are so ready for me, beautiful. So ready for us," he whispered, while, as he'd done only once before, he slid a finger inside her, stroking in and out leisurely and using the pad of his thumb to press against and caress her clit.

"Sugar, give me your eyes," he murmured to her. "I want to see you while I love you." Her brown eyes opened, the irises darkened with her desire. "So beautiful," he whispered against her jaw, concentrating on touching her and bringing her to climax on his hand.

Her hips moved, arching up into his touch and he pulled his hand back, eliciting a short noise of disappointment from her that was quickly followed by a deep moan when he thrust two thick fingers deep into her core. Moving them slowly inside her, he was stretching and easing her open when he heard her breath catch. Curious, he repeated the movement that caused the sounds, and watched as her eyes fluttered closed, eyelashes landing on her flushed cheeks.

"Give me your eyes, baby," he reminded her, and her eyelids opened halfway as she looked at him with a sexy curve of her lips. He watched, rapt as they parted slightly, and he echoed the gasp that escaped. She pressed her head back into the pillow, tilting her chin up, and he shifted his position a little, stroking his fingers into her faster, continuing to circle her clit with his thumb.

He propped up on one arm, absorbed in watching her passion as it played out across her face. He whispered to her, dipping his head down beside her ear. "Come for me, baby. I want to feel you clench down on my fingers and come on my hand. Give me you. Let yourself go."

She drew in a quick breath, and then her legs stiffened, trying to close tightly on his hand and arm as he drove his fingers into her faster and deeper. Covering her mouth with his, he swallowed the cries she released as she came hard on his fingers, her hips arching up and holding taut.

Rob swiftly slid between her legs, moving his hand and pressing his pelvis hard against her, grinding into her clit. He wrapped his wet, slippery fingers around his cock, stroking up and over the head, and then down, pulling back and aligning himself with her entrance.

She was still coming down from her explosive orgasm when he pressed himself partway into her. She lifted up to meet him instinctively, drawing him deeper inside. He was breathing hard, holding still as he whispered to her, "God, so hot. I didn't know you'd feel so good, baby. So fucking hot and tight, Andrea." He was panting, trying to retain control, speaking in fractured sentences. "Wet for me. Mine. My first. Your first. So right. Love you. Sugar."

Slowly, his cock slid into her welcoming heat. He paused every few seconds and pulled his hips back a bit, then pressed relentlessly ahead, murmuring and crooning to her all the while. Finally, reaching what he thought was the obstruction he'd been seeking, he stopped and looked down at her face. "Drea, are you okay? Is this okay? Am I hurting you?" Punctuating each question with a kiss, he watched her eyes and face for hurt or discomfort. He wanted this to be something they both remembered with love, not pain.

Andrea tilted her head back, offering her neck to his mouth as she said, "I want you, Rob, all of you. Don't you dare stop now, babe."

He withdrew a couple of inches, then thrust into her and retreated again, setting up a quick, shallow rhythm that was torture. "So fucking tight. You're so tight, like a fitted glove. I don't know if I can—oh, baby." He paused and held still for a minute, panting again.

"Sugar, I'm going to go deep." His voice was harsh, hoarse, and gritty with the strain of holding back. She nodded, seemingly unable to speak as he drew back that couple of inches again and then pushed hard and fast into her, moving past the barrier until he was buried deep inside her. She cried out and tightened, closing her eyes as her hands fisted in the sheets. He stopped moving and watched as a single tear rolled down the side of her face. He kissed it away, and through gritted teeth, he whispered a careful, "Let me know when you're okay."

Stroking her cheeks and jaw with one hand, he brought the other to his mouth and got his first taste of her; sweet and smoky, a little spicy, she tasted as natural on his tongue as the finest whiskey. "Mmm...you taste so good. I can't wait to make you come with my mouth," he murmured into her ear, and it was quiet enough in the room for him to hear how her heartbeat sped up as she listened to him talk about wanting to love her.

"Let me know when you're okay," he whispered again. "Let me know when it's okay to move." He felt her nod against his shoulder and shook his head in answer. "No, I need your words," he told her. "Tell me when you're ready."

She took in a deep breath that pressed her breasts hard against his chest, and said, "It's okay, Rob. It's good. It's easing now, and I want you to move. I want to feel you inside me. Love me."

Rob closed his eyes, leaning his forehead against hers for a second before he moved, thrusting into her again. "Oh, baby, I do love you, no mistake about that. My whole life. Love you. I won't last long. I can already tell. I've wanted this so long—you—ohhh."

Hips shifting up and out, and then down and in, he smoothly slid his cock in and out with deep and long, smooth thrusts, ending each with an arch to his back that massaged the head of his cock against the front wall of her pussy. "You are so hot, like a—" Losing track of what he was going to say, he finished with a groan. "Mmmm."

Her legs tightened again, neck arching up, her head thrown back, and he increased the pace marginally, not wanting to be too rough with her. Sweat dripped off his nose onto her neck and he leaned down, licking across her skin. She moaned and he felt her walls tightening around him deep inside her in the area he'd been certain to stroke against, where his fingers had drawn the greatest response. He'd study her the rest of his life if it meant making her happy. "Feeling good, yeah? My sugar. Love you. Come for me, baby. Let go if you can. Let me love you. Mmmm."

Holding deep, he ground his pelvis against her clit again, his mouth stretched in a small smile as he heard her groan and felt her tense against him more, her hands moving to stroke his biceps and over his shoulders as she trembled underneath him, calling out his name.

"Oh, goddamn, baby," he said, gripping the soft skin on her shoulder lightly between his teeth. "I can't wait; it's too much. I'm gonna come. It's too good. You're too good, sugar. Made for me. Baby." He groaned, sliding his lips across hers and burying his face into her shoulder as he thrust deep and shuddered, the waves of pleasure rising from the base of his spine and spreading across his body. "So good. Love you, my wife. Love you."

He pushed in hard several more times, pausing with each stroke when he was buried as deep inside her as he could go, feeling her arms tighten across his sweat-slick back in response. He came explosively deep within her while she clenched hard around his cock, burying his groan in her neck as he shuddered and shook.

After a few minutes of attempting to catch his breath, he realized he was still holding her tightly and shifted, rolling them onto their sides, face to face. "Andrea," he whispered, kissing her lips, "I love you."

She smiled back at him, eyes hooded with satisfaction, and her tongue slid across his bottom lip. "I love you, too, Rob. Was it okay?"

"Oh, baby, so much better than okay. That was incredible. You are amazing. Everything I've imagined, everything I wanted. Made for me...you were made for me." He nuzzled against the side of her face, dropping small kisses across her cheekbone to her ear.

Her eyes fluttered closed, and he asked with a note of affection in his voice, "Tired?" She nodded, adjusting her body to lay more comfortably against him and then made a noise of disappointment when his cock slipped out of her, having softened in the aftermath of their lovemaking. Shivering as the air moved across her damp skin, she snuggled into him even more.

He kissed her forehead, and then moved off the bed, accompanied by her complaining groan. "I'll be right back, baby." Going to the bathroom, he cleaned himself up and then wet a washcloth with warm water. Returning, he shifted her onto her back in the bed, moving her legs apart with his as he knelt between them. "Cleaning you up, sugar," he explained when she made a questioning noise as he used the wet cloth carefully. *She doesn't seem to have words left,* he thought in amusement. *She's all moans and groans, hmmms and mmmms.*

Surprised at the amount of blood, as he finished wiping and cleaning her off, he asked, “Are you hurting, Andrea?” She shook her head, but he gently caressed her labia, separating and pushing a finger inside her, and he winced as she flinched a bit. Headed back to the bathroom, he dug into his bag for a minute, coming out with a bottle of over-the-counter pain medication.

Grabbing one of the water bottles from beside the bed, he shook two tablets into her hand and pressed the water into her hand. “Take these and we’ll have a nap,” he murmured to her, stroking his fingertips up and down her side, dragging them across her ribs teasingly. “We’ll have a nap. I think we’re both pretty tired.”

She twisted to put the water back on the nightstand, and then snuggled into his side with a smile on her face. “That was pretty good.” Quietly spoken, she waited on an answer.

“I’m glad it was good for you, because for me, it was amazing. So good,” he crooned into her hair. “Made for me.” Tightening his arms around her, he held her as she dozed off, and fell asleep, tumbling into his own sweet dreams soon after.

3 - In the Navy

He'd known from listening to Joel talk that basic training was tough, so he wasn't surprised by that aspect of the experience. He knew it would be hard, and expected he'd be challenged every day. What he hadn't expected was that he'd enjoy it so much. The drill instructors pushed the recruits to the edge every day, forcing them to stretch their capabilities to the max, and he found he was excelling at both the physical challenges and the mental ones. One would think something called 'basic seamanship' shouldn't be that tough, but while it was the most difficult thing he'd ever done, he loved it.

It didn't seem right he'd been here eight weeks already, but tomorrow was graduation. His team had made it through Battle Stations training last week, and they'd earned their U.S. Navy ball caps. All that was left was putting on their dress uniforms and standing in rows in the sunshine for the commanders and their families. Andrea would be here, and he'd get to touch her for the first time since their wedding weekend. They'd been able to talk on the phone only a couple times while he was in basic, and not at all for the last month.

Up for PT early the next morning, there were no days off at basic, no matter the importance of the day's events. By seven a.m., he and the rest of the recruits had readied themselves for the upcoming ceremony. After standing in the sun at attention for a long time, and being officially recognized as no longer recruits but sailors, they were released for liberty call to find their families and loved ones.

He stood still, turning in place and scanning the crowd until he saw familiar white-blonde hair and a wildly waving arm. Keeping his eyes on her as he moved through and past the groups of people between them, he caught partial glimpses of her face, which looked like she was smiling widely.

Rushing the last few steps to him, Andrea wrapped her arms around his neck, lifting up on tiptoes to press her lips against his neck in a series of soft, quick kisses. "Rob, I've missed you." She mumbled, "Love you, love you, love you."

"Oh, sugar," he whispered into her ear, "I've missed you too. God, you feel good. It feels good to hold you. I love you so much, Drea."

Pulling back, she peppered his face with kisses while he grinned at her. "I guess you did miss me, huh?" There was a hand on his shoulder, and he turned to see his father-in-law, Andrew Graham, standing alongside his mother.

He shook Andrew's hand, receiving a head nod along with it, as well as a gruff, "Proud of you, son. Good job." Rob smiled at him as he pulled his mother into a tight hug while keeping one of Andrea's hands in his.

"Hey, Mom," he said. "I did it. I made it."

She stepped back, wiping tears from her face with one hand, and holding onto him with the other one. "I never expected anything less, Rob. I'm so proud of you." Andrea's other hand was on his back, and she pressed her cheek against his arm. He was happy to have her touch him; it felt so good.

"Let's go grab some food," he said. "I have a lot to tell you guys. We've been given liberty until nine."

"Rob," his mother offered, "we can talk on the drive home. Why don't you show us around."

"That's part of what I need to talk about," he grimaced. "I won't be driving home with you. In a couple days, I'm headed to tech training. They want me to do both A School and Power School. They're gonna put me on a submarine, and I have to learn a lot in a short time if I'm going to become a nuclear propulsion plant machinist mate." He grinned at the confusion on his mother's face.

He heard a muffled sob from behind him and gathered Andrea against his chest, holding her gently. "Oh, sugar. Don't cry. Baby, tech training is only six weeks, and then I'll get a week off to come home." He soothed her, stroking her hair slowly. "I didn't know for sure about the evaluation test results until this morning, and it was too late to call and let you know."

"Drea, it's a good opportunity for me...for us. There's a lot of room in this engineering specialty for bumps and promotions. Some of the other jobs they offered are so full people don't move up in rank for years. With this, I'll make E4 fast, and that means more money for us. I want to be able to take care of you, baby. I want you to be proud of me."

She was sobbing against his chest and talking through her tears, but he couldn't understand anything she was saying. "Andrea, easy, now. Easy." He spoke quietly, stroking her hair down her back, pulling her close into him. "Easy. What is it? Is it the six weeks? We'll talk lots. I promise. Tech school is different from boot camp. Easy, sugar. Tell me. Talk to me."

With one hand fisted in his crisp shirt and one hand curled around his neck, she pulled him down to place her mouth beside his ear. "I'm pregnant," she breathed, her voice still hiccupping with sobs.

Rob froze and asked softly, "We're going to have a baby?" She nodded her head, her soft hair grazing the side of his face and neck.

A grin spread across his features, and his joy and pleasure were apparent on his face and in his voice as he spoke louder, no longer questioning. "We're going to have a baby!" He dropped his head down to kiss her neck, whispering into her ear, "I love you, Andrea Crew. A baby. Our baby."

He vaguely heard his mother asking questions, and realized from her tone she hadn't known the news. Turning to look at Andrew's face, he saw surprise there too. His heart swelled as he realized his girl had kept quiet about their baby and told him first.

Arching back, he looked down at her, cupping her face in his hand. "A mother. Andrea, you're going to be a mother. My baby is in you. I can't believe it; this is...wonderful. You are the only woman for me. My love, made for me—the mother of my children."

She smiled up at him, pulling in a shuddering breath as she calmed, his reaction reassuring her. "I'm so glad you're happy, Rob. I didn't know how to tell you. I was afraid you'd be mad. We haven't had much time to ourselves yet, and now we're adding a baby to the mix so soon."

"Oh, baby, how could I ever be mad at you?" he asked softly. "Andrea, you are my breath, my life, my wife." Kissing her leisurely, he reached a hand down to press it flat against her belly. "My baby."

***

"I know, sugar," he said quietly into the phone, speaking over the barely audible sobs, "but it's only another two months and I'll be home. That's only eight weeks, baby. Fifty-six days. You can do this standing on your head." He hated when Andrea cried like this, even if he suspected it was the pregnancy making her moody.

"I'm going to talk to your dad. We need to get an apartment and get you set up in it. Gotta get the princess' room ready, too," he told her. "I know Kelly likes having you as a roomie, but we need more space with Ashley coming."

He heard a hiccupping snort of laughter over the phone and responded, "Yeah, go ahead and laugh, but I'm liking Ashley this week. I keep trying it out. 'Ashley Marie, go to your room', or how about, 'Come to Daddy, Ashley,' for when she's learning how to walk? Yeah? I'm liking Ashley this week."

"You are impossible, Mr. Crew," she told him. "Last week, it was Tiffany, which I hated by the way. There was a Tiffany in my class in grade school, and she was mean. I'm not naming our child Tiffany."

"So definitely not Tiffany, then?" he asked.

"Definitely not, and not Coralee, either. I didn't like that one," she countered.

"Yeah, it didn't have staying power. Coralee only lasted a day." He laughed. "Ashley, though...Ashley has been around for six days so far, and I'm still liking it. Both my angels with 'A' names seems fitting. Andrea and Ashley, my angels."

"It didn't work, you know. I'm not distracted," she told him. "I'm still not happy they extended you by eight more weeks. You've already been gone five months, counting tech. That means I'm going to be almost at term with this pregnancy when you see me next. I'm already so huge you won't know what to do with me."

Rob sighed. "I know, sugar. I'm not happy about it either. We're going to be blacked out for communication most of that time, too, but it's not for long. Remember, fifty-six days and the boat will be in Norfolk and I'll be there with you, right in time for Ashley's grand entrance into the world. And, baby, come on. I know you; you are not huge. You are right-sized for a mamma-to-be. I want pictures, lots of pictures of that belly. And your beautiful face."

"I'll email every day, Rob," she said and he laughed. Being on a sub meant they hardly ever got physical mail, and even email was notoriously unreliable.

"I know you will," he told her. "I'll respond as I can. I gotta go now. I love you, Andrea. Rub your tummy for me, and tell Ashley that Daddy loves her too."

"Crazy man," she muttered. "I love you, too, Rob. Be safe and come home to me."

"I will, sugar. I gotta go," he said again, pausing for a minute. "Hang up for me?"

"God, I hate when you do this," she half-yelled and then was sobbing again. Taking in a deep breath, she said, "Okay, here we go." She hiccupped a sob. "I love you. We're hanging up in three. Two. One." The line was disconnected.

He dropped his head back, looking up at the ceiling. "You done, man?" asked the guy behind him. "Yeah, it's all yours," he said as he moved away from the phone provided for the sailors. Today, they were in Rota, Spain, but they'd be headed back out to sea tonight.

He had watch in about three hours, which left him barely enough time to head onshore and buy Andrea a gift. Maybe he'd get something for Ashley too. He grinned as he realized the name truly was sticking with him.

4 - Staying power

Rob knew he had a crazy grin on his face, but couldn't help it. He was standing in Andrea's hospital room, holding their daughter. Their gorgeous, exquisite daughter. Both his angels were exhausted, and he was slowly pacing, cradling his tiny princess, watching over them as they slept, their protector. Staring down at Andrea in wonderment, he leaned over the bed, tracing her face with his fingertip, and smiled when she wrinkled her nose in her sleep.

The labor had seemed to go on forever, and she had been exhausted near the end. God, she had been determined though, and even the doctor had praised her toughness because she was so strong. After being in the labor room with her for hours, holding and supporting her body while she strained and shook trying to bring their child into the world, Rob was in awe of his wife. He'd wanted to take away the pain when she cried out, and had welcomed her crushing grip on his hand and arm when the contractions grew in strength, since the only thing he could do to help her was be by her side.

Then, in that first instant when he heard their daughter's voice raised in a squalling scream, he'd known an exhilaration that he felt could never be surpassed by anything. Andrea had fallen backward into the bed, and he'd kissed her over and over, stroking the sweat-wet hair away from her face while she ignored him, craning her head to see their baby. He'd told her with complete honesty that she'd never been so beautiful to him.

He was thrilled to have been there when the nurse first laid their naked baby on her bare chest, skin to skin. As he watched Drea, seeing how her face softened as she focused on their daughter, it felt as if he'd been granted a front row seat to see someone fall in love. Together they counted tiny fingers and toes, traced the bowed lips and miniature chin with soft touches, and kissed each other over their daughter's head as she lay cradled between them.

Once the hospital assigned them to a room, Rob had made the announcement phone calls. He expected their families to descend on the hospital at any minute, but for right now, it was just him and his angels.

Looking down at his daughter, he saw her eyes were open and she was staring up at him with a calm, clear gaze. "Hi there, little Ashley," he whispered, his big hand cupping her fragile head. "How you doin', little one? Mommy's sleeping, but Daddy's got you. Yeah, Daddy's got you, baby girl. Never let you go, sweetness."

He caressed the curve of her cheek with a fingertip, marveling at how petite and beautiful she was. Touching her open palm with his little finger, he smiled when her hand curled around it, grasping and holding onto him. "I think it's the other way around, sweetness. I think I'm wrapped around your little finger already." He leaned in, nuzzling gently with his nose and taking in the clean, fresh scent of their newborn.

Straightening, he watched her intently, her cupid-bow lips moving faintly as her eyes slowly closed. He brought the swaddled bundle up to his face again, kissing her forehead reverently. Cradling her close to his chest, he bounced slowly and gently from foot to foot, crooning nonsense to her.

The door pushed open and he saw his mother's face peering around. Recognizing him, she smiled and came in. Moving to his side to peer down at the baby in his arms, she whispered, "Oh, Rob, look at her. She's perfect." She leaned in, rising on her toes to kiss his cheek. "Congratulations, Daddy," she said with an affectionate smile.

Placing Ashley in her arms, he watched as tears slipped down his mother's cheeks. She said, "I know that all babies are precious, but she's something special. Look at her, so beautiful." Looking up at him, she asked, "What did you and Andrea decide to name her?"

He beamed, "I told all of you the name had staying power. Your granddaughter's name is Ashley Marie."

"Well, little Ashley Marie, welcome to the world," she said, pressing a kiss to Ashley's cheek.

***

"I don't know, Andrea. How much are the lessons?" Rob asked, looking around at the chaos that surrounded him on the dock as dozens of sailors disembarked for shore leave here in Haifa. He stepped aside, staying out of the way of the men who'd been in the biggest hurry to change out of their blue coveralls and into a regular uniform.

"My mom and dad offered to pay it, Rob. I just wanted to be sure you are okay with her going to dance class," she said carefully. Rob knew he was sensitive about being able to support and provide for his family, and she evidently didn't want him to say no only because he didn't want her parents to pay for it.

Truth be told, he knew her parents wanted to help out lots more than they were given the go-ahead to do, and most especially where their only granddaughter was concerned. He grinned, remembering Drea's email from last weekend about grilling in the backyard with her folks. Ashley had them twisted around her little fingers. She'd wanted s'mores over a fire, so her Grandpa headed straight off to the store to get everything needed.

"She's only four; you think she'll have fun in the class? What can she learn at that age?" he asked.

"Kelly's daughter is going and has a blast. She was trying to show Ashley how to stand like a ballerina when we saw them at the park. That's what got me looking into it. They were having a really good time." He could hear her holding her breath. Not only would Ash have a good time, but Andrea would get a chance to visit with her friend while the girls were taking the class. He decided he wouldn't follow up on the cost question, since it meant so much to her.

"You know I'll want pictures, sugar," he surrendered with a grin, so she could hear it in his voice. "Tell your folks thank you."

"She's going to have such a good time. And yes, I'll send pictures. I love you, Rob," she said.

"Andrea," he started speaking, and then paused.

She waited for him to resume, and when he didn't, she asked him, "What, babe?"

He took in a deep breath, blowing it resolutely back out. "Sugar, are you sure you are okay with me re-upping? They're pressuring me for a final answer, even though it's nearly a year away. Since our assignments are three years, they need to know pretty soon in order to line up a fresh puke from the next class if I don't."

She couldn't hide the distress in her voice as she replied, "We've been through this, Rob. *I know* you love being a Nuke, and you are passionate about the Navy. But, *you know* I want you home, and I want Ashley to be with her daddy more than just a few weeks a year." Here, she paused for a second, clearly collecting her thoughts. "Baby, if you want to re-up, then I support your decision one hundred percent. It's a stable job, you are safer than some of the other naval specialties, you're good at what you do, and you love it. I also know you love us and you hate missing out on so much with Ash. Don't forget you want to have more babies, but I'm not doing that alone again, so you have to weigh the tradeoffs. I do support you, Rob. I'm your number one cheerleader."

Wetting his lips, he told her, "All valid observations, sugar. It's only three years, and we can do that," here she joined him, saying the words along with him, "standing on our head." They both laughed, and then he sobered, continuing, "There's a nice bonus for not only re-upping, but letting them know early enough to sort out the recruiting class of pukes. We can use that to pay down the house loan, or put some aside to start saving for Ash's college. It's good for our family, even if it's hard on us personally."

"So what's your decision, Mr. Crew?" she asked, and he already knew what he was going to say.

"I'm going to let them know tomorrow they can count on me for another assignment. It's too much money to pass up, Mrs. Crew. There's still lots of room for bounce, too, which I like. More rank, more money, less work."

He heard her sigh and knew she was forcing a brightness into her voice, probably pulling her ponytail over her shoulder nervously as she said, "One hundred percent support, babe. I love you."

5 - Coming home

The stars are brilliant tonight, she thought. Edith Morgan was sprawled on the roof of a small rental house she lived in with her mother out here in the desert, along where the borders of California and Nevada met. Facing upwards, her eyes swept in a pattern from horizon to horizon, tracking planes and satellites through the nighttime sky while she watched for wish-worthy shooting stars.

Moving here from San Diego nearly two years ago to escape an unmanageable situation, so far they'd been successful in their bid to make a clean break from the past. Their life now was relaxed, comfortable, predictable, even boring—but safe. One day, she'd have her own kids, and this is the kind of life she would want for them. Safe. *Always safe.*

Listening closely, she heard a low moan from the open window of her mother's room below her, and the shuffle of a visitor coming through the attic, the gable window still gaping wide from her escape. She sighed, knowing her freedom was on a short leash this evening.

"Eddie, you need to come back inside, hun. I need to talk to you." That was Melissa, her mother's hospice nurse addressing her through the attic window.

"On my way," she called quietly, sitting up and scooting sideways along the roof towards the opening. Gripping the overhead sash with both hands, she came through the window feet first. Standing, she turned, closing the window and flipping the latch before glancing over at the pleasant-faced nurse and asking, "What did you need to tell me, Melissa?"

"Let's go to the kitchen. I've made some tea," came the smooth response and Eddie nodded, biting the inside of her bottom lip. In the kitchen, she wrapped her frigid fingers around the mug Melissa slid over to her and sat in one of the chairs pulled up around the table, cradling the warmth in her hands.

"It's not a good report," the nurse started speaking and Eddie closed her eyes. "There's only so much her body can take, and she's beginning the process of letting go. Kimberly isn't what we would call actively dying yet, but it won't be long, Eddie. I hate that you're alone in this, and at your age. Are you certain there's no one you can call to be with you during this time? Someone to help you bear the responsibility of easing your mom's passing?"

"No, there's no one but me that cares about her." Eddie opened her eyes, staring at Melissa before flicking her gaze back down to the table. "How long does she have?"

"That's nearly impossible to say with any certainty, but we believe it's weeks and not months. It could even be days, hun. I talked to the case supervisor, and we're going to add a medication that will help keep her more comfortable. I've called in the prescription and I'll write the instructions down for you." Melissa reached across the table and wrapped one hand around both of Eddie's where they cradled the mug of hot tea. "I'll schedule the doctor for mid-week. We can see what she has to say, okay? Meanwhile, you need to finish out the semester with passing grades, so I expect to see you working on homework and projects every time I come over. I want to come see you graduate."

Shaking her head, Eddie lifted her gaze to Melissa's face. "God, school seems ridiculous right now. I know I'm a senior and I should care, but it doesn't feel relevant anymore."

Melissa looked at her with compassion. "I know school and your education seem unnecessary with what's going on with your mom, but finishing school is important. To her, as well as you. She knows it will give you the chance to go anywhere, be anything you want to be. Keep trying and doing your best. Ask for help if you need it, hun. I could talk to the school if you want."

Shaking her head, Eddie clamped her lips shut. Shutting her eyes, she took one slow sip from the trembling mug, and then another as her hands steadied. Lifting her face to the nurse, she said, "I'll do what I can."

An hour later, Melissa was gone for the night and Eddie was alone with her mother again, sitting on the floor and leaning against the hallway wall outside her mom's bedroom. She was tapping the phone against her thigh, deep in thought when her mom's voice came from the bedroom and startled her, making her jerk and drop the handset.

"Call him," she heard her mother say, accompanied by a low moan of misery.

"No," she whispered, thudding her head backward against the wall. "Mom, I can do this. We've managed for two years. I don't need him." She swept her dark hair over her shoulder, twisting it into a loose knot.

"Baby, call him. It's okay," her mom told her, shifting the covers restlessly over her legs. "We need his help."

Eddie picked up the phone and saw her hands were shaking. Slowly dialing the long-distance number from memory, she held her breath until a gruff voice answered, saying curtly, "Yeah?"

Her tongue slipped out, wetting her lips before she said in a small voice, "Shooter?"

The tension pouring down the line was palpable; she could almost hear the phone creaking in his hand as his grip tightened on the handset. His voice, when it came again, was considerably softer, more hesitant than she'd ever heard it. "Eddie? Tell me where you are. Is Kimberly with you? Honey, tell me you're okay."

The tears that had been threatening since Melissa called her inside and off the roof began welling in her eyes, spilling down her cheeks as she hiccupped into the phone. "I'm sorry. It's bad. She's bad and I don't know what to do. I just don't know what to do."

"Tell me where you are. Let's start with that, okay? Everything else can be worked out, but I need to know where you are so I can help." He spoke the words evenly, his voice stronger now.

"We're in Nipton," she choked out, another sob tearing up her throat.

"Give me a phone number," he said and she heard an indistinct noise, realizing he'd covered the handset speaker on his end. She heard muffled voices and then a couple of sharp shouts, and abruptly he was back on the line with her, repeating his plea. "Honey, tell me what the phone number is."

Rattling off the number, she sat still, quietly waiting until he said, "Tell me now. I'll be there before you know it."

"I love you." She barely breathed the words into the phone and pulled it away from her head, but not before she heard his reply of, "Love you more. Talk to you soon."

She was still sitting on the hall floor four hours later when she first sensed the shaking in the wall at her back, something other people might have worried was an earthquake. Closing her eyes, she felt the vibration grow in strength, evolving into an audible roar that rattled the windows, as well as the floor. Taking her time climbing to her feet, she glanced into the bedroom as she walked past, catching her mother's eyes in a look of shared dread.

Making her way down the stairs, she went to the front door and swung it open, inviting a powerful cacophony of noise inside as she stepped out onto the small front porch. Nipton was a small town, and their house was on the main street in what was normally a quiet, sleepy neighborhood.

Now, for as far as she could see in either direction in the streetlights, there were motorcycles parked on both sides of the street. Some of the men who had ridden into town were already off their bikes, standing alone beside their rides, or clustered in small, tense groups while others still straddled their bikes, looking about watchfully.

She knew every man...each *rider*...wore a vest with patches on the back that read *Outriders*, the name of a motorcycle club based out of San Diego. The avid attention of dozens of men swung to her as she stood silhouetted in the doorway, wrapped by light from within the house.

A group of about seven men were coming up the sidewalk in front of the house, their faces flowing through darkness and light as they traveled through the shadows she cast. The man in the lead drew in a deep breath as he neared the porch, his voice gravelly and rough with emotion as he softly said, more benediction than greeting, "Eddie, doll baby."

Sweeping her into his arms, he crushed her to his chest, locking into stillness and holding her in place for several long minutes. The other men broke formation and flowed around them into the house, but she couldn't hear what they said or did; she couldn't hear anything over the harsh exhalations beside her ear. His arms were bands of steel coiled around her, and they tightened and loosened with no rhythm she could identify, bound by the overwhelming turmoil within the man who held her.

He took a breath in and held it, relaxing his arms imperceptibly, and then took another breath in, seemingly to prove to himself that he could as he slid his arms from around her, clutching her upper arms with his hands. Staring intently down into her face, he asked in an anxious tone, "Where is she?"

"Upstairs," Eddie spoke her first word since stepping out of the house. He shifted her bodily, urging her towards and through the doorway. She led him up the stairs to her mother's room, gesturing at the doorway, and he released her, entering the room. Suspended in place, she listened to the rustling of the men in the house and the murmurs of a brief conversation coming from the bedroom only three feet in front of her, but a world away.

The man came out, and he tenderly wrapped an arm around her shoulders, guiding her down the stairs and into the kitchen. Seating himself in a chair at the table, he pulled her down onto his lap, her legs draped over his tense thighs as he enveloped her tightly in his arms again. "Shooter," she began, but he interrupted her with a faint, "Shhhh. Give me a minute, doll baby. Shhhh."

"Okay, Daddy," she murmured, and slipped her arms around his neck while she buried her face in his shoulder.

They sat that way for a half hour or more. She stirred on his lap a couple of times, and he shushed her again, gentling her with a stroke against the fall of her hair or down the length of her back. The other men gradually filtered into the room, drawing out chairs to sit or leaning patiently against the countertops and walls around the room.

He eventually shifted in the chair, easing back and taking in a deep breath, which he hummed out in satisfaction. "*Goddamn* it feels good to hold you, Eddie. Missed you so much. I didn't know where you were; we couldn't find you. I've been so worried, baby. Why—how'd you wind up here?"

"Mom thought this town was small enough you might not find us, might not look for us here," she spoke directly and brutally, giving a little one-shouldered shrug. One of the men in the room drew in a dismayed breath at her words and she felt Shooter tense under her. She looked up at the man, locking gazes with youthful grey eyes that were exactly like hers, precisely like their father's, and she scrambled off

Shooter's lap and away, turning to face him from across the room. "You brought him with you? Out of all your options, everyone you can think of, you brought *him*?" she shouted the question and heard the chair scrape loudly across the floor as her father abruptly stood, his face twisted in fury.

"He wanted to come, Eddie. Everyone in this room, every brother riding at my back, wanted to come. Hell, needed to come. It's not a chore for any man with me, because they are all your family, not just me." He didn't shout in response, but his voice was intense with his anger and some other unspoken emotion, raw and painful sounding. "I rode in here with sixty brothers, not because I'm their President, but on account of you being their daughter—their sister—their family."

Her gaze pivoted back to the young man standing across the room, staring at her. "Luke, I'm sorry. None of this is your fault. Shooter was—"

She was interrupted by her father, who was shouting now. "Shooter was what? Wrong to acknowledge his blood? Crazy to want to do right by his family? Stupid to think you'd see past that to how much he loved you? How much he loved your mom?" He scoffed, throwing his hands up into the air in frustration. "Tell me what 'Shooter was', doll baby. Let me know exactly what you believe."

She shouted at him, "I think you had Luke and Roxy, your other family. Actions speak, Daddy, and yours were screaming that you didn't need us. You didn't need me and Mom, because you had what you'd always wanted, what I couldn't be...a son." A hush fell in the room, and she could sense the weight of the men's stares on her skin like pressure from an approaching storm. Her voice weakened. "You didn't need us...me."

"I love Luke like I love you, Edith. He's my son, you're my daughter, and I love you both. But Roxy was nothing to me, and your mother knew it." He shouted her down, jaw thrusting forward angrily.

"Knowing that was what *you said*, didn't stop what *you did* from hurting her. Every time she looked at you, she saw you fucking Roxy. I held my mother when she cried because she wasn't enough for you, couldn't keep you happy, when she thought she was losing you, had already lost you, wasn't pretty enough. Every time she looked at you, it tore her up, because she saw you as you really are, instead of what her ideal had been." Her chest was heaving with the emotions she'd been suppressing for years, but finally getting it all out wasn't making it less painful; it seemed to hurt worse now than it ever had before.

Still shouting, he pounded his chest with each uttered word, hammering so hard he rose on the balls of his feet with every strike of his tightly clenched fist. "I. Thought. You. Were. Dead." Staring at her, the emotion twisting his face a mix of fierce anger and paralyzing fear, he roared the words, "Because. Of. *Me*."

Her breath hitched and she reeled, because when they'd left and run away, she'd imagined he wouldn't care. After all, he had his other family to take their place. She recognized how wrong she'd been in that assumption, and she broke into tears when he repeated himself, softly saying the words as if they were a secret. "I thought you were dead, because of me. I thought another club had swept you up, and then when there were no demands, when nothing came, no word, I *knew* you were dead at their hands. Both of you, God, I knew you had to be. Because of me. Had to be dead, because you were important to me. Because I loved you both. All this time, I have been mourning you, but still hoping for a call. The call came tonight. Your call."

"Doll baby, I love you and your mother so much. I can't even tell you...can't quantify it. It's crazy—I've been crazy these past two years." He moved towards her, and seizing her shoulders in his hands, he bent his knees, bringing his face down level with hers. "Let me get you home. Let's bring your mom home, where I can take care of her."

Nodding, she stuttered through her sobs, "O-okay. L-let me pack a bag—"

He interrupted her, fingers clenching painfully on her shoulders. "No, everything comes. Not a bag, like this is a temporary fucking trip. Every fucking thing that matters to you or her comes with us tonight." Swinging his head, he looked at one of the men standing nearby. "Tug, I know you aren't mine to order anymore, but I need you to take Eddie back to the clubhouse now. Take my girl home."

"You got it, Shooter." The response came from a man with salt-and-pepper hair and a well-groomed handlebar mustache, who stepped across to wrap his arms tightly around her. Tug kissed the side of her head, saying, "Eddie girl, good to see you."

She breathed in his scent, familiar and reassuring. "Uncle Tugboat," was all she said, and he moved them out of the house and into the street before she could react. Lifting her, he sat her on his bike, shifting to straddle the seat in front of her and start the motor quickly. Within a minute of her father's request, she was on a moving bike, headed out of town into the darkness.

"Tug, go back. I have to help them get Mom ready," she shouted into his ear, leaning against his back with her arms around his waist. He shook his head, not slowing the bike down. She shifted, grasping his belt with one hand while she balled up her fist and thudded it against his shoulder, trying to get his attention. "Take me back! I have to show them what to do. There're medicines and equipment to deal with."

He shook his head again, and she thudded her fist against his shoulder another time, beginning to get angry. "Take me back, Tug," she yelled beside his head. Looking at him, she saw his face was resolute, eyes staring straight ahead of them as he ignored her pleas. Turning loose of his belt, she lost control, pounding on his back with both fists and screaming at him to take her back to her mother, back to their home. He reached a hand down to grab her thigh, gripping her leg tightly in order to keep her balanced on top of the bike.

She continued to beat at him, unaware she was crying, sobbing out her fear and sadness as her fists again and again found their mark. When she finally quieted, they were only a few minutes from the Outriders' clubhouse, and she was exhausted, covered in sweat from her exertions in spite of the whipping wind from their journey. Sagging forward, she wrapped her arms around his waist, laying her head against his back as he patted her thigh in sympathy, seeing for the first time his patch didn't say Outriders, but Rebel Wayfarers.

6 - For always

*Babe—before I forget, here's a kiss from Ashley: XOXO. She wanted to make sure you got that first. I took her shopping last week. She's grown another inch taller and all her pants were high-waters…again. The dance recital is next weekend, and we found out at class last night that she got a solo! Isn't that great?! She's the only seven-year-old to be selected, and the part isn't long, but I think the experience will be good for her. I wish you could be here to see it, but I'll take pictures, and if there's anything in the paper, I'll cut it out and save it.

*Mom and I got her signed up for school next year. She's going to be in second grade, if you can believe that. No more naptime, but she won't have to change classrooms yet. That will be third grade, ugh. Not looking forward to that. I'm so glad you'll be home in a few weeks! I can't wait to wrap my arms around my man. Knowing you're coming home helps me keep things moving forward here. We love you, Rob. So much.

*OH—you'll love this. Or maybe you won't, I'm not really sure. I got a call from the school earlier today. Ashley had to go to the office and see the principal this morning. Some kid was being mean to a little boy on the playground and she yelled at him and pushed him down. I asked what grade the mean kid was in and they said fourth grade. Can you imagine our little Ash standing up to a boy nearly three years older? I asked her what she was thinking, and she told me, "He needed to sort himself out, Momma.

Don't nobody need to be that mean. I told him he was just angry at himself and he needed to go look in the mirror before he came and talked to Henry again." (Henry is the little boy she protected.) I like to think that's you coming out in her, because you work so hard to keep everyone safe.

*We love you, babe. -Andrea and Ashley

With a big smile on his face, Rob finished reading the email from Andrea for the third time. He typed up a reply, wanting to make sure she got his directions before this weekend.

*Hey, Drea - Buy one of those mini-cameras and tape the recital on Saturday, then mail me the tape. We'll be in port in another thirty days, and it should be waiting for me. One of the guys has a player and I'll be able to watch her dance. I can't believe she got a solo. She's amazing, but you are her mom, so she comes by it honestly (grin).

It's hard to believe she's gonna be in second grade in the fall. She's growing up so fast. Every time you send pictures, it looks like she's grown another foot. Taller, not like a third foot (grin). Nothing new here, just the same routine with new people. Same old, same old. Tell my littlest angel I love her, and make sure her mom knows I love her, too, okay? -Rob

He pushed back from the computer, standing and stretching for a minute before he headed out to the rec room. He wished he could be there to watch her dance on stage. The last time he'd been home, she'd put on one of her dance outfits and given them a private performance in the living room, but he knew it wasn't the same. He'd found time kept flowing past, like the seas around the sub, and she grew whether he was there to see it or not.

Briefly, he considered sending another email to Andrea, letting her know he'd made the decision this was his last assignment. He was going to leave the Navy when his time was up and go home to his family. She'd be ecstatic, he knew, even though they'd already talked about what they could use the bonus for if he re-upped again.

For the most part, she talked like that to humor him, and keep him from knowing how hard it was with him away all the time. He'd gotten to see remote and exotic places in the world, like he'd told himself he would, and was proud of his service and the work he did, but he often felt like he was missing out on all the most important things at home.

They'd worked hard to make sure Ash had good experiences with him and their families when he was home, building memories by going to the beach or the zoo every chance they got. He'd taken her camping the last time he was there, just him and his girl. They'd set up their tent far from their house in Bayonne, near Norfolk in the Great Dismal Swamp, laughing at each other's guesses of how the park got its name. Then, after it got dark, they told each other spooky stories around the fire until late in the night.

She hadn't been afraid, even when there were noises in the darkness stretching beyond the flickering light of their fire. He loved that Ashley was brave, and proud beyond words she wasn't afraid to stand up for people who needed someone...like that little boy on the playground. *My little heroine. My littlest angel.*

He'd pulled third watch all week, so he would need to get some bunk time before reporting for his six-hour shift. They were at full-capacity crew-wise, so every day, he spent extra time working on maintenance, because he had to wait for a bunk to open up anyway. He'd always thought he might as well be productive while he was waiting. Most of the guys hated hot-bunking, because even though the bunk curtains afforded an illusion of privacy, having the bedding and mattress still warm from another body made it impossible to ignore the fact there wasn't anywhere on the sub to get away from people.

Two days later, and he still hadn't gotten a response back from Andrea. Not unheard of, because email was still unreliable while they were at sea, but the other men were getting messages. Rob asked the duty officer if he could send a family-gram using the normal messaging systems and got an okay. He reported to the operations compartment and wrote out what he wanted to say, ***buy mini-video camera, send me a tape of recital***, and received a reassuring nod from the operator when he asked if it would be delivered before Friday.

Saturday, when he checked email, he saw Andrea's name. *Thank God*, he thought, *she got my messages*, and clicked on the email to open it.

> *Hey babe, I found a mini-tape video camera on sale and bought it like you said. I've addressed an envelope and I'll mail the tape as soon as we leave the recital. That way, it will get to you faster than if I bring it home. Ash reminded me to send you kisses, so here they are: XOXO, and she said the last one has extra spit, so you know it's from her. Ugh, I'm gonna tell her that's gross.
>
> *They had dress rehearsal today, and her costume for the recital is so cute. It's a white tutu over a half-black, half-pink leotard. When she pirouettes, the black and pink look pretty cool as she spins around. Did you decide yet on what the Navy asked? You know what my vote will be, but you also know I support you, babe. Like I said eight years ago, 'With love and affection, respect and honor, trust and faithfulness. I love you, Rob, for always', For always, babe. We love you. -Andrea and Ash*

Closing his eyes, he remembered their wedding day and how nervous he had been standing at the front of the church. His wife. He never got over how lucky he was she had picked him. Luckiest man in the world. He had a wonderful woman who loved him, a beautiful daughter who was the light of his life, a career he enjoyed, and friends the world over.

Three weeks later, they were docked and waiting for shore leave to be announced when a message came for him to report to the duty officer right away. He shook his head, because he knew one of the recent inspections hadn't gone well, but it wasn't his watch that had screwed up and he hoped the NCOs knew it. Stepping into the operations compartment, the duty officer looked up, acknowledged Rob, and motioned him over. "Need you to report to the CO's stateroom, Petty Officer."

"Yes, sir," was Rob's response, and he headed back the way he came. The duty officer called after him, asking, "Do you have any particularly close friends on board?" Rob shook his head in confusion. "Sir, Petty Officer Gibbs has served with me since boot camp. I would consider Bruce my closest friend in the Navy, sir." Picking up the receiver, the duty officer asked for Gibbs to be sent to the CO's stateroom.

Being dismissed again, he wondered about Bruce as he moved down the sub towards the officers' quarters. *Why would they need both of us?* A clanging noise reverberated through the sub and he knew they'd finally docked. This was going to eat into his time, and he really wanted to be there for mail call first thing. Knocking on the CO's stateroom, he heard a curt, "Enter," and opened the door.

The CO was standing, holding a piece of paper in his hand. Gibbs was in the room, standing off to one side in the cramped space, subdued, his face white. Rob looked at him and Bruce dropped his eyes. *Whatever it is, this is bad,* he thought.

The CO motioned to the lone chair, saying, "Petty Officer Crew, have a seat." Rob sat, feeling uncomfortable. This was not standard operating procedure and made him anxious. "I have some bad news, son," the CO went on, "and there's no good way to tell it."

Rob tensed, clasping his hands tightly together, waiting. The CO exchanged glances with Gibbs, who swallowed hard and took a half-step forward. "Rob, man," Bruce said, his voice strangled with emotion. "There was an accident. Andrea and Ash were in an accident three weeks ago. They're gone, Rob. I'm so sorry."

Looking up, he saw both Gibbs and the CO's lips moving, but their words were lost to him in the clamor of a loud, buzzing noise. He shook his head, *What are they talking about*? With a clueless look on his face, Rob waved a hand and they stopped speaking. At least he thought they stopped, but since he couldn't hear them, he had to go off the fact their mouths stilled.

"Excuse me? Come again?" he tried to say, but wasn't sure he'd gotten anything out. He couldn't even hear his own voice. Nothing Gibbs had said made sense. *Where did they go if they were in an accident?* Standing purposefully, Rob waited. He shook his head; the buzzing wasn't getting any better. *Where did they go?*

Muted, as if through a powerless megaphone, he heard the CO's voice from far away. "Son, I'm sorry. Your wife and daughter were killed in an automobile accident twenty-three days ago. The report indicates their passing was immediate and they did not suffer." Rob heard an echoing as again and again the CO's voice told him, *They did not suffer. They did not suffer. They did not suffer. They did not—* and then, everything went black.

***

Sitting in a troop transport plane on the tarmac at Ramstein Air Force base in Germany, Rob held onto the webbed harness with both hands. He was headed home. Thoughts rolled around in his head, unmoored and random. He had contended there was no need, arguing against going back since everything was already taken care of. His angels had died and been buried, and he hadn't been there. He'd been stuck in a tin can under the ocean, and not at home.

Talking on the phone to Andrea's parents had nearly torn him in two, but he'd locked it down. Since he couldn't be reached in time, they'd had to take care of all the arrangements. Her mom, Diana, kept apologizing to him, saying she hadn't wanted to make the decisions and she hoped he wasn't upset at her.

He wasn't mad; he was just lost. So lost. She'd wanted to talk to him about the service; she needed his approval, even though it had already happened. She and Andrew had decided on a joint funeral to make things as simple as possible. Ash was buried in one of her dance costumes, but it was closed casket, so no one saw her.

What did that mean? Closed casket. Closed. Did that mean my littlest angel was so damaged by the accident that no one would want to see her? He wanted to be able to see her, but he couldn't, because he was too late. *My sweetness. My baby girl.*

Closed casket. Diana kept talking. She said they'd had a beautiful picture of his girls on display for people to look at. Andrea's casket was closed too. *What did that mean?* They'd bought burial plots in the cemetery at their church in Bayonne. *Andrea Crew, nee Graham. Their daughter. My wife. My daughter. Their granddaughter. Closed caskets.*

Is she still my mother-in-law, even though her daughter died? He thought so, since he didn't regard himself any less of a father now. She was still a mother without one of her children, like him without his daughter, but still a father. "Did you hear me, Rob?" she'd said into the phone, and he had to admit he wasn't listening. She repeated, "Rob, I can't go in the house. You'll have to get someone else to help you go through their things."

"Why would I want to go through their things? I want their things left alone. Don't go in the house, Diana." He told her what he wanted and she broke down crying, handing the phone to Andrea's dad. "It's going to take me nearly thirty-six hours to get home, Andrew. Don't let Diana go in the house. I think it makes her sad," he said and heard agreement from his father-in-law. "I'll be there soon," he told him, and then hung up.

The taxi let him off in front of the dark house. It shouldn't be dark. The house was never dark. Ash had been afraid of the dark when she was younger, so even at nighttime, there should be a faint glow of her nightlight from her upstairs window. The house was dark. *Closed casket.* Lifting his duffle onto his shoulder, he walked up the driveway towards the side door. Reaching above the doorframe, he grabbed the key and used it to open the inside door, sliding it absently into his pocket.

The stench was what hit him first and had him gagging and retching. The odor was rank; it smelled like something had crawled in-between the walls and died. Clamping his mouth shut tightly, he quickly walked through the kitchen and into the living room, turning lights on as he went.

Everywhere he looked, it felt like his emotions were under attack, taking hits to his chest where his heart used to reside. There were little tennis shoes tidily arranged side-by-side below the coffee table, waiting for feet that would never put them on again. Andrea's coffee mug was sitting on a table near the couch, half-full of evaporating, congealed, moldy liquid. The smell wasn't as bad in here, so he stood for a few minutes, breathing through his mouth as he studied the room.

Ashley's book bag was sitting beside the front door, ready for her to grab it on her way to catch the bus. The book Andrea was reading sat next to her coffee mug, lying face down and open; she didn't care if she broke a book's spine, saying it showed they were well-loved. He smiled; the cover had a tattooed man's naked torso on it, so he knew it was one of what she called her 'guilty pleasure books'. She loved to read him passages out of some of them, and they'd either laugh at the language or reenact the erotic scene, depending on the mood.

Closed casket.

His smile faded.

Everywhere he looked, there were reminders they'd expected to come home and continue their lives. Continue living. But they didn't, so all of these things were evidence that life had been cut short—brutally short—for his wife and daughter. Ash would never be able to grab that bag, never ride the bus again, bouncing on the seat in excitement. The litany of things she would never have a chance to do ripped through his mind. She would never date, or have the drama of her first breakup. Would never graduate high school. Never go to college. Never get married. Have her own babies. Grow up. She would never anything.

He closed his mouth on a sob, and when the smell assaulted him as he drew air through his nose, he absently opened his mouth again. *Did not suffer.*

The pictures of Ashley on the mantel caught his attention. Taken every six months or so, they tracked her growth and development. Andrea had attached the final picture in the series on the wall to her last email, and his eyes returned to it again and again. He should have argued more about the dance lessons. *Did dance kill her, or was it really the truck?*

Going upstairs, he avoided their bedrooms, putting his duffle on the bed in the guestroom. The bed was smaller than the one he shared with Andrea, but it was much larger than the bunks onboard the sub; those things weren't much bigger than a casket. *Closed casket. What did that mean?*

Back in the kitchen, he quickly found the origin of the smell in a variety of mold-covered food in containers and dishes in the refrigerator, and a rotten, forgotten roast in the oven. Thank God Andrea had used the timer, or it could have burned the house down. *If the house had burned down, I wouldn't have to be here.* "They did not suffer," he mumbled aloud as he went through the house and methodically opened windows, venting out the smell and reducing the heaviness in the air.

Locating garbage bags in a drawer, he used one after another to throw the bad food from the fridge away, container and all, wanting to reduce the stench, but not caring about salvaging the dishware or plastic storage sets. As he was pulling the roast out of the oven, it sloughed sickly away from the bone, appearing to dissolve into the jellied juices in the bottom of the pan, and he had to quickly set it down on the counter to turn and vomit into the sink.

After three trips to the dumpster in the back alley and nearly four hours of scrubbing and bleaching the kitchen and bathrooms, the smell was principally gone. He reached into the cabinet and found a glass, filling it under the kitchen faucet and turning it up to his mouth twice before his thirst was satisfied. There wasn't anything edible in the house; he hadn't thought that far in advance in the cab on the way here. He'd have to go to the store tomorrow, but he'd need to check in with the base first, find out how long he would be allowed home. *Hardship leave. Closed casket.*

Tomorrow. With that one word, a mental list of everything he needed to do began organizing in his mind. Call the base. Go grocery shopping. Drive to the cemetery. Visit his mom. See his in-laws. Talk to the lawyer about Andrea's will. Go to the bank. Go to the post office. Dammit, there was a lot he had to get settled and fast. He knew his time here had an expiration date, because it always did.

He'd write it all down tomorrow, and run through it as if it were a mechanical inspection checklist. That way, he wouldn't forget anything. He'd start with grocery shopping, because he had to eat regardless. Opening the cabinet over the fridge. He realized there was at least one thing to drink in the house as he pulled out the unopened bottle of whiskey.

***

"Nooo," he slurred. "Gimme back. Now. Gimme 'em back. I wan 'em back."

Waking with a start, he looked around the guest bedroom in confusion, his head pounding. He'd been trying to grab Andrea and Ashley off a carnival ride. The black-dressed bastard running the ride had kept them just out of his reach. In his dream, Ash's face looked so scared, and she kept calling out for him to come find her.

He flipped over in the bed, lying flat on his back and breathing hard. As the full memory of everything that had happened settled back into him, tears rolled from the corners of his eyes and down the sides of his face. His angels were far out of reach, just like in the dream.

***

Grasping the outstretched hand, he barely heard the thanks from the realtor. His three weeks were nearly up, and settling the house was the last thing he had to resolve before leaving for Norfolk in two days. Since there was no way he could sell the house in that amount of time, on his lawyer's advice, he'd signed papers for giving full power of attorney to his mom. That way, she'd be able to keep things progressing, even after he'd gone back to sea.

He thought he could barely tolerate sleeping in the house for two more nights, or not sleeping, which was the case more often than not. Hiring a moving company to come in and pack everything up had made a small difference, and he'd found he could at least rest a little. He put the furniture in storage and hauled the few boxes of personal things to his mom's attic. Everything else—the clothes, books, toys, and dishes—went to Goodwill. The house was now stripped of all character and looked as if anyone...or no one, lived there. His air mattress would be the only thing left in the house when he was gone.

Once the realtor drove away, he looked up at the house. Andrea had really liked it, but he couldn't bear to live here without her. Selling it was the best thing he could do, and he believed the house needed a family living in it.

Walking up onto the porch, he frowned at a brown envelope slanting against the door. Leaning down, he had the package in hand before he recognized the handwriting, and dropped it as if it were on fire. It landed face up, and he squatted down slowly, extending one hand and tracing the lettering on the front with a fingertip. It was addressed to him, supposed to go to the next port of call, but it had come back here instead.

Andrea's handwriting scolded him from the front of the package, admonishing him to pick it up, to open it. Her script was so smooth and flowing, soothing, like she was...had been. He flattened the package under his hand, feeling a small, rectangular item inside.

Closing his eyes, he picked up the package without looking at it, and then stood, holding it for a moment. Gathering his emotions into check, pulling them back into line with the stoic façade he'd been presenting to family and friends, he walked into the house.

He opened the package carefully, using the blunt edge of a knife to slide under the sealed flap. Easing the two edges apart, he saw the black rectangle tucked inside a plastic sandwich bag down in the envelope. There was something shiny at the bottom of the package, and when he turned it upside down, the plastic bag with the video tape slid out, along with a handful of glitter and a piece of folded paper.

Ashley's recital. That's what was on the tape. Drea had said she was going to mail it before going home, and they'd only been five miles from the house when the cement truck ran a red light. She must have already mailed it when the accident happened. Carefully, slowly, reverently, he unfolded the paper to see two sets of handwriting marching across the unlined page.

Andrea's note said, *Rob, I hope you are ready to watch magic, because our princess was amazing tonight. I wasn't the only one standing and applauding, babe; she's really good. Email me when you get this. Let me know what you think. I love you ~A*

The other half of the paper was covered in Ashley's half-script/half-print scrawl. *DADDY, the glitter is from my wings. I wish you were here. I was an ANGEL tonight, just like you always say. I love you, ASH. XOXO*

Rob's legs unhinged, and he collapsed onto his knees on the kitchen floor, the paper held to his chest. Swaying back on his heels, he stayed there unmoving until there was a pounding on the door. "Rob, open the door, son." He heard a woman's voice. "Open the door and let me in."

There was a high-pitched sound in the house, rising and falling from low volume to much louder, and then low again, building and descending back and forth. He heard a scrabbling at the door and it swung inward, revealing his mother with a key in hand, purse dangling from a strap draped across her forearm. She stood for a moment, looking at him before her face crumpled, and then she was moving across the room, falling to her knees and pulling him to her chest. She slowly rocked him back and forth as he cried, howling out his grief and loss.

He heard the paper crinkle between them and grabbed at it, frantically smoothing it out, cautiously touching it with the flat of his hand. "Andrea wrote me," he said, taking in air with loud whoops. "She sent me a tape of Ashley's recital." His mom's arms tightened around him, pulling him close without saying anything.

"I miss them. I want my angels back," he wailed again, teeth clenched hard as he glared at the ceiling. "I want them back, my girls," he cried. "My angels." Stroking the back of his head, his mom made soothing noises, but didn't try to stop him from talking or crying.

Rob buried his head in his mom's neck, finally moving to put his arms around her as his words turned to wracking sobs that shook his frame. They remained on the kitchen floor for hours, only moving from their knees to sit side-by-side, her arms never leaving him.

***

With a start, Rob woke up and realized he was lying on the kitchen floor, his head pillowed on his mother's legs as early morning sunlight streamed through the window. He sat up, feeling the stiffness and kinks in his neck and back as he looked at her. Still awake, she was propped against the island, eyes red and swollen. "Mom, I'm so sorry—" he started and was surprised when she lifted her hand and smacked his chest, interrupting him.

"We needed that, Robby," she said. "Both of us. I'm sorry you're going through this, but you aren't alone, son. Never alone. Don't you forget that."

***

There was little satisfaction in working with pukes. Those sailors barely out of boot, who hadn't gotten their dolphins yet, the pins that signified they'd passed the qualification process for submarines. They were the worst sailors, because they either wanted to work exactly by the book, which they didn't yet know, or they wanted to be the big man on the boat, which they clearly weren't. Rob had pulled a terrible group of non-useful bodies this time, but he had eight months to train his replacement, if he could find one in this pile of NUBs.

He wasn't sure yet what he was going to do once he got out, after he was done with the separation and retirement counseling. That was a weeklong class where they taught you how to create a resume, how to interview for jobs, connect you with organizations for support, and tried to show you how to live life on the outside of the Navy. He'd been in so long now it was hard to think of doing anything different, but he absolutely couldn't stay. His only reasons for staying in this long had been his family, and that was gone now.

As the months went by, he'd gotten to know one of the sailors fairly well. They'd go to rec at the same time and play cards, or go to the weight room and work out together. Carter LeRoy was a hardworking kid who didn't expect any favors or special treatment. He'd completed each phase of study on his qual-card in good time, never winding up as a dink on the delinquent list.

He didn't talk about his family much, other than his Uncle Mike. They were from Chicago, and his uncle still lived there. Rob got the feeling family life was tough on the boy growing up, and he was glad to see LeRoy putting in the effort to be successful in spite of what he might have been surrounded with before the Navy.

As his separation date neared, Rob became certain he'd found a good replacement for his job in LeRoy, and told the CO as much, giving the sailor his vote of approval.

One night, as they worked together to annihilate another pair of sailors in a game of cribbage, LeRoy asked Rob what his plans were once the separation process had run its course. "I don't really know," he said truthfully. "I want to do something like what I've been doing, working with my hands on machinery, but I'm not sure what that will look like."

"Are you headed back home to Bayonne?" LeRoy asked.

"Nope, I'll find another place to land, just not sure where yet," he responded.

"I have an uncle; you've heard me talk about him." Rob nodded at LeRoy to continue. "Let me write him to see if he can help you out. He works for a shop in Chicago, and he's always complaining about how poorly things are maintained there," LeRoy said, shaking his head and laughing. "He's a little bit of a drama queen, but that man knows people," he continued. "If he doesn't have an opening, he may be able to find one for you."

"I'd be okay with Chicago. I remember it some from basic," Rob said, musing. "Email him, see what he can do. I have twelve weeks left to get my shit together, and I'll take all the help I can find."

7 - Serendipity

Standing beside the guard shack at the entrance to the base, Rob waited on the taxi he'd called to pick him up. He had a heavy canvas sea duffle with his few possessions on the ground near his feet and a small wad of money in his wallet. Grinning wryly, he imagined this was a bit like someone leaving jail and then the smile faded, sliding off his face as he thought that while he might be out of the Navy, he was still in hell.

The taxi dropped him at a nearby pub and he walked in, dropping his duffle by the bar. He pulled up a stool on the far end away from the door and ordered a beer. Pulling his new cell phone out of his pocket, he smoothed the instructions on the bar, reading how to add contacts and use the various applications that came preinstalled on the phone. Tapping the screen, he quickly added numbers and information for his and Andrea's families. He pulled out a small piece of paper from his shirt pocket and input that, too, including Mike LeRoy's phone number.

No time like the present, he thought, and tapped the button that would dial the number. It rang twice and a deep voice answered, "Tug, whatcha need?"

Caught off guard, Rob stuttered and said, "Must be the wrong number. Sorry." Ending the call, he compared the number on the recently dialed list to the one written on the paper, verifying they were the same. *Maybe it was a friend who answered*, he thought as he hit redial. "Fucktard, you need somethin'?" the voice growled.

"I'm looking for Mike LeRoy," he said. "Is he available?"

"Who the fuck is calling me on this number and knowing that name?" came a barked response.

"Rob Crew," he replied. "I served with your nephew recently. He was supposed to email you about maybe finding a job for me in Chicago."

"Nuh uh, didn't get no email, man," the deep voice answered. "What's my nephew's name?"

"Seaman Carter LeRoy, serving on a submarine in the Navy," he responded.

The voice on the phone started laughing hard. "Fucking kills me. Reminds me of the joke about the Army-Navy game and why folks liked to watch it. 'Seamen, seamen, seamen, all over the field.' Fucking Seaman LeRoy, U.S. Navy. That boychild did not email me, man. How the hell's he doing?"

Rob grinned. "He's doing really well. Learns fast and knows his shit. He's dependable, too, which will take him a long way in the Navy."

An appreciative noise came through the phone. "Thanks for that, man. What kind of skills do you have?"

"If it's mechanical, I can fix it. Give me a wrench and I can handle almost anything. Things I don't know about, I learn real quick," he said. "I don't have a degree or anything, but I have nearly nine years in the Navy working on a nuclear reactor as a propulsion plant engineer. I finished out as an Engineering Watch Supervisor. I'm not afraid of hard work, and I'm not too proud for anything; I just want something to do."

"This a good number to reach you at?" the voice, which he now had to assume belonged to Mike LeRoy, grumbled into his ear. "I'm not promising anything, but we have a hole here and it sounds like you could fill it; not at this shop, but with some friends of mine. You ever worked on bikes before?"

"Bicycles? Only growing up, when I'd fix the chain and shit," he began, halting when LeRoy interrupted him with more laughter.

"Naw, man. Motorcycles. I have friends who opened a second garage for bikes, and they need someone who can tear down and fix an engine."

"Oh, yeah." He made a humming noise. "Yeah. With those, you're looking at two-stroke or four-stroke motors, with varying configurations of V and flat. I can deal with those," he said, not bragging, just stating facts as he saw them.

"Where are you now?" LeRoy asked.

"In Norfolk, I only separated today, so I don't have a lot going on," he responded.

"Okay, gimme fifteen minutes. I'll call you back," the voice said, and the call was disconnected.

Rob ordered a bacon cheeseburger, along with another beer, and settled in to wait. He didn't have to long. Within a couple of minutes, the phone rang, and he answered it with a swipe across the screen. "Yeah?"

"No can do, man. Sorry," LeRoy said. "If something opens up, I'll give you a call. Good luck."

***

In Chicago, Davis Mason was looking at Tug like he'd lost his mind. "Are you fucking kidding me? You wanted to bring a citizen into the new garage on his say-so, not even your nephew's, man?"

Tug, aka Mike LeRoy, had the good grace to look sheepish, tugging on one earlobe. "I can verify with Carter pretty quickly, and the man sounded like he knew his stuff," Tug said. "We need another set of hands at FWO2, and if he's used to working on engines the size of a house, he will probably be okay with a bike." Grumbling, he continued, "You know we *need* that other set of hands, Mason. There's no fucking way all the orders are going to get out on time, not with the delays for the retrofits. We're currently about a month behind, but I see that growing every day we don't have another good wrench."

Mason stood unmoving, watching Tug. His arms folded across his hard chest; the two-day scruff on his jaw made him look dangerous, and the rest of his body backed up that assessment. This was not a man to fuck around with. If he didn't like you or want you around, you would quite willingly go away. He was surprised at Tug's attitude. The patch seldom argued with anyone, and to disagree so vehemently with the President of his club was fucking odd. He'd been part of Mason's club almost since it was formed, was an officer, and Mason would readily trust the man with his life.

"Tug," Mason stared at his brother, "what's the deal?"

Shaking his head, the man reached up and scratched the back of his neck. "I don't really know, Prez. He sounds like he needs a friend," he cut his eyes over to Mason, "and I know how that feels, brother."

***

Staring down at his phone, Rob shook his head. That opportunity had folded faster than expected; in fact, it wasn't an opportunity at all, but just another way of life fucking with him. Looking up at the bartender, he asked, "Know anybody who needs a mechanic by chance?" Laughing at himself, he picked up his burger and finished it, paying his tab and walking out. Standing on the curb, he shoved his hands in his pockets, pondering what his next steps should be.

"Hey," came a call from behind him, "I think you forgot this." Turning, Rob saw a tall, dark-haired man with broad shoulders walking towards him with his left-behind duffle in hand.

"Yeah, thanks. Would've been bad to lose that," he said, lifting the duffle's strap onto his shoulder.

"I couldn't help but overhear your question in there," the dark-haired man said. "How good a mechanic are you?"

"As good as the Navy could make me," Rob answered with a shrug.

Nodding, the man continued, "My brother and I have a taxi service, and our uncle's been our mechanic. He's off for a while, had a heart scare a few days ago."

Rob grimaced, asking, "He gonna be okay?"

Smiling, the guy nodded, "Yeah, but he can't work for a while, so we need a mechanic."

Rob shifted, looking down for a minute. "I don't have any tools, but I can fix nearly anything that runs on gas or diesel." Looking up at the man, he held out his hand, introducing himself, "Rob Crew, your new mechanic."

Laughing, the man extended his hand to grip Rob's, saying, "Dennis Baugh, your new boss."

Dennis released his hand and pointed down the block. "Come on. Our shop is around the corner. I'll show you the place." Looking Rob up and down, he asked, "You need a place to stay too? There's a little apartment over the shop. We haven't used it for much other than an occasional crash pad, but there's a bed."

Rob scoffed as he shook his head. "Are you for real? Yeah, I just separated today and didn't sort any arrangements yet. A place to work and sleep in one package seems like someone should be jumping out yelling, 'You've been punked' as a joke."

Dennis covered his mouth with a hand. "Ha. No punking, we really do need a mechanic." Walking down the sidewalk, he pointed across the road at a diner. "Here's a tour of the neighborhood, the short version. Bethany's is a good place for food. Mediocre seating, tepid coffee, lackluster service—but the food?" He made a puffing sound, blowing out air. "Man, the food is excellent. And that's the tour." He laughed. "Here we are."

Dennis pulled open the doorway to a storefront, and Rob was surprised it didn't look like a garage from the street. The sign on the window said *Baugh Brothers Taxi Service*, so it had to be the right place. There was a single desk in the small room, with a phone and a lamp sitting on top of it. A hallway led down the left-hand side of the space, and Dennis yelled, "Donny, you here? Got someone I want you to meet." Lowering his voice, he told Rob, "Just inside the hall are the stairs for the second level. That's where the apartment is."

A roar came up the hallway at them, then shut off abruptly. A wash of exhaust followed the noise, and a much smaller version of Dennis walked into the light. "Rob, this is my brother Donny," he began the introductions. "Donny, this is our new mechanic, provided he can do what he claims."

Rob hiked the duffle up higher on his shoulder and stuck out his hand to Donny. As the small man came further into the light, Rob couldn't help but notice the poorly-repaired cleft palate deformity embedded within his features. They gripped hands, and Donny responded nasally, "New mechanic? About time you did something right, Dennis." Shifting his gaze to Rob, Donny tightened his grip aggressively. "Where ya been working, Rob?"

Stepping back to reclaim his hand from the crushing hold, Rob unobtrusively shook his hand, trying to reduce the throbbing. Dennis laughed and slugged his brother in the shoulder. "Donny, knock it off. Everyone can see you're a he-man. You don't gotta prove it every time you meet someone."

Flashing a misshapen grin, Donny stepped into a dark room and a light flickered on then off. He came back holding three beers, handing them out to his brother and Rob. "Let's go into the garage," he suggested. "We can see what Rob knows about maintaining abused taxis."

Rob hitched the duffle again with one hand and held the beer in the other as he followed the brothers into the cavernous space behind the offices.

***

Donny shrugged, responding to a question from Rob. "Nah, it doesn't bother me anymore." He took a swig from his beer. "I had a feeding tube until I was almost sixteen. Otherwise, I'd probably be as big as the rock star here." He bumped his shoulder into Dennis, nearly knocking him off his stool. "Nutrient liquids will keep you alive, but they do *not* satisfy." He laughed, taking another drink from his beer for emphasis. They were sitting in the garage, near the workbench that housed all the tools, parts, and supplies used to maintain the fleet of taxis the brothers owned.

"Our aunt and uncle tried to get a doctor to do reconstructive surgery on him, but by the time we had moved in with them, he was too old. At least they were able to fix it enough so he could get off the tube." Dennis tilted his head, leaning his elbows back on the bench and looking up. "Mom and Dad didn't do enough; they left it too late. Too focused on their own shit. Sucks for Donny." He paused. "But," he looked over at Rob, "at least I'll always be the bigger man."

Donny laughed and hit his shoulder. "Shut up. You're supposed to be supportive, brother." Rob shook his head. *These two had a relationship like Joel had with…*

His face fell, and he almost dropped the bottle held in his hand.

Donny and Dennis both marked the change in mood that swept over him, looking at him quizzically as Dennis asked, "You okay, Rob? You look like somebody hit you in the gut, man."

Taking in a deep breath, Rob pasted on a smile that he didn't think would fool anyone. "What's with the 'rock star' comments? That's about three times tonight you've called Dennis that."

Donny laughed, rolling his head over to look at Rob. "Denzel here is in a band. Plays guitar, if you can believe that."

Dennis slapped his hands on his thighs. "Don't call me that, Donovan, and I'm far from a rock star. I'm not even in a band. I play in the bar from time to time. Nothing fancy, just fun."

He stood. "Who's hungry? I'm starving. We need to go to Bethany's for dinner. I'll show you where you can stow the duffle you've had a stranglehold on all afternoon, and we'll all walk across the street." He looked at Donny, asking, "Who's dispatching tonight?"

Donny twisted to look at a board on the wall beside the door. "Alex, but she'll be late; she always is. I'll see if Mike can stay until she gets here." He hopped down off the stool and walked across the garage to the real office of the business, where the dispatcher sat with blackboard slates and chalk, keeping track of the pick-up requests and dispatched vehicles.

Standing and stretching, Rob followed Dennis. "Thanks again for the opportunity. I needed this, all of it." He blew out a long breath. "I sold my house in New Jersey a few months ago, put the money in the bank. I just...have no interest in returning to where I grew up, back where my family still lives."

"That's too bad, man. Family is important." Dennis had paused while he spoke, then continued walking. Following a quiet Dennis up the stairs, Rob looked around the small space carved out of a storage area on the second floor. Pushed up against one wall was a double bed, and near a narrow window stood a mini-fridge with a hot plate set on top of it. An open door in the hallway revealed a glimpse of a tub and toilet; the sink was probably in there too.

Rob tossed his duffle on the floor beside the bed, observing the sheets looked crisp and clean. Pointing at the bed, he asked, "Were you expecting company?"

Dennis laughed. "My aunt changes the linens every week, even if no one has slept up here. She's a hoot and set in her ways...that's for sure. Wants to always be ready for anything." He paused and looked at Rob. "Family, right? They took on a lot when they volunteered to raise me and Donny. I'm glad we were able to move in with them when we did. I think it probably saved his life. I'm also glad that even though they're sisters, she and my mom aren't anything alike. Mom's got issues."

"All right, girls, are you coming down voluntarily, or do I have to come up and get you?" Donny called up the stairway, making a racket with his hands on the walls. Dennis and Rob were laughing as they clattered down the narrow stairs, and the three new friends walked across the street to the diner.

8 - Up tempo

"Seriously, Dennis. I want to learn how to play, but I won't take your flattop. I'll buy one from the pawn shop so you can teach me." Rob rolled out from under a taxi on his mechanic's creeper. "I've heard you play enough times to know you're good. Now you gotta spread that wealth around, help me out."

Sauntering into the garage, Donny yelled at them from across the room. "Quit gossiping, you two biddy hens. Get back to work, slaves! Back to work!" He made a noise like a bullwhip cracking—*wuh-PSH!*—and laughed.

"You're a useless sack, you know that?" Dennis shot back at his brother. The *wuh-PSH!* sound came again, followed by more peals of laughter.

He'd been working for the brothers more than a year now and had grown accustomed to their relaxed and playful rapport. It had been hard losing the Navy; there was security in the known, and having a strict understanding of what was expected of you made life comfortable. Fortunately, while the brothers at first had only a vague idea about schedules and maintenance, they'd been okay with everything Rob had recommended. With him running the garage, things were now regimented, planned out tightly, and that helped him cope most of the time.

The nightmares were still the hardest part, and they had gradually gotten more intense and frequent when the anniversary date of the accident approached and passed. It was impossible to believe it had been so long since he'd last seen his angels.

A few weeks ago, he'd finally broken down and talked to Donny about Andrea and Ashley. They'd been sitting on the stools near the workbench as they often did, chatting about nothing in particular, and it seemed natural to share with his friend. Donny, more than anyone, knew life wasn't always fair, but the man was a study in how to get past terrible experiences or circumstances without becoming bitter. Things seemed to get a little easier for Rob after that; at least his nightmares had settled to some degree.

Donny could try and joke all he wanted about being a slave driver, but even if he honestly was one, it was because he wouldn't let anyone give less than their best at anything. He went into every project and job expecting superior service and work from everyone on staff, most notably himself. He had a brilliant mind and kept many details about the day-to-day business in his head, only writing things down if he had to assign them to someone else. He could perform virtually any function in the shop, and was a one-man whirlwind when it came to getting drivers out the door for their shift.

Dennis was easygoing and seemed comfortable in more of a mentor role, and Rob hoped he'd agree to teach him how to play the guitar. It would be something Rob would be able to practice by himself, and now that he was settled into the routine of work and life here in the shop, he found he needed more distractions to keep his mind exhausted and hands busy.

Rob stood, using a rag to wipe the brake fluid off his hands. He looked up at the board to see what other maintenance jobs were planned for that day, and found this was his last car. "I'll bleed the lines on one-four-six," noting the car's call number, "and then I'm done for the day. After that, I'm going to shower and then go buy a guitar, and I'll meet you back here. Don't tell me no, man. I'll even buy the beer, Dennis. Come on, spread the wealth. Share the riches." He held his breath, smiling in relief when Dennis nodded.

Walking back into the shop about an hour later, he carried a guitar in his hand and a case of beer under his arm. Dennis and Donny were sitting on stools, waiting for him. "All right, give it up. Hand it over. Lemme see what you wasted your money on, Robby." Dennis relieved him of the guitar case, carrying it over to one of the taxis and carefully placing it on the hood.

Flipping the latches, he opened the case and whistled low. "Holy shit, Robby. This is a PRS acoustic. What did you have to shell out for this one?" He lifted the guitar, grinning widely. "Wow. It nearly humbles my Taylor, man. Pretty, pretty!"

"So I picked out a good one? I strummed across the strings on several, and this one sounded okay. Fifty bucks, was that a good deal?" Rob asked.

"Holy shit! Yeah, that's a good deal. And really? 'Okay?' It's so much more than just okay." He repeated himself with a smile, "Pretty, pretty!"

Dennis held the guitar loosely and closed his eyes as he plucked the strings, tuning them before he launched into a fast instrumental. His fingers danced across the strings as he used a combination of techniques, both strumming and picking; his fret-hand slid, moved, and clamped swiftly to pull the song from the instrument.

He stopped mid-song and opened his eyes, smiling. "This is a sweet one. Listen to the resonance. The sound is so rich." Closing his eyes again, he played a few bars of *Always,* a popular hard rock song by Saliva.

Donny laughed at him, poking his elbow into Rob's ribs. "He's in lust. Look at the desire on his face. Imagine that, Dennis the Great, brought low by some common wood and varnish."

"Speak not thusly, ignorant knave," Dennis shot back in the same spirit. "Thou knowest not what thou sayest. 'Tis artistry I hold in me hands, the marriage of wood and humidity, acoustics and space; listen...the heart of the wood weeps for your words." Laughing, he looked up at them. "Or something like that."

Rob laughed so hard he was holding his sides in pain. "That was so bad, Dennis. Like a mix of Shakespeare and English done in a slight Irish brogue, with a small side of science thrown in for good measure. You're a fucking weirdo. Gimme back my guitar and get your own out. Show me how to play something before the beer gets too warm."

Dennis pulled his guitar case out of the backseat of his car and brought it over to the workbench area. Clearing off a space, he opened it and took out his Taylor, holding a pick between his teeth as he reverently attached a shoulder strap to the guitar. Talking around the pick, he asked Rob, "Probably the easiest thing is to learn specific chords that go with a song you want to play. What song do you want to attempt?"

"Something easy, I guess. I don't know. Um..." He thought for a minute. "I know the intro is hard, but what about the regular part of that Black Crowes song, *She Talks to Angels*?"

Dennis nodded his head unhurriedly, and Rob could see he was working the song out in his head. "Yeah. That wouldn't be bad. It's a sad-ass song, but it's like three chords and open-chord strumming once you get past the intro. Lemme tune a second, I think..." His voice trailed off while he slung the guitar strap over his shoulder. He stood for a moment, then took the pick from his mouth and put his hands to the strings.

A few minutes later, their instruments were tuned to his satisfaction in what he called an open E, and he was showing Rob the fingering on the frets for the chords. "You're almost always strumming down, not on the up. Like this...dooown, dooown, down, up, down, down—and then my part, da...da...da...dada, and then back to you—dooown, dooown, down, up, down, down. Do you hear the phrasing? It's awfully slow, but good." He listened and played with Rob for a minute. "Yeah. Yeah, like that," Dennis said encouragingly.

By the end of the night, Rob's fingers were blistered and hurting, but they'd played the song through several times. Dennis played the intro with complex, intricate notes that sounded like a waterfall, and then they'd played the verses and chorus of the song together, blending their voices as they sang along.

Rob lifted his head after the last rendition, surprised to see they had an audience of off-duty drivers as well as Donny. The smattering of applause was rewarding, and Rob looked at Dennis with a broad smile on his face. "That was awesome. Thanks for your patience, man." He shook his hands out, only now realizing they were cramping.

"I didn't think I'd enjoy teaching someone, but you learn fast. That was pretty good. Now you have to work on toughening up your tips, so we can keep going," Dennis advised him as he put his guitar back into the case, removing the strap.

Rob picked up the bottle in front of him, making a face when he took a drink and got a mouthful of warm beer. Glancing down, he realized most of the case was gone, and looking around, he saw Donny had handed bottles out to everyone. With a grin, he put the guitar back on his knee and started strumming again, singing quietly as he watched these people who'd become his friends smile encouragingly at him.

Lying in bed that night, Rob reached over and pulled an envelope out from between the mattresses. He knew the men's Aunt Judy had found it early on when she changed the sheets, but she'd never asked him about what was in it. Every week, she simply left it on top of the pillows for him to put away.

Resting the envelope on his upper body, he covered it carefully with both hands, pressing it gently into his chest. "Hey, sugar. How you doin' tonight? I bought a guitar today...gonna learn how to play from Dennis. I've told you about him and his brother, how they helped me out. They remind me of you and Joel all the time, how you'd pick on each other. I should call Joel this weekend; I haven't talked to him in a while."

"He misses you, ya know? So do I, sugar. So, so much. Miss both of you. Tell that pretty girl standing there with you that her daddy loves her. She's my sweetness. Sugar and sweetness, my angels. I love you both so much." He became aware of the tears streaking the sides of his head, soaking into his hair, and he reached up, swiping across his eyes with the back of one hand.

Rob rolled over and tucked the envelope containing the unwatched dance recital tape and his last letter from his wife and daughter back between the mattresses. With a sigh, he settled down for what he expected to be yet another sleepless night.

***

"I don't know, Dennis," Rob disagreed. "I only know three songs, and only play those well if you're helping me out." He pulled his head out from under the hood of a taxi, making a gesture to the driver to crank the engine. When it started, he closed the hood with a firm push of both hands, then wiped where he'd touched with the ever-present rag from his pocket.

Dennis cocked his head, looking at him. "Robby, you're ready. I wouldn't propose this if I didn't think you were. If we weren't. It's my ass up on that stage, too, ya know." He grinned, cocking his head back the other way. "But you're ready, and I want to show off my teaching expertise."

Looking up at the board, Rob groaned when he saw there were two more vehicles on the roster for the day. Gesturing up, he said, "I don't agree with you, but there's also the fact your slave driver of a brother thinks I can work twice as fast as is humanly possible." He raised his voice until he was shouting across the garage. "Forget the reality of being a mechanic and the time it takes to do a good job. Your brother thinks I should be able to service a transmission in fifteen minutes and he's *CRAZY*."

Hearing laughter, both men looked up to see Donny coming their way, and heard the *wuh-PSH* sound that accompanied him when he was in a good mood. "Little fucker thinks he's funny," said Dennis, and Rob laughed.

"Resorting to short people jokes again, brother? Running out of your own material?" Donny retorted with a snicker.

Turning to Rob, he leaned in conspiratorially. "I gotcha a present, Robby."

"Oh, yeah? Whaddya get me, boss?" He laughed, not knowing what kind of practical joke to expect today.

Turning around, Donny yelled towards the back of the shop, "Bring it in, boys."

The overhead door slid up, opening to the outside, and Rob saw a small group of men standing there. Once it had opened sufficiently, they pushed in a...well, it looked like a motorcycle, but without some awfully important parts, like handlebars and a seat. "What the hell is this, Donny?" he asked with a nervous laugh.

Donny grinned. "This," he said, with a sweep of his arm towards the bike, "is your new project. You're getting bored, and I think this will suit you. First, agree to the gig with my brother, then get started sorting out the bike." Preparing to leave, Donny shot a glance back over his shoulder. "No fucking excuses, Robby. Just do it." Stunned, Rob stood in silence, watching him walk away.

"I can only apologize for my brother; he's a bossy little man," Dennis began, and Donny's head popped back out of the hallway.

"Again with the short jokes? I'm gettin' tired of your shit, brother." They faintly heard the *wuh-PSH* sound again from the front office of the shop and both laughed.

"Okay, I'll go to the pub. *And*, if it's not too crowded, I'll play the three songs I know *with you*, not by myself. It's only the three, Dennis," he reiterated.

Dennis nodded. "Yeah, yeah. Your angel songs. I get it. We'll do them at the end of my set. I'll want you sitting on a stool while I do the first songs. That way, you don't have to walk in or leave, and we can flow from my songs into the duets without drawing too much attention to you." Rob realized Dennis had given this some consideration and was warmed by his friend's thoughtfulness in understanding how it made him nervous to be the center of attention.

Seated on stage that night, Rob watched the faces in the crowd as they enjoyed Dennis' performance. He was playing long-time favorites, and a large number of the customers were singing along. Sitting on a stool like Rob's, he was wrapped around his guitar and kept his mouth near the microphone, lost in his music and seldom looking up at the audience, much less referring to the set list taped to the floor.

Rob kept looking down at his list, going over it again and again, anxiously counting the songs through the whole set. This was the last one for Dennis, and then they would be playing his angel songs, starting with the most difficult one he'd learned so far, *Angel* by Jack Johnson. Hearing the vibrations from the strings on Dennis' guitar slow and still in the relatively quiet air in the pub, Rob sat up a little straighter. It was time for their two guitars now, and he apprehensively saw some of the faces in the audience swing over to look at him.

Watching Dennis for his cues, he began strumming out the main melody for the song, and in sync with his friend, Rob leaned up to the microphone and opened his mouth to sing. Within a few moments, the sounds of the pub and customers all faded away, and all he could hear was only himself, Dennis, and their guitars playing the song. Rob hadn't realized he'd closed his eyes until they finished and the sounds of the environment fell back in on him with a rush, forcing his eyes open wide. He saw that not only the people crowding the stage were applauding, but even the men at the bar were standing and clapping, and Rob looked at Dennis in awe.

They moved into The Black Crowes' song next, *She Talks to Angels*, penned by brothers Chris and Rich Robinson. The crowd hushed when they heard the familiar notes coming from Dennis' guitar. Joining in on the main verses and choruses, eyes closed again, Rob lent his tenor to the song. Together, their singing lifted the sad reality of sordid addiction to poignant sentiment with the emotion of loss and longing clear in their voices.

Not allowing the crowd time to applaud or respond, Dennis transitioned quickly from that song to the last of the set, *Calling All Angels* by Train. Keeping his eyes open this time, Rob saw the people in the audience joining in on the chorus, seeing as their mouths formed the words over and over while he and Dennis strummed their way through the extended version they'd been practicing.

Then it was over, and the acclaim from the crowd seemed deafening in the small space inside Mickie's Pub. Dennis stood and reached over, pulling Rob into a hasty, congratulatory hug, and then waved at the crowd in front of the stage as they turned to walk off.

Donny met them in the back hallway that led to the small storage room doubling as a green room for visiting musicians. "That was amazing, boys. They couldn't get enough of you, Rob. Dennis they've seen before; he's a repeat offender, but you—fresh meat and talented, too? No way you're going home alone tonight. No way." He clapped his hand on Rob's elbow, patting his bicep.

Rob rubbed his forehead with the back of his hand, laughing weakly. "That had to be the single most frightening thing I've ever voluntarily chosen to do. More terrifying than standing next to a nuclear reactor while hundreds of feet under the ocean. What the hell was I thinking?"

Donny handed him a towel and then pointed both index fingers at him. "Doesn't matter if you were thinking or not—you pulled it off. What you guys did up there tonight was damn good, and Mickie wants to talk to you both when you get cleaned up." He walked out of the stifling room and back towards the front of the pub.

Dennis sat, leaning back in a folding chair and wiping his face with a towel. "I've never seen the crowd as excited as they were for those last three songs. Your voice is good, Rob. You're talented, and their reactions should show you what I mean. This was a lot of fun, man. I hope we get to do it again soon." He stood, clasping one hand on Rob's shoulder, squeezing lightly before he walked away.

Watching Dennis follow his brother into the public area of the pub, Rob thought about what Donny had said about not going home alone. It was no secret he hadn't brought any women around the shop in the time he'd been living in the little apartment on the second floor. Rob knew he was a good-looking guy with his dark hair and green eyes, and his single state wasn't for lack of opportunity.

No, it wasn't scarcity of selection that kept his bed empty every night. His mother would more likely call it *lackawanna,* because he simply couldn't seem to drum up interest in any woman. Intellectually, he could look at a woman and tell himself she was beautiful and he should be attracted to her, but realistically, he could not get past the fact they weren't Andrea. It wasn't even a feeling of being unfaithful, more that he wasn't interested. A lack of wanna.

He rolled his shoulders, stacking his guitar case on top of Dennis', and then he wiped his face one last time before tossing the towel down and following the brothers out front. Time to see what Mickie thought and accept the congratulations of his friends.

9 - New era

"Delivery for you, Crew," called Alex, one of the dispatchers. She'd worked for the Baugh brothers for several years and had developed a comfortable, friendly relationship with them. Early on, when he started working in the garage, she'd declared Rob her pal and had adopted him as one more surrogate brother alongside their bosses.

He walked over and picked the box up from beside her desk, taking it to the workbench where he cut the strips of tape holding it closed. "Oh, cool, the handlebars finally came in," he called to Alex and heard her laugh.

"You still trying to fix up that hunk of junk Donny shoved off on you, Rob?" she asked.

"Why not? I don't have much else to do. It's not like I work for a living or anything," Rob called back to her, and they both laughed hard when they heard the familiar *wuh-PSH* sound from behind the closed office door.

Donny's muffled voice came through the door. "You *won't* work for a living much longer if you keep that attitude."

Carrying the handlebars over to the bike, he stood for a bit and looked it over, proud of his handiwork. All the dirt and rust had been removed, and if it couldn't be eliminated, then the ruined part had been replaced. The chrome was shiny, and the new leather seat was crack-free and supple. These handlebars were the last piece needed to complete the rebuild of the bike, and he was looking forward to seeing it finished. He wasn't sure what Donny intended to do with it, but it had been fun working on the bike.

He didn't understand how Donny had known what he had needed, but working on the bike had been good for him. It had steadied him, giving him something to focus on, and he'd relished every challenge, such as pulling together the needed parts, not stopping even when there were some he couldn't locate. Rob had dusted off his high school CAD drawing skills on the shop's old computer, working for hours to draft and tweak designs for some of the alterations he wanted to make. Donny had been able to find a machinist to fabricate every part to specification, and hadn't balked at the cost of anything, which was a surprise, because it was unlike him.

Tightening the bolts that held the handlebars in place, Rob finished attaching them and stood back, admiring the look of the bike. Using a graphic art program, he'd designed and created a stencil for the paint job. The tank and fairings had a pretty metallic-blue swirl as a base coat, with a red, flaming trident overlay that symbolized his naval career, serving on submarines and diving underneath the oceans. With its classic lines, the Harley Davidson FSX Super-Glide was gorgeous, especially when paired with the paint job and modifications. He ran a hand over the tank and seat, excited the 1987 bike was finally ready to ride.

Rob turned the key and jumped on the starter, grinning wide when the bike fired up on the second kick. Standing to one side, he revved the motor a couple of times, listening to the rack and ring of the pipes. A change in light alerted him to the overhead door opening, and he turned to see Donny standing beside the controls, waving at him. He killed the bike reluctantly, and walked over to see what Donny needed.

Before he even got there, Donny was already talking. "Don't get pissed. That one is yours, won't sell it, won't give it away—can't make me. Don't get pissed, Robby. That Super-Glide is yours, free and clear; the signed title will be in your next pay envelope."

Rob shook his head. "What the hell you talking about, Donny? The bike? You paid for all the parts, man. That's not my bike. I can't take that. It's not—"

Nodding wildly, Donny interrupted him, "No arguments, Rob. Can, will, did. Debate-free, that bike is yours. But, these?" Here, he paused and pointed into the parking lot behind the building, drawing Rob's attention outside. Sweeping his arms wide, he made a popping noise and then said with satisfaction in his voice, "These, we will sell."

Rob looked out and saw at least a dozen bikes in varying stages of ruin and neglect. Looking closely, he saw that each was a classic Harley—or at least the original chassis were. Some of them had aftermarket modifications that were poorly done, or had cheap replacement parts.

Dennis walked up, whistling low. "I see the delivery finally got here. Donny, that's a lotta bikes, man. You sure about this?"

Punching him in the bicep, Donny scowled up at him. "Did you see the bike he built? Did you *see* the fucking bike? Something like that will go for thousands more than the cost for parts and labor to put it together. Each one will be unique, a one of a kind. A Baugh Brothers Bike, with some Crew thrown in for spice."

Rob stood silently for a few minutes, going over what Donny had said. Then he walked out among the bikes, taking mental notes about what was needed to restore each. After a span of time, he strolled back over to where Donny and Dennis were standing. Studying the bikes, he folded his arms across his chest with a deep sigh. "BB and C," he said cryptically.

"Done," crowed Donny, while Dennis glanced between the two of them with a bewildered look on his face.

Rob took pity on his friend's confusion, telling him, "Baugh Brothers and Crew. That's the name of the custom bike shop we're opening. Your money, tools, space, connections—my talents."

***

"Claudia, do you have a copy of the parts shipment invoice from Decker's? I want to see if they claim they shipped the whole order. I can't find the engine crash bars I need for the FXB Sturgis we're working on," Rob said. He was standing at the half-door that opened into the office, speaking to the manager they'd hired almost a year ago, when profits from the custom bike business became the norm instead of an exception.

Blowing out her breath in exasperation, she reached back and pulled out a file cabinet drawer. Quickly thumbing through the information in a folder, she retrieved and offered him a sheet of paper, pointing with one crimson-covered nail at the note on the bottom, where it indicated the crash bars would take an additional week. "I swear, Rob. I told you, or maybe I told Donny. I know I told somebody." She shrugged, refiling the paperwork and turning back to her desk.

Rolling his eyes at her attitude, he was silently amused. Claudia was more than competent as an office manager—as long as everything was written down. Unlike Donny, she couldn't hold details in her head for more than a few minutes, and their differences in management styles had caused some pretty spectacular fireworks in the beginning. Donny had quickly realized they complemented each other both inside and outside the office, and things had heated up even more as they began dating. Over time, things in the shop had gradually settled down into a routine, and the office ran more efficiently than ever. If you listened to Donny, their relationship in bed was still full of fireworks and far from routine.

Rob huffed in irritation, because he really wanted to get the Sturgis done and out the door so he could spend more time on his new bike. He looked across the garage, studying the effect of his work from a distance. It was a 2002 Harley Softail Heritage Classic he'd modified and customized to be exactly what he wanted. He still loved riding the '87, but the Softail had more kick and more real estate for paint, which was what he was working on now.

He walked back to his workbench, staring at the picture on the computer screen. Intended for the tank, it showed the figures of two angels embedded in clouds and dressed in gossamer gowns as they looked towards the seat, where the rider would be. The larger angel had white-blonde curls wreathing her smiling face; her wings were streaming in the wind, blowing and swirling around the two figures like smoke.

In the picture, she was holding the smaller angel in front of her, arms wrapped around her waist. The smaller angel was nearly bent double, relaxed in the security of those arms, holding a large, overblown dandelion in her outstretched hands and blowing the seeds loose into the wind. Her white-blonde hair was pulled into a ponytail that draped forward over her shoulder. The front fairing would have clouds swirling across it, while the back would have swirls of the same color, along with a dozen dandelion seeds in great detail.

He was struggling with the wings for the smaller figure, he hadn't been able to render them the way he wanted, like they were in his head. Reaching up, he touched the face on the screen, dragging a fingertip across those little lips puckered to blow the seeds, and he softly said, "Sweetness." Turning away from the computer, he sighed as he picked up his mug of coffee and took a deep drink.

Donny burst into the garage, holding a piece of paper between his thumb and fingers, waving it over his head like a flag. "Hey, hey, hey, Rob! This is fantastic! Come see," he called across to where Rob was sitting.

Knowing he didn't have to move, because Donny was already headed his way, Rob held out his hand, snapping his fingers impatiently. "Hurry up! I don't have all day, Donny. I've got work to do," he said in a mock-serious voice.

As Donny handed over the paper, he made the whip sound that had become so standard in the garage, and both men laughed. Rob quickly looked the paper over and raised his eyes to Donny's face. "Is this for fucking real, Donny?" he asked incredulously.

As he carefully reclaimed the paper, plucking it out of Rob's hands, Donny responded, "I think so. God, I hope so. Everything checks out. I've run as much information as I can get on this dude, and he looks like he's a legit customer. Granted, he's not a consumer, but this is a new market we hadn't counted on. Selling parts and custom paint to another bike shop? Genius! I wish I'd have thought of it; we could have kept this as only BB, and left off the C."

"Watch your mouth, little man," Rob growled out, and Donny laughed.

"So predictable—you and my brother both. If you can't think of a comeback, you go for the short joke," he snorted. "But, hey! I'm sitting here holding an order for more than a hundred thousand dollars. Go ahead and make all the jokes you want as long as you tell me we can fill this order, Rob."

"Lemme see it again. Does Dennis know about this yet?" Rob held his hand out, and once he had the order again, he took more care reviewing the details, seeing Donny shake his head. Rob weighed options in his brain. "I'm not sure about the availability of original parts for some of these models. If we can't find them, you'll need to see if he's okay with fabricated to original spec. Who is this guy? Davis Mason, owner of FWO and FWO2 in Chicago?" He looked over at Donny, "What does FWO stand for?"

“No idea. I’ll ask when I call to find out about the fabrication. Anything else jump out at you? I’d like to have a complete list of questions or concerns before I place the call.” Donny stretched and arched his neck. “Better yet, you can ask him yourself. He’ll be arriving next week to talk about orders beyond this first one.”

Blowing out a breath, Rob said, “Okay. We’re performing at the pub tonight, so let’s talk to Dennis after the show. He’s gone over to check on Aunt Judy, said she wasn’t feeling well.” Rob looked at the paper again. “That’s a lot of work to do in a short time, but if they are okay with fab when I can’t find original, I can do it. I’d suggest you go ahead and give the guy a call.” Peering at the paper, “This Mason…it’ll save him a trip if it doesn’t work out.”

10 - Partnerships

Hearing voices from across the garage, Rob raised his head to see who was invading his space. Using wide, sweeping hand movements, Donny was engaged in an animated conversation with the man he and Dennis were escorting, a big guy with short, dark hair. Dressed casually in motorcycle boots, jeans, a black leather vest, and a dark blue Henley pullover, he looked relaxed and comfortable, the sleeves of his shirt pushed up, exposing tattoos on his arms.

Rob straightened up from his computer, where he had been working on final touches to the angels picture for his new bike, and caught the man's gaze. There was a snapping crackle across his senses as he became fully aware of this man's authority and presence.

"Rob, this is Davis Mason," Donny introduced them. "He's come from Chicago to talk to us." Stretching his hand out in greeting, Rob was aware of the weight of the man's gaze on him. It felt as if he was being judged and measured, and it was not unlike the calculating looks Naval Officers would turn on him during inspections or exercises—evaluating, appraising, and assessing. Straightening his shoulders with a jerk, he gripped Mason's hand when it finally met his palm and firmly shook it twice before releasing.

"I'm glad to finally meet the artist behind the fucking work," Mason told him, and his eyes turned to the computer screen. "May I?" he asked respectfully, while already stepping around Rob to look at the picture of the two angels. There was silence in the room for a moment; the brothers hadn't even seen his design yet, but it felt right for Mason see his tribute to his girls, his angels.

"This means something to you." Mason muttered the words, not really making it an inquiry, but Rob answered him anyway.

"Yeah," he said quietly, "it's for my bike. My wife and daughter."

"Fucking hard, man. That's fucking hard to see, but tougher to live through, right?" Mason looked at him as he asked the question.

"Yeah," was all Rob could squeeze out through his abruptly tight throat.

Mason gazed at the screen again. "You do this from a picture?"

He shook his head, "No, my memories of them are vivid and strong."

Nodding, Mason stared for a minute more, and then asked, "You got other stencils ready to go? You should have the specs for what I need. I sent those a couple weeks ago."

Rob leaned over to save and close the file on the computer, and then with a few clicks of the mouse, he launched a gallery of images, setting them to scroll across the screen. "I have a few designs done up and ready. I think some of the dimensions may change, but if we can fabricate the tanks, we can standardize certain elements and go to templates. That will make it easier to create additional designs going forward."

He stepped back, allowing Mason control of the computer. After watching silently for a few minutes, tapping his thumbnail against his bottom teeth, he reached out and clicked the mouse, pausing the scroll of images that was flowing across the screen. "I've seen enough. I'm good," he said, twisting to look down at Donny. "One of my brothers bought a ride from you last year, so I know the craftsmanship you put into the bikes. Now that I know customization is feasible at the scale I need, I'm good."

Looking at him expectantly, Rob asked, "Which one?"

“Which what?” Mason asked in return.

“Which bike did your brother buy?” He cocked his head, waiting for an answer.

“Red bought a Sturgis. His bike has a biomechanical look to the paint job, as if there are gears breaking through from under the paint. He calls it the T-1000.” Mason shrugged. “The bike itself is solid, man. The alterations to enhance the power are genius. Red is the envy of the club.”

“Club? I thought you said he was your brother?” he questioned.

Mason shouted with laughter, tipping his head back in amusement. “He *is* my brother…my patch brother. I’m the national president of the Rebel Wayfarers MC, and he’s a member. We have a number of businesses to help support the club; the two bike shops are only a small part of the whole.”

“FWO and FWO2?” Donny spoke for the first time since they’d stopped in front of the computer.

“Yeah, Fucking Wide Open shops one and two. Our bike shops.” Mason smirked, and Rob found himself mirroring the look of delight.

Over dinner in the pub, the conversation had gradually shifted to talking about life outside of the bike shops, and Rob was telling a story about how to have a foot race on a submarine by running around the reactor bay. Mason lifted his beer and took a sip, then said, “One of my men has a nephew in the Navy, Carter LeRoy.”

Rob’s head shot up. “No shit? I served with LeRoy. A few years ago, I trained him as my replacement, in fact.”

Mason looked at him with a level gaze, muttering, “No fucking way.” He spoke louder, asking, “Did he tell you to call his uncle in Chicago about a job?”

He nodded. "Yeah, it didn't pan out, but Dennis was here in the bar that day, and we talked—and here I am. It all worked out like it was supposed to, I think."

Rubbing his hand across his jaw, Mason looked pained. "No *fucking* way. That was you? Goddammit. I could have had you in my shops all this goddamn time?" Shaking his head, he spoke to himself, saying, "Shoulda listened to Tug, dammit. Fuck."

Laughing in bemusement, Rob asked, "His uncle works for you? I thought he managed a shop, but then when I called, he talked about bikes. I wasn't sure what he was going on about, and then he called me back to tell me there wasn't a job for me." He shrugged. "Like I said, everything worked out like it was supposed to. I started as a mechanic here for Donny and Dennis, and then Donny had the bold idea for the bike shop, so we opened BB&C. It's been satisfying. They've been good to me." He looked over at Donny, who had started laughing, saying, "Shaddup, shorty."

Dennis waved to him from the stage, and then Rob turned to Mason. "Time for the show. You gonna stay and listen?"

Mason pulled the corners of his mouth down dismissively. "What show?"

He pointed to Donny. "This jokester can fill you in, but if you can stay, you should. We're pretty good."

Standing, he made his way to the stage, dodging between chairs and customers, meeting Dennis by the back entrance. "You'll never believe this, Dennis. You remember that day I got out of the Navy, when we met here in the pub?" He pulled his guitar case up to place it across the top of a crate. Hearing an agreeable noise from behind him, he continued, "That call I made was to a member of Mason's club. The job I got turned down for? It was in one of his bike shops. Small world, huh?"

He turned to see Dennis gaping at him and heard him say, "No way! That's too weird. What are the odds, Rob? That's crazy."

"Yeah, I know." Taking a deep breath, he bumped fists with Dennis. "Okay, let's do this." They walked out onto the stage, where they now sat side-by-side as equally-skilled musicians. He still got nervous before they played, but was more certain of his abilities now. Their set tonight launched with a technically challenging but rewarding song by Fink titled *This Is the Thing*, and ended over forty-five minutes later with back-to-back Hot Tuna classics, a bluesy *True Religion* followed by the laidback *Hesitation Blues*.

Standing in the artist's area behind the stage, he used a towel to wipe the sweat off his face and neck. Hearing a sound behind him, he turned to find Mason leaning against the wall. "What'd ya think?" he asked, carefully putting the PRS back into its case.

"The two of you are fucking outstanding, man. That was impressive," Mason said, nodding firmly.

Holding out his hand, Mason told him, "I've worked out the details on that first order with Donny. We're good to go with your recommendations, Rob. At some point, I'll want you to come to Chicago and see the set-up we have there. I think you'll have some suggestions for changes once you see it. But that's not today, that's for the future. Right now, you're holding an order of parts and paint for fifty bikes." He reached out to grab Mason's hand and found himself gripped by the wrist instead, pulled into a one-armed shoulder bump.

"Good to meet you, man. Like I said, y'all were really awesome on stage too. Fucking brilliant," Mason said, and then he walked away.

***

"Naw, Rob, don't worry about it. Whatever you decide is needed is gonna be okay with Mason," came a drawled response to his question. Slate, Mason's second in command, was on the phone and had just granted Rob carte blanche on altering the parts order for fully half the bikes.

"But, it adds an extra nine hundred dollars per bike, and that's multiplied by twenty-five bikes, Slate," Rob continued. "You confident Mason's gonna be okay with that?"

"Aww, fuck yeah, he'll be fine with it. We've all seen the genius that is Rob Crew, and we are believers, brother. Drink that Kool-Aid." He laughed and Rob grinned in response.

"Changing the dimensions on the intake manifolds for the eleven-hundred and twelve-hundred engines like this gives us a significant amount of additional power. I fabricated the part a couple weeks ago and put the mod on my bike. The fucking thing squats when I crank it open now. One test ride and the bikes will sell themselves," he justified.

Slate laughed down the line again. "Preaching to the choir, brother. I want one of your bikes in the worst way. Make me a wicked Fatboy, man. I need to retire my Indian."

He responded promptly, "So...yeah, I can do that. Send me what you want, I'll start drafting specs and changes, and then I can run them past you for approval. Got any concepts for your paint?"

There was silence on the line for a minute, then Slate said haltingly, "Yeah, I do, but we can talk about that when you're here in a couple weeks. You still set on making that road trip, man? Long way to ride by yourself—I know from experience."

"Then fly out here and ride with me, Slate. I have Winger's bike ready. If he's okay with it, you could ride it back, instead of me having it shipped. Help keep me in line on the trip," he joked and then chuckled.

He heard a series of staccato pops through the phone that seemed as if they came from a distance, and Slate spoke brusquely, all humor gone from his voice. "*Fuck me.* Rob, I got business. Gotta go." Rob made a face as the call suddenly ended. *Biker business*, he thought and shook his head, wondering at the noises he'd heard in the background.

"Donny," he yelled, "we got changes to the FWO order. Slate gave me the go on the phone. You gonna take that at face, or verify before I place the fab order?" He laughed quietly. "FWO...Fucking Wide Open...only bikers would name a business something like that."

The office door banged open and Donny strolled through to the garage. "Go ahead and do the fab order. I'll send a change request over for Mason's signature with a note that Slate verbally approved."

Donny stood there for a minute, quiet, his face thoughtful, and then asked him, "Rob, do you—are you enjoying the work? Working here, I mean? I keep thinking about how you wound up here with me and Dennis. If things had gone differently that day in the bar, if Mason had given you a job, we'd have never met. And just look how our business has changed...morphed, because of you, us augmenting the taxi business with the bike shop. This has been huge for us, and it's because of you. Now here we are, hooking up with the guy who turned you down for a job, which was how we met? Life is weird, man. *Good*...but weird."

Puffing out his cheeks, Rob let out a breath, feigning irritation. "Was there a question in there, Donny? You kept talking nonsense, so I couldn't tell if you really wanted an answer."

"Fuck you, Rob," he said without heat. "Are you enjoying the work?" Donny asked, reaching up and punching his shoulder.

"Yeah, I like the work. It keeps my hands busy and my mind occupied. I need this. I get lost designing the paint jobs and look up to find it's five hours later. It feels like this is where I'm supposed to be right now. So, I'm not going anywhere, unless you kick me to the curb." Then, he asked, "Are you kicking me to the curb?"

Tilting his head to one side thoughtfully, Donny took a minute to answer. "Not today," he eventually declared with a firm nod, and Rob laughed with him.

Sitting on his bed that night, Rob cradled the PRS across his lap, absently plucking the strings as he mulled over the earlier conversations with Slate and Donny. Slate's easy acceptance of his recommendations was unsettling. He wasn't accustomed to people behaving in that way when they'd never even met him. In his mind, their trust of him was unwarranted—and since he hadn't done anything to earn it, he didn't know what would cause it to fail. If it were based solely on his relationship with Mason...well, he'd found out the hard way unexpected things happen.

That bond with Mason had been easy from the beginning, almost as if they were good friends who had been apart for a long time and had fallen back into a well-established relationship after an absence. That sense of friendship and comradery had quickly spread to include the rest of the Rebels with whom he had interaction, and that's where a lot of his difficult-to-diagnose uncertainty about the level of trust came in.

Donny's anxieties, however, were more easily understood and addressed. Rob's designs had grown in popularity, and as demands for his services were increasing, it was normal and maybe even expected that he'd be unsure if Rob felt like he was settling by staying with the brothers.

Changing key, he strummed with more purpose, the music less meandering as humming, he eased his way towards the song in the back of his mind. What Donny didn't understand was the job here with the brothers had permitted him to keep his sanity. They'd given him a home and a family at a point in his life when it was desperately needed, and he would never turn his back on their confidence and faith in him.

Because of them, the pain of losing his angels was less intense now, less acute. It hadn't gone away; it was still in residence...still affected him, like a deep wound that had first scabbed over and then scarred. But it was less severe, because some of the raw spaces around that loss had been salved and healed with the brothers' friendship.

Sliding his hand down the neck of the guitar, he used his fingers to create a barre chord and eased into *Aeroplane* by the Red Hot Chili Peppers. The song was upbeat in tempo, but the lyrics revealed his state of mind, unsettled and needing...something.

11 - FWO East

The rumble of the bike's engine filled the garage, revving, rolling and echoing in the space. Claudia had to shout for Rob to hear her, and she was wildly waving the phone at him. He reached over and twisted the key off, killing the engine noise abruptly, so her voice was unexpectedly too loud. "—the phone for you," she shrilled, and then clapped a hand over her mouth.

Raising his eyebrows, Rob questioned her silently as he strode over to accept the handset. *Mason*, she mouthed, and he nodded. "This is Rob," he said into the phone.

"Hey, brother, it's Mason. I wanted to touch base and see how things are coming there in Norfolk at FWO East." He laughed at his own joke.

Rob snorted and replied, "FWO East, huh? Do the Baugh brothers know you've renamed the shop now?"

Mason laughed louder, replying, "Naw. No need for them to know. It's my secret plan to take over the world. Hey, man, I'm sending Slate your way next week. He said you offered for him to take a run with you and ride Winger's bike home. We had some shit go down up here a few days ago, and it was a fucking mess. The run sounds like a good idea. He's a solid kid; getting away from Chicago for a few days will help clear his mind."

"What kind of shit?" Rob asked.

"The terminal kind," Mason said bluntly. "Tell me about the bikes, man. How are things coming with the scoots? I've got a good audience up here. Need to keep these fuckers fed with pretty, shiny things so they continue laying their money down on the table."

"Bikes are looking good. I'm pleased with the progress. Fabrication is complete on the parts we're modifying, and I'm beginning the assembly process now. It's only me, so it's kinda slow, but I'm working my way through them all one-by-one. Paint will be the last thing, but I've got stencils for every bike now. I plan on sending those to you for final approval by tonight. Everything's moving along," he concluded, upbeat.

There was silence on the line for a long minute, and he could practically hear the gears turning in Mason's head. "Is there a hotel or motel close by the shop? Naw, never mind. They can bunk there. I'm sending Slate down a week early, and he'll bring Tug and Pike. They'll help you with the assembly. You need to tell me if they fuck shit up. No goddamn arguments, man. I gotta go get them on the move. They'll be there tomorrow." The call ended abruptly. *What was it with the Rebel members and hanging up the phone without a sendoff?*

He massaged his forehead with his fingertips, squeezing his eyes closed tightly. There had been no chance of telling Mason no, so now he had the task of telling Donny they were about to be descended upon by bikers who, by the way, were going to move into the garage. *Fuck*. Maybe the apartment was better. There was a second room that was currently unused. It meant they'd be in his living space, but it would let him work early and late without worrying about disturbing sleeping men in the shop.

"Claudia," he yelled, getting her attention, "we need some bunks in the back room upstairs. Call that cousin of yours with the furniture store and tell him I need four beds by noon tomorrow. Get Aunt Judy to buy mattresses, sheets, and shit." He watched her gape at him for a moment, and then she picked up her cellphone and dialed a number, speaking as she turned away. He nodded, glad that was handled, and went to find Donny and Dennis to tell them what was going on.

He could have predicted their responses. Dennis was laidback, so everything was okay with him as long as things got done and he could play his shows.

Donny, on the other hand, was offended by the thought Mason felt they weren't moving fast enough. "Doesn't he realize this *is* our sole focus right now? We're running a lean shop. How much quicker does he want the bikes built than what we're doing? He knew the set-up when he signed on, and we're ahead of the promised delivery timetable by nearly a week," Donny ranted. "Do we have to pay these men to come into our place and work on his order? I need to call him, figure this shit out. What a pile of steaming—" He interrupted himself, looking over at Rob. "Why aren't you pissed? He's essentially saying you can't move fast enough."

Rob shrugged. "I'll get his men to do the parts of the job I don't particularly enjoy, and it *will* move faster with four sets of hands. I don't know about the payment stuff, but he didn't say anything about it. He only wanted to get off the phone so he could get things in motion for them to come down. It doesn't bother me, Donny. But, if it bothers you, then you need to call Mason and straighten shit out."

Dennis dropped full beer bottles down on the table between them, gathering up the empties and stowing them in the recycle container next to the door. "Donny, stop it," he said firmly. "It's a gift; take it as one. Call Mason and see if we can pick them up at the airport in the morning. Call Claudia and see if she got the beds. Call Aunt Judy and see if she got the shopping done. Hell, *call me,* but stop winding yourself up over nothing."

Grumbling about men of immense stature but miniscule intelligence, Donny made almost all the calls Dennis had suggested, beginning with one to Mason. That one-sided conversation was brief but to the point. "Mason, it's Donny Baugh—" A pause. "Yeah, Rob said you ca—" There was a longer lull in the exchange.

"Well, thanks. Do you need us to do anyt—" Another break, followed by, "Sure, we can pick them up at eight." Donny rubbed the back of his neck. "No, thank you, Mason. Good idea, man."

"Plane lands at eight in the morning. I'll take the van to pick them up." He sighed. "Shut up, Dennis. I can hear you thinking from here." Dennis and Rob were both still laughing as he made his next call.

Rob was sitting on a short stool next to a bike the next morning, working to get the fittings in place for one of the parts. He'd struggled with the installation, because his hands were too big for the space where it mounted. There was a commotion at the back door and he raised his head in time to see Donny strutting into the garage followed by three big men. They seemed to all wear the same standard biker uniform of black leather boots, tight blue jeans, and shirts covered by leather vests.

He watched the three men enter the room, noting how they spread out in a small arc so they wouldn't foul each other's sightlines as they carefully assessed the place. These were men who looked accustomed to fighting together, like they entered every situation as if it were potentially hostile. It made him wonder about their world, and he thought again about those noises he'd heard in the background of the call with Slate the other night and the fact Slate had to go right after with a terse comment about club business. The same business Mason had later deemed 'terminal'.

Tilting his head as he continued to watch them unobserved, he saw how the men were aware of each other, the way a good team should be. This is what Mason meant when he called them his brothers, an undefined connection between the men that spoke of their protection for and commitment to each other.

Standing, his sudden movement drew their gazes across the garage and they focused on him. The man in front had brown hair and a lean build, but was powerful looking. He turned and gave his companions a silent chin lift before striding across the floor to Rob. "You must be Rob, resident genius. I'm Slate, Mason's lieutenant." He reached out a hand to shake, and Rob read the script tattoo on the man's forearm, *We live with the scars we choose*.

Meeting Slate's grip with his own, Rob acknowledged the introduction. "Hey, Slate. Welcome. Yeah, I'm Rob Crew, but I won't touch the genius comment."

Breaking the handshake, Rob gave a brief wave to the men who stood near the door. "Do you have bags? I can show you where to put them." The older of the two made a hand gesture that had the other one turning and walking back outside.

Striding across the garage, the older man held out his hand and gripped Rob's wrist in a tight warrior's handshake. "Hey, Rob, I'm Tug." He grinned. "I believe you know my nephew Carter LeRoy."

Rob said, "Hell yeah, I know him. I think I even talked to you one time about four years ago."

Tug nodded. "Yeah. Wasn't meant to be at the time. But, it's good to meet you motherfucker, I've heard a lot about you from Mason." There was a noise at the door, and Rob saw the other man coming in with several bags in his hands. "This is Pike," Tug said shortly and turned back to Rob. "You got a place for our shit? We need to get started wrenching for you, but I'd like the two-penny tour first, if you don't mind."

Seeing Slate had turned his back on them, facing the door again, he looked up as one of the drivers strolled in, staring down at his phone. "Who the fuck's that?" growled Slate, cutting his eyes over to Rob.

"An employee, we have several hired on the taxi business side of things," he explained. Raising his voice, he called, "Merritt, whatcha need?"

Without looking up from his phone, the man pointed at the soda machine along the wall near the office. The four of them stood and watched as he dug change from his pocket, agonized over his sugary drink selection for what seemed an inordinate amount of time, and then recovered his reward from the bin at the bottom of the machine before walking back out, never having looked up from his phone once.

"They do that a lot? Wander in and out like that?" Slate asked, his brow wrinkling in thought.

Rob answered, "I don't know, honestly. I don't pay a lot of attention unless there's an issue with one of the vehicles. If I'm working on the computer, hell...a bomb could go off and I'm not sure I'd hear it."

"Can we curtail their access while we're working here? I'd hate to have any unfortunate misunderstandings." Slate looked genuinely worried and Tug scowled, studying him intently.

"Sure, I guess," Rob agreed without conviction. "I'll talk to Donny; he can let them know. We have an office manager on this side of the wall, and she works every day." He raised his voice, calling, "Claudia."

The door opened and she took one step before going stock-still, rocking back on her heels. "Claudia, this is Slate, Tug, and Pike. They'll be staying here for a few days, like we discussed yesterday. Gentlemen, this is Claudia, the office manager for BB&C."

Slate laughed quietly and Rob thought he heard Tug say under his breath, "FWO East," but ignored it.

The men all spoke politely to her, and Claudia gave them a nervous wave from where she stood by the office door. At Rob's nod, she retreated quickly back inside, and he imagined she was slumped in her chair as soon as the door closed behind her.

"We put some bunk beds in the back room of the apartment upstairs. Let me show you where things are. Time for that two-penny tour, as you called it," Rob said. Leading them into the front rooms, he pointed out the showers and bathroom, then preceded them up the stairs to the small space above. "I live in this room," he pointed to his bed. "Down that hall is another bathroom, and then the room where you'll be staying."

Pike moved down the hall, flipping on lights as he went. Rob saw the top patch on his vest said *Prospect,* and wondered what that meant. Pike called back, "Two up, two down. You two taking the downs?"

Tug replied to him, "Yeah, and you ain't sleeping on top of me, so put your shit on the bunk over Slate. Privilege of age, motherfuckers."

Rob heard Slate and Pike laugh, so he smiled politely. He was comfortable with these men, and he found himself envious of the easy rapport between the three. "I'll leave you to get settled. It's not hard to find your way around, so come down when you're ready," he said, turning to go.

A hand on his shoulder surprised him, and he turned to see Slate with his arm outstretched. "Thanks for putting us up, brother. We'll be more productive this way, but I hate we're taking over your house," Slate said, seeming sincere in his words.

"It's no big thing," Rob answered. "It's only for a few days. I can do that standing on my head." Only after the words were out of his mouth did he realize what he'd said, and his breath stuck in his throat and chest, his muscles immobile with pain. He saw Slate looking at him with concern, but it was Tug who responded to his sudden paralysis.

Moving close, Tug reached out a hand to clasp Rob's bicep loosely. "Mason said you lost your wife and kid. I know how that feels, man. My old lady died twenty years ago, but a word or phrase can bring back the loss until that fucking ton of shit is sitting on my fucking chest, choking me. *Breathe, man*. It will pass. Just fucking breathe; get that shit off your heart. Let it go and breathe."

Nodding without words, Rob was embarrassed by the tears welling in his eyes, but Tug wouldn't let him look away. "No, man. That honors them. Be proud of that love. My old lady died from stupidity. Wrong medication at the wrong dosage, and all I got was 'We did all we could'. That fucking phrase echoed in my head for years, popping up at odd times and triggering the shit that takes my voice and my breath.

Someone made a mistake, they did all they could, and they still took the light out of my life.

"Shit's hard, man. This shit is fucking *hard*, and remembering the bad makes it worse. I try to remember my Nytro as the badass old lady she was, and hold those memories tight." Tug's words wound to a stop and he released his hold on Rob's arm.

Without thinking, Rob blurted, "Mine is 'They did not suffer'; that's what my CO said when he told me. They'd been dead three weeks by then, man. The funeral and everything was long over before I even found out they were dead. I should have known, ya know? I should have had an idea something was wrong. But I didn't. I went about my days like nothing was off beam. For twenty-three days, I was oblivious. What does that mean? What does that say about me?

"My angels, Andrea and Ashley—Ash was only seven. They had to have closed caskets. That thing I said, that I can do this standing on my head? That's what Drea and I would say every time things got hard at home, or with me in the service. We could do anything if we took it one day at a time, and with that approach, we could do everything. As long as we had each other, it meant something. Now...I just miss them. It's been four years, and I miss them as much now as I did the first day I knew they were gone."

He closed his eyes and stood for a minute, controlling his breathing and forcing peace in place of the panicked pain swamping him. Drawing in a deep breath, he blew it out and opened his eyes, saying, "Come down to the garage when you're ready." Turning to leave, he felt like there was a rubber band pulling him back with every step he took down the stairs. He fought that draw to go back to see again the sympathy and friendship in Tug and Slate's eyes, continuing on to the bike he'd been working on earlier. He sat, picked up his tools, and started back to work.

It was some time later when he felt a stirring of the air at his back and knew Slate was standing behind him. “Ready to get to work?” he asked, dropping his elbows to his thighs and bending his neck to look over his shoulder.

Slate’s gaze never stopped sweeping the garage, looking for a threat or something else…exactly what, Rob didn’t know. The other two men stood behind Slate as he nodded, saying, “Tell us what you need, brother. We’re your monkeys for the next week.”

He took his time showing them the parts, explaining how the assembly worked on the engines. He showed them the locking solution to use on the bolts, and clarified the check-out/check-in system for the bike keys and paperwork. Once he was confident they understood the process, he demonstrated the installation of one of the manifolds, pointing out the challenges and letting them watch closely when he finally got the part to fit correctly.

“There’s a one-in-seventy failure rate, so if the part doesn’t seat properly, call me over. If the fittings crack when you tighten it down, call me over. If it leaks when you crank the bitch up, call me the fuck over. We don’t ship out shit that’s fucked up, and everyone is responsible for their own quality assurance checks. When it was just me that QA was easy, because it was all on me to make sure things were right. Now, you’re doing some of the work, but it’s still my responsibility, and the fault would be mine—so get it right, or call me over.”

Looking at the three men, he said, “Let’s get this party started, guys.”

He walked back to the bike he was working on and overheard Pike asking Slate, “What the fuck was that? You gonna let him talk to you like that, brother?”

“Pros, you got no idea what you are stepping in. You got no leeway or space to question me. So, shut the fuck up, get a key and paperwork, and get to fucking work. Do not embarrass, Prospect.” Slate’s tone was harsh, but had the desired effect, and Rob watched as Pike swallowed hard before he gathered the materials needed for his first bike.

Things had gone smoothly throughout the day, and by early evening, Rob was about ready to call an end to it, but wanted to give everyone time to finish the bike they were working on. Dennis came into the garage and yelled, "Robby, where are you? Mickie called; he'd like for us to play a set tonight. You up for some singing?" He looked around, belatedly realizing they had an audience. "Oh, hey. I'm Dennis. You're the guys from Chicago, right? Mason's...um...what do I call you?"

Slate chuckled, saying, "Rebels. Call us Mason's Rebels. That works. Or call us by our fucking names." Pointing to himself, he said, "Slate." He introduced the other two men and asked, "Where's this show at tonight?"

Dennis nodded, repeating, "Mason's Rebels, okay. Slate, Tug, Pike...got it. Pub is around the corner. We usually eat at the diner across the street after we're done. That way, Mr. Sensitive here doesn't puke backstage." He punched Rob's shoulder and laughed when his hand was swatted away.

"Yeah, I'm up for playing. What time does he want us to go on?" Rob started wiping his hands with a rag. He'd been done with his bike for a while now, but had been waiting on the rest to finish.

"He said anytime between seven and eight would work," Dennis said as he walked away, calling back over his shoulder. "I'll meet you there, man."

Rob addressed the men, "When the bikes you're working on now are done, go ahead and put up the tools and get the paperwork lined out. If you go out the front door and take a left, you can't miss the pub." He wrote his cell number down on a piece of paper and laid it on the workbench. "In case you do get lost, here's my number. Text me your name so I can add you to my contacts. See you at the pub."

He walked out to shower and get ready. He realized with surprise that leaving the men unsupervised didn't bother him; after spending only hours in their company, he trusted them. Trust equaled access in his mind, and giving them access to the garage seemed natural. He had a thought and stuck his head back in. "The front door locks behind you after five. I'll dig out a spare key and put it on the table upstairs. See ya."

Standing on the stage, Rob was a little more nervous than usual. He and Dennis were adding two new covers to their set list tonight. The songs were different, but both were difficult. He liked the power chords used in *Mona* by The Bloody Hollies, but recreating the organ section using only their acoustic guitars had proven challenging, so he hoped they could pull it off.

Of the two songs, his favorite addition by far was their acoustic version of Howie Day's *Collide*. A poignant piece, he and Dennis had found the song was well-suited to their style and he was excited to see the reaction of the crowd tonight. Watching the audience, he saw an odd emptiness near the back wall, not far from the pool tables. Looking closer, he saw the void was a buffer of space surrounding a table, and was amused but not surprised to find Slate, Tug, and Pike were seated at the table that provoked such respect.

Placing his PRS in the stand near the front of the stage, he walked back and grabbed their stools, bringing them downstage, one in each hand. Dennis effortlessly leapt onto the waist-high stage from the floor and picked up his Taylor. "We ready, Rob?" he asked.

Nodding, Rob sat and ran through his tuning routine quickly. "Ready, set, go, man." Closing his eyes, Rob let the opening bars of their first song sweep over him, the music traveling down and across his body, and out through his fingers as he lost himself in the melody.

***

"Slate, can you come here a minute?" Rob called across the garage. Turning back to the workbench, he went over the numbers again.

"'Sup, man?" The query came from beside him as Slate looked down at the papers.

"We're moving faster than I expected. A lot faster. This is great. I'm going to drop out of assembly and get started on the paint, okay?"

"Uhh...okay? What the fuck you doin' asking me? You're the genius; I'm only a wrench monkey, man," Slate said with a laugh, wagging his greasy fingers.

Rob rolled his eyes. "I'm not asking permission, just seeing if it makes sense to you. The three of you are working on a good average of three bikes each per day. We have Tug and Pike for another four days, and that should see everything put together. If I start on the paint jobs now, I can finish them all before you and I leave next week. What do you think?"

Slate pulled out his phone and pressed a speed dial icon. "Prez...yeah. Bikes assembled in time for Tug and Pike to go home...four days." He paused. "Paint jobs done before Rob and I hit our run. Toss in a couple days for curing the last ones and you can have the truck come pick them up by a week from Saturday."

He paused again. "Uh huh. You hiring local or sending from Chicago? Okay, lemme see." He pulled the phone away from his face, asking Rob, "Do you know of a local trucking company we can hire?"

Nodding, Rob said, "Yeah, Dennis' cousin has an over-the-road company. He's hauled bikes for us before, knows his job. He's dependable."

Slate turned back to the phone. "Got it covered, Prez. I'll arrange everything and talk to Myron. Yeah, me too. It's been a good trip. See ya."

Rob shook his head in amazement. The Rebels seemed to take everything in stride. Within a ten-word conversation, they could solve complex problems and answer questions that would take most businesses days in committee.

The next few days passed quickly. Rob became immersed in the process of turning computer-generated stencils into airbrushed designs on the bikes. It took him a few hours that first afternoon to get all the tanks and fairings into the paint prep room. Then, after the prep work was done, he moved them into the main paint room in batches, positioning the heat panels to speed the curing process of each lot as they were primed with the base coat, becoming a blank canvas for his pictures.

Once the painting process was finished, the tanks and fairings had been installed on the bikes, and Rob was beginning to think ahead to the next big order from Mason. Looking up absently as someone called his name, he saw Slate standing there with a set of keys swinging around the index finger of his right hand. Furrowing his brow with an unspoken query, he waited for Slate to communicate what he needed. "Did you even hear me, fucker? Come on." He stepped forward and touched Rob's shoulder. "Let's get some food."

Seated in a booth at Bethany's diner five minutes later, Slate picked up in the middle of a conversation they'd begun two days before. "It's nearly nine hundred miles, Rob. We'll break that into three days; otherwise, my ass gets tired and I get cranky. Believe me when I tell you," he leaned across the table conspiratorially, "you do *not* want to see me cranky."

"You're the boss here, Slate. I'll follow your lead," Rob said, honestly. The road trip, this *run*, as Slate put it, seemed old hat for him, and that quiet confidence soothed any nerves Rob might have otherwise felt. He would be taking his cues from his friend, because he had significantly more experience than Rob did.

"Winger's bike is road-ready. I only need to change the oil in mine. I can get that done tonight. We're gone in the morning, right?" Rob asked.

His mouth full of omelet, Slate nodded. Swallowing and taking a sip of his coffee, he said, "Yep. If we get on the road by eight or so, we'll be set up good for the day. Get ready, brother." His tone grew wistful. "Riding cross-country lets the world wrap around you in a different way. You're close to everything you see, not buffered by glass and steel, not caged. You're totally engulfed in the experience. Best feeling in the world, man. Best ever."

12 - Chicago

Pulling into the parking lot alongside Slate, Rob allowed himself to feel the exhaustion that plagued his body. In the three days since leaving Virginia, they'd covered the miles that separated Norfolk from Chicago, and Rob was sore in nearly every muscle from the effort and stress of riding for so long.

Slate pushed the bike he was riding backward with his feet, parking at the end of a line of bikes. He motioned Rob to park next to him, and was sitting at ease by the time that was accomplished. "Sit for a minute, man. Shake the road off." Slate grinned, shifting his hips and putting his feet up on the front pegs of his parked bike before stretching.

Rob sat, enjoying the silence for a moment, and then complained, "*Fuck,* my ass is numb." He tipped his head up, looking at the buildings reaching above them, seeing the closed curtains of nearby apartments with backlit shadows moving inside. He heard a strangled noise from beside him and saw Slate's face contorted. "Fuck, man. You okay?" he questioned, and was taken aback when Slate burst into laughter. "What?"

"Fuck me, Rob. You said that like it's the very first time. As if you haven't said that every time we stopped for the last nine hundred miles. '*Fuck,* my ass is numb' has become your theme song. You're fucking hilarious, man. Abso-fucking-lutely hilarious." He dismounted the bike. "What say we head inside and see if Mason's here tonight?"

Rob stood, reaching for his bag, and Slate stopped him with a motion. "You can leave it. No one fucks with Rebel shit, and you're parked in one of our spots. Now, if you had parked over there," he gestured towards a collection of bikes with a single individual watching over them, "you'd have to worry." He saluted briefly, calling out, "Hey, VD, you on watch duty tonight?" He laughed when he received a grunt in reply.

"He's a member of the Skeptics. That means Bones, the president, is presumably inside, which raises the likelihood of Mason being here by quite a bit." He pointed over to another group of bikes with their own watcher. "And that's Tree. He's a prospect for the Dominos, which probably means Hawk is also inside. Shit can go sideways fast when you mix Skeptics and Dominos. Let's go in and watch the show."

"And Hawk is—?" Rob asked, walking beside Slate.

"President of the club, and a good one, but their territory borders on the Skeptics, so rubbing causes friction and discord," Slate answered as if his explanation made sense.

"Is that common? To have three presidents of different clubs in one bar at the same time?" Rob was curious; he still hadn't sorted out how all the club business worked, but Slate had patiently explained many of the perplexing questions uncovered by this trip.

"Here, yeah." He indicated the marquee, which held the word 'Jackson's'. "This bar is a neutral location. We get a lot of patches in here, as well as plenty of folks like you, who are open-minded but not affiliated with a club. We call them citizens to distinguish from those like me, people who live the club life. You guys exist in a separate world with different rules from us."

Rob scowled, not certain he wanted to be described in that way, and convinced he was unhappy having it pointed out that he didn't share in the brotherhood Slate enjoyed.

Slate wrenched the door open, permitting a wash of noise and music to rush from the building. As they entered, closing the door behind them, the sounds other than music muted, conversations pausing mid-sentence. Slate rocked back on his heels, raising his face and voice to yell, "Mother*fuckers*. What's a guy gotta do to get a fucking beer in this place?"

There was a yell from across the room, and Mason strode around the end of the bar. "Goddamn, Slate. You took your time. Not sure you deserve a beer after that." He was grinning though, and pulled Slate into a one-armed clench, thumping him on the back. "Welcome back, brother," he said in a quieter voice, turning to the bar. "Merry, get these brothers a beer."

A tart, "Yes'ir, bossman," came from a woman near the cash register, and she pulled frosted mugs from a cooler.

Mason looked at Rob, reaching out to shake his hand with a forearm grip, pulling him into the same kind of clench complete with fierce thumps on his back. "How the hell are ya, Rob? Fucking good to see you. Glad you could make it, man. I hope Slate wasn't too big a pain in the ass."

Rob laughed. "Nah, he's okay." Seeing Tug and Pike approaching, he pitched his voice to carry, "Tug, though, he's a bitch when he hasn't had his coffee. You could have warned a man." There was laughter from the men around them, and an amused smile on Tug's face as he greeted them.

Rob considered that sense of comradery later that evening, as the crowd in the bar began to thin. He'd met all the Rebels present, and it seemed that the entire bar had trooped outside to see the bikes he and Slate had ridden on from Virginia. Bones, the president of the Skeptics, wanted one much like Winger's, but with a modified paint job. He had put in an order with Mason, and after having a man run an errand, had paid cash in advance for the thirty-thousand-dollar bike.

"Mason," Rob called, "I have a question for you."

Mason strolled down the bar, wiping idly along the top as he came. "Yeah?" he grunted in response.

"Why didn't you give Bones a discount? That would seem to be a good way to cement relations between the clubs," he asked.

Mason answered on a laugh. "Because he didn't want a discount. It was a calculated move, and he planned it well. He wanted everyone in the bar to see how quickly he could front the cash and how he wasn't afraid of the expense. He also got the first non-Rebel custom order in the door, which means he has bragging rights. He then got to work directly with you on his specs and design." Mason pointed at the napkin in front of Rob that held his notes.

"He did all this in the middle of a neutral bar, confidently and apparently without fear of rejection, which tells everyone he has a good relationship with the Rebels. If he'd wanted a discount, he would've approached me privately, like Hawk did." He slapped another napkin down on the bar. "Here're the details on his bike, but we work on Bones' first."

Rob woke the next morning without the hangover he'd anticipated, but with a near-visceral need for coffee. Rolling out of the rack, he stood naked and unashamed as he stretched and rolled his shoulders and back, finding strained muscles still from the extended bike ride. A feminine voice came from behind him and he jerked, seizing a pillow from the rack to hold in front of his cock. Looking around, he saw an older, red-haired woman standing in the doorway. He hadn't focused on what she'd said, which was obviously a question, given the tilt of her head.

"Umm. What?" he asked her, still clutching the pillow to his crotch.

"Guys sent Winger to wake you—" She got that part out before a roar in the hallway outside the door interrupted her.

"What in the fuck are you doin', woman? Get your head out of that goddamn room and get back to the kitchen. You better fucking hope—" The voice trailed off as a man pulled her out of the room, looking inside for himself and shouting at Rob this time, "This is my fucking old lady. What the hell are you doing naked in front of my old lady?"

The woman's voice came from the hallway. "He didn't do anything wrong, Winger. I should have waited for you."

The big man turned in the doorway, his hands fisted tightly at his sides. "Goddamn right you should have waited on me. What the hell were you thinking, DeeDee? This was a bullshit move, and you'll answer for that later. For now, get back to where you were supposed to be and fucking stay there. You better goddamn well keep Lockee and Melanie the fuck away, too. This guy's big as a damn bear. If his cock's that big, those girls will get ideas."

Her laughter moved away from the room, trailing back up the hallway. Rob stood in the same place, the pillow still clutched in front of him. He was not sure what the protocol was in these circumstances, but he did not want to misstep. The man, Winger, seemed relatively volatile, and he didn't want to provoke him further.

He recognized Mason's voice, hearing him ask, "Miscommunication with your woman, Winger?"

"Fuck you, Prez. I rode bitch all the way up here on her bike. I'm in a piss-poor mood, and your fucking man was naked in front of DeeDee." He swung to look at Rob again, moving aside when Mason forced his way into the room.

Laughing when he saw Rob's position, protecting his lovelies with a pillow, he spoke to Winger in an easygoing tone. "She needs to keep out of shit that isn't her concern, man. Take her in hand before you go to the clubhouse tonight. This shit won't fly in that place."

Seeing his agreement, Mason glanced over at Rob, asking Winger, "Hey, what did you say about Rob? Big as a what?"

Winger barked a laugh. "Big as a fucking bear, man."

Mason crossed his arms across his chest, glancing up at Rob again, saying, "Good name." He walked out while moving Winger ahead of him and called back, "Breakfast and coffee in the bar, Bear. Get a move on it, man."

Dressing quickly, Rob made his way out into the bar and found it full of bikers, not only Rebel patches, but several different ones, including the Skeptics and Dominos insignias he remembered from last night. Seeing Slate talking to Mason, he walked over to them and received a chin lift in greeting while they continued with their conversation. "I'm telling you, we *will have* the fifty bikes up here in three days. I got confirmation yesterday that the truck picked up the loaded trailer. What we *don't have* are bikes today. You need to put this shit off until we have bikes to sell, Mason. Tell these douche canoes to tie a knot in it and wait the time," Slate growled, his eyes roaming over the crowd restlessly.

Rob spoke up. "I'll want a day to test them all after they've shipped. Make sure nothing went wrong during loading or transit. If you could give us five days before you do whatever it is these people are here for, that would be the best thing."

Mason looked at him, annoyed. "Bear, that's a day longer than the math indicates. Why not four? Four puts us at Friday, which is good for auctions, because banks are open."

"We'll need willing hands to unload and test them, then—" he began and was interrupted by Mason's shout.

"Listen up! Rebels, need fifty hands here on Thursday early to offload the truck. Everybody else, auction starts at eight a.m. sharp on Friday. Get your shit in order before you show up, these motherfuckers won't go cheap. If you haven't seen Bear and Winger's bikes yet, we're rolling them inside now, so hang around."

The noise level increased in the bar as people discussed the information they'd been given, and one man, not a Rebel, called, "Who the fuck is Bear? How did he rate a bike already?"

Mason stared at him, snarling out, "Buckshot, you questioning me?"

"Oh, fuck naw, Mason. Sorry, man. Respect." The man was verbally backpedaling quickly, racing to find a safe position. "I just don't recall a Rebel named Bear is all. Sorry, man."

Holding his hand out and pointing to Rob, Mason stated, "This is Bear. He's the fucking genius behind the bikes, has built or had a hand in building every one of them. He rates a bike, because he built it." Mason shrugged. "Not a Rebel, nope." Smirking, he glanced over at Rob. "At least, not yet."

Bones strolled up, his tattooed head as distinctive as his personality. He was as internally self-aware as he was of everything transpiring around him, and his every action and expression appeared studied and deliberate. Rob understood now that what Mason said about him last night was true; his arrangement and discussion about the bike was a visible declaration to everyone that he was in command, his club was profitable, and he had influential supporters.

Fingering a piercing in the top curve of his ear, Bones looked Rob up and down lazily. "I heard something this morning, my friend from out east. I learned that Winger nearly removed your head for looking at his old lady nude and uncovered. That does not appear to be something you would do, Bear. Reassure me that you have more regard for the man than that."

Rob shook his head. "She had clothes on, I swear. I was the one naked. It was merely a misunderstanding." He hesitated, thinking, then asked, "I'm wondering something; maybe you can help me out. Why is everyone calling me Bear? Is that like a nickname, like Bones?"

Jerking his head backward as if he'd taken a heavy blow to the face, Bones spoke coolly, shaking his head and pulling on his black goatee with his fingers. "Bones is *not* a nickname to me, Bear. It is me. My *persona*. Bones is who I am, who I've been for years."

He continued, smoothing his goatee down his chin. "It is a badge of respect to be so named, and like yours, my name was granted to me by my president. That means something to me, so please do not belittle it by declaring it a nickname. To some, it is a road name, but *to me*, it is *my* name. The *only one* I claim. I no longer answer to my government name."

Rattled, Rob tried to interrupt and apologize, but Bones persisted. "Also, I am pleased to hear you did not disrespect Winger's old lady. He fights hard to deserve her, and he would probably have had to kill you if you saw her naked."

Rob's wide eyes turned to Slate, and he and Mason burst into laughter as Slate said, "Bones, my friend, stop scaring the genius. Jeezus, look at his eyes. You scared the shit outta him." Rob chuckled as he realized Bones had been making a joke at his expense. He stopped laughing as he traced that thought to its conclusion, because it dawned on him that Bones was treating him like a friend would.

***

The auction went well. Mason had hired a professional auctioneer to come in and run the event at Jackson's, and even had about a dozen conservatively-dressed young women working the crowd, standing near the bidders to guarantee no bids were missed in the rush.

The next two days were packed as Rob gathered details about individual custom orders. Evenings were spent riding the roads around Chicago, finishing at the bar to close things down. He had good memories about Chicago from when he was in basic, and the Rebel members were delighted to introduce him to some of their favorite places too.

Now, it was time for him to get under way, going home to Norfolk. Clasping forearms with first Mason and then Slate, he said his goodbyes, settling his bike into formation with the Fort Wayne Rebels who were returning home. He'd travel with them as far as their clubhouse, spending the night there tonight. Winger's daughter, Lockee asked if she could ride with him, and he'd obtained Winger's consent before letting her on his bike. He'd never had a passenger before, and was terrified he would screw up, so he found himself being more careful than usual.

At their first rest stop, she waited for him to slow as he pulled into the parking lot, but then before he could come to a stop, she stood tall on her pegs, gripping the shoulders of his jacket tightly, shouting, "This bike is *awesome*. Smooth as shit, and soft on the ass. Daddy, I want one!"

The men around them laughed at her, and Rob cautiously guided the bike to a careful halt. Her best friend, Melanie, was riding with Winger and she rose, too, laughing. The girls leaned over to high-five each other as Winger pulled to a stop next to Rob.

Winger grimaced, looking over at him. "Sorry, Bear. They are always like this. Baby girl, maybe you should ride with Bingo instead." Bingo was an older man, president of the Fort Wayne chapter of the Rebel Wayfarers, and his bike had a rigid frame, transferring every bump to the riders' asses.

Lockee tipped her head back and yelled, "No way, Daddy. I'm in love with this bike, not getting my ass off it until the Fort."

Rob smiled tentatively at Winger. "It's okay. I'll keep her safe."

Laughing, Winger let Melanie dismount and Rob copied his movements, holding one hand up for Lockee to grasp and steady herself. "You got kids, man?" Winger nonchalantly asked him, and Rob responded as if someone had booted him in the throat. He couldn't catch his breath, couldn't utter a word. Toeing down the kickstand, he let the bike lean over into it, struggling to reply.

"I did," he eventually choked out as DeeDee walked up, having alighted from her own bike a few paces away.

"Oh, fuck, man. I'm sorry. Mason said something about your family and I still stepped in that shit and stirred it, Bear. Fucking sorry." Winger was conscience-stricken, taking in the expression on Rob's face.

DeeDee lifted a hand and lightly brushed the backs of her knuckles down his cheek, telling him with tears in her voice, "I'm sorry, Bear."

She walked away, and Winger said in a hushed voice, "We tried for a long time to have Lockee. DeeDee lost more than one baby, some even after feeling them move in her belly. I know it's not the same, but we feel it every day, man. Sorry."

"It's been four years," Rob said tightly. "I still miss them every day. I get it, Winger. No worries." Standing, he swung his leg over the bike and walked into the store.

When they pulled into the clubhouse in Fort Wayne, a prospect held the gate open for the group, swinging it closed after everyone was off the street. There were a number of bikes already parked on the lot, and Winger waved Rob to one of two spots near the door. He repeated his earlier motions to hand Lockee off the bike, and was startled when she leaned into him, embracing him tightly from where she stood on the ground.

His attention was drawn back to the gate, where a solitary woman was walking past the compound. Her long, dark hair was unbound, draping down her spine, and she looked like a student, carrying a messenger bag. As if she sensed his gaze on her, she raised her head and met his eyes across the distance, her grey ones locking onto his greens. There was a crackle of awareness that blazed across his skin when their eyes met, and he saw her falter and trip, her feet keeping her from falling with a jerky stutter-step. Then she was gone out of sight, walking past the compound lot and behind the next building. He felt himself incline forward a few inches, as if he were drawn to where she'd disappeared, and then found himself pulled back by Lockee's arms snug around his chest.

"Thanks for letting me ride with you, Bear. I felt...safe," she told him with easy confidence. He nodded, looking over at Winger and catching a quick smile crossing the man's face. Glancing back to the gate, he wondered about the woman and his reaction to her, thinking to himself, *That was weird.*

They dismounted, stretching the road kinks out of their muscles as they walked into the clubhouse, Rob with his bag in hand. The girls went into a back room, but DeeDee paced alongside Winger into the main room, her hand carelessly tucked in his back pocket and his arm slung around her shoulders. Their casual intimacy and affection set up an ache in his heart, and his mind turned again to the dark-haired woman.

After a quick discussion with a member behind the bar, Bingo came over and informed Rob, "Deke will show you where to put your bag. We'll eat before long, but meantime, help yourself to the booze, or get a prospect to serve you. You're a guest in this house tonight, but not a member, so don't go straying into places you've not been shown. Shit's gonna get wild here in a bit, once the old ladies go home."

DeeDee laughed and said, "I'm leaving shortly, boys."

A man Rob presumed was Deke motioned him over towards a staircase. "Guest rooms are on the second floor, right at the top of the stairs. It's got a shitter and a shower, so you're good to go. What time are you heading out in the morning?"

Rob answered, "I dunno. When I get up, I expect. You need me out by a particular time?"

"Naw, Bear, this ain't no fucking hotel. I'm just trying to make sure we'll have a breakfast for you before you hit the road, man. You can fucking stay all day if you want. Bingo's made you welcome." Deke laughed a little.

"Hey, I have a question for you," Rob started, and waited for Deke's encouraging nod. "Bingo said things are going to get wild? What does that mean, exactly?"

"Drinking, fucking, dancing, drinking...probably fucking some more." Deke shrugged. "If you aren't interested, just come up to your room. Most of the bitches will respect a closed door. If you want company though, you can leave it open. You'll tempt one in quick that way."

Rob nodded, not truly understanding, but he was now positive he'd be spending the evening in this room. He was right about where he stayed; however, the noises and sounds of the unrestrained party emanating from the main room downstairs fed his dreams, filling them with dark hair and grey eyes, and he woke in the middle of the night so aroused and engorged that his cock hurt. He wondered if anyone was still around, and got up to open his door slightly, acting without wasting too much time rationalizing it.

He got back in bed, and loosely cupping the shaft of his cock in his hand, he deliberately palmed it up and then down, circling with finger and thumb around the sensitive head. Hips thrusting restlessly, pushing his cock into his hand as he tightened his fingers slightly, still holding it loosely. His eyes were closed to enhance the sensations, so the first indication he had company was when the edge of the bed dipped. He froze, opening his eyes and looking to see a pretty, naked brunette resting quietly on the mattress, sitting with her legs crossed, her pussy in dark shadow while her full breasts were on proud display.

Seeing she'd gained his attention, she reached up and cupped her bare breasts. "Bear," she called his name and moaned as she twisted her nipples between the forefinger and thumb of each hand. His cock jumped at the sound, and his hips thrust impatiently again, his fingers now tighter around the hard length of his cock. She shifted, looking as if she was going to move towards him, and he growled out, *"Stay there.* Keep doing that. Keep touching yourself." He couldn't see her eyes, but knew they weren't brown...or grey.

She smiled and nodded, her hands once more cupping her breasts. Molding and pressing them together, she massaged and pinched her nipples again and again, pulling them into erect peaks and drawing another low-pitched moan from her own lips. Rob's back arched, his shoulders pressing into the mattress as he slid his hand quickly up and down his shaft. Holding tightly at the base with one hand, he slipped the fingers of his other up to the head, rapidly jacking the rim of his cock, imagining the small hands of the woman today as she'd clutched the straps of her backpack.

The brunette slid a finger into her mouth and sucked, pulling it out with an audible *pop*. She stroked her nipples with the wet fingertip, and he watched her areolas pebble and tighten with the stimulation. Blindly, he reached out with his left hand, scarcely spanning the space between them, his fingertips tracing the outer curve of one breast.

She made a sound in the back of her throat, using her hands to raise and lift herself into his touch. As he cupped the warmth and softness of her breast, trailing the pad of his thumb gently around the erect nipple, he groaned deep in his chest and stilled. His hand and fingers tightened around his cock as he came, shooting thick ropes of semen, painting his chest and stomach with his hot come.

He felt the bed shift, and thought she was leaving, but her voice came from beside his head, humming with awe in her tone, "That was beautiful."

He jerked to a sitting position on the edge of the bed, elbows on his thighs and head in his hands. He asked her quietly, "Can you leave, please? Shut the door?"

"Sure, baby. Want me to clean you up first?" she asked as he felt the mattress move again, hopefully confirmation of her pending departure.

"No," he responded to her curtly.

"Okay, baby," she replied sweetly, seemingly unflustered at his selfish behavior and tolerant of his request that she leave. He hadn't even asked her name, hadn't worried about her pleasure. He sat there silently until he heard the door close and latch in the frame.

"Fuucck," he ground out between clenched teeth. He'd touched her. He'd reached his hand out and...touched another woman. Not even someone he knew, or cared about—just some random woman. What the hell was wrong with him? Surging to his feet, tense with anger at himself, he went into the attached bathroom and turned the shower on as cold as it would go. Standing in the freezing water for as long as he thought he could manage, he gritted his teeth and pushed himself to stay another five minutes, then ten—not yielding until his teeth were chattering uncontrollably and the muscles in his arms and legs were shuddering with cold.

Resting on the mattress, he tapped his still-icy fingertips against the place over his heart where the envelope would be if he were at home. His mind empty, the taps kept cadence with a heart not his own, a restless, phantom heartbeat.

13 - Forced changes

Sleepless for the remainder of the night, Rob readied himself quickly when light leached into the room around inadequate drapes across the sole window. Zipping his bag closed, he looked around the bare, impersonal room one final time, ensuring there was nothing of himself left behind, and he walked out, leaving the door standing wide behind him.

Silently treading down the stairs, he entered the main room of the clubhouse and halted in his tracks. There were men and women on every available horizontal surface around the room. Most were still sleeping, but there were a few men awake and moving, some sitting at the bar with plates of eggs and fried potatoes in front of them. Dragging his gaze across the room as he walked to the bar, he saw the naked brunette from last night asleep alone on a pool table, curled into a tight ball with one hand tucked between her legs, cupping her pussy protectively.

He dropped his bag near the bar and was directed with grunts and chin lifts down a corridor to the left, where he followed voices and noise to the kitchen. Quickly making himself a plate of food, he stood against the wall, holding the plate at chest level with one hand while the other made short work of shoveling his breakfast into his mouth. It was a familiar pose from his time in the Navy, where on a sub, space was at a premium, and even though meals were served in shifts, there were never enough seats to go around.

Rinsing his dishes, he placed them in the dishwasher and left the room. The entire exercise had taken about five minutes, and had been conducted entirely in silence, which suited him this morning. Back in the main room, he grabbed his bag and headed towards the door, surprised when an inquiry came from his right. "Ya headed out then, Bear?"

Continuing to walk, he responded with, "Yeah, I'm gonna get on the road. Tell Bingo I said thanks for the place to crash."

"Will do," came the voice again. "Happy trails, brother."

He paused, looking towards the door. "Yesterday, when we got here, there was a girl walking by on the sidewalk. Dark hair, backpack. You know her?" He didn't know why he was asking about her; he'd probably never be back in this town.

"Yeah, I've seen her. She's back and forth to classes. The River Riders watch her." The reply surprised him and he looked at the man, who he thought was called Pinto. He was seated in a chair, a nearly naked woman draped across him, his hand moving idly between her legs.

"River Riders? Who are they? Why do you think they watch her?" He told himself he was curious. It seemed unusual for what sounded like a club to keep track of someone they'd consider a citizen.

"No fucking idea. She's probably on somebody's radar. Riders are another club here in the Fort," the man confirmed his suspicions and shrugged, turning back to the woman on his lap.

Outside, Rob strapped his bag into place and straddled the bike, starting it as he pulled on his gloves. He saw movement out of the corner of his eye, but wasn't prepared for the full-body hug from the slight feminine form that flung herself at him. He recognized Lockee and his arms went around her in a reflexive move, steadying and supporting her, holding her upright but not against him. Hands under her arms, he set her away from him and frowned. She was so immature and impulsive, and after the way they first met, he suspected her dad wouldn't like if it he saw her in Rob's arms.

"What are you doing, girl?" he asked in a gruff, annoyed voice, feeling the decade of years and experience between them.

She grinned and ducked her head. "Thanking you again for the ride yesterday. Daddy doesn't ordinarily let me ride with anyone but him or Mom, so it was a lot of fun, Bear."

Rob frowned harder, his brows lowering over his eyes at the thought rolling around in his head. This girl was younger than Andrea had been when she died. "You already thanked me. So, again, you're welcome, Lockee. Tell your dad I appreciate the hospitality. I gotta get going if I'm going to cover miles today. You take care."

He rolled out of the parking space and up to the gate, pausing as the prospect on watch opened it for him to motor out and into the street. Opening up the throttle a bit, he pushed south on surface streets, working his way over to the interstate, ready to get home.

Two days later, he was about an hour out of Norfolk when he stopped for dinner. He had made good time on the trip and was looking forward to collapsing into his own bed when he reached the shop. Digging his phone from his pocket, he saw he'd missed five calls from Donny since lunch. Muttering to himself, he dialed the number, waiting through three rings before a man answered. It wasn't Donny.

"Is Donny around?" he asked, uncertain who this man was. "Tell him it's Rob."

There was a noise on the phone and then he heard, "Rob?" and recognized the voice of the guys' aunt, Judy.

"What's wrong?" he asked, immediately turning around to climb back on the bike, his desire for dinner forgotten in a rush of anxiety at the palpable anguish in her voice. "Where's Donny?" He bit out the question, because she hadn't spoken after that one word, and unless he could get her talking again, he didn't have any way of knowing what had happened.

"Judy, what's wrong? Where's Donny?" he repeated when she was persistently silent, and after the third iteration, he heard her take in a quick breath.

"Donny's okay; he's here. We're at Sentara Norfolk and he's with the doctor, Rob. It's Dennis," she choked out.

"Okay, okay. Slow and easy. Take in a breath, Judy. Breathe with me, okay? You're doing great. Why is Donny with the doctor? Slow and easy, all right? You're doing great. What happened to Dennis?" He had to keep her talking or get her to hand the phone off. He was in a panic to understand what was going on.

"Dennis took a shift late last night; a driver got sick and had to go home," she said, her voice quavering.

"In one of the taxis? Dennis was driving? Was he in an accident?" His anxiety level skyrocketed at the thought of an accident. He could almost hear the grinding metal and harsh screams of tires on pavement...like in his dreams. He was trying to piece things together to form a picture, but she hadn't given him enough information yet, no framework for the image. "Who's there? Who's with you, Judy?"

"He wasn't in an accident, Rob. He was carjacked. They shot him," she said. Her voice trailed off, and then came back hoarse and pain-filled. "They shot him for forty dollars." There was noise in the room with her, a loud clatter, and then silence as the call was disconnected. Rob took in a deep breath, ramming his hands back into his gloves. He put the phone in his pocket and was swiftly back on the road, covering the distance to the hospital much quicker than the laws allowed.

Parking outside the main entrance, he went to the information booth, only to find they wouldn't tell him anything; they wouldn't even concede that Dennis was in the hospital. *Fucking privacy laws*, he thought angrily, dragging the phone out of his pocket again. Dialing Donny's number, he sagged in relief when his friend answered.

"Donny, I'm at the main entrance. Where are you guys?" he asked quickly.

There was silence on the phone, and then he heard Donny say flatly, "I'll come get you." The call terminated, and Rob stood expectantly near the elevators, keeping himself from pacing with some effort.

As the elevator doors hissed open, he saw Donny standing inside the car, shoulders slumped and his normally neat clothing looking uncharacteristically rumpled and creased. He stood staring in shock for so long the doors began to slide closed, and Rob jerked, holding out a hand to force them back open. Stepping into the elevator, he wrapped an arm around Donny's shoulders, pulling him in for a tight hug. "Tell me," he pleaded.

Donny's tongue swept out between his lips and he opened his mouth. Nothing came out at first, and he took in a deep breath as the elevator stopped on the third floor. "It's bad," he said finally, pulling away. "They don't know why he's not dead already." Rob followed him off the elevator as Donny shook his head, saying, "The guy shot him in the head; he shouldn't still be here. A cop found him just before lunch in an alley not far from the docks. They had to bring him in a chopper. They Nightingaled him here and weren't convinced he'd even survive the transport, but he keeps hanging on."

Taking a deep breath, Donny said, "Aunt Judy's here. We've been sitting with him...Uncle Paul, too. Come on. Denny'd want you here." He looked up at Rob, unshed tears standing in his eyes. "He looks bad. They've got these tubes coming out of his head, and his face is so swollen it's hard to see Denny under there."

"Okay," Rob said on a loud exhale, then repeated it in a softer voice, "Okay." His mind was grinding through the information Donny had given him, circling away from and avoiding the fact Dennis wasn't expected to live. That wasn't right. His friend couldn't die. "All right. Positivity. Dennis would demand positivity. So...*fuck*...people beat the odds all the time, Donny. If anyone can, it's Dennis." Nodding his head, he had more confidence in his voice as he continued, "He can kick this to the curb, man."

Donny looked at him with bleak eyes as he shook his head, sighing and saying only, "Come on. Come see him."

Stepping into the hospital room, Rob looked first around the periphery, refusing to see the patient lying in the bed, central to the scene. Judy was there with her husband Paul, as were Donny's girlfriend Claudia, and Alex from work. Donny walked over to the bed and stepped up onto a small stool, where he looked back impatiently at Rob. *Fucker, you can do this,* he thought to himself, hardening his courage. *For Donny, you can do this.*

Stepping to the bed opposite where Donny stood, Rob looked down at Dennis' face for the first time. His features were swollen, the entire right side of his face a painful purple, and so dark it looked black in many places. There was a wide swath of gauze around his head, holding a large dressing in place along his right temple, and a larger bandage on the back of his head.

Donny's hand came into view, bearing a sponge on the end of a stick. Bringing it to Dennis' mouth, he used it to swab the inside of his lips and along his gums, avoiding the tubes that drew down the corner.

"It went in there on the side of his head," Donny said, his voice faltering over the words. "The brain doc said the bullet rattled around in there, then came out at the back, over there. There are entire sections of his brain untouched, but the parts where the bullet went through are bad, just shredded...destroyed. Doc called it TBI, traumatic brain injury."

He took in a breath and continued, reflexively slipping back and forth between talking to Rob and speaking to his brother. "They did a test this morning, said there's not much left of Dennis. He's not quite what they'd call brain-dead, but there's limited activity. The doc said you are essentially gone, Denny. He said you can't hear us or feel us. Doc told me there's no chance of him waking up. It's only a matter of time before his body realizes what his brain already knows. Time to pull the curtain, Denny. End of the show. Time to go home."

"We can't do much," he heard Judy's voice say. Rob was helpless to look away from Dennis, reluctant to miss a breath. He understood Donny had to be right when he quoted the doctor's statements about not surviving this injury. There was no way anyone could live through this.

Abruptly, Donny said, "I brought your PRS. Can you play for him? He's so proud of how quickly you've learned. Told me a year ago that meeting you and delivering you to the shop was one of the greatest things he'd ever done." Addressing Dennis, he said, "Rob has an excellent habit of soaking up the knowledge, doesn't he, man? We're pleased with him, huh?"

Rob raised his eyes to gaze at Donny, who remained looking fixedly down at his brother. The suffering on his face was at odds with the relaxed tone in his voice. His anguish made the imperfection of the scar on his top lip stand out against his features, holding the upper part of his mouth immobile against the grief ravaging the rest of his face.

Rob looked around the room, seeing as Judy lifted a hand to indicate the corner where the guitar case stood abandoned. He walked over and squatted down, opening it flat on the floor to take the instrument out. Lightly strumming the strings, he quickly tuned it and rose, seeing a chair against the wall near him. Perching on the edge of the seat, he closed his eyes, smiling as he remembered the day he'd brought the guitar home, when Dennis' role expanded from being his friend to also his tutor and mentor.

"Dennis, I've sweated over these for a while. I want you to tell me what you think, brother." He murmured the words softly as he strummed his way into Aerosmith's *You See Me Crying*. He said, "I understand there's really no replacement for the horns, but listen, man.

I believe I got this right." He fingered the intro again as his foot tapped out a strong, steady rhythm. "I think the pub would love this, especially when we put our duet on it. There're a bunch of Aeroheads in that place, and you know it."

He finished the song, playing the outro, and there was only the sound of steady beeping from the medical equipment in the room. Peering up, Rob saw Dennis lying in the same position as before, Donny's hand delicately running through the hair on top of his head. "Got more, Robby? He'd like to listen to more, I think," Donny said without looking up from his brother.

"Yeah. Um...there's another one I've been working on. No modification needed from other instruments to acoustic, it's already here—it was born acoustic. Listen, Dennis, you know this one; it's by the master." Taking in a deep breath, he altered the tuning of the guitar strings and picked out the opening bars of the melody. Singing the first words to Eric Clapton's *Tears in Heaven,* his voice broke and he abruptly stopped singing, continuing to cycle through the mellow musical introduction until he regained his composure, and then he began again, playing and singing the song through to the conclusion.

Seated as he was, he couldn't see reactions from the people in the room, so he tucked his chin to his chest and continued playing softly. Moving into his own headspace, like he did when they performed, he played through the night, transitioning from song to song. He gradually worked his way through most of the material he and Dennis had learned for their shows over the years. Eyes closed, he played for hours, reliving the reactions of the audiences and seeing Dennis' shining pride in their performances. "Robby," he heard Donny call his name, jarring him out of his thoughts.

Looking up, he kept his fingers gliding over the strings, enabling the music to continue to push back the stillness that hovered along the edges and corners of the room. Donny was standing in front of him with his hand outstretched. "Give it to me, Rob. I need you to stop now and come here." Turning his head, Rob handed over the guitar as he saw the medical staff crowding around the bed, gently handling Dennis as they monitored machines and readouts. "Go say hello, Robby." Judy reached out and took the guitar from Donny.

Standing, his body unfolded sluggishly with complaints from being held in a single position for so long. He took a pair of stutter-steps towards the bed, following Donny into a space created for them. One of the staff carried the stool back over, placing it near the head of the bed, and Donny stepped up on it without a pause or word. Rob saw some of the swelling had left Dennis' features, making him more recognizable. As he watched, Dennis' eyelids fluttered and then opened, staring up unfocused and blinking.

"Okay, Denny. It's okay now," Donny crooned. "You hung around, man. We're good. It's okay." Rob reached over and clutched Dennis' hand, shivering as his friend gripped his in acknowledgment. They saw the hitch in his breathing at the same time, and both Rob and Donny drew in an enormous gulp of air, as if they could force Dennis to remain breathing along with them. He coughed, and they held their breath until it eased.

"You've got a tube breathing for you, Dennis. You gotta stay still, okay? Calm and still. Let the medication and docs do their job." Rob spoke confidently to his friend—his brother. "You've done the hard part, honestly. We love you, man. Glad you're still with us."

Rob looked up at Donny's face, seeing the look of understanding that crossed his features before he looked down at his brother, fingers tenderly ruffling the hair on top of his head again.

***

"I'm closing the shop," Donny announced, tipping his beer up to take a long drink. "I've got enough money saved up, and with Denny's insurance, he'll never have to work. I just don't have the desire to be in business any longer. I talked to Mason, and if you are willing to relocate to Chicago, he's got a place for you." Rob was speechless; this was the last thing he expected when Donny said they needed to have a discussion. He felt like he'd taken a punch to the gut.

Pushing ahead, Donny continued, "If you want to keep the bike shop here, you can buy me out. I'll make you an attractive deal. But I'm done, Rob. I can't be here. I need to focus on Dennis, not a business that drains me."

They were seated side-by-side on the workbench, a small bucket of ice between them containing the remaining four bottles of beer. Donny had let the other employees go home early, something he'd begun doing often in the months since Dennis was shot. Finishing his beer, Donny sat the bottle behind the bucket, away from the edge of the workbench, and pulled a fresh one from the ice.

"We'll finish out the latest batch for the Rebels. I figure we're about three-fourths done with the seventy-five they ordered, and then there are a half-dozen custom bikes in the queue. If we can get all of them done about the same time that would work out best for me. It would help give me a clean break from here. Oh, hang on...I almost forgot. Gimme a sec." He twisted and jumped off the workbench to the floor, walking over to the office and bringing a guitar case back with him.

Handing it to Rob, he climbed back up to perch on the edge of the surface, picking up his beer. "Denny remembered yesterday that he bought this for you. He thinks he intended to give it to you on your birthday, but didn't want to wait. There's a note in there with some music on it, but I couldn't decide what he was talking about. You can ask him tomorrow, but I left it, in case it makes sense to you."

Dennis was in a long-term care facility, struggling to regain his strength and capabilities. Donny and Rob had officially agreed to alternate days to go see him, but Rob went every day if he could make it happen.

Speech was difficult for Dennis, and he had to work hard to make himself understood. Written communication was no less challenging than spoken; it was the words themselves that became bound and trapped in his brain. The same mind that held the melodies and lyrics to hundreds of songs now struggled to communicate what he'd had for lunch. He was determined to recover and had worked his way back to playing simple melodies, and the two of them played together frequently.

Rob clutched the handle of the guitar case in nerveless fingers; he was still stunned and hadn't spoken since Donny announced he was closing the shop. Finding his voice, he asked through anger-twisted lips, "So you're closing the doors in about three weeks?" He was pissed, and thought, *God, this feels like a betrayal.*

Shaking his head, he scoffed and continued, "Fucking hell, man. I can be out of your hair before then. I'll look for a place to live first thing in the morning, then see if I can line up a position somewhere. That way you can finish the bikes at your own pace. You'll be able to deal with Dennis' stuff easier, too, without dancing around me. Finally kicking me to the curb. *Damn*."

"Rob, that's not my intent—" Donny started, sounding irritated, but Rob cut him off.

"No, your intent is to shut yourself off from anything that hints of before, and I'm one of those things. I get it; this is hard, but you still have him in your life. Donny, he's my best friend. But, more—you're the brother I'd never had, and closing the business kills both of those. You'd know that, if you paid attention at all. But hey, if you want to close off, I'll let you. If circumstances are too hard with the way everything shook out, I'll make it easy on you. I'll slam the motherfucking door."

Sighing wearily, Donny massaged his forehead between his thumb and forefinger. "Rob," he said patiently, "I want you to stay and help finish out the bikes. I'm not going to leave you stuck, man. I need you.

God, you're my family too. There's an apartment in my building that I've already talked to the super about. If you want to buy the shop, great. If you don't, that's great too. Want to stay in Norfolk? Great again, I can hook you up with that apartment. Want to move to Chicago? Better than great, I know you and Mason get along well. I think he'd be good for you."

He leaned forward, looking Rob in the face. "But I can't keep the business. It's too difficult to do everything. This isn't about me closing off, or isolating myself. It's just that I have to help Denny get better, and splitting myself like I've been doing is killing me. I can't do it all." Drawing in a deep, ragged breath, he said, "So what are you thinking? Stay, buy, leave, or Chicago...you've got lots of options here, Rob."

The anger slowly faded, disappearing as he realized Donny had given this a lot of consideration and had the right focus—family. Shaking his head, Rob muttered, "No idea right now, Donny. I need to think on it a bit."

"Fair enough," Donny agreed. "Now open your present. I want to see your face."

Rob propped the case across his knees, opening the clasps that held it closed. Inside he found a beautiful PRS guitar. It was used, but well cared for, and he picked it up as he set the case aside. Standing it on his knee, he looked the guitar up and down, seeing the master craftsmanship evident in every line of the instrument. Without a word, he cradled the PRS in his lap, strumming gently as he painstakingly adjusted the tuning.

He turned it flat on his lap, flipping it upside-down to see the serial information on the back of the headstock. Donny watched him as he wordlessly communed with the guitar, settling back on the bench and propping one foot on the back of a nearby chair. Beginning a warm-up routine, he alternated between vertical and stepped chromatics as he strummed and finger-picked his way through several sequences.

Eventually satisfied with his performance, he slowed the tempo and picked his way through a series of arpeggios that sounded like a waterfall, finally strumming into *She Talks to Angels*, the first song he learned from Dennis. Finishing, he listened to the sounds echoing around the open space, the air quivering into silence as the song died away.

"This is an Angelus," he said. "It's a gorgeous guitar, man. The tone is exquisite, and the strings marry to the frets; you can't hardly make a mistake playing on this guitar. Beautiful piece." Twisting his body, he reached into the case and pulled out the single piece of paper that had been lying under the guitar. He was quiet, his lips moving as he read, and then he barked a laugh, looking up at Donny.

"What is it? I didn't understand any of it," Donny complained.

Rob grinned. "Dennis is such a card, man. He's always looking to be a funny guy, but his humor is so dry it's hard to explain. This is a musical cryptogram. I think he's used the Bach and Latin, but can't be sure right now. It's probably something stupid like happy birthday, but I'll have to do some pen work to decide and decipher."

Donny laughed harshly. "Figures. The last thing he communicates to you before he gets hurt, and he makes you work for it. Just like he does everything else, yeah?"

Rob shrugged, setting aside the paper and strumming the instrument. "Good things are easy to work for." He looked up at Donny. "You sure about closing the place, man? That seems like a drastic step to take. If the work is too much, we could hire someone to do the pieces you don't want to do."

Shaking his head, Donny demurred, "It's not just the work. I'm as capable of whipping myself into action as I am someone else."

Rob made the *wuh-PSH* sound and Donny laughed.

"It's not sudden. I've been thinking about it almost since I got the call about the carjacking. If we'd moved to the bike business sooner, maybe Denny would still be okay. But, what about the next time? What if it's one of our guys with kids, a wife...how can we live with that? Between needing to be there for Denny and worrying about the drivers...Rob, I just need out."

Adjusting the guitar on his leg, Rob eased into another song he and Dennis had played often, an old Hot Tuna song, *Death Don't Have No Mercy*. "I don't want to buy the business, Donny. I'll help you close it down, but after that, I don't know. I'll call Mason tomorrow, talk to him and Slate." He stopped playing abruptly and grabbed his beer, muttering as he drained the bottle, "Fucking *sucks*, man."

"Amen, brother," Donny murmured. "Amen."

***

"Goddamn, the hits just keep coming, Slate," Rob said softly, holding the phone tightly to his ear. "Both of them? Holy shit, man. How's DeeDee holding up?"

"Fucking hard, man. We've got nearly three hundred brothers coming for the funerals. Patriot Riders are sending a cadre, too, since Winger is...was retired Army." Slate's voice was hoarse with emotion.

Rob hadn't been able to talk to Mason, so he'd called Slate, hoping to feel him out about coming to Chicago. After his talk with Donny last night, his first waking thought was about his future, which now seemed so inane. Winger and Lockee were both dead, killed in a car accident yesterday. He shook his head, thinking about her excitement at riding pillion on his bike, her innocent enthusiasm and uninhibited hugs. "She was younger than Andrea was."

"Your wife?" Slate asked, jarring Rob out of his thoughts. He wasn't even aware he'd spoken aloud.

Shaking his head, he said, “Yeah, Lockee was two years younger than Andrea was when she died.”

“Mason’s in the Fort at the club, if you called Bingo or Deke you’d get him, I think. We’ve got shit to settle with DeeDee, make sure she’s taken care of, along with that gal that lived with them.” Slate sighed. “Fuck me, this is fucking hard.”

“I don’t want to bug Mason now, I’ll talk to him in a few days, give things time to settle out.” Rob looked around the shop, seeing the bikes in various stages of assembly scattered around at workstations.

“Maybe I can answer your questions, man. Whacha need?” Slate asked.

“Donny said he’d already talked to Mason, so I don’t think it’s a secret.” He paused, deciding how to proceed. “He’s closing BB&C. Needs to focus on Dennis’ recovery, he said. Leaves me with nowhere—“

“Yes.” Slate interrupted him and Rob barked a harsh laugh.

“You don’t even know what I was going to ask, man.” Rob shook his head again.

“Yes, come to Chicago and work in our shop. I’ve only ever heard Mason say he regretted two things, man. One was not knowing about his son until the kid was a teenager. The other one was turning Tug down when he first approached him about you working for us. The answer is yes.” Slate’s tone was definitive, leaving no room for argument.

Rob was silent for a moment, then said, “Okay. After this last order is shipped, I’ll plan on heading that way. We can work the details out—“

Slate interrupted him again, “I’ll come down to pack and load. We’ll travel back together. Road trip number two.”

"Okay," Rob spoke softly, overwhelmed by this gesture of friendship from Slate. "Let me know if DeeDee needs anything, okay?"

***

"That's the last of 'em, Slate," Rob called up into the semi-trailer.

"I didn't think we'd get them all on one truck. That's a lotta rolling iron, brother," Slate marveled. "Had to fucking go dry to get the weight right, though. No gas in any of them. Even now, I'm nervous, but I think we've at least got it balanced okay, since we've dropped some eight-eighty three's up in with the bigger bikes. There's a chance we'll have to offload a few and put them in the straight truck, but we can deal with that if we have to."

He wiped sweat off his forehead with a bandana. "It's a pretty load, Bear. These are impressive looking bikes. But, what the hell is that VRSC doing in the mix, man? That don't even look like a fucking Harley."

Rob laughed. "The V-rod is for me. I think it's sleek and pretty. It'll be quite a different ride from my other two." His face changed, becoming troubled as he said, "Mason okayed it going on the truck, Slate. I'm not trying to get shipping for free."

"Fuck you," Slate shot back. "Like I'd give a shit if you loaded your goddamn crap on the truck. In fact, why don't we do that? Pack your shit up in boxes and put it in the straight truck. Get you moved while we're finishing up here. Hang on a sec."

He pulled out his phone and made a call. "Pike, call that club here in Norfolk and see if they'll loan their club pussy for packing duty. Let's get Bear moved to Chi-town." He paused for a moment, then said, "Okay, lemme know, brother."

He looked over at Rob and grinned. "See, Bear? That is how you get shit *done*! Mission accomplished. Let's get some food. I've been slaving all fucking day while you stood there and supervised. Fucking shovel-holder…feed me."

The next morning, Rob stood looking around the room that had been his home for the past several years. All his things had been efficiently packed up by several young women who'd come over prepared with boxes and tape. The room was empty of personality now; a simple, small efficiency apartment with a bed and a hotplate, it looked just as it had the first time he'd seen it.

He'd come upstairs to make sure nothing had been forgotten, and with a set look on his face, he walked over to the bed. Reaching down between the mattress and box spring, he felt a little shock of panic when his fingertips didn't touch the expected brown envelope. Pulling up one edge of the bare mattress, he still couldn't find the package. Tossing the mattress and then the box springs completely off the frame, he was so engrossed in his frenzied search he failed to hear Slate enter the room.

"Looking for this?" he heard, and turned to see Slate holding his envelope between his finger and thumb. Lunging at him, he snatched the precious paper from his grasp and found himself clasping it tightly to his chest. "What the fuck is in there, Bear? What are you hiding?" Slate asked him.

Shaking his head, Rob closed his eyes as he tried to even out his breathing. "It's sentimental…that's all."

"That's a fuckuva lotta sentiment then, brother. You looked like you were losing your mind when I walked in here," he said, causing Rob to look around the room at the wrecked bed. His eyes compassionate, Slate asked him, "Your wife and kid?"

Rob nodded. "Yeah. She mailed this the night of the accident. It made its way to me several weeks later, showed up on the doorstep of our home just as I had decided to sell. It's a recording of my daughter's dance recital."

Slate smiled. "Was she good?"

Rob shook his head, shrugging. "I never got to see her dance. I was always deployed when her recitals happened. I heard she was good, but I never got to see her."

Cocking his head, Slate looked at him intently. "But you watched that tape, right?"

Dropping his gaze to the floor between his feet, Rob shook his head again. "At first, I couldn't stand to think about it. Now, I can't find a camera that the tape will play in. Like I said, it's sentimental."

Rubbing the back of his neck for a minute, Slate offered a solution. "We got a guy in the club named Myron. He's a wiz at electronic shit. We get to Chicago, let's hand it over to him. He'll have it set up for you in no time. That way, when you want to watch it, you'll be able to.

"We've all lost people, Bear. Not trying to downplay your loss or grief ever, man, 'cause that shit's real as it gets. Everyone grieves and recovers at their own pace. Look at DeeDee, man, look at the difference there. She lost her husband and daughter, and she's working her way through, but she's got the support of the club to back her. Winger and Lockee, that was a huge hit on everybody that knew them. My own mother never got over Daddy's death. She checked out and is lost in a sea of shit right now. Addiction and drink own her." Slate took a breath and Rob nodded, understanding what his friend was telling him.

"I know all that—logically, intellectually, but getting past it is fucking hard, man." He shook his head and cleared his throat, attempting to speak past the lump that had developed there. "When you told me the news about Winger, I couldn't believe it. Him and Lockee both, that's crazy. A lot like my angels, they are both gone because of one person's stupid inattention. So much…just gone. I talk to DeeDee every couple of days, check on her to see how she's doing. Slate, if she ever needs anything, you guys have only to ask, you know?" He tipped his head down, chin to his chest, hiding his pain.

Grunting in acknowledgement and swinging around, Slate headed back downstairs, calling over his shoulder. "Yep, same goes the other way, two-lane road, man. But for now, let's get in the wind, motherfucker. I need to get my knees in the breeze."

Taking a minute to straighten the disheveled bed, Rob followed him down the stairs, surprised to find Donny, Claudia, Alex, and several other employees waiting in the garage. Over the past few weeks, he'd used most of his downtime to see Dennis, but he and Donny had kept missing each other and now he was glad they'd at least be able to say goodbye. Looking around, he saw there were more people over beside the office, and then Judy rolled Dennis into view.

"Lazy bastard, why aren't you walking?" he asked Dennis, grinning and gripping his hand in a fierce shake. His friend's face held a broad smile, and he jerked his head backward, indicating Judy was the reason he was in the chair. "Oh, I see. Made it easy on Aunt Judy? What a nice guy you are." He laughed at Dennis' welcome, comfortable smile.

Hugging Judy, he quietly reassured her, "If you need me, I'm only a plane ride away. Okay?"

She nodded, kissing his cheek. "Okay, Robby. You take care, son."

Shaking hands with the drivers, he said his goodbyes and wasn't surprised when both Claudia and Alex demanded hugs. He'd worked his way through everyone present, and then realized he didn't see Donny any longer. He frowned, thinking he'd missed his opportunity to talk to him until he heard a noise and turned to see him quietly standing, hands in the pockets of his suit and a reserved look on his face.

"Donny, man. Thanks aren't enough, ya know? What you and Dennis did for me, taking me in fresh out of the service, giving me opportunities like you did, I just..." He shook his head. "Thanks aren't enough, but they're all I have. So thank you, from the bottom of my heart. You changed my life."

Donny's face twisted, and Rob thought for a moment he was going to lose it, then his sardonic personality took over and he said, "Don't forget we paid you to learn this shit. *Paid you.* Slacker all the way, man."

Reaching down, Rob shook Donny's hand. "Learned it from you, little man." He heard Slate's bike start, the low rumble in the background reminding him it was time to go.

"Typical. Short jokes to mask your despair at leaving Norfolk and the glory that is the Baugh brothers. One of these days, I'll introduce you to sarcasm. I think you'll like each other. Be safe, Rob." He grinned up at Rob and pressed down hard on his hand, giving him a fist bump when Rob winced, grinning, and then pulled away.

Looking around the garage one last time, Rob took in the faces of his friends, feeling humbled at the genuine affection they had for him. He walked over to the bike and straddled it, securing the envelope in a saddlebag. "You ready, Slate?" he called, starting the motor. In response, Slate rolled his bike out through the overhead door opening and into the alley, lifting one gloved hand in farewell to the folks gathered to see them off.

Bear followed him, lifting his hand in an echo of Slate's gesture, turning the front wheel towards the street and Chicago.

14 - Moving on

Sitting propped in one corner of her couch, Eddie dropped her head against the cushions, pushing her glasses up on top of her head and knuckling her eyes roughly. Angling forward a little, she fluffed the throw pillow behind her and leaned back, settling the laptop more comfortably on her knees. She still had three evaluations to write up and was determined to finish them before she passed out in her bed from exhaustion. Reaching up, she settled her glasses back in place and took her curly, dark hair out of the hair tie, shaking it out. Putting it back up in a high ponytail, she yawned and shook her head, ready to finish the day's work.

Over the past thirty-six hours, she'd been cussed at, kicked, punched, scratched, and bitten...and it was only Tuesday. *Just another day at the office*, she thought and sighed. She reached over and grabbed her phone, texting ***Is it wrong to be pissed at GenEd because they can't do physical restraint?*** She laid her phone down, but before she could get her hands back on the laptop keyboard, there was an answering chime indicating an incoming text.

She leaned over, reading, ***Don't dis the nice teachers. Are ya beat up, Pookie?*** and snorted a laugh.

Little bit, she replied.

There was another chime, and she saw the message pop-up, ***Walk on the wild side tomorrow?***

Biting her lip, Eddie hesitated before responding, ***Thursday—taco and tequila night?*** and hit send.

In a short time, the reply ***Hells yeah!*** came back, and she settled into the couch, ready to tackle the paperwork that evolved from her job.

Typing her name and credentials into the form, she stopped for a minute, reading what she'd written: E. Morgan, M.Ed. Special Education, Autism Itinerant Sp.Ed. Those few letters encompassed years of college and learning, on the job training, and practical application of her skills. Rubbing her bicep, she tugged up the sleeve of her shirt, looking at the shiny black ring of bruises. All that knowledge, and she was still bitten by an eight-year-old girl today. Not for the first time, and she'd been out of school and working for only a few months. She thought to herself, *Surely it gets better? At least she didn't break the skin!*

Sighing heavily, she continued to work her way through the forms for one of her elementary school students, Raphael Foscan, inserting interpretative documentation where needed, and writing her recommendations in a combination of plain English and the linguistic torture of acronyms, knowing most of the attending parties would interpret LRE, BIP, ESYS, ASD, ODD, and ITP as least restrictive environment, behavioral intervention plan, extended school year services, autism spectrum disorder, oppositional defiance disorder, and individualized transition plan. It was an alphabet soup outlining the qualifying diagnoses, as well as the services the boy badly needed.

Finally finished, she picked up her phone again and launched the music program, rewarding her hard work with a shuffled playlist of favorite songs, grinning as Avril Lavigne's vocals on *Anything but Ordinary* rang through the apartment. She looked at the clock and scoffed at herself. It was only eleven o'clock. *Whatever will I do with the rest of my night?*

Closing her laptop and placing it on the floor, she scooped up her phone and a tumbler with a half-inch of tequila-flavored melting ice. Turning off lights as she retreated to the kitchen, placing the tumbler in the sink, and then headed upstairs to her bedroom, she set the phone and her glasses on the bedside table, wasting no time changing into her comfortable sleep shirt. Turning down the bed covers, she slid between the sheets, sighing in relief as her body gradually relaxed to the sounds of one of her favorite lead singers, Josh Todd from Buckcherry, as he sang about *Lawless and Lulu*.

Flipping over on her side, she reached out a hand and turned off the light, tucking her elbow close to her body as she settled into her spot on the mattress and fell asleep to her eclectic selection of songs. Her dreams that night were filled with mesmerizing green eyes, still pictures flashing through her mind like slides from a moment she remembered vividly—a bare five seconds from the day her gaze locked with a handsome biker who'd been wrapped up in the arms of a beautiful young woman.

The next day actually *was* better as she audited classrooms to observe students who the general education teachers, or GenEd as they were called, had potentially identified as requiring additional services from the school district. In one of the three cases, she quickly agreed with the teacher and began the paperwork process of initiating a formal evaluation by informing the parents the school felt their child's behavior warranted focus and attention.

Walking out of the school building to her car, a bright yellow Honda Accord, she moved with lethargic steps and held her laptop bag loosely in her left hand. Hearing the buckle of the shoulder strap dragging along the ground, but not caring enough to lift it, she thought the vibrant color of her car had more energy than she did right now. Hearing *Fish Heads*, the ringtone she'd set for her dad, she started digging through her jacket pocket for her phone. She answered the call, wedging the phone between her ear and shoulder. "Daddy!" she cried, forcing more energy than she had into the response.

She heard motorcycles approaching, and looked up with a tremor of fear, seeing a half-dozen bikers rumbling unhurriedly down the street in front of the school. Her eyes caught on one man, and a shiver shook her frame for a different reason. His dark hair was cut short and he wore a black leather jacket that accentuated his broad shoulders. She knew if she could see his eyes they would be green, and it was as if her dream had called him to her.

She watched them cruise up the street and out of sight before she could pull herself back into the moment and focus. Belatedly, she remembered she was on the phone with her father, an event which typically needed one hundred percent of her concentration.

Unlocking the Accord, she set her bag on the floor behind the driver's seat and closed the door as she heard him reply, "Hey, baby girl. How you doin'?"

Smiling, she eased into the seat and leaned back, closing her eyes, saying, "I'm good, Daddy. Work is good; the apartment is good. Everything is good. Gooood. It's goooood."

He laughed at her attempted humor, and she could hear the smirk in his voice. "Yeah, I can tell it's goooood. You just now getting off work, or are you out somewhere? I thought I heard bikes."

"Yeah, I'm headed home now. Barely crawled into the car. There were some riders going past the school right as you called." She yawned loudly and then clapped a hand over her mouth. "Daddy, I'm so sorry. That's nearly as rude as burping on the phone. Gah." She heard his laughter echoing off the walls of wherever he'd called her from, and then caught a male voice in the background asking a question.

"In a minute," he said brusquely to someone and returned to the phone, his voice growing deep as he told her, "I won't keep you, Eddie. Just wanted to hear your voice, baby girl, see how things were going. I don't like there being bikes around your work like that. Anything happens, if you need anything, you call me...hear?"

She made agreeable noises into the phone and he countered, "Eddie, I'm not fucking around here. You feel me? I have friends in the

Fort; I can back you up with one call. You need *anything*...you fucking call me."

"I get it, Prez. I got you," she said quietly. "I gotta head home, Daddy. Love you."

Shooter, her dad, president of the southern California chapter of the Outriders motorcycle club, responded as he always did, "Love you more, baby girl. Talk to you soon."

The call disconnected and she sat there with her phone in hand, wrists draped over the steering wheel, staring off into the distance. Eyes unfocused, her pupils were wide and dilated as if with fear. In her mind, she heard him again telling her he had friends in town and could sweep in and cover her with just a word.

She hadn't expected him to extend his reach like that. It was one of the reasons she'd accepted this job after going to school here. Fort Wayne, Indiana was small enough that his club had no interest in it, sitting all the way over in the middle of the continent. She knew there were other clubs here in town, and some along the bottom edge of Michigan, but there were no Outriders here—at least that she knew of.

She'd come here to escape the relentless pressure of being Shooter's daughter. She wanted a chance to be herself, away from anything to do with biker clubs. How ironic that she found herself hopelessly attracted to a biker she'd never met, someone she'd glimpsed outside the Rebel's clubhouse one time.

Her phone buzzed, breaking her from her reverie, and she looked to see a text, ***It's Wednesday. Do you know where your tequila is?***

Laughing, she replied, ***In my freezer at home,*** and hit send. Starting the car and pulling from the lot, she heard another chime from her phone and ignored it until she was parked in the carport assigned to her apartment.

Then that's where I'll be, she saw and grinned.

Opening her door, she was greeted by salsa music and the smell of hot peppers and onions cooking. Shaking her head, she looked across into the kitchen and saw her best friend, Willa, dancing like mad in front of the stove as she rapidly stirred something in a skillet. "Willa," she called in a singsong, dropping her bag by the hall table as she took off her suit jacket. "Honey, I'm home!"

Eddie was glad she wasn't any nearer to her friend when she spun around, spatula in hand, yelling over the music, "Someone's late. I hope fajitas are okay." She handed Eddie a tumbler half-filled with a clear liquid and made motions for her to drink it. "See if you can guess which one I used." She turned back to the skillet with a softly spoken, "Fuucck," briskly stirring the contents.

Toeing off her flats, Eddie leaned back against the kitchen cabinet, sipping from the tequila in the glass. Swallowing easily and smiling, she said with authority, "Milagro, Select Barrel Reserve, anejo."

"How the hell do you manage to guess it every time? That's freaky, Eddie." Willa complained, "I can't ever beat you. You're a tequila freak of nature."

"Wills, you use *my* tequila to taste test me. I buy what I like, and I drink what I buy...it stands to reason that I'd know the flavors of what I like too." She was laughing as Willa spun around again, spatula at the ready.

After silently opening and closing her mouth a couple times, Willa faced the stove again, muttering, "Jackass."

"How long until supper, Wills? I need a shower," she questioned. Willa didn't turn around again, but waved the spatula over her shoulder, so Eddie walked down the hallway to her bedroom, laughing.

Stepping into the bathroom, she looked in the mirror, cleaning the light makeup from her face, removing her contacts and gazing into her grey eyes, so much like her dad's. Climbing into the shower, she quickly washed her hair and was rinsing as she heard Willa calling from the kitchen. Drying off roughly, she dressed and wrapped a towel around her wet hair.

"What are we watching tonight?" she asked, moving past the kitchen into the living area. Calling back to Willa, she said, "I have three new movies to choose from: *Seven Pounds*, *Ironman*, and *Twilight*. Which do you wanna watch? I'm agnostic; it's like super-serious, versus hot guy with funny, versus sparkly-vampire mega hit."

Carrying two plates full of sizzling meat and vegetables, Willa pushed the coffee table closer to the couch with her foot. "Go grab the tortillas? I choose...*Ironman*."

"Two hours of hottie fun coming up." She slipped the disc into the player and brought the tortilla warmer back to the couch. Rubbing her hair briskly with the towel, she bunched the terrycloth up in one hand and tossed it into the hallway.

Two hours later, Willa was slouched on the couch, head tipped up so she was looking at the ceiling. "I'm so fucking full. Why did you make me eat that last fajita?" She moaned, lazily rubbing her belly with one hand.

Eddie laughed at her, saying, "I didn't make you, Wills. You thumb-wrestled for it and won. I try, but even I can't always save you from yourself."

"It's Wednesday night, and we're hanging out on the couch alone. How sad is that?" Willa asked only half-jokingly.

"Evidently, it's not too-much-fajita sad. Or maybe, it's just-enough-tequila sad?" Eddie smiled at her, asking, "You going home, or crashing here?"

Tucking her feet up onto the couch cushions, Willa promptly closed her eyes and feigned sleeping, complete with hearty snores and snorts that had Eddie laughing at her again. "I'll get you comfy, sweetie," she said, casually unfolding to her feet. Gathering up blankets and a pillow from her storage ottoman, she picked up Willa's head, stuffing the pillow underneath.

"Owww, bitch! Easy on the hair!" Willa howled, grabbing at Eddie's wrists.

"Sorry! Lemme go and I'll cover you. I gotta go to bed, Wills. Tomorrow comes early." Blowing out a breath, she broke the tenuous hold her friend had on her wrists and laid a blanket over the top of her, followed by a warm comforter.

Leaning over her friend, she fondly kissed her temple, whispering, "Sleep, Wills. Love you, girl."

She heard a mumbled, "Lub joo, Ed," and smiled as she walked up the hallway to her bedroom, picking up her still-wet towel as she went, idly wondering why she hadn't mentioned seeing *him* to Willa.

15 - Troubleshooter

"I'm telling you, Mason, he's solid," Tug said, picking up his mug of beer and taking a long drink. "He's been working at FWO for more than a year now and has been a prospect almost that long. I want to take him on a run to Fort Wayne again soon, get him more comfortable with Bingo and the men. We can meet with Judge if I can arrange it, so we can get a feel for that shit while I'm down there."

Seated on a stool behind the bar, Mason's eyes continually roved across the crowd gathered by the pool tables. He glanced over at Slate, where he was sitting near the front of the bar, and saw when he recognized the bubbling discontent over some shit there. Putting one foot on the floor, Slate partially stood, eyes focused on the arguing men. As a unit, their heads swiveled and looked at him, their shoulders rounding in unconscious submission as they dropped the volume level of their voices.

Slate sat down, his chest lifting in a silent huff, glancing over at Mason with a one-sided grin. Acknowledging Slate's long-distance mastery of assholes with a two-fingered wave, Mason turned back to Tug, narrowing his iron-colored eyes. "Yeah, take him with you. He's been a good pros, never a peep or argument out of him. I like getting military guys in; they understand the need for protocol and standards, and Bear's better'n most."

He took a drink of his beer, motioning to Merry, his longtime waitress at Jackson's, to bring him a refill. "I talked to Slate last weekend and we agree; if you can wait to leave on Sunday, Bear will be going with you as a full-patch brother. He and Tequila are gonna get patched in Saturday, and we'll vote on shifting Nelms and Stewart from hangarounds to prospects."

Tug nodded his head in approval. “Good deal. I’m always happy to see the club grow with worthy brothers. I know Bear’s still got some shit to deal with, but he’s doin’ good. Like I said, he’s solid, and so is Tequila.”

He took a drink of his beer, setting it down on the bar deliberately. Cutting his eyes over to Mason, he worded his inquiry carefully. “You get any sense for how well Bingo’s doin’ down in the Fort? I know Winger was glad he folded his little MC in, and that was a thing well done, especially before he passed. But I’ve heard there’re issues with the River Riders in town. You think that shit’s gonna settle, or blow up?”

Mason rolled his neck and shoulders in exasperation. “I got no idea, honestly. Since his sister died, Bingo’s focused on her kids more than anything, and it shows in the shit he’s letting slide. Fuck, he didn’t even know Judge was Outriders until I told him. It should have been on his radar way before it was on mine. Instant dad is one thing to deal with, but he’s gonna have to step it up for the club. I’d have never expected to think about replacing a chapter president, but it’s on my mind now for fucking sure.”

Slate stood again, drawing both men’s attention as he stalked across the bar towards where a table of businessmen—citizens—were harassing one of the waitresses. They heard a low growl of words from that direction, and the men all stood, dropping bills on the table as they left the bar. Slate pulled the waitress into his side, giving her a little hug and a shake, picking up the money on the table and tucking it between her titties, making her laugh.

Sliding his mug back and forth in the condensation on the bar, Tug pressed his lips tightly together and then blew out a breath. “Slate could do more, ya know,” he said.

Mason nodded, turning to face the room with a small smile curling the corners of his mouth. “I know he can. He will. Saturday, he’s gonna take on a national role.”

Tug jerked his head, looking at Mason in surprise, asking, "He know that?"

"Fuck no!" Mason laughed. "He'd try to talk his way out if he knew. Motherfucker is seriously underwhelmed by himself. So national lieutenant first, then maybe chapter president. I'll miss the bastage; he's got a touch with the fucktards that come in here. He's also a goddamn genius when it comes to putting together a plan for pretty much anything though, and I get the feeling we'll need him in Fort Wayne before long."

16 - Patching in

It was midmorning, and Bear was standing on the shop floor at FWO2, looking up at the job board on the wall. This was where all the custom bike orders were listed out individually, with assignments and tentative timelines associated with each step of the process. He had one hand on the back of his neck, rubbing and pulling, trying to loosen up the muscles. There was no way this board was right, and it was making him crazy, because he couldn't find where it was fucked up.

Tats came over, standing a half-step behind him. "Whatcha lookin' at, Bear?" he asked smoothly.

"I'm not sure, man. Shit's not adding up," he said, still looking up at the board.

"What the hell's wrong?" Tats questioned, eyeing the same board with a shrug.

"There's nothing on here for me after Saturday morning. I know I have at least three paint jobs coming up, and I thought there were some parts for Dino's Fat Bob needed some tweaking, but the files aren't in my folder on the server anymore. I'm also missing my notes on the Softail for Deke in Fort Wayne, and another bobber that was on my radar."

He looked at Tats. "I know club church is Saturday. Did I fuck something up, Tats? Are you guys kicking me to the curb?" His stomach was in knots waiting on the answer, but it was the only thing that made sense to him. He had to have transgressed in some way, causing them to conclude he wouldn't be a fit, the way he did with poorly-machined parts, tossing them in the scrap heap.

Tats burst into laughter, throwing his head back in his amusement. "For a smart guy, you are fucking dense sometimes, Bear," he finally said as he turned and walked away, pulling out his phone.

Bear watched after him as Tats strolled through into the office area, leaving him alone in the garage. Looking back up at the job board in annoyance, he picked up the information for the scant projects that were still assigned to him and moved towards his bay. Each regular mechanic was assigned their own station, so they could set things up to best facilitate their work. There were several open bays, and club members regularly used those to work on their own bikes on an as-needed basis.

Spreading the paperwork on his workbench, he got started on the CAD drawings for several requested modifications, preparing the documents to send to the machinist with illustrations and measurements.

Hearing a noise behind him, he turned to see Mason standing there, arms folded across his chest, an amused expression on his face. Bear glanced at the clock on the garage wall and realized it was after eight. He was expected at the clubhouse in less than forty-five minutes. He'd been at the garage for not quite ten hours, lost in his work. *Fuucck*, he couldn't be late.

"Hey, Prez. Sorry," he said apologetically, snatching up the papers he was working on and stuffing them into a folder beside the computer. "Lost track of time, sorry. I know I gotta get my ass in gear to make my shift. I'll be there; you can count on me."

He stilled with dread as Mason pulled his phone from his jeans pocket, dialing a number and talking into the phone. "Yeah, tell Tequila he's on at nine in the clubhouse. Until I fucking say he's not, that's how long." He hung up and slid the phone back into his pocket.

Bear's stomach began churning, and he felt a shudder of fear dance down his back. This was it. This was where Mason told him he hadn't cut it in the prospect period. His skills in the garage didn't make up for the fact he wasn't a hardass like most of the members. He'd rather sort problems out by watching and listening than have any kind of physical fight.

"I got a call," Mason said, staring Bear in the face.

"Yeah?" Bear grunted, helpless to string words into coherent sentences.

Mason continued, his eyes narrowing, "Heard you were worried about shit getting done."

"Yeah. The job board is fucked up," Bear told him, sweeping an arm out to point at the wall in question. "Shit's not assigned right anymore, and I can't find my files."

"Ever think that was intentional, Pros?" Mason drawled.

Dammit, he thought, steeling himself and squaring his shoulders, looking Mason in the eye. "I gotta admit it's crossed my mind," Bear said, grimacing, his mind going back to the first time Mason had called him that.

"Pros," Mason shouted across the clubhouse, "get me a fucking beer." Bear was sitting on a stool near the bar. It still struck him odd this private building had a fully-stocked bar, with volunteers as bartenders. He was hanging out with the Rebels at their Wisconsin clubhouse, which felt more like a fortress with its cement walls and wire-topped fences. He was hoping to become a member, and had talked to Slate about it a few weeks ago. Bear had ridden up here a few hours ago with him, and had been told to stay in this room.

Mason, Slate, Tug, and several others had gone into an office off the main room, closing the door against interruption, and Mason's yell was the first indication their meeting was over. Bear looked up, surprised no one had jumped to get the beer Mason demanded, and then he realized everyone was looking at him.

Drawing on years of experience garnered from public inspections, Bear lifted his chin, squared his shoulders, and called back, "What fucking kind, Prez?"

The room erupted into laughter, and as he went behind the bar, he saw a leather vest, complete with the main club patch and a 'Prospect' rocker, laying on top of the beer cooler.

He quickly stepped around the bar, sliding his jacket off his shoulders and draping it across the back of a stool before he picked up the cut. He slipped his arms into the open holes and felt the chilly leather settle across his shoulders. It was stiff and new, and he listened to the slight creak it made as he slid the cooler open, grabbing two bottles of beer in each hand.

He looked up to find Mason and the rest of the members had come over to the bar and were standing looking at him. Bear grinned at Mason, saying, "Beer," as he opened the first bottle and slid it over towards him. He set the rest of the beers on the bar, pulling out another half-dozen and handing them across until everyone held a bottle dewing with condensation.

"Fucking amazing," he said gruffly, and Mason reached across the bar to rest a hand on his shoulder.

Gripping him tightly, Mason told him, "Welcome, Brother." Bear listened in awe as the phrase was echoed around the room.

Pulling himself back into the present, Bear waited for Mason to tell him what was going on. He rocked back on his heels when Mason held out a hand to him, reaching out to grip his wrist. "Brother," Mason said. "We intended to wait for Saturday, but I decided to move the timetable up a little." There was a noise from across the garage, and he saw Slate, Tug, Tats, Red, and a dozen more Rebels crossing the space.

Slate had something in his hand, and as he got closer, Bear realized it was a bottom rocker, part of the three-piece patch the Rebels used. The one on his back right now said 'Prospect,' and what Slate held said 'Chicago—Mother Chapter'. Pressing it into his left hand, Slate gripped his right tightly, pulling him into a one-armed shoulder bump, fist thudding hard on his back. "Tawny'll sew it on for you tonight," he said, referencing one of the girls that hung around the clubhouse in Chicago as he pulled back to look into Bear's face. "Welcome, Brother," he said.

Overwhelmed, Bear accepted the greetings each man offered, and could say nothing but a muttered, "Thanks," as they congratulated him. Turning to look at Mason, he blurted, "Still doesn't explain the job board, Prez."

He grinned as Mason laughed loudly. "Fucker, you worry about the oddest shit. Most guys would be happy to have time to wrench on their own bikes, but you're tore up you can't make your pretties. Here's the skinny—you and Tug are going on a run Saturday, after you join us for church. We need you. Gonna spread you thin, motherfucker."

Nodding his head slowly, Bear swung his gaze to Tug, and then back to Mason, asking, "Where we headed?"

Tug stroked his mustache and grew solemn. "Fort Wayne for a start. Gotta go see what's up with the River Riders. DeeDee said she needed you to look at something on Winger's bike too. She's keeping it in a storage unit, but rides it once in a while. We'll be gone at least a couple weeks; we'll know more Saturday."

17 - I'll get right on that

"I still don't know what you have against motorcycles," Willa said conversationally, turning her head to watch the dozen bikes traveling the other way down the street.

"I don't have anything against the equipment." Eddie laughed. "I simply have an aversion to the jockeys."

"Yeah, whatev." Willa looked at her. "Rephrasing...what do you have against men who ride motorcycles?"

Turning on her blinker, Eddie changed lanes, preparing to drive into the parking lot at Marie's, one of her favorite restaurants and bars. "Not all riders," she clarified, pulling into a parking space, "only the ones in MCs, in clubs." Nodding her head as she killed the engine and removed her keys, she felt the weight of her friend's gaze and turned to look at her.

"Seriously, not all riders, just the ones patched into the one-percenters...the lifestyle clubs, Wills," she said, opening her door and standing.

Willa climbed out on her side and looked across the top of the car at her friend. "But why? When have you even gotten close enough to a man to even know what he drives or rides? I haven't even seen you have more than a two-sentence conversation with someone of the male persuasion in...what...two, nearly three years?" Willa questioned her. "That's a long dry streak, Eddie. I'm just sayin'. Why would you eliminate any portion of the population until you know for sure what your favorite segments might be? The club my folks are in is full of nice people."

Shaking her head, she grinned at Willa. "Your folks are in a riding club, an RC, not an MC. There's a whole world of difference, Wills. Come on, let's go inside and discover a hot Hispanic romance with tequila and tacos. I'm hungry, and need a bit of a buzz before we continue this conversation. Food first, talking second." Willa met her at the corner of the car, tucking her hand through Eddie's arm, and together, they walked into Marie's.

Sitting in one of the tiny booths, they ordered dinner and drinks, by tacit agreement waiting to continue their talk until after the alcohol was delivered to the table. "Okay, bitch. Spill it," Willa demanded, bringing the margarita glass to her mouth and daintily licking around the rim, capturing some of the coarse salt with her tongue.

"So...I might have some personal experience with motorcycle clubs...MCs," Eddie began her explanation, speaking quietly.

Willa's eyes grew large and round, and she responded, "Nuh uh. No way. You've been my friend for what...years? You'd have told me, right? Before now, I mean?"

Shaking her head, Eddie said, "Prolly not. It's part of my life I've been trying to push aside for an extremely long time. I was reminded of it when Daddy called yet again, so it's been on my mind. Hence, the convo."

"What kind of 'personal experience'?" Willa asked, raising an eyebrow as she made air quotes around the two words.

Looking at her, Eddie tried to decide how much to tell her friend. It would probably be enough to say she'd grown up around a club, which was both true and plausible. She didn't need to go into detail about her dad. Lifting her eyes to meet her friend's and preparing to speak, she was startled when Willa started shaking her head negatively.

"No fucking way. You do not sugarcoat it, and you don't fucking lie, and editing is lying," Willa told Eddie sternly.

Eddie took a drink from her own glass, savoring the flavor and burn of the straight tequila over ice. "I'm not going to sugarcoat it," she argued, lifting her glass again.

"The fuck you were not," Willa stated, raising her eyebrow. "I see your brain working, and I know how you are. You can't scare me, Pookie."

"Okay, edit-free, here it is then. Straight at you." She took another drink, preparing to tell a story she hadn't spoken of for longer than she cared to remember.

"My involvement...I grew up around a club, an MC," she began, and was surprised when Willa remained silent, attentively listening. "The members were always everywhere. Anywhere I looked, everywhere I went," she said. "Protecting me, watching me...smothering me. It didn't matter what I did, the men—the people my father called brothers—were always there. I couldn't do anything or go anyplace without one of them knowing upfront, or finding out what was going on—usually when I least wanted them to. Wills, one of them took me to the store to buy my first bra, and another time to purchase tampons. They were always in my life."

With a small smile, Eddie said, "I loved them...most of them, and they were good to me, like favorite uncles. I adored being around them, knowing they cared, treated me like a treasure—but at times, they were also into bad shit. That scared me. I never knew from week to week who was going to be hurt, or worse."

The smile flickered and dimmed. "I got tired of being afraid, so when Mom got sick, we left, walked away, and we went to a town they couldn't know, wouldn't figure out, so we could disappear. Daddy had cheated on my mom; he had a whole other family, so I thought he wouldn't really even miss us.

"I raised myself for a couple of years, tried to do a good job caring for Mom. But then, when she got sick, like really bad sick, I couldn't do it on my own anymore. By then, I was old enough to recognize the facts for what they were, so I called Daddy. He rolled into town with a shit-ton of bikers at his back, coming to bring us home."

Cutting her eyes up at Willa, she said, "He is president of the club, the leader. Everyone follows him without question, so when he told them to rent a van and load Mom up, they did. When he told someone to put me on the back of a bike and take me home, that man picked me up and put me on the bike without hesitation—or my permission."

"Mom only lasted another couple of months. She died before I finished my last year of high school. I didn't have anywhere else to go, so I stayed with Daddy. But then, when I graduated, suddenly I had all these options."

She shrugged. "My GPA and test scores were decent enough to land a good scholarship to a state college back home in Cali, but I saw the program here in Indiana and decided to apply. It's a long way from where Daddy controls things, and I thought I was far enough away to really *get* away, but I found out long ago he's got eyes and ears here in town. He's keeping an eye on me and reminds me of it every time he calls."

"So, if anyone even looks like they are messing with me, he'll have an Outriders member breathing down their neck, pronto. Or a local member of a club sympathetic to the Outriders." She shrugged. "The downside of all this is like I said; he's watching me again, or I guess, still. My whole life has been lived with someone watching me, weighing and judging my behavior and decisions. If I were to ever have kids, a family...I can't imagine having them live like that."

Their food came, along with a second round of drinks. Eddie pushed her tacos around the plate with her fingers, picking out the diced tomatoes and eating them one-by-one, leaving the rest untouched. "I thought I'd gone far enough, you know? All through college, I didn't have any idea he was keeping track of me. Then, when he called this last time, I heard him say, 'you feel me'. He says that same thing every time, but this once, it all came socking back home. He's everywhere."

Willa looked at her from below her eyebrows, her face tilted down towards the tabletop. "What kind of bad shit?" she asked quietly, cutting her eyes to the bar.

Eddie turned to look, and she saw a man with longish, dark brown hair and a River Riders patch sitting nearby, but no Outriders in sight.

"Shit I'd rather not talk about, Wills." She evaded the topic, picking up her glass and draining it.

"Okay," her friend hissed, cutting her eyes over towards the bar again.

Eddie looked once more and met the amused grey eyes of the River Riders biker who'd turned around, propping his elbows on the edge of the bar. He was younger than she'd thought at first, and she took in his dark brown hair, which was tucked behind his ears. He had a couple days of scruffy beard on his face, and she thought he looked vaguely familiar, but wasn't easily able to place him. Maybe he was a parent of one of her kids. He was about the right age.

He grinned at her and stood, padding over to their booth. Leaning down, he rested both fists on the table, knuckles folded under, biceps flexed.

Eddie looked up at him; she was sure she had a quizzical look on her face and thought she saw an instant of disappointment flash across his features, but it was gone before she could actually classify the emotion. "Can I help you?" she asked politely, waiting for his response.

"Depends," he said cryptically.

She sighed in irritation, rolling her eyes a little, and prompted him, "Depends on what?"

"On what you remember, Eddie," he said, locking onto her face with his eyes.

"How do you know me?" she asked him, her back straightening as she pushed back from the table as far as the booth would allow.

"Shooter sent me," he said, flicking his gaze across Willa's face, and then back to Eddie's.

"You're full of shit," she said with hesitation. "You're not an Outrider, not one of Shooter's."

It wasn't a question, but he responded anyway. "Looks can be deceiving, Eddie, but you are correct. I'm not patched into Outriders. However, the River Riders have an arrangement with Shooter. Longstanding arrangement...for years now." He laughed harshly. "Yeah, years."

"I don't need you," Eddie spoke more assuredly, picking up her drink and rattling the ice around the bottom of the empty glass. "You can tell my father. I don't *need* you," she repeated her words, daring a look over at Willa. "I have friends who can watch out for me." Nodding, she reached over and grabbed Willa's margarita, draining it. "I have friends in the Fort."

The man threw back his head, surprising her with his laughter. "Yeah, I'll get right on that. I'll be sure to tell Shooter exactly that. 'Hey, man. Your daughter don't need you. She said so, and she's got a friend...so it's all good. Sorry you bothered to check in on her.' Yeah...naw. I like my nuts where they are, thanks."

He stood, stepping back from their table. "Just wanted you to know we're here for you, Eddie. If you need us, you call Shooter. He'll roust a response."

"Why have the middleman?" she asked him caustically. "Why not give me your cell, and if I need you, I can simply call?"

Laughing again, he pulled his phone out of an inside pocket of his cut, tapping a few times and then her phone buzzed. "Now you get me." He nodded at her phone as she picked it up. "Now you get me, Eddie."

He walked out of Marie's, looking over at a booth on his way out. She glanced that direction, and saw as the two bikers sitting there gave the asshole a chin lift in recognition.

"Fucking shit," she muttered, using the mirror behind the bar to watch the two men. They were chatting casually, sipping their beers, and stealthily looking at her. "Hey, Wills? Wait here for me, okay? I'll be riiiiight back." She stood, keeping her eyes on the mirror, and saw both men become more alert, waiting to see what she'd do.

Walking towards the bathrooms, which happened to be beyond where the bikers were sitting, she walked past their table, and then whirled back on them. "I need you to tell Shooter he doesn't need to have me watched, followed, guarded, or caged." She ground the words out between gritted teeth, "I'm fine. I'm always fine. I don't need you, and I don't need *him*." She watched for a reaction and saw the one she'd expected and dreaded...fear. Not of her, but of her father.

She said, "I'm going to go to the bathroom. I'd like it if you weren't in here when I come back. Just...tell Shooter I wouldn't put up with his shit. Blame it on me. It's all good."

One of the men laughed. "Hell, I'll tell Shooter anything; just don't make me tell Judge that shit."

"Who's Judge?" she asked, knowing she wouldn't be happy with his answer, even as she asked the question.

"He just hiked his ass outta here," the other man said solemnly, and she leaned her head back and groaned.

***

"Ms. Morgan, I'd like you to explain your recommendations for this student, please." This was from her supervisor, who was trying to distance herself from Eddie's suggestions. She knew good and goddamn well what this kid needed, but because it was a variation of what the district had identified as appropriate services, like always, it was going to be an uphill battle to have it approved.

Three hours later, she'd managed to salvage the services, but knew she'd traded in some markers for the win. That's okay, because this kid, Raphael, would benefit, and he needed all the help he could get. She'd worked with him for more than a year now, and his family life sounded really tough. Eddie knew from his address that he lived in a part of town where gangs and drugs were prevalent. The fact that, yet again, no parent had shown up for today's meeting was another indicator of challenges the boy faced.

Turning to stuff her laptop and paperwork into her bag, she knocked her phone from the front pocket. Bending down to pick it up off the floor, she saw from the display she'd missed fifteen calls during the meeting. Pushing her glasses up her nose with one fingertip, she flicked open the lock screen to see the initial two were from Judge and the rest from her dad. Sighing, she closed her eyes tightly for a moment, deciding to wait until she was home to call back.

She knew letting the tequila talk last night had been a bad idea, even as she'd opened her mouth. Now it would come back around to bite her in the ass. *Hard*.

Everything packed away, she offered the expected professional words of victory, subtly acknowledging the future debt she incurred. Right before she left the room, she asked the GenEd teacher who'd come to the meeting if she knew anything about Raphael's home life. Eddie hadn't been ready for the answer, and her head was still spinning as she pushed the doors open to access the parking lot.

"Yeah," the woman had responded, nodding her head. "He lives in a rough part of town. Gangs, drugs, violence, bikers...lots of bad influences around there. His dad is in a gang, and because of the violence in the household, Rafe stays with his grandmother more than he is at home. But she lives way out on Main, so he has to take public transportation to school when he does."

She asked, "What kind of gang is his dad in?"

"He's in a biker gang." The teacher buzzed with tension, her pupils dilating; she was clearly titillated at the thought of men in leather.

"A local club? Do you know which one?" Eddie pushed, because she was afraid of what the answer might be.

"Rebel Wayfarers," the woman nodded. "They've got a house in town."

"A clubhouse?" Eddie asked, and saw the answering nod. Her heart sank, because this meant she'd have to deal with the entire club if the kid's dad wasn't doing right by him. That's the way they worked. They didn't call each other brother because it was a game; families were protected, even from members if need be. At least it wasn't the River Riders.

In the parking lot, she adjusted her computer bag's strap on her shoulder and almost slapped herself in the face with her purse when she reached up to move the collar of her shirt. Laughing silently at her own antics, she was surprised when she heard a low chuckle from ahead. Looking up, she saw Judge leaning against his bike, which was parked in the space next to her car. She stumbled to a stop several feet away, glancing around the parking lot warily.

"I'm alone, Eddie," he said. Frowning, he asked gently, "Have I given you reason to be afraid of me?"

She shook her head, but instinctively knew he needed a verbal acknowledgment, much like her dad, so she replied, "No, I'm not afraid of you, Judge. But, I'd like to know why you chose to call me today, when you've clearly had my number for a while, if your little act in the bar last night is to be believed."

"Shooter got wind of some of the things you said," he shrugged. "I wanted to warn you before he talked to you."

On cue, her still-silenced phone vibrated with an incoming call and she pulled it out of her jacket pocket, sending it to voicemail after checking to see it *was* her dad again. Raising an eyebrow at her, he tilted his head, and with that one facial expression, he became more than familiar to her—she knew *exactly* who he was.

"I know you," she breathed. "You're Roxy's boy," she said, a smile beginning to lift the corners of her mouth. "Luke Morgan." Her strides ate up the distance between them and she wrapped her arms around his waist, laying her head against his chest as his arms came up to hold her. "My baby brother."

***

Flopping onto her back on the floor, Willa propped her feet on the couch between Judge and Eddie. "Tell me everything, dahling," she said, using a fake, sophisticated accent, and then kicked his thigh, continuing in her regular voice. "Seriously. Tell me why you are here and why you didn't get in touch with our Pookie sooner? Why make her feel like she's alone? That seems kind of a dick move to me."

Eddie laughed as Luke—Judge, she had to get used to calling him by his road name—rolled his eyes at Willa. "Well, first, I don't typically answer interrogations from a crazy woman, but I'll make an exception in your case." His tone was joking, and Willa stuck her tongue out at him. "Second, I'm here in case Eddie needs someone. I didn't push her, because she wanted some distance, and we all knew it. I'd have swooped in and pulled the brother card earlier if needed."

He looked over at Eddie with pride. “But there wasn’t a need. She did great, first in school, and now in her job. But…” here, he paused and looked back at Willa, “…I’ll need you to tell me later about the Pookie thing, ‘kay?” She nodded, giggling.

He stared at Eddie with a quizzical look on his face. “Did you honestly think Shooter wouldn’t keep track of you? He sent me here weeks before you even left for school. I’d been settled in town for nearly two months before you moved in on campus.” He laughed.

Willa puffed her cheeks out and asked, “Why’s he called Shooter?”

Judge was already looking at Eddie, so they at least didn’t have that guilty reaction to feed Willa, but Eddie sure as hell wasn’t going to tell her the real reason. Speaking to her friend, but continuing to look at Judge, she said, “He was a marksman in the military and the name stuck.” She saw the corners of his mouth tense and watched as an expression she could only categorize as disgust swept across his face and was gone, tamped down and smoothed over in a moment as he looked away. *What the hell?* she thought, wondering why he’d be upset with her.

“I has mo’ questions, kids.” Willa giggled. “Why didn’t you recognize this fine specimen of a man last night in the bar?”

Judge turned back to Eddie, saying, “That is a good one, and I’d like to know the answer too. Why didn’t you recognize me? I thought for sure you would know me if you saw me, so all this time I’ve been careful to keep in the background and use other members whenever we were doing close protection.”

Eddie laughed hard for a second at that. “Close protection? Really? Me? What makes you think I need close protection, Luke? For your edification, I’m a freakin’ teacher, not a rock star.”

“Shaddup,” he mock-growled, then became serious. “You’re Shooter’s girl. Gotta keep you safe.”

Shaking her head, Eddie grinned as she answered them, "Luke—" He frowned at her repeated use of his name, so she corrected herself, "Sorry—Judge. Yeah, so, our moms weren't the best of friends."

He snorted, saying, "Understatement."

She nodded in agreement. "True. They hated each other. So Judge and I only got to see each other around holidays. Couple of years in there we didn't see each other at all. We had different schools, different family functions—the only things in common were Dad and the club. I haven't seen you in—I dunno, maybe seven years? We've both done a lot of growing up in that time." She felt a wrench of melancholy. "I know it's what I wanted, but it feels like I've missed a lot."

Willa kicked her leg this time, asking, "How did you finally recognize him?"

Eddie grinned wide, leaning back and laughing. "I dunno if I should disclose that information. It's a secret, like a poker tell."

Kicking her harder this time, Willa grunted, "Spill it, biiiitch."

"Dad has this thing he does with his eyebrow when he's trying to figure out what you might not be telling him. He raises the one and tips his head just so," she tried to demonstrate, but both eyebrows raised as her eyes squinted, making them laugh at her, "and Judge has the exact same mannerism. It was as if Dad had dropped from the sky in front of me, and I simply knew."

He barked out a laugh, saying, "What the hell? I didn't know I did that."

Willa squirmed backward, scooting to a sitting position, leaning against the ottoman. Staring hard at Judge, she said, "Do it. Right now. You must show me! Doooooo et!"

Judge raked her with a glance and asked out of the corner of his mouth, “Is she for real? Like an adult and everything? Holds down a job?”

Laughing, Eddie nodded. “Yep. She works for the same school district as me.”

He turned a horrified face towards her. “Oh, holy hell. No. A teacher and molder of minds? She influences our youth?”

Flailing with her legs on the floor, Willa yelped when she finally connected with his foot, kicking his boots with her bare toes. “I help protect them from the wilds of the world, not take them into the barrens,” she laughed, rubbing her foot gingerly.

Eddie leaned into him, resting her head on his shoulder. “She’s IT support, practically the entire department and the only knowledgeable one in the bunch.”

Judge blew out a huge breath in exaggerated relief. “Tech geek is much more acceptable for that warped personality than teacher. I’ll sleep better knowing the impressionable minds are safe from her twisted sense of humor.”

“I’m getting another drink. Anybody else?” Eddie stood, stretching her back and feeling it crackle and pop. “I need to talk to Shooter eventually, but I want another little bit of liquid courage before I make the call.”

“Beer,” came from Judge, but Willa shook her head.

“None for me. I have maintenance in the morning, so six o’clock will be here sooner than I’d like. I’m not leaving until I see the eyebrow thing, though.” She sat up and put the soles of her feet together, tucking her feet into her body in a bound angle yoga position. “Nope, sitting riiiiight here. I can do this all night. Waiting, that is.”

Eddie stepped into the kitchen, reaching into the refrigerator to grab Luke—Judge's beer. Opening the freezer, she pulled out the bottle of one of her favorite tequilas, a Casa Noble's anejo.

She heard the low rumblings of conversation and laughter continuing from the living room and smiled, glad her best friend and not-so-little brother were bonding over humor. Pouring three-fingers of chilled liquid into the glass, she sipped her drink, topping it off before returning the bottle to the freezer. Hearing her phone singing *Fish Heads* in the other room, she made a face, knowing for sure Judge was gonna answer it...and yep, it stopped ringing way too soon. *Dammit!*

"It's good, Shooter," he said into the phone as she walked back into the room. Shaking her head in frustration, she tossed the bottle of beer to her brother, who reached up reflexively to catch it in mid-air. Tucking it between his legs, she saw Willa's gaze resting right above the bottle for what Eddie felt was a moment too long.

"Not happening, Wills," she discouraged quietly, shaking her head, and received an innocent gaze in response.

"You know I like bad boys, Eddie," she wheedled, not bothering to lower her voice and laughing when Judge turned his eyes down to her, raising one eyebrow in astonishment. He was still talking on Eddie's phone, but at least her dad hadn't demanded to speak to her.

Bah, she thought, *spoke too soon,* as she saw Judge extend the phone towards her with a commanding flip of his wrist. She scowled at him and shook her head, but knew she wouldn't get off that easy. He frowned and shook the phone at her again with a mimed act of forcefulness. She sighed and took it, teasing him by holding a fingertip right above the disconnect button, but then put the phone to her ear, brightly saying, "Daddy," as she watched Judge gingerly open his beer.

Shooter sighed reproachfully. "Baby girl. I got a phone call last night that disturbed me. It wrecked my sleep, and you know how pissed off I am when I don't get my sleep."

She switched the phone to her other ear, preparing to walk away from the couch, but felt fingers wrap around her wrist. Judge pointed to the couch cushion, apparently wanting to hear at least her side of the conversation. She sat. "I'm sorry you didn't sleep well."

"It's kinda hard for an old man to sleep after he's been told his baby girl don't need his shit. When he's informed she don't need *him*. That hits hard, Edith. You know I only want you to be safe, and I'm always going to take steps to make sure that happens. You don't have to like it, but you can't fight me on this." His voice dropped, growing rougher as he spoke. "I lost you once, and that shit's not happening again."

She drew in a breath to respond, but he continued speaking. "My boys know you clocked 'em, and that's okay. It's good you're watching and know you're covered. But they're not gonna keep trying to be background noise anymore if you confront them in public like that again. We've been tryin' to be considerate of you and your friends, but you know I won't fucking hesitate to pull you back into the fold if you fuck with me on this, Edith. Now hand the goddamn fucking phone back to Judge before I lose my goddamn shit with you."

Without saying anything, she extended the device to Judge, dropping the phone into his outstretched hand. He responded to what he heard on the call with a series of grunts and 'yeah' statements, closing his eyes at one point and shaking his head slightly. "I got you, Shooter," he said finally, and then held the phone out to her.

"Yes, Shooter?" she asked when she had the phone again.

"Baby girl, you know I love you and want you happy, right?" His voice was softer than before, questioning.

She sighed. "I know, Daddy. I love you too. It just took me by surprise you'd reached out here and had people on me. I hadn't expected it."

"Aww, baby girl, you know I'll always make sure you're safe. Don't matter what it takes. You're my doll baby, my kid. Both my kids there in the Fort, I'll have to come visit. Maybe soon?" He paused, waiting for an answer.

She smiled, because she did love her dad, and when she could get past the parts that pissed her off, she was always glad to see him. "I'd like that, Daddy. Let me know when and I'll take off work."

"Will do, Eddie. Real soon, expect it. You need anything, you call me or Judge. You got me?" His voice dropped an octave, becoming the frightening growl she remembered from her youth.

The smile faded from her face as she responded, "I got you, Prez."

"All right, then. Go ahead and tell me, and we can wind up this call. I got shit to do." His voice turned chilly for a second, but she knew it wasn't directed at her.

"Love you, Daddy," she told him, and listened to his warm response.

"Love you more, baby girl. Talk to you soon."

She ended the call and looked over at her friend, not surprised to see Willa's wide eyes staring at her. She tried to laugh it off, saying, "Family. Assholes or not, they're yours, right? Whatcha gonna do? Can't kill 'em all; can't make 'em into stew."

Hearing Judge's growl made her eyes close in dismay. She hadn't meant to include him in that statement. "I only meant Daddy, asshole. Don't get your panties in a bunch," she shot at him without moving.

Taking in a deep breath, she forced a smile, opening her eyes to see them both looking at her. "Like we always say, morning comes early. I'm headed to bed. Willa, don't forget we have that tech thing tomorrow in Kalamazoo. We need to leave right after you finish your maintenance. All right, kiddos, there are blankets and pillows in the ottoman. Help yourself and get horizontal, or lock the door on your way out." Turning to Judge, she smiled more convincingly. "I'm glad you're here. It's good to see you, Luke. Love you, brother."

"Love you more, Eddie," he answered her with a half-grin, finally pulling a real smile from her.

He stood, gathering up his empty bottles and the plates from their dinner, taking them into the kitchen. Willa watched him walk away and looked over at Eddie. "So it wouldn't be okay if I hit that?"

"Fuck you, Wills. No. Just no. Hell no." She laughed as she pulled her friend to her feet.

"Okay, not sayin' I wanted to, but just clarifying for future reference," Willa said and yawned.

"You stayin'?" Eddie asked, gathering up the rest of the detritus from their impromptu party.

"Yeah, it'd take me an hour to get home and in bed, and I can be asleep here in ten minutes. Gimme." She took the food containers from Eddie as they both walked towards the kitchen. Standing in the doorway, she watched her friend and brother work comfortably side-by-side, as if they'd done this a dozen times.

Spinning and walking to her bedroom with a smile on her face, she left them to sort things out, more content than ever with her life and the decisions she'd made to get here.

18 - Judge & jury

Settling into the chair opposite the president of the River Riders, Bear swept his gaze across the room. They were at some shithole of a bar north of Fort Wayne proper, having another sit-down with the other club based out of Fort Wayne. Bootleg had finally brought Judge to a meet, and Bear watched an interesting dynamic develop between the two bikers. Instead of the younger man being deferential towards the older, higher ranking officer, things seemed turned on their heads, with Bootleg conceding to Judge on many topics.

Bingo had put him and Tug on this meeting, not bothering to attend himself, which could have been seen as an insult by the other club. Fortunately, they seemed to know a lot about Bingo and his situation, and were unfazed by his absence. Bear knew he was expected to only observe today, and had no plans to interact, even though Tug had deftly maneuvered him into the lead seat at the table.

After a series of desultory exchanges about people they knew, recent accidents, and the little information they were comfortable sharing about several of the different clubs' businesses, Bear felt the tension level at the table increase dramatically when Judge addressed him directly, eyes boring into his face. "So you're the famous Bear, the whiz kid behind the FWO bikes? You don't talk much, do ya?" he said, flicking a glance at Bootleg.

Bear saw Bootleg's lips thin, noticed a slight tightening of the muscles at the corners of the man's eyes, and knew he was nervous about what was coming next. Judge smiled wide, looking back at Bear, and then without waiting for a reaction to his questions, stated, "Kind of a shit deal you didn't invite any Riders to the auction y'all had last month. I guess only Illinois and Wisconsin clubs were invited, huh? Oh, wait, I think a Michigan club went too, wasn't there? Highwaymen? No River Riders, though. Seems a shit deal to me."

"We invited those who expressed interes—" Tug began to speak, but was interrupted by Judge.

"Fuck that, Tug. You knew we wanted in on that auction."

Tug rolled his neck, stretching the muscles. "As I was saying, we invited those who expressed interest in the specific bikes available at the auction, *Judge*." His name came out as a sneer, and Bear saw with interest that Bootleg flinched at the tone, but Judge did not.

"As I remember it, the bikes your club are interested in will be in the next lot. Tats or Red will be in touch, just like they are with all the rest of the clubs who want the softails." Tug smoothed his mustache and laid his hand on the table palm-down. "No insult was intended, none was given, and you fucking know it—you got a question, then ask it. You got an issue, go through your fucking president." He angled his head looking squarely at Judge, but speaking to the other man at the table, "Bootleg, if you don't pull your officer back into line, we're gonna have a problem pretty goddamn quick."

Judge laughed and leaned back in his chair, real relaxation gradually releasing his muscles from the tense state in which they'd been held. "I wondered how long it would take you to call me on my shit, Tugboat," he said with a straight face.

"Fuck you, Judge. You can't rile me. I knew you when you were a gleam in your daddy's eye, and then I wiped your snotty-ass nose when you were growing up." Tug leaned back, matching Judge's state of ease. Bear saw a look of confusion on Bootleg's face, and suspected the same look was probably on his own as he thought, *What the fuck just happened*?

"How's Shooter?" Tug asked, taking the first drink from his beer. None of the men had touched their drinks during the initial exchange, and Bear reached out and gripped his bottle, bringing it to his lips.

"He's good. Dealing with shit south of Diego, but he's got a handle on it, like always," Judge responded, tucking his hair behind his ears.

"You've been in town...what? Eight...ten years now? We've talked to Bootleg a dozen times, and this is the first time I've seen you at a sit-down to talk to. What the fuck are you doing here, man? And, no offense to your Fort Wayne club, Bootleg, but Judge—damn, what the fuck was Shooter thinking letting you patch out of the Outriders? I heard you were in line for national officer, and now you're in Fort Wayne?" Tug laughed, draping one elbow over the back of his chair. "Had to be a shock after SoCal. You've stuck through a bunch of shitty winters; most guys would've bailed by now."

Judge tilted his head, looking at Bear, and asked, "Hey, whiz kid, which question do you think is the most important one? If you wanted me to answer just one in that shitpile Tugboat posed, which would it be?"

Bear shot a look over at Tug and gravely considered the puzzle. "What the fuck are you doing here? That's the question I'd like answered, but then I have a few that are different from Tug's, if we get around that far."

His lips twisting in the resemblance of a smile, Judge looked Bear up and down. "You got a brain, that's for sure." He laughed. "My sister came here several years ago. I've been on goddamn escort duty ever since." He gestured towards his president. "Bootleg allowed me to patch in, knowing it's not long-term. Soon as we can get Edith to go home, I'll be back in the land of sunshine and sand. No more fucking snow."

Leaning forward in interest, Tug rested his elbows on the table. "Edith's here in Fort Wayne? How long has she been here? I didn't realize. How's she doin'?" He sat back a little, asking, "You keeping her presence need-to-know?"

"Naw, not need-to-know from Rebels. She's good, man. She's a fucking teacher, Tug. Makes me laugh knowing how she hated everything about school, and now she's in one all the time." He put truth to his words, laughing along with Tug.

The mirth fled from Judge's face and he leaned his elbows on the tabletop to match Tug. "But, Shooter's coming into town in a few weeks, Tugboat. I'm wanting to get things hammered out between Riders and Rebels tonight, so I don't gotta think about any shit except keeping Edith safe and healthy 'til the old man gets here."

"Tell me what the fucking problem is with Bingo, then. We'll hammer all that shit out," Tug said, shrugging. "Can't fix shit if I don't know shit."

Judge leaned back, looking over at Bootleg for a long minute, his grey gaze level and steady. Bootleg barked a laugh and leaned up, resting one elbow on the table. "Mother*fucker,* you gonna put this shit on me now? All goddamn right, then. Tug, Bingo's distracted. He's not taking care of business and it's starting to seep onto us. He's letting bangers shuffle within feet of the compound gate, and he's not protecting territory. It's sloppy, and it's shit." Bootleg rubbed one hand across his pectoral muscle roughly, his grease-stained nails scratching at his nipple through his shirt. "He needs to take care of his club. He's not paying attention, and he fucking needs to."

There was a long pause, then, his voice icy, Tug said, "So lemme see if I got this right. You called for a sit-down so you could complain about how a Rebel chapter president is taking care of his own fucking club? This isn't about shipments, or territory, or even an insult to a member? It's you sitting there and goddamn whining at me, 'Waaah, Bingo doesn't play the way I want him to'? I expected there might have been bad blood about how we folded Winger's old club into the Rebels. Or there'd be disappointment about the fucking auction. I never expected whining from you, Bootleg." Tug sneered, and Bear saw both Bootleg and Tug tense, tightening their muscles in preparation for a physical altercation.

"Tugboat, man, listen. He lets the bangers in, and we can't push them out as effectively," Judge explained, sitting forward, delicately defusing the moment. "That's what it boils down to. We only want him to take care of his territory in a way that doesn't make our life harder."

"Oh, yeah, I get that, brother, but goddamn. I didn't need to hear it from you," Tug replied as he intentionally relaxed, crossing his left ankle over his right knee and propping his arm across the back of the chair again. "I'll fucking deal." He blew out a breath, then said, "With Shooter coming in, if you do an all-hands party, you better let me know. I haven't seen that brother in years; it would be good to get him fucked up again."

"You got it, Tugboat," the young man said, tucking his hair behind his ears again. "Hey, I gotta go. Meeting some members at Marie's in a bit. I'll let you know, but we'll probably have an all-hands party."

Seen this way, he didn't look at all like a deadly force to be reckoned with, but his name had come from his penchant of being judge, jury, and executioner, and Bear knew it wouldn't pay to underestimate him.

19 - Don't be mad

"We gonna slide to Detroit while we're over this way, Tug?" Bear asked cautiously. Their conversation with the River Riders hadn't gone as he'd expected, and only a portion was due to Tug's evident familiarity with the players. The biggest surprise had come from the other club's willingness to call the Rebels on what they saw as inadequate club leadership in Fort Wayne. Bear knew Tug had spent a fair amount of time on the phone last night with Mason as he brought their president up to speed on all the chapter issues.

Receiving a noncommittal grunt from Tug, Bear pushed him warily. "I've got a question for you. Can you help me out? Yesterday's conversation was odd. Judge took lead until he forced Bootleg to say what they were both thinking. Since when does a junior officer's words carry more weight and credibility than the president's? Is it based on who Judge's old man is? What'd you call him...Shooter?"

"Don't disrespect Judge, man. He's as solid as they come. Me and his old man go way back. Hell, I was an Outrider long before I was Rebel. You make lifelong friends...brothers, like that. I'd probably still be there, but Nytro died, and it just—"

His voice trailed off, then picked back up, more assertive. "After my old lady passed, I had all I could stand of the familiar places, so I got permission to go gypsy. Six months later, I met Mason in Chicago and patched in right away. I was an Outrider for a long time though, and I saw Luke born and raised up until I left Cali. His mom Roxy was a bitch on wheels, man. We never understood why Shooter would hook up with her, when he had a solid old lady at home."

Tug's face had a thoughtful expression, and he cocked his head looking at Bear. "Only good thing Roxy ever did was give that boy to Shooter, but it caused a fuckton of misery with the rest of his family. Then his old lady, Kimberly, got sick, and she took off with their daughter, Edith, for almost two years. Edith went along, because she was pissed at her old man for stepping out on her mom.

"That man was fucking beside himself, because no one knew if they'd been scooped up by a rival club or wrecked out—if maybe their car was in a ravine in the mountains somewhere. I was out there on a run for Mason the day Edith called Shooter, telling him they needed to come home. We stormed into a little town on the California-Nevada border where they'd been living, all roaring pipes and pissed off bikers, our riding lines splitting on the main drag as we parked bikes on each side of the street.

"Kimberly was pretty out of it, and you could see Shooter's shock at what the cancer had done to her, his pain from the time he'd lost with her and Edith. She was...ravaged, man. He told me to pick up Edith and take her to the clubhouse in San Diego. She fought me like crazy, and me driving and trying to make sure she knew I wasn't about to hurt her the whole way back—and it was four long hours, brother. She beat at me with her fists, fighting even though there was nothing she could do. I was fucking sore for a week." Tug laughed dryly.

"It wasn't long after he got her home before Kimberly passed. That'd be about seven...eight years ago. Damn long time. Sounds like Edith's been living here since high school. She's a strong-ass girl, taking on shit like she has all her life. Taking on her old man, too—that's a certain brand of crazy, for sure."

Bear's head lifted as he heard clear, pealing laughter drift from across the room. Turning to look, he saw two women sitting at a high table, alternately putting their heads together to whisper, and then shifting back in their seats laughing. He thought they must be friends out for a drink, because even though they both had brown hair, they didn't look like sisters.

They were both attractive, but the one with darker hair caught his attention, her features delicate and elegant, her hand gestures expressive as she used them to describe something to her tablemate. Recognizing her, he drew in an unsteady breath. It was *her*, the woman he'd seen years ago walking past the Rebel compound here in town. The woman who had populated his dreams since then.

He realized he was staring when she scowled in his direction and turned her face into the side of her friend's head, speaking into her ear. He wondered what she'd said, because both women leaned back, looked his direction, and laughed hard. *Fuck*, he thought, *it's really her*.

She carefully slid off the stool, and the level of care used to ensure she was steady on her feet revealed the fact she was slightly drunk. Bear grinned, watching her deliberate saunter towards the bathrooms. He poked Tug, saying, "Watch this one, Tug. If she makes it back up onto the stool, I'll buy the next round."

***

Eddie grabbed the handle on the bathroom door, pushing firmly, and was surprised when her chest slapped into the door. *Why didn't it open?* Scowling at the sign, she saw the word 'Pull', and giggled at herself, tugging at the door to open it. Checkerz wasn't a bar they generally frequented, but after spending all day at an assistive technology seminar in Kalamazoo, this place seemed a good option. It was both close enough to home and conveniently on the way.

If she'd remembered it was a biker bar, she'd have held out for Marie's. *Ugh. At least we don't have an escort*. She wondered what Judge thought about her ditching his boys this morning in the parking garage and giggled, thinking, *I bet he's pissed. A whole day of not knowing where I am. Ermaghard!*

She managed to navigate the stall successfully, and then was standing at the sink, gazing at herself in the small mirror on the wall. Beginning to de-silver, the mirror reflected her with a haze over her face. *I look like a zombie*, she thought, and made little moaning sounds for a minute, giggling at herself. "I might need to think about stopping drinking about now," she muttered aloud, turning away from the zombifying reflective surface.

Pushing the door open, pleased she'd remembered the directional swing, she walked back out into the bar and paused for a moment, settling her eyes on Willa, who was half-reclining in her chair at their table. Eddie plotted a course she hoped would keep her out of trouble and began snaking her way through the crowded tables and chairs, sidestepping feet, purses, legs, and at least one hat.

Nearly there, she thought, *wait, was that a hat?* She was looking back at the hat just as her feet tangled with the legs of a chair she could swear wasn't there a moment ago. Reaching out to grab the edge of their table in an effort to remain upright, she saw it tip towards her as their glasses began to slide across to the edge. The thought, *Save the tequila!* flew through her mind, making her turn loose of the table as she fell on the floor, landing squarely on her ass with a thump.

Face red with embarrassment, she looked up and around, realizing with gratitude that only a few people had witnessed her humiliating fall. Of course, one of them would have to be the good-looking, dark-haired biker she and Willa had been watching earlier. For a while, she'd thought it might be her mystery biker, but she hadn't been able to get a good look at his face and had discounted the idea as too far-fetched. What were the chances, after all this time that they'd be in the same bar?

"Fuucck," she growled, kicking the offending chair out of the way and looking up to see Willa's head pop over the edge of the table.

"You okay, Pookie?" Willa said with an unrestrained giggle. "Whatcha doin' down there on the floors?"

Scowling, she glowered at Willa. "I attacked the floor. Backward. Because I'm freakin' talented like that. What the fuck do you think I'm doing down here?"

A burly bouncer stooped down beside her, going down on one knee as he reached out to grasp her arms, asking, "Ma'am, you need some help?"

She flapped her hands at him, pushing and waving him away. "No, no. I got this. You should corral that chair, though. It jumped right out in front of me. Terriblest thing you ever did see." She continued to mutter as she pushed herself back upright, dusting her ass off before she climbed back onto her stool.

"You sure you're okay, miss?" the bouncer persisted, hovering nearby as she settled herself at the table.

"Yes, I'm fine. Everything is fine. My ass is fine," she responded, feeling vindicated as he finally gave up and turned to walk away. That lasted about five seconds, then she heard male laughter from nearby and knew it had to come from that damn biker, especially when she overheard a deep voice say, "That ass *is* fine."

She tipped her head backward, gritting out, "Why me, Lord?" Eddie looked over at her friend, seeing Willa's lips were held tightly between her teeth while her eyes were squeezed shut. "Are you fucking laughing at me? Willa Grace Shipman, my former friend," she teased halfheartedly, "are you laughing at me?" She glanced around the room as she picked up her drink, trying not to focus on that damn biker.

"Pookie...you sure you need that?" Willa asked her, trying and failing to put a stern frown on her grinning face.

Eddie laughed, draining the tequila in one gulp. "You look like you're gonna fart," she told her. Leaning her head back with closed eyes, she tried to get her laughter back under control and failed miserably, giggling uncontrollably.

Willa shrugged, draping an arm across her shoulders. "I fart, you fall—we're a pair! And you are toasty."

Eddie chimed in, "A farting, falling, fracas-causing, fun-filled, fucking friendship." Dixie, the bar manager, came over, moving her gaze between the two hysterically laughing women, first opening and then closing her mouth, then with a grin, she shook her head and walked away.

"I'm fine, Wills. It was just that damn chair." Reaching up with one hand, Eddie poked at her own nose with a finger. "I can still feel. I can feel the tip. Of my nose. I'm good. How about you? Can you feel this?"

She reached over and poked Willa's nose, laughing when Wills crossed her eyes and said, "K-nope, k-not a thing. I'm fully k-numb. Got a k-nife, a k-nob, a k-anoe?"

Shaking her head, Eddie told her, "Canoe begins with a 'c', not a 'k', doofus. Are you too drunk to spell?"

"Least *I* didn't fall on my ass," retorted Willa, setting them both off into peals of laughter again. "Oh, hey, I got one. What did the floor say?"

"I don't know. What did the floor say?" Eddie heaved a sigh, waiting for the punch line. Willa's jokes were always immature, but usually funny.

"If you fall, I'll be there." Willa leaned back, her stool tilting precariously before she yanked herself back upright, laughing riotously.

Once they had calmed down, Eddie looked around the bar, asking, "Okay, where were we before my oh-so memorable attempt at water closet visitation? Had we done the bikers yet?" She and Willa had been playing a game of Guess the Creep Factor, where they graded men based on their creep-o-meter ranking on a scale of one-to-ten.

"Nope, they are next. So—creep-o-meter rating? They don't scare me, so I'd give them no more than a two. Maybe even as low as a one," Willa declared, turning her head to look at the men in what was probably supposed to be a stealthy manner, but actually looked more like she was having a seizure.

"No fucking way," Eddie snorted. "Your meter is broken. My creep-o-meter is fully active and engaged. I'd give the mustache a four, and peg pretty-boy at an eight. At least an eight. Fully creepy, fully meter...y. Totally a creep-a-zoid. Even if he is pretty. Wish I could see his face better. I thought he might be my mystery biker. He's a pretty-boy, pretty biker."

"Nu huh. Cutie pie was getting up to help when you fell, but the bouncer got there first," Willa disagreed, vigorously shaking her head back and forth, hair flying in a corona around her. "That kind of compassion should take a bunch off the meter. He's a nice guy; I can tell from here. I took a picture of him while you were in the potty. Wanna see it? Nice guy. They're both nice. Nice boys. Hmmm." She paused, laughing quietly at whatever was in her head. "Pretty boys, nice boys. Legs around your neck boys," she sang, slightly off-key. "Cocky boys, hard boys, eat them up yuummmm."

Laughing, Eddie asked, "Really? Was that the worm song? But you made it about fucking? Seriously, woman? That's a particular level of twisted I did not even know *existed*."

Willa smiled widely as she sang, still off-key, "Existed, twisted, assisted, and persisted. Resisted, insisted, eat them up yuummmm."

Eddie turned away from her crazy friend to look at the men again, seeing a fresh round of beers and shots delivered to their table. There seemed to be an argument over who was going to pay, and both bikers pointed in her direction as they dickered. The dark-haired one indicated the floor, while the older man with the mustache flung a hand towards her stool. They laughed good-naturedly, and the dark-haired biker paid the tab, while the older man lifted his beer bottle towards her in a salute.

"I think those men bet on if I would make it back onto the stool," she huffed, turning to face Willa.

"Well, you did fall on your ass. But...you also are currently sitting on said ass in the stool. So maybe they both won?" Willa grinned at her.

"Whatever," she said. "I'm toasty. Getting ready to head out, Wills. Gonna call a cab. You gonna be okay getting home?"

"Oh, fuck no." Willa giggled at her again. "I called Judge while you were in the bathroom. He's gonna come get us."

"You did not! Oh, Willa. Tell me you didn't call my brother." Eddie rolled her head back, looking up at the ceiling again. Without looking back over at Willa, she continued, "You did, didn't you? You called Judge...Luke. Little brother Luke. Little Lukie. Lukie Pookie. Shiiitt. He's gonna be pissed. So pissed. He *is* pissed; I know he is. I wasn't supposed to ditch his boys, you know. You just got me into a world of trouble, my seriously former friend."

She stood, swaying for a second before she grabbed her purse. "I gotta go before he gets here. Text me when you get home." Without giving Willa a chance to argue, she walked towards the front door of the bar, and then stopped, hearing the rumble of a bike approaching. Flashing a look of fear towards Willa, she walked instead towards the kitchen, praying there was a backdoor exit.

***

Bear watched the woman with interest. Obviously exasperated with something her friend had said, she was walking to the front door with purpose, apparently intent on leaving. He was disappointed; he wanted to keep looking at her, memorizing her face, but knew he had no right to interrupt her night and approach her. How weird would that be? 'Oh, hey, I saw you for five seconds a few years ago, and I haven't been able to stop thinking about you. Sometimes I jack off when I think about you.' *Yeah, nothing about that screamed stalker or weirdo at all.* But being able to watch her, see her reactions...hear her laughter. *God.* Something distracted her on her way out, and she now headed towards the swinging doors leading to the kitchen. Tug spoke up, "Bike outside."

The woman still sitting at the table bounced lightly in her seat, gently clapping her hands together and staring at the door. A smile lit up her face when it opened and Judge walked in. *What the hell?* Bear thought, seeing the Riders' officer impassively sweep the room with his gaze. He frowned, remembering Pinto had told him his dark-haired woman was on Riders' radar. Judge acknowledged him and Tug with a chin lift, but he zeroed in on the quietly excited woman staring at him.

Bear watched him stalk over to talk to her, and realized he'd lost sight of his dark-haired woman in his surprise. The door leading to the kitchen was still swinging, so when Judge looked back up and at them with a raised brow, he pointed at the door with an impassive face. Receiving a brisk nod in reply, he watched with interest as Judge tugged on the woman's wrist, pulling her off the stool and across the room towards them.

"Tugboat, watch her a sec, would ya?" He spoke to them as he approached, and picking the woman up with an arm around her waist, he placed her on a stool at their table, telling her firmly, "Wait. Here."

"But my drink is back there." She pointed, pouting, then laughed aloud when he produced it from his other hand. "Never mind," she said, reaching to pick it up as Judge walked away.

“I’m Willa,” she introduced herself, holding her glass loosely in one hand. Looking between the men, tilting the glass back and forth, she asked with a grin, “Did you bet for or against my friend?”

Tug barked out a laugh. “For,” he said shortly.

She pointed at Bear, glaring at him. “That means you bet against. She’s right; my meter is broken. ‘Zoid.” She stuck her tongue out, blowing a noisy raspberry his direction. “I was hoping you were the mystery biker, but nope, you’re just a ‘zoid.”

He tilted his head, looking at her in bemusement. “Maybe you’ve had enough to drink, Willa. What’s your friend’s name?”

“Oh, probably,” she retorted, ignoring his question to lift and drain her glass, “but lookie. That is no longer an issue, ‘Zoid.” Setting it down, she looked over his shoulder and her face sobered. “Uh oh, I think Judge is pissed.” She blew out a breath, making a brief raspberry noise again. “Wishin’ right about now my dialing finger was as broke as my meter is. *Fuck*.”

“Thanks, Tug. Willa, come on. We need to go. Let’s get you home.” Judge ground the words out between gritted teeth, reaching for her hand. She didn’t respond, simply slipped from the stool and waved goodbye at Bear and Tug. As he pulled her away, Bear heard her say, “Don’t be mad, Lukie Pookie. She’d never have…” Her voice faded as they moved out of range, and then out the door.

“Fucking interesting night,” Tug muttered, taking a drink from his bottle. “I can’t even remember what the hell we were talking about before the show started.”

“Me neither,” agreed Bear, cutting a glance over at the kitchen door with a smile. *Mystery biker?* Maybe he wasn’t the only one with memories of their shared glance so long ago.

20 - Heading home

The sit-down in Detroit went well enough. Tug had him call ahead and ask for a welcome into the Highwaymen's clubhouse, and Gasman agreed. The parking lot had been almost full when they pulled in, and they followed a prospect's wave towards open spots near the door.

After they had parked, Tug leaned over and said, "We wear our colors inside, but only because we have an arrangement with the Highwaymen. Anywhere else, we'd pack them out of respect for their clubhouse. Keep your back to a fucking wall, don't speak unless asked a direct question, and even then, you need to treat any questions as hostile. So keep your responses to 'yes', 'no', or a fucking 'ask Tug'. You got me, brother?"

Bear nodded, briskly wiping his unexpectedly sweaty palms down his jeans. "Yeah, I got you, Tug."

The door leading into the clubhouse opened, and Gasman strolled out. "About fucking time, Tug. Old ladies are all pissing and moaning the food's gettin' cold." He reached out and grasped Tug's wrist as he shook it. "Good to see you, old man." This last was said with a smile that pierced the fierceness of his face.

Looking over at Bear, his face grew hard again and he grunted, giving a chin lift and saying only, "Hey." Bear nodded at him, rising off his bike and waiting for Tug to precede him into the clubhouse. Inside, the room was crowded with men, faces he didn't know or trust, and he remembered Tug's advice to get a wall at his back. Knowing he wasn't expected, or probably even allowed to remain with Tug while he talked to Gasman and the other club officers, he glanced around the room and rested his shoulders against an open section of wall near the door.

Keeping his gaze moving, he tried to not look overly long on any individual, instead skimming across the room while maintaining an awareness of where Tug was over near the bar. A tall, powerfully built man stepped between them, looking fixedly at him, and Bear locked his gaze on the man's face, unsure if this was a challenge or something else. The man seemed familiar, but was out of place here. Bear gave him a chin lift, and had abandoned the staring contest to begin his slow sweep of the room again, when he heard the man ask, "Rob? Rob Crew?"

His eyes shot back to him, startled, because with the voice came a wave of recognition, and he knew why the man had felt familiar. Bear felt a slow smile curl the corners of his mouth. "Petty Officer Gibbs, good to see you, man." Offering a handshake, he reached out to clasp wrists with his Navy buddy. "Bruce, how the hell are you?"

He asked the question as a brusque voice snapped out, "Nugget," and saw his friend's face darken, closing down further, and he grimly said, "Good." He then turned away, dropping the handshake with a low, hissed, "*Fuck*."

Belatedly, Bear recalled his instructions from Tug and clamped his lips tightly, settling his shoulders against the wall and pressing his spine into the wood. *Great*, he thought, *exactly three minutes in and I'm fucking up. Dammit*. Dragging his eyes up, he was staggered at the number of hostile stares turned his way, including a somewhat less hostile one from Tug, who was settled in across the room with Gasman and the other officers.

Tug jerked his head in a silent command, and Bear moved towards him across the room, angling to where he stood with a group of men near an interior door. Threading his way between the bodies and furniture, his mind briefly returned to the pretty, dark-haired woman from the bar yesterday, and her failed negotiation of the walking hazards there.

Giving himself a mental shake, he brought his mind back to the work at hand, which was helping Tug mediate an understanding with the Highwaymen regarding Fort Wayne. His focus was definitely *not* supposed to be thinking about a woman he'd likely never see again. A woman whose laughter thrilled him. A woman with a history with the River Riders. A woman who had a crazy friend who knew Judge well enough to call him by his given name.

"Gasman, this is Bear," Tug voiced a one-way introduction, and Bear returned the chin lift he received, following the other man's lead.

"You know Nugget?" The question came from one of the other men, standing a half-step behind the Highwaymen's president. The room quieted around them as their conversation became the focus of the assembled members.

"Yeah," he responded, glancing around and remembering to adhere to Tug's request to keep his answers brief.

The drawn-out silence that followed gradually became uncomfortable, and the same man gave a disgusted shake of his head as he asked, "Yeah? Know him long?"

Thankfully it was another yes or no question, and Bear was able to respond with an additional, "Yeah."

The uncomfortable silence fell upon the group more quickly this time, settling around them like a smothering blanket, and he saw the tiniest impression of amusement flash across Tug's face. "Y'all friends?" came the next question, asked in an exasperated tone with an out-flung palm from the same man.

Bear answered with conviction, "Yeah." Tug started laughing, his teeth glinting whitely behind his dark mustache.

"This motherfucker ever say anything except 'yeah', Tug?" the man asked him, swinging away from Bear in irritation.

Throwing his head back, Tug laughed harder, finally pulling himself under control enough to respond, "Yeah."

His answer set off a corresponding wave of laughter through the group, and Bear relaxed slightly. Tug slapped his shoulder and asked him, "Where do you know Nugget from? He's a fairly recent prospect into the Highwaymen, so how you know him is curious. I gotta admit it's a thing interesting to me, too, seeing as how I know you've hardly been out of the garage in over a year." He looked at Gasman. "Fucker sleeps beside his bike, I swear. He's always at FWO or FWO2."

"Navy," Bear responded. "We did boot together, and then served on the same sub. I haven't seen him since I separated from the service years ago." His head snapped around as he heard several soft cries of "Hooyah!" from around the room, and his wary posture subtly changed, easing as he nodded to each of them, recognizing them as Navy brothers, even if they had never served together.

Tug looked at him, the corners of his mouth pulling down slightly. "He know Carter?" Bear grunted in affirmation, nodding and seeing the look Tug shot across the room. "Call him over, Gasman. I got a question," he said quietly.

Bear stepped to the side, marginally behind Tug, watching as Nugget was directed their way. "Bear said you're Navy." This was a statement from Tug, not a question, and Nugget inclined his head, cutting his eyes over to Bear.

"I am," he responded with a frown.

"You know Carter LeRoy?" Here was the question that mattered, and Bear held himself still.

"I do. Petty Officer LeRoy is a good man," Nugget said, rocking back on his heels and tucking his thumbs into his pockets. "Proud to have served with him, as I am with Bear," he concluded with a firm nod.

"Carter talk to you about anything important? He tell you about club life, or any shit like that?" Tug questioned further, and Bear wasn't sure where this was going.

"Nope, I know the kid's from Chicago, but that's about all I know other than he's a fucking genius at cribbage." Nugget grinned.

"Little motherfucker's gonna get a piece of my mind next time he calls," Tug was grumbling. "He should always be talking up the Rebels, dammit." He laughed, looking between Nugget and Gasman. "Carter's my nephew," he explained, and there were hoots and grins from the group of men.

Gasman gestured at the door behind him. "Tug, let's get down to business, now that we have the pleasantries and shit out of the way." To Nugget and Bear, he said, "Pull up a chair, sit, and catch up if you want." Someone handed Bear a bottle of beer and pointed towards a row of chairs along the wall. He reached out and grabbed one, passing it off to Nugget as he pulled out a seat for himself.

"When did you get out, Bruce...Nugget? Have you been in Detroit long?" he asked, curious.

"Last year," came the answer. "I put in fifteen. Seemed like a good number to call it quits on, and they were still buying out some of the specialties, so I got a nice package. I've only been here for about four months. I separated with a couple of guys who wanted to go to the woods, so we spent a while hiking along the east coast. I followed them—it was an easy decision, and hiking is about as far from military life as you can get. Detroit...well, I chased someone up here, but that didn't work out. Found the Highwaymen, and it felt like I found myself. Ya know?"

Nodding, Bear said, "Fuck yeah. I stayed around Norfolk for a while, working for a pair of brothers as a mechanic. We got off into custom bikes and got the notice of the Rebel president, Mason. Shit fell apart there, and he told me I'd have a place in Chicago. Fucking crazy ride, man, but I know what you mean. The club is like coming home."

The conversation turned to a series of 'do you know where' and 'what did so and so ever do' as they caught up on each other's lives. There was a comfortable silence, and then Nugget asked quietly, "So how you doin', Rob? Did you ever find anyone after your wife...you know?"

Bear felt as if he was on an express elevator that had suddenly dropped a dozen floors at once, the blood leaving his face in a rush and nausea pooling low in his stomach. Eyes wide, his breath seized in his throat, and he lurched gracelessly to his feet, one hand slapping the wall behind him to steady himself.

Nugget jumped up, his concerned and anxious gaze on Bear. "Sorry man, fuck...look, I'm sorry. I didn't know it still—"

Bear interrupted him with a hard, "No, I'm still a fucking widower." Stalking out of the room, he was searching blindly for the bathroom, outside exit, or any-*fucking*-where but where he was when Bruce asked that question, because now that space was filled with echoes of the CO's voice saying, *'They did not suffer.'*

He staggered outside, dragging in raw gasps of air before collapsing backward to the wall of the building, his shoulders and elbows colliding painfully with the cement that supported him, preventing his fall. He stood there for a long time, tightening his fists again and again, occasionally pounding the back of his head against the hard surface behind him.

Several hours later, Tug exited the building to find Bear sleeping restlessly on his bike, arms crossed on the tank, pillowing his head. He looked at his friend sadly for a moment, seeing the pain-twisted features he wore even in his sleep, then reached out, but thought better of touching him.

Bear startled, hearing a voice close beside him say, "—ride?" Picking his head up and blinking owlishly, he looked at Tug, "Whadidja say?"

"Ready to ride, Bear? Let's head home," Tug told him, straddling his own bike and starting it with a couple of easy kicks. Bear scrubbed at his face with both palms, rubbing the last traces of sleep and his dreams away. He shook his head; some of his dreams had been welcome tonight, filled with dark hair and grey eyes. Sitting up, he stretched his back and started the bike, pulling out on the road behind Tug, headed home.

21 - Too far, too fast

"Dammit, why can't shit just keep between the lines for once?" The rhetorical question hung on the air of the Rebel clubhouse in St. Louis, and Bear shook his head at Mason. The man was on a rant again and, as always, you just needed to stay out of the way and keep your mouth shut until he'd worn himself down. Bear had some concerns about where the wind-down point of this one would take them, but he'd ride it out as far as was needed.

"I see that shit. Don't you do it. Don't you fucking try and handle me, Bear. I'm not putting up with this kind of bullshit. These dickless mother*fuckers* want to be Rebels, but they can't be bothered to keep the fucking charter?" He roared, "This is *my house* and I'm going to fucking clean it. They won't know their goddamn, motherfucking assholes from a posthole in the fucking ground when I'm done with them." Mason tugged his beanie off, wiping his forehead with the fabric before tucking it into his back pocket.

He leaned against the closed door of the office, gaze sweeping the men seated and standing around the room. "You assholes know the charter. It's short, to the fucking point, and goddamn easy to follow. This is shit and you goddamn well know it. Ain't a one of you has respect for the colors on your fucking back. If you forget what we stand for, all you gotta do is look at the fucking patch. Three prongs on the shaft of that skeleton, shows you it's central to *everything*. We got three rules to unlock membership, three rules to keep us free. They are our warded lock." He'd referenced the main patch of the club and the skeleton key held clenched in the teeth of a grinning skull. "You got no respect for the brothers sitting at your side. Should cut 'em all."

There was a collective gasp in the room, and leather creaked as men shifted, hands instinctively and unconsciously moving towards weapons as their membership in the Rebel Wayfarers club was threatened. *Fuck,* thought Bear, freezing until he caught Slate's eyes from across the room. The man shook his head almost imperceptibly, remaining in a relaxed posture, propped on one corner of a table against the wall.

"Well? Is that what you fucking want? Gimme a fucking answer, Pike," Mason snarled, slamming his fists down on the chapter president's desk with a loud crash before standing and taking a step back, hands resting arrogantly on his waist, elbows akimbo.

There was a scraping noise as Pike shoved his chair back, drawing himself up to his full height to look Mason in the eyes. He swallowed audibly, his Adam's apple moving in his throat as he prepared to speak. "No, Prez. I do not want that. Not for any man here." He swept his arm out, indicating his officers and senior members. "*Fuck.*"

Shaking his head, he said, "I fucked up. If you gotta bust someone out, then bust me. It's my leadership that allowed this to happen. Tender, Pipes, Hammer, and the others here don't bear the same responsibility."

He pointed a stiff finger at a man who shifted and made to speak. "You shut the fuck up, Tender. Doesn't matter if you are lieutenant or not, this is still my name under the President patch." He poked his vest with his finger, indicating the patch saying 'Pike'. "St. Louis is my chapter. My responsibility. My duty, the charter my charge." He shifted back to face Mason, nodding resolutely. "Mine."

The two men stood staring at each other for several minutes, and Bear could almost see the gears humming in Mason's head as he examined and rejected different tactics. He, Mason, and Slate had outlined several possible scenarios this morning before riding in, but none of them involved finding out some of the members were selling fully automatic weapons. At a high profit, it was true, but that was one of the three tenets Mason wouldn't ignore being broken. They were in uncharted waters, and Bear didn't know which way the winds would cant the sail.

"Well, all right then," Mason said, and reached out to grasp Pike's shoulder, shaking him back and forth slightly. "Let's fix this shit." Bear drew in a deep breath of relief as the two men sat down to begin the hard work of reclaiming trust from what Mason regarded as the most serious type of disloyalty.

Hours later, Bear was on the clubhouse rooftop, seated on top of a picnic table strumming softly on a borrowed guitar, when he heard the scuff of boots behind him over his quiet music. He'd been up here for an hour or more, watching as the sky deepened from palest blue to indigo, and then to the velvet black of current. Twisting, he saw Mason and Slate headed towards him, both walking with exhausted strides. "Prez, Slate," he greeted them, turning back and moving the guitar to stand it between his legs.

"Today could have been bloody," Mason said without prelude. "I don't even know how we recovered today, and it's hard to see my way to salvaging this chapter. I've let us grow fast. Too fast. And now it's impossible to keep tabs on all the fucking chapters." He climbed onto the bench, turning to sit wearily next to Bear on the tabletop. "We're what, two years into this expansion, and shit is already falling apart? I just want to give everyone a place to fucking own, not have to reform the chapters every six fucking months."

Slate stood in front of them, his thumbs tucked into his back pockets as he studied the toes of his boots. He shrugged indifferently. "So we close this chapter, move the brothers home, or around, or something. I agree, you fucked up when you agreed to have Pike lead this chapter. He's not seasoned enough. Hell, he's only been a full patch for a handful of years, and he was a challenger all through his prospect period. Gave me grief more than once. Maybe we've been too easy on the prospects? Need to kick ass more, fucking nurture less?"

Bear shook his head. "I say figure out a way to save this one. It makes sense to have chapters along the main interstates in these large cities, and we've got lucrative businesses supporting each one of them so far. They legally contribute to the greater whole, which makes the entire club stronger as long as they keep the charter." He leaned forward and put his elbows on his thighs as he asked, "Did Tug have anything to offer?"

Mason had been on the phone with Tug after the meeting in the office, laying down short-term plans for the chapter. In the time since Bear had patched into the club, he'd come to depend on Tug as much as Mason did, and valued the man's opinions highly. Mason said, "He agreed with me, and I agree with Bear. Goddamn, I lean on that man, as well as you two." He scrubbed his face with his palms. "We publicly cut the six members tomorrow, deal with the rest afterwards as needed. If I close the chapter, it's a fuckton of work for Myron and you two, and a pain in the ass to divest ourselves of the businesses. What really torques me over is these men all have good lives here. They make a good living, have brothers to depend on, a club that has their backs...and then they fuck it up like this."

Shaking his head, Mason sighed. "We're already under scrutiny in every city we house a chapter. People in the neighborhoods know we're there for them, keeping shit safe and clean within a reasonable radius of the clubhouse, but local LEO is wary, and always looking for any reason to call in the feds and fuck with us.

"This club is my life, man. Shit like what was happening here will get it dismantled fast as hell. We have to fly under the radar as much as we can, show ourselves helpful to the communities. I have no doubt we're tapped and watched everywhere they can get a paper. If these pussy motherfuckers realized the rules are in place to protect everyone, not to try and keep them from making a buck, they'd kick their own asses when they fuck up like this." He sat upright, tightly gripping the edge of the table with both hands.

"I'm not going to let the club spiral down like the original one did. It's taken years to come back from that damage, and when I think about it, *goddamn,* the bitter is still in my mouth. We've built something to be proud of, a club to lean on, filled with brothers we can trust...for the most part." He shook his head ruefully.

"So tomorrow, we cut," he said with a sigh. "We cut rockers and patches. They'll have thirty days to cover or remove club tats, if they have them." He looked at Bear, frowning, his lack of a club tat was a sore point with the Prez. "Pike stays. Tender stays. I'll shift Tats down here to keep eyes on all this shit steady for six months or so. Playing fucking sentinel—should make it a new fucking office in the club and call it Watchman."

Shaking his head, he continued, "We'll rotate you two and Tug in and out of here, Memphis, Little Rock, and Fort Wayne to look out for shit. Spreading you thin, I know, like I have been for the past few years." He rocked backward then forward. "I'm gonna make a call, an executive decision." He snorted humorlessly. "We grant no new chapters for a while, brothers. We lid this goddamn shit here and sit for a spell. Fucking sit tight."

***

Beginning the next week, Bear began spending weeks at a time in the various outlying chapter clubhouses, swooping back to Fort Wayne frequently, where it began to feel more and more like his home base.

Every visit, he'd feel a familiar pressure begin to build and would watch for even a glimpse of the dark-haired woman, stalking Checkerz night after night until he either saw her or was directed back out of town. He still didn't even know her name, but just seeing her and knowing she was okay eased something in him. He frowned, remembering their most recent encounter from a month ago.

He'd been walking in the backdoor and saw her exiting the bathroom, drawing his mind back to the night she'd taken a tumble and he smiled. Following her into the room, he watched as she walked up to the bar, standing between two regulars, Reno and Blake. Reno was an affable man, officer in a local club, wearing his colors on his cut, fingers filled with silver rings and signature yellow glasses on. Blake, while a rider, was not in the lifestyle. He knew both were good men in committed relationships, and Bear watched as his not-Willa flirted harmlessly with them and Brad, another regular sitting nearby.

The men kept up a steady stream of flattering and sometimes coarse conversation with her, noting she seemed to be giving as good as she got, garnering repeated shouts of laughter from all three men. Bear frowned and watched with growing jealousy as she touched each man casually, a hand on Reno's bicep, trailing a hand across Brad's back, and leaning in to kiss Blake's cheek.

Lifting a hand, he signaled to Dixie that he wanted his usual beer, moving to sit at a nearby table where he could watch the woman unobserved. He'd still never approached her, preferring to remain distant, keeping his fascination a secret. When Dixie brought his beer, he reached out, pressing a bill into her hand. Her attention now firmly fixed on him, he asked, "The woman talking to Reno, what's her name?"

She looked, then twisted back to him, frowning. Placing the money carefully on the table, she shook her head. "She's a friend of mine, and I know her a lot better than I know you. If you want her name, she can give it to you, Bear. You running a tab?"

He nodded, frustrated, and handed her the money again, saying brusquely, "Keep it, Dixie. God knows you earn it twice over when Brent's in here." He pointed out the front door where the patio was, indicating another regular.

She looked outside, lifting her lip and making a growling noise deep in her throat. "Oh hell no," she said softly. "That just makes my goddamn night." Looking down at him, she smiled and paused before walking back to the bar. "Thanks, Bear. Hey, here's a thought. Why don't you just ask her what her name is next time she's in? She watches you, too, you know?"

He turned with a jerk, not really surprised to see his not-Willa was gone. Shaking his head, he grinned ruefully. Seemed like she was always just out of reach.

22 - Riptide

Bear startled, hearing a pounding on the apartment door. Putting the guitar back in its stand, he stood, stretched, and walked to the door. He pulled it open and saw a big man standing in the hallway, recognizing the figure as Mason. Reaching out to clasp wrists with his friend, he hissed, only realizing his fingertips were raw when they stung upon touching the man's skin. He must have been playing the guitar for a long time since waking early once again from his recurring nightmare.

"Mason, good to see you," he said, releasing the handshake. He glanced at the clock and winced at the hour; it was late afternoon. He'd lost nearly twelve hours this time. He stepped back, opening the door wide. "Come on inside. Want a beer, brother?"

"Wouldn't turn one down," Mason told him. "Heard you playing through the door. It's been so long since you played out somewhere. I forget how good you are, man. You should come into the bar and play one night. It would be a nice change from the jukebox at Jackson's."

He shrugged, grabbing two beers from the refrigerator and passing one over to Mason as they stood in the kitchen. "It's just something to keep my mind busy when I can't work on the bikes. It's no big deal," he said, tipping the bottle to his lips and taking a long swallow.

Mason glanced over at his hands and tilted his head, leaning one hip casually against the counter. "It keeps your mind busy, huh? If that's the case, then keeping busy looks like it fucking hurts, brother."

He opened his mouth, but Mason cut him off. "That ain't why I came over. Your business, not mine." He took a drink from his beer, then said, "I do have some Rebel business I'd like you to handle. I need you to come down to Jackson's tonight, sit lead on a conversation with Hawk. He's looking to affiliate, and I got to know if that's in our best interests, being he's in the same fucking town."

"Relations with the Dominos have always been friendly, but distant. We haven't had any trouble between us, but that's because we all mind our lines. An alliance is different, and I don't get what's in this for us. He's obstinate, saying the meet needs to be tonight, and I got some other shit to deal with up in Milwaukee."

He thought for a long minute, and then nodded, agreeing with Mason. "I don't see an upside, not for the Rebels. But, I don't see a downside either. Unless there's something going on in their club that Hawk wants to nip in the bud. The other option would be to fold them in, but I can't see us easily absorbing their members; that'd be too many to convert to our ways. All right, boss, I'll head over to the bar in a bit, bring Buzz and Hoss with me. We'll sort it out, Prez."

Mason straightened and set his empty bottle on the countertop. Moving towards the door, he stopped and turned around, a somber look on his face as he sighed and said, "You need anything, brother, I'm here. I hate to see you still tearing yourself up like this. You're killing me. Tug told me what happened in Jackson's last night. It's clear to all of us you got shit festering inside you, brother. Fucking talk to someone, man."

Memory of the casual question that drove him out of the bar in an anxiety-filled panic swept over him. *Do you have kids?* It happened less frequently than it had in years past, but when the feeling swept over him, he was lost. Tongue trapped between his teeth, he bit down hard. With a crunch, he tasted copper and felt enough in control to respond with a hoarse grunt. "Yeah."

Closing the door behind Mason, he leaned against it and looked back into the apartment. There were only a few things to indicate it was actually occupied. It looked much like he felt inside: empty. It had been this way for longer than he could remember. He'd believe he was finally finding his center, as if he were regaining a balance that spread throughout his life, steadying him. Then there would be an event, an incident—and as if he were an out of control rollercoaster, he'd be rocketing down again. He'd only found two things that could anchor him when that was happening: the guitar and the bikes.

The hardest thing to reconcile was that there was nothing to rage against. The other driver, sure, but he'd determined long ago that was ultimately futile. The man had paid and paid and paid, losing first his job, then his family when his wife left him, and eventually his freedom when he was convicted of manslaughter, all because he didn't see a red light. Then the man had lost his life, but he hadn't lost that so much as taken it.

With nothing to grab hold of, Bear's grief kept washing around inside him. Similar to the ocean, it receded periodically, as outside influences pushed or pulled it out of focus. But like a powerful, irresistible surge that ran before a storm, when it rushed back in, the grief could be overwhelming, rolling his emotions in a churn along the edge of the surf, pushing him under until he was drowning in the loss again, pulling him along with it, helpless in a riptide of pain.

Physically shaking his head to free himself from the crippling sadness, Bear made his way to the bedroom, refusing to look at the picture on the dresser. It was straight out of his dream, a photo of the three of them sitting on their blanket at Ocean View Beach in Norfolk, his arms around both his angels. Efficiently stripping off his sweat-rank clothes, he roughly pulled on a clean shirt and jeans, stalking out of the room, headed to Jackson's.

23 - Shoulda had boys

"Not a merger, not at all. What I'm looking for is a way for us to work together, instead of existing alongside." Hawk looked at him from across the table, a sheen of sweat on his forehead and upper lip.

Bear watched him carefully and blew his breath out in exasperation. "I hear what you're sayin', Hawk, but what I don't hear is why this is beneficial for the Rebels. I see where it looks good from that side of the table, because there's a lot of sway and push that comes with being affiliated with us. Keeps bangers off your shit, other clubs off your six, prides up the members...that's all real good for the Dominos. But Hawk," he paused, thinking, *I have to remember we aren't equals; I'm just a long-time member sitting down with a club president,* and then asked, "what's the shine for Rebels?"

"I've got eighty men I can bring to bear on your behalf—" he began, but Bear interrupted him.

"I got two hundred here in Chicago, another eighty in Fort Wayne, a hundred twenty in St. Louis. Hawk, you know I could go on and on naming the chapters. What's in this for Rebels?" he repeated his question, his slipping control giving his tone a sharp edge.

"We have pull with other clubs," Hawk said, beginning to look panicked as he watched Bear already shaking his head.

"We have markers from Machos, Disciples, Outriders, Highwaymen...fucking name the club; I can play that tune too. What's in it for my brothers?"

"If we don't, I'll have to go to war with Disciples. That shit will fuck Chicago up for everyone," Hawk silenced the bar as he half-stood and shouted across the table at Bear. *"Fuucck,"* he whispered, dropping back into his chair.

"There we go," Bear uttered quietly, and then demanded more assertively, "Tell me."

"We gotta do this here, man?" Hawk asked, looking around the bar at the dozens of curious and concerned faces turned their way.

"Naw, let's hit a room," Bear agreed, standing and pointing to the first private meeting room door on the wall behind the bar.

Once inside, Hawk found a chair and sat abruptly, his limbs strangely loose and unhinged.

"Tell me," Bear repeated his demand in a quiet voice, standing with his arms crossed over his chest.

"Mange fucking overstepped. I fixed it. I fucking fixed it, but the motherfucker's on a vengeance run for my goddamn head." Licking his lips nervously, Hawk looked up at him.

"I'd like the whole story, man, not the bits you think I need." Bear said this with a growl. He thought tiredly, *How does the man expect me to help him with his problems if he's not going to be honest?* It had slowly turned into a long day.

"Fuck. Okay, Bear. Okay. You know me and Houlihan have three girls?" Hawk waited for Bear to nod before continuing. "My oldest, Olivia, she just turned twenty-two. Mange is fucking thirty-five, way too old for my girl. He caught sight of her and started a chase. She didn't tell him no, and he took it as a yes. He stopped short of fucking her, but now Olivia thinks she's in love with the motherfucker. I shipped her off to relatives—no phone, no internet, no contact—and he's fucking crazed, man. I thought he'd thank me for getting her crazy ass out of town, but he's threatening war if I don't bring her back."

He ran a hand over his face, tugging fingers roughly through his hair. "My Houlihan believes I'm nuts. She thinks it's okay for them to be together. She should have had boys. None of this fucking shit would've happened." Hawk's tirade was beginning to wind down, and Bear had to fight to keep a smile off his face.

"My next girl? Kecia? She's as pretty as Olivia, but she's got a mouth on her. Goddamn sixteen and a mouth like that already. Says she's done with school in a year, and she's trying to tell me she don't need no college. Fucking kids, man. Judy is the sweetest one. She's eight and hasn't started growing titties yet. When they grow titties, I think they go crazy."

"Hey, Hawk," Bear called his name, interrupting the man's introspective commentary. When he looked up, Bear offered him a grin. "Want a drink, brother?"

"Fuck yeah," Hawk said with a groan. "Fucking kids. Fucking *girls*."

A few hours later, Mason called, and Bear reported the sum of what he'd learned, hearing quiet snorts of laughter coming from the phone. He'd sent the short version to Mason earlier via text, knowing he would be talking to the Disciples' president at some point that day.

"That matches what I got from Mange up here," he said. "Thanks for the heads-up today, brother. Could have been a cluster otherwise. Glad you helped Hawk sort things out. He gonna send for the girl now? Mange is going nuts wondering where and how she is."

"Yeah, he already made the call. She was over in Rockford, and she'll be home by now or near enough." Bear yawned and cracked his neck. "I'm headed home myself, Prez."

"Hold a minute, brother," Mason said, and then it sounded like he hesitated. "Tomorrow, I need you in Fort Wayne. Word is Shooter's headed that way again in a couple of weeks. I want you settled in the clubhouse before he shows. I'll be down for the actual meet, but need you to have a read on things before I ride in."

"Fucking hell, Prez. Why not Tug? He's friends with the bastard." Bear yawned as he lodged his complaint casually, then straightened as he heard the whip crack in Mason's voice.

"Because I fucking told *you* to, Bear. If I want Tug there, then I'll fucking send Tug. You don't want to do this, then we need to have a goddamn chat."

"Dammit, Mason...Prez. You know that's not the problem. I just...I want to work on the bikes, man. Working like I do keeps my head straight. I'm *shit* right now, and you saw that this morning." He pleaded, "I want to work on the bikes. I've been gone so much I can't even see the pictures in my head anymore. I just need the bikes, Mason."

"And I *just* need you in the Fort, watching shit as only you can. You and Slate have a way of analyzing people and their actions, and I want that level of scrutiny looking outwards as we head into this meet alongside all the other shit already going down in the Fort. I can't spare Slate right now; he's got too much to deal with here, and that means you are next in line for me to lean on, brother. Let the change in scenery help you pull your shit together, and fucking get your head on straight."

His voice softened. "I know you struggle, man, but you gotta keep moving forward. You can't hide in the garage forever." Mason's voice regained the edge it had lost as he spoke, turning steely and unsympathetic. "Bingo's already expecting ya. Get your ass on the road early. Ride safe, brother." The call ended abruptly, and Bear was left looking at his phone in frustration.

24 - The Fort

"Man of my fucking word," Bear grumbled to himself, pulling into the clubhouse parking lot in Fort Wayne mid-morning. "Bingo here?" He called the question to the prospect on lot duty, receiving a non-committal answer in response. His mind went to a conversation with Slate not long ago, and he wondered how much time Bingo actually spent around the club. He'd been the president since the chapter's origin nine years ago. It should consume his life, because the brothers all depended on him and the club, but he sure didn't appear to be committed.

Grabbing his bag off the bike, he headed into the building. Stepping inside to allow the door to close behind him, he had paused to give his eyes a moment to grow accustomed to the dim, indoor lighting, when he heard a raspy, "Bear, good to see you," from one side of the room. He swung his head to find Deke standing there. Raising a hand, he headed over, seeing a group of men standing near his friend.

Two of the men were leaving as he walked up, and he recognized Rabid and Ramone angling towards the door he'd just come through, and gave them a chin lift in acknowledgment. He greeted the rest of the members, gripping forearms with Gunny and Diablo, meeting and greeting a few he didn't yet know.

"What ya doin' here?" The question had come earlier in the visit than he'd expected, but he'd prepared a response on the way, deciding to be honest to a point with the members here. "I need somewhere to get my head on straight," he said, looking Deke in the face. "Chicago's not doing it for me, except in the garage. Hopefully FW will suit me better, at least for a while. Mason agreed, so here I am."

Deke's eyes narrowed, and Bear worried for a moment that Mason had messaged and he was about to be called out on his lie by omission, but the reaction from his friend and brother startled him, causing his heart to clench in his chest. "I lost my sister and nephew, man. Stupid accident, not really anybody's fault. You need to talk, I got ya." He reached out and clasped Bear's shoulder. "I got ya, brother."

Nodding, Bear wordlessly acknowledged the support and went upstairs to find a room and dump his bag.

Wandering back down to the central area, Bear was surprised to find Melanie sitting at a table. She'd been like a daughter to Winger and DeeDee, and Lockee's best friend. She looked different now, harder, warier. The last time he'd seen her had been a few years ago, not long before Winger and Lockee were killed.

When she caught sight of him, she jumped up, squealing as she raced across the room. This was more like the Melanie he remembered. She and Lockee had been a wild pair. She launched herself at him, locking her legs around his waist, and he grabbed her in reflex, wrapping his arms around her while trying to keep from falling on his ass.

She was laughing as he eased her down, setting her feet back on the floor. Bear found himself smiling along with her, standing quietly and listening as she talked animatedly, asking him countless questions without ever waiting for a reply. Her eyes were downcast, but she flicked her gaze up again and again, occasionally gifting him with her easy smile.

He shook his head at her silliness and looked around the room, his gaze stopping at Deke, who was frowning their way. Unsure what line he was edging toward, he took a step back from the girl and she swung her head up to look him in the face.

"Nuh uh, Bear," Melanie said, reaching out to tug on the edge of his cut. "No running in the clubhouse." She continued laughing until she saw the look Deke had on his face. "Deke, stop it," she shouted at him across the room. "You're scaring the Bear, man."

"Goddammit, Mel. You can't fuck with him; he's a brother—patched into the club. Leave him the fuck alone," Deke yelled back, and she looked up at Bear in surprise, fear flooding her face. She hung her head as if expecting a blow, taking a step backward and putting her hands behind her back.

"I'm sorry," she breathed.

"For what?" Bear asked, holding his hands out to the side in confusion.

"I grabbed your colors, Bear. I shouldn't have; I'm sorry. I'm sorry," she repeated in a whisper, cringing. "I'm sorry."

He understood now. The last time she'd seen him, he hadn't even been prospected into the club, and now he was a full-patch member. Fortunately for her, he was undoubtedly one of the more laidback men, and the insult hadn't even registered with him. "It's okay, Mel," he responded. "Just a mistake. No harm, no foul."

Her voice was barely audible when she said with a sob, "Lockee would never make that mistake."

He sobered, recalling Mel was only a handful of years older than Ashley would have been, and she carried so much grief and pain. He well remembered vibrant Lockee, Winger's daughter and Melanie's best friend. He realized that she, like his Ashley, would never get a chance to grow older, and he felt a soft wave of sadness break over him again for the loss.

Reaching out, he gathered the girl into a gentle hug, folding her close and holding her against him until they could both breathe without gasping. "I miss her," he confided raggedly against the side of her head, knowing they remembered different people, but their shared pain connected them. She nestled her face into his chest trustingly, her arms folded up between them, the tension in her muscles easing slowly as she stood in his comforting embrace.

Pulling away, he looked down to see his shirt was damp and using his thumbs, he wiped the shining tear tracks from her cheeks. Reassuring her in as soft a voice as he could manage through a throat clogged and tight with tears and sorrow, he said, "It does get easier. It never stops hurting, and I don't think it should. But you'll be okay, Melanie. We won't ever be the same, but it gets easier. Let yourself be okay, all right?" As he stepped back, he looked up to see Deke watching them carefully. He finally set her aside with a gruffly spoken, "All right, then. See ya around, girl."

He spent the balance of the day casually, visiting and telling stories with the members as they made their way in and out of the clubhouse. By evening, Bingo still hadn't made an appearance, which surprised Bear, but didn't appear to faze anyone else.

Deke and Gunny good-naturedly harassed him until he agreed to go get a few beers at a bar they said was biker-friendly. Riding and following the lead of his brothers had become second nature, and it wasn't until they pulled into the bike parking in the back of the building he realized it was Checkerz. This was where the dark-haired woman had been, where Judge came to retrieve her and her friend, leaving with only the one. The one place where he'd seen her sporadically, but repeatedly in the years since those initial encounters. *Maybe she'll be here tonight*, he thought.

He followed the two men inside, listening to the friendly and welcoming calls they received from people sitting at the bar and various tables. His companions were recognized and their club respected, and that felt good.

There was a vibe to the air, and he looked more closely around the bar. Seeing her, he felt a smile creep across his face. She was here, sitting in the top section, which was elevated by a handful of steps from the level where he was. Her confusing friend was with her, and there was a biker sitting at the bar beside them. It looked like they were having a drinking competition.

Nudging Deke, he pointed at the women and asked, "You know those two gals, man? Saw them in here a few years ago when I was with Tug. Judge came in and retrieved the one on the left, but the other one had gone out the backdoor. He did not look pleased."

Squinting up the room, Deke shook his head. "Naw. Can't say I know them. The guy with them is Bulldog. He's a River Rider." They watched as a man approached the women from behind, putting his hand on the neck of the darker-haired woman, his not-Willa. It was Brent, the bar's most obnoxious asshole, and Bear tensed, holding himself stiff until she laughed and brushed his hand away, driving him off with her words. He saw Bulldog easing himself down off the same kind of tension, and Bear wondered what not-Willa was to him.

"I'm gonna go introduce myself to the Rider," Bear said. He wanted to see not-Willa up close, and maybe this time he'd get the nerve to ask her name and get a chance to figure out if she was with the biker sitting beside her.

"Sure, no reason to stand on ceremony. You want a beer?" Deke looked at the bar, giving the pretty bartender a chin lift to call her over. She raised a finger in recognition, picking up a tray and heading over.

"Yeah, draft is fine, Dixie knows my usual. I'll be back," Bear said, sliding off the stool and walking towards the upper bar.

***

Eddie had clocked her biker when he walked in the bar. Wait...*her biker*? When had she taken ownership of him? She'd watched him while he sat with the two Rebels for several minutes before he saw her. She'd been observing closely enough to have even been able to identify the moment he recognized her. She thought of him often and caught glimpses of him frequently enough that he still made appearances in her dreams.

She'd agreed to come here tonight, not simply to shut Willa up about going out, but also in the hopes he'd be here again. She leaned back, looking at Willa, and used her eyebrows to try and convey that the mystery biker was here.

"You got something in your eye, Eddie?" Willa asked, and Eddie sighed, thinking, *Wills really is hopeless sometimes*. Thank God she had friends to help her blow off steam from work.

Bulldog laughed, asking, "This your way of saying you're done before we start, Eddie girl?"

"Dawg, man. No fucking way can you outdrink me. I'm a pro. You ready for this? Hmmm?" she taunted him, pleased with the idea of a shooter war, knowing he'd already had a few beers before they arrived. He was another Outrider transplant, and she'd known him all her life.

"Fuck yeah! Shooter war," he said, yelling downstairs at the bartender. "Bring the bottle of 1800, Dixie."

"Willa, you joining in?" She turned, seeing the negative headshake and shudder. Willa preferred anything except straight tequila and could really only stomach it in a weak margarita. "Suit yourself," she said to her friend, calling out to the bartender, "Bring six shot glasses with you, Dix."

Lining up the little glasses, she filled each one level with the top, eyeing Bulldog out of the corner of her eye. "Don't forget loser buys. It's eighteen dollars a round, man. Is that too rich for you?" He shook his head, eyeing the shot glasses.

"No? Good. Oh, I almost forgot to ask...Dawg, you gonna need pussy limes or salt? Just wanna make sure you've got everything you need to be successful. Don't want you grousing later that it wasn't fair," she laughed, trying to disguise her amusement as solicitude.

"Fuck you, girl. I was shooting tequila before you could walk," he barked back at her and picked up the first glass with a little smirk. She matched his actions and watched as he grimaced before tossing the liquid to the back of his throat, swallowing hard with a shake of his head as he smacked the glass onto the bar.

Waiting for him to look at her, she teased the edge of the glass with the tip of her tongue, dipping it into the liquid and drawing it across her lower lip. Easing the glass to her mouth, she tipped it up smoothly and swallowed slowly, savoring the flavor and bite of the liquor. "Fucking hell," he muttered, watching her make a meal of the drink.

"Next?" she asked, picking up the second glass to begin the routine again. He grabbed the glass in front of him and tossed it back, making the same shudder and grimace before he followed it with the third shot. By the time he had his third glass back on the bar, she'd matched his actions, thumping hers down a fraction of a second before his hit the bar.

There was a touch on her shoulder, followed by a hand grasping the back of her neck. She flinched sideways and reached up instinctively to brush the hand off her, leaning away from the face which appeared next to hers, belatedly recognizing it as a man who had bothered her the last time she'd been in this bar. His name was...she struggled to pull it from her memory, finally nodding to herself. His name was Brent.

He wore leathers, but no patches, so was probably a wannabe. This meant he was fair game for teasing, especially if he was an ass. And it looked as if he certainly was an ass, at the least.

"Hey, baby, want to go for a ride?"

His voice was as obnoxious as his words, and she pulled a face before she told him, "Not a chance, Lance. Find a different gal." He grumbled and mumbled a few more words, but eventually walked away.

She turned around to face front again in time to see her biker easing back off the edge of his stool. Huh. It almost looked like he was about to come up here and rescue her. He was still watching her, and her gaze was caught by his, heat flashing across her skin.

"Hey, Willa, do you remember 'Zoid?" She smiled, waiting for Willa's response.

"Hells yeah, I 'member 'Zoid. We only talk about him all the time, bitch. 'Sup?" Willa twirled a lock of hair around her finger, looking absentmindedly around the bar.

"If memory serves, you said 'Zoid was about to play the hero that day and help me up when I managed to climb up on my own, right?" They'd fallen into the habit of referring to him with the diminutive version of creep-a-zoid that Willa had used on him.

"Uh yeah, I remember that. But your meter was good, mine was broken. Don't *you* 'member?" Willa looked back down to her phone, where she was playing a word-find game.

"Yeah, I remember. Just wondering," she said, breaking her gaze free from him and turning to Bulldog. "Ready for more, Dawg?" she asked as she reached to fill up the six shot glasses again.

"Fuck yeah, Eddie. Let's chase this bitch," he snorted, picking up the first glass and beginning his ritual of slam, shudder, shake, and smack.

She picked up the first glass, tipping it smoothly into her mouth and swallowing easily as she lifted the second glass to her lips, already reaching for the third with her other hand. Once again, she was seconds ahead of her competitor in smacking the third glass back onto the bar.

"Round two goes to Eddie." Willa laughed, reaching across and picking up the bottle of tequila to start filling up the glasses again. "That's both rounds to her so far, Bullfrog," she reminded him, grinning at her friend.

A hand came down on the edge of the bar between the girls, and Willa jerked back, dropping the bottle on its side as Eddie turned to find Brent had returned. "Lemme buy you a drink, pretty lady," he said, leaning in towards her side. He reached his hand out to touch her hair, and she swatted it away.

"I can buy my own drinks, thanks." She tried to be nice in her brushoff, but she was definitely going to lose her cool if the guy didn't leave her alone.

"I'll buy you whatever you want—" he started, but Bulldog interrupted, tugging her towards him with a hand on her shoulder.

"Pour the fucking shots, gal," he told her, then pointed at Brent, snarling, "Back the fuck off, man." Brent walked away again, grumbling, and she had a sinking feeling this wouldn't be his last trip to Rejectionland.

Eddie lifted the bottle from the bar, thankful that little had spilled. Eyeing the contents, she decided there was still enough for another round of shots. Finishing filling the glasses, she looked over at Bulldog, raising an eyebrow when he paled a little looking at the liquor.

"Remember our bet, Dawg?" she asked him, tapping a fingertip against the napkin on the bar, but was denied an immediate answer when her biker sat on the next stool, facing her little group. Only he wasn't looking at her, just at Bulldog. *Oh, club business*, she thought.

She took in a quick breath; he was cuter than she remembered, having molten green eyes and a strong jaw covered by rough beard. His face had rounded cheeks, with a mouth made for laughing. *Too bad he's here for a club thing*, she thought, sighing. *He is gorgeous.*

"Hey, man, wanted to come introduce myself," he said. "I'm Bear, down from the Rebel's Chicago chapter for a few weeks. Rode over with Deke and Gunny, and they pointed you out."

Bulldog eyed him, saying shortly, "Bulldog, Fort Wayne, River Riders."

There was a silence, and the biker—*his name is Bear*—leaned up and spoke across the group in his deep voice. "Willa, good to see you again. It's been a while."

"Yeah." She cut her gaze up from her phone and sucked in a breath. "Hey, 'Zoid! Yeah, good to see you too." She poked Eddie in the ribs with her elbow, laughing. "I was wrong! Totally broken meter. Not mine, yours. Hey, Bullfrog, you gonna drink that last round?"

Eddie looked at Bulldog. She needed to keep the game moving before he lost that lovely shade of green he had when thinking about drinking another shot. Bear opened his mouth, but she cut him off. She couldn't focus if she looked at him, so she spoke directly to Bulldog. "Yeah, you ready Dawg? Shooter war, remember? What was our bet? Loser buys winner's choice? You ready to lose, man?" She was egging him on, biting her lips until his hand shot forward to grab the first glass.

He muttered, "Bull*dog*, Willa."

Reaching out, she pulled the first shot glass to her mouth, again running her tongue around the rim before dipping it into the liquid. As she deliberately drained the glass over her lips, savoring the taste, she heard a harsh intake of breath and slid her gaze over to see Bear had stilled, his hushed attention riveted on her mouth. With a small smile, she picked up the second glass, drinking it down more quickly, watching Bulldog in her peripheral vision, and saw him hesitate over that second shot, his hand hovering in the space above.

"Fuck it," he hissed out, pulling his hand back. "I'm done. Dammit to fucking hell. What the fuck do I gotta buy you, girl?" he yielded, and she

did a little shimmy in her seat to celebrate her win. She'd opened her mouth to explain what she wanted, when Brent was suddenly in her face again, shoving himself into the narrow space between her and Bulldog.

"Dance with me. I played this song for you. Dance with me." He circled her wrist with one hand, his grip crushing as he held on tightly, trying to drag her from the stool. She shoved at his chest, and it only took a second to detach him, pushing away while twisting and pulling her arm roughly out of his grasp.

Gritting her teeth, she channeled Shooter's cold, harsh voice in her head to say, "No. Not just no, but *hell no*, Brent. Fuck no. No drinks, no rides, no dances. Now *get the fuck away from me*." Her voice went quiet and icy. "You got me?"

She heard the scrape of barstool legs from the other side of Brent, but before either of the men could react, the man had already shouldered back in, turning his back on Bulldog as he pushed his face closer to hers, glancing over at Willa before hissing, "What's the matter, girl? Do you just not like dick?"

She looked around at the faces turned towards them, and still using her best impersonation of Shooter's emotionless voice, laughed and said, "Oh, Brent, sorry, man. I do like dick. In fact, I like dick *a lot*. I just don't like *your* dick."

Scattered laughter came from around the bar as her words were repeated, causing a wave of humor to sweep across the room. The man's face reddened in embarrassment, and it only worsened when Bulldog yelled at the bartender, "Hey, Dixie, lemme buy Dick here a beer."

And that was all it took. Bulldog's statement was the genesis of a dozen jokes and remarks in the next five minutes, all calling the man Dick, effectively renaming him and running him from the bar, at least for the night. Eddie cringed a little, and then thought to herself that he'd brought it on himself. He could have walked away at any time, but chose not to. *Dick*. She snorted a little and laughed, picking up the remaining shots from the bar and pouring them over the ice remaining in her original drink glass.

She looked over at Bear, seeing him gesture to his friends down on the main floor as he rose from the seat. "Well, that was entertaining. See ya around, Bulldog," he said, tapping the bar with both hands before pushing back from it decisively. "Willa," he said as he angled his head politely, and turned to Eddie, saying, "Good to meet you—" He paused, leaving her an opening to respond.

"Good to meet you too, Bear," she said quietly. Looking into his face, she traced across her bottom lip with one fingertip. He swallowed and walked away without another word. She watched as he climbed stiffly onto the stool next to his club members.

"I'll bring it in tomorrow, Eddie," Bulldog said petulantly, holding the napkin on which they'd written their desired winnings. "I can't believe a little girl like you beat me. What the hell?" he grumbled, standing and walking away.

Willa laughed softly, leaning over to speak into her ear. "When will he realize it was his six-pack of beer that bested him, and not you?"

Eddie hugged her. "Hopefully never," she laughed, turning back to the bar and beating out a steady rhythm with her thumbs. "Bear is nice, yeah? He's cute." Willa made a so-so motion with her hand, and both women grinned.

"Better than Dick, that's for sure," Dixie said from across the bar, and the three women laughed loudly.

***

"Lover, don't tease me." A voice filled with the heady rasp of desire came from behind her on the bed, heat from a man's body radiating against her back as his strong fingers dug into her hips, pulling her backward as he shifted forward.

"I'm not," she said, gasping. She was resting her forehead against her crossed wrists, ass in the air, her body moving and shifting as he thrust into her. She felt the slip and slide of their skin together as he ground into her, and he smoothed one hand up her back, burying his fingers in her hair and using his grip to arch her neck backward, the pleasant pain making her sigh.

"Baby, you let him touch you." Beside her ear, the voice spoke, dark stubble grazing the side of her face with a delightful scrape. "Here," she felt fingertips tracing her neck. "And here," strong, callused fingers tenderly wrapped themselves around her bruised wrist. "He touched you." His stomach was pressed tightly against her back, his weight crowding her flat onto the mattress, even while he continued to push his cock deep inside her.

"You're mine. Don't ever forget that. You're mine. Only mine." He thrust into her again, burying himself deep and holding there, pressing her into the soft, giving surface of the bed. "Mine," he repeated, pulling back and plunging forward again. "They don't get to touch what's mine."

"I'm not," she repeated her words nonsensically, tugging her head against his hold in her hair, trying to look behind her. She wanted to see his face, wanted to see him. She heard music coming from somewhere nearby.

"Yes, you are, baby. Eddie, you're mine. You've always been mine." His voice caressed her as his fingers loosened their hold on her hip, stroking gently down and under her belly to tease the bundle of nerves between her legs.

"I'm not," she said again, and then gasped as he slammed into her, deep and hard. "I am," she said as the dream dissolved around her, leaving her clenching her thighs together and breathing harshly. She rolled over and reached out a hand to silence her alarm, Gretchen Wilson singing loudly about being a *Redneck Woman*.

25 - Rafe

It had been a couple of weeks since he'd rolled into town, and Bear was sitting across the desk from Bingo in the clubhouse office, staring at a printout of an email. "There ain't nobody else, Bear," Bingo said, palms flat on the desktop. "Rabid's gone to Chicago. Mason wanted to see him, and I got no idea when he'll be coming back. This teacher won't let shit go until he gets to talk to someone responsible for the kid." The email was from the school Rabid's oldest son attended, and it emphasized the need for a parent or guardian to be present at a meeting the next day.

Bear ran the tip of his tongue along the edge of his teeth, shaking his head. He tossed the paper back onto the desk. "I'm not responsible for the kid, not legally. The teacher won't be able to talk to me. There're all kinds of privacy laws and shit. Dammit. You're raising a passel of kids. Why don't you go?"

"Tyler, my nephew, has football practice. I gotta be there for that." Bingo rubbed his forehead with his palms, saying, "Kids are a fucking handful. I don't know how my sister did it by herself for so long." He sighed. "I need an old lady. I also need you to do this; there isn't anyone else remotely qualified. Look at all the hard shit you've handled for the club through the years. One little piss-ant of a teacher shouldn't even make you break a sweat."

"Tell you what, I'm gonna think about it, but first I want to talk to the boy. It's been a couple of years since he's seen me. I'll let him get a feel for what's going down. Then, if it's okay with Rafe, you'll have to get Rabid to write a letter, or better, why don't you get Myron to draft a power of attorney that we can sign. That keeps us on the right side of the line. No reason to draw attention on small shit like this, right?" He couldn't believe he was going to agree to do this.

Ten o'clock the next morning, Bear was sitting in a local Greek restaurant with a cup of coffee, waiting on the teacher to show. With the morning rush over and the lunch crowd a couple hours away, he was the only customer, and there was nothing to distract him from his thoughts. The teacher's name was listed as E. Morgan in the email, but the guy had signed the email informally as Eddie, so hopefully he wouldn't have a stick too far up his ass and this wouldn't be excessively painful for a Monday.

He'd talked to Rafe for a long time last night, and was impressed by him. To look at him, you'd never know he struggled with anything, but Bear had learned the boy had a crippling insecurity stemming from the knowledge he was different from other teenagers his age, the ones the grandmother called neuro-typical. Autism was a subtle bitch when she wanted to be.

The boy had asked no fewer than a dozen inappropriate questions about sex and fucking, making it clear that the neighborhood they lived in was giving him as much of an education as the school programs. Bear felt they couldn't move that family out of there soon enough, and he was glad Myron had mentioned an open apartment in one of the club-owned complexes. Some of their brothers and old ladies were over there right now, boxing shit up and moving it. By nighttime, Rafe would be sleeping in his bed in a new place, one that was a fuckton safer.

He'd given Rafe's grandmother money for his medicine, and she was supposed to be picking it up on her way to the new apartment. Rabid hadn't been doing right by his family, but the club would take care of things and make sure everything turned the corner towards okay. That kid—all those kids—needed any help they could get, which was why Bear had agreed to meet with the teacher and smooth things over at school.

He saw a bright yellow car pull into the lot and watched idly as it pulled around to park in the front, out of view from his table. He was eyeing the door as it opened, and winced from the flash of sunlight that blasted in, drawing a halo around the figure walking inside. He blinked a couple times as the door closed, and as he focused on the face that was glancing around the restaurant, he thought, *No fucking way.*

The beautiful, dark-haired woman who had been haunting his dreams for so long stood shaking out her hair and settled her gaze on him, subtly shaking her head back and forth in disbelief.

He caught his breath, watching her, slowly rising to his feet. She'd grown from the pretty girl he'd seen outside the clubhouse into the teasing and poised woman he'd seen in the bar. Now, seeing her up close, he could appreciate the elegance and beauty of the woman standing confidently before him.

His not-Willa turned, looking all around the room, even going so far as to step behind the hostess station and ask the gal a question before gazing back at him, shaking her head again. *Well, that's kinda insulting,* he thought with a frown.

Visibly straightening her shoulders, she composed herself and strode across to where he was waiting to meet her, reaching out to grab his offered hand. When their palms made contact, a shocking jolt ran up his arm, making him catch his breath as he felt her fingers curling around his hand. He slipped his other hand around hers, cradling her small hand between his two large ones, his thumb stroking across the back of hers. *God*, he wished he'd touched her the first time he'd seen her. He'd been missing this all along. *Her.* Seeing her lips part as she took in a quick inrush of breath, he knew she felt it too.

With a crooked smile, he said, "I'm Rob Crew. Good to finally meet you, Eddie."

She was even prettier than he remembered, her grey eyes sparkling with intelligence and what looked like anger. Her lips were pressed together tightly, but he could tell they were full and lush, complimenting her delicate features, which had only the barest hint of makeup to accent her beauty. Her tongue slipped out, trailing along her bottom lip and wetting it nervously, his gaze locked onto that small movement. It reminded him of watching her drink tequila, when his cock had gotten stiff from seeing her mouth on the shot glass.

He felt her grip loosen, and he swallowed hard because he didn't want to let go; he wanted to continue touching her, holding her hand. Instead, he allowed her to pull away, ending the handshake and making him immediately miss the touch of her skin on his.

"Eddie Morgan, nice to formally meet you, too, Rob," she introduced herself, and the corners of her mouth twisted down as she pulled a folder from her bag. "So, you are Rafe's dad." Her voice tight, she made it more of a statement than a question, and she was watching him closely, a little frown creasing her forehead.

"No, I'm a family friend," he responded. She took a step backward, frustration clear in her face. Her mouth opened and he interrupted her before she could dismiss him. "Not quite a guardian, but I have power of attorney. You can talk to me about Rafe. I'm here to help. He needs someone in his corner, so let me be that person. Please, let's sit down and look things over." He gestured towards the table and she nodded, gaze locked on his face for a moment, her expression unreadable.

Sliding into the chair across from her, he opened the conversation with, "You teach Rafe? He's a good kid. How's he doing in his classes?"

She tipped her head to one side as he spoke, her gaze flitting from his mouth to his eyes, and then back. She bit the inside of her bottom lip for a moment before responding. "Honestly? He's not doing great. Things are better than a couple months ago, but not great. I'm frustrated for him, because so much of what influences his behavior is out of his control. How much do you know about him and what's going on?"

Watching her, he said, "I've known his dad for years, and like I said, Rafe's a good kid. I understand he has problems at school, but I don't know who wouldn't, given the situation. Rafe is frustrated with unsettled issues at home, and I think he'll benefit by living with his grandmother full-time, which is happening."

Rob tapped a fingertip against his top lip contemplatively as he paused. "She said there are meds he's supposed to be on, but they haven't been filled in a while. I expect that doesn't help. That's being fixed. I can promise you his home life has begun to improve as of yesterday, when I became aware of the problems he was running into."

Silently chewing the inside of her lip again, she listened to him and seemed to come to a conclusion, nodding absently to herself before responding, "I'm not a teacher, per se, but a special needs advocate. My title is Autism Itinerant. I negotiate on the students' behalf, both with the school administration and my boss, the director of special services, to ensure they can access the programs and services needed for their individual situations."

She took a breath and continued, "In this case, that student is Rafe, and the services include counseling, speech therapy, the right to use the resource room, and extra help in the classrooms among other things. I know quite a bit about him, because I've been working with him and his teachers for several years, since he was in middle school. You are absolutely right that how things are at home serve to severely compound the problems he experiences during school hours."

She tilted her head down, and her voice softened. "He's a good kid; you're right. He tries hard and is willing to work with us to craft a successful strategy. Things are just going against him right now. Rafe's afraid of the bangers in his neighborhood, and not having the meds made it so he was swinging from emotional highs to lows, cycling frequently during the day.

"All of that means he's not as successful as we need him to be at school in order to remain qualified for the special services. He has to show progress." She gestured with her hand. "As our kids age into the grades, the expectations increase with each year. Most high-functioning kids gain in emotional maturity, not at a rate consistent with their physical age, but with at least an appreciable increase year over year. Rafe plateaued a couple of years ago and hasn't been able to keep up with the standards applied to his age group.

"As a sophomore, he needs to stay in class long enough to receive direct instruction before leaving for the resource room, but he's so stressed out he can't sit still or focus for any time at all. He's holding it together, but that is one fragile thread from complete breakage. He's one of my kids, and I really want to see him succeed, so please tell me—what do you mean his home life is going to improve?"

She glanced up as the waitress stopped at the end of the table, and she ordered hot tea, tucking her hair behind her ears. Rob held up his nearly empty coffee cup, asking silently for a refill and the waitress nodded.

Still not smiling, she looked at him again, prompting, "How are things going to improve?"

He sighed, not sure what she'd understand about club life, even though he'd seen her associating with members of the Riders club. "His dad is a close friend of mine. Me and some other friends didn't realize how bad things had gotten around where they lived. We're moving them somewhere safer right now, so Rafe doesn't have to worry about or deal with the bad stuff in that neighborhood," he finished, thinking the explanation was about as generic sounding as he could make it.

With a smirk, she let him know just how much she knew about how things worked in his world when she said, "So the club is taking care of business. Are the brothers moving them to the clubhouse, or another property? How can you ensure the same issues won't arise where you're moving them? Because if it is into the clubhouse, then catching glimpse of one party could be far worse than what he'd see on any street in his old neighborhood."

The hair on the back of his neck rose in a wave and he narrowed his eyes, looking at her. He remembered her confidence in the bar and that she was on the Riders' radar, and he was now considering it might be as a claimed partner. "I find myself wondering exactly how you know about clubhouses and clubs, and the parties that happen there, Eddie. You've managed to surprise me."

He paused for a second, then said, "I have a friend who owns some rental properties here in town. Those apartments are where they're going. We're also moving Rafe's grandmother in with them, so even when his dad's out of town, like right now, Rafe can stay in his own bed at night. It's a protected area, and we won't let shit touch him. I can promise you that. Kids are a priceless gift, and they need to be taken care of. I know that well."

As he spoke, he watched as a smile finally began to curve up the corners of her mouth. She ducked her head, and he thought she was trying to hide her amusement. When she looked up again, she had been unsuccessful, and he saw her face held a broad smile that reached her eyes, crinkling the corners and lighting them up, making them sparkle. She was *gorgeous*...his not-Willa, this dark-haired beauty. *His Eddie*. He imagined those eyes barely awakened, sleepy and loving, hooded with desire, fluttering closed, dark lashes brushing her cheeks, sated.

Shaking the images from his head, he focused on her mouth as she nodded approvingly and said, "Sounds like you're taking care of family."

With those few words, pain and panic knifed through him. *Family*. He didn't deserve her approval. He hadn't taken care of his own family; what made him think he could take care of somebody else's kid? *God. Andrea—how did I forget? How did I lose sight of Ashley? My angels.* He had to get out of there.

Reeling abruptly to his feet, he threw money on the table and said grimly, forcing the words past the choking lump in his throat, "We're done here. You know things will be taken care of, so you should have all you need." Her tea hadn't even been served yet, but he couldn't stay. He couldn't breathe. *My angels*. She scooted her chair back, preparing to rise to her feet in reaction to his hasty exit, but he curtly motioned her to remain sitting. *I can't wonder about her. I shouldn't want her*. He had to move; this was one of his worst fears, a waking nightmare.

Her brow furrowed, she raised a worried gaze to meet his, and opened her mouth, her lips moving. He knew she had to be speaking, but he couldn't hear anything but the roaring silence in his own ears. He walked away, leaving the restaurant without looking back.

***

"Rob, wait," she called. "I want to ask—" Seeing her request would go unanswered, Eddie's words trailed off as she stood still for a moment, watching him walk away, every line of his body taut with pain. She ran their brief conversation back through her head, analyzing it, but couldn't identify anything that would justify his sudden departure.

Biting her lip, she slid back into her chair while she thought back to the shock that filled her when she realized who was waiting for her. To say she'd been startled to find him here would be an understatement, and if she was honest with herself, while she'd been surprised, the encounter had wound up being a pleasant one.

He was gorgeous, with his short, dark hair and striking green eyes, jaw covered with a delectable scruff, broad shoulders and strong arms, and when they had finally, *finally* touched for the first time, shaking hands, there'd been an immediate and strong connection. Which she'd hated.

She'd been furious and embarrassed, and had tried to hide both emotions. Furious, because if he was here for Rafe today, it meant he must be the parent absent from all those meetings. Embarrassed, because it meant she'd been attracted to someone who acted that callously to a child. Then she'd found out he wasn't even a relative, but a man who cared enough to try and make a difference—and that cemented her feeling that he...that *Rob* was special.

His eyes were full of sorrow, she thought. She'd never met anyone who wore grief so plainly and agonizingly on his face. She wondered what the story was behind him walking out like that. There'd been a constant, powerful attraction between them every time they'd encountered one another through the years, and the draw had seemed so much stronger today. She sighed. *I thought the interest was mutual, but given the way he just walked out on me, clearly I'm the queen of miscues.*

She looked down, and as her gaze traveled across the table, she realized he'd forgotten the folder he'd brought to the meeting, leaving it behind in his haste to flee. Reaching out, she dragged it across the table with one fingertip, automatically making room for the teapot when the waitress appeared with her order.

Without looking, she held up the money he'd left to the waitress, distractedly asking her to go ahead and cash out the bill. She wouldn't be eating tonight, at least not here, not with her mind racing and rushing a dozen distinct directions with every thought.

There'd been a definite connection, she *knew* it, and her palms grew sweaty just thinking about him. *God,* she had not had this kind of reaction to a man in a long time—maybe ever, and it had to be a biker? Scoffing, she laughed at herself, because if she acted on it, she'd be breaking one of her own rules against getting involved with someone in the life.

Looking down at the folder lying on the table in front of her, she thought, *I shouldn't open this. Whatever is in it will likely be private*. But, what if it could help Rafe? It might be what was needed to bolster her efforts in ensuring he received the assistance needed to be successful.

Snorting with light laughter, she realized she was using advocate-speak to talk herself into doing something she knew she shouldn't.

Tapping one fingernail against the file, she yielded to her internal negotiations and flipped the top of the manila folder open, seeing a letter granting power of attorney on top of the stack. It listed Robert Crew as durable POA for one Emanuel Foscan, Rafe's father. That meant he had the capability to make decisions for Emanuel and his dependents until the POA was revoked.

Rob's phone number was listed, and she punched it into her phone, creating a new contact. It wasn't an Indiana area code, but since her own number was California still, she didn't think it was odd. She lifted the sheet of paper and peered at the one below.

That one was a rental agreement for an apartment on the north side of Fort Wayne, within the school district where Rafe currently attended. She smiled, thrilled; this meant he'd be able to ride the school bus and wouldn't have to take public transit anymore. The residents were listed, and it looked as if there was an older sister, as well as two younger brothers. No female adult other than the grandmother was shown on the paper, so Rafe's mom must not be going to live with them. She wondered what the story was there. The owner of the building was listed as Mason Enterprises out of Chicago, and she made a note of that so she could look it up later.

Flipping back to the POA, she paused for a moment, studying the document. Rob's address wasn't shown as Fort Wayne, but Chicago. She remembered him introducing himself to Bulldog at the bar a couple of weeks ago. He'd said he was in town for a short time, so he must be helping out with something to do with the club.

He won't be in town much longer, she thought with alarm, and stroked her fingertips across her lips for a moment, it had gotten hard to breathe and her stomach nearly rebelled. *I hope I'm not getting sick,* she thought as she stared at the door, idly rubbing her tight and aching throat with one hand.

Finishing her tea, she stood and walked out to her car, shoving both folders into her bag. She sat for a moment in the car, resting her head against the seatback and thinking. Rob—Bear—was in the life. He was a member of a club, a big one. One with more reach and influence than even her dad's.

She had long ago promised herself she wouldn't turn into her mother, wouldn't allow herself to get caught up with the wrong guy by following her emotions. She sternly reminded herself that physical attraction wasn't everything. Stability, as a relationship requirement, was far more important. *Sure, I'd like to have the whole package, and Bear seems to be just that.*

Her thoughts trailed off for a moment. She shook her head, breaking the reverie. She was certain she could find it in someone outside of a club almost as easily. Something about him drew her though, and she sighed. Since their first encounter years ago, their gazes meeting on the street, she'd found herself thinking about him, drawn to him. She remembered his quiet confidence as a stranger in the bar when he approached Bulldog, his relaxed manner with members of his own club. And he *was* good looking. She was definitely attracted to him. In fact, he'd shown up in a few fantasies, and lately, his face with that oh-so-sexy scruff was the one she was most likely to imagine between her thighs when her fingers brought her to a solo climax.

Scrubbing at her face with both palms, she shoved those thoughts aside and reached to turn the key just as a fist pounded hard on the passenger window, startling a yelp and flinch out of her. Whipping her head to the right, she saw her brother grinning in at her, leaning against the side of the car with one hand on her mirror. Rolling down the window, she scolded him, "*Jesus*, Judge, you scared the shit outta me. You can't just knock like normal people?"

He reached in across the width of the car and tapped her cheek with his fingertips, taunting her, "Red, red, red...lookit your cheeks. What in the world have you been thinking, big sister?" He barked a humorless laugh, then ordered, "Unlock, lemme sit a minute with you." She flipped the locks and he opened the door, climbing inside as Mel McDaniel's *Louisiana Saturday Night* came over the speakers.

Without looking at her, he reached over and turned the sound down, and then grabbed her bag, delving into it and drawing out the two folders of information on Rafe. With a frown, she reached to pull them from his hands, saying, "Give those back. You can't look at them, dammit. They have private information on a student. What the hell, Judge? What do you need?"

With bitter emphasis, he said, "What. The *fuck*. Are you doing meeting with a Rebel without telling me first? You didn't think this was something I'd want to know? Need to know?" He turned his head, locking her down with a stare. He was glaring at her, and she saw from the steel in his eyes that *this* was the real reason he was there. "Do you know how it looks for my sister to have a meeting with a Rebel? Bulldog called me twenty minutes ago when he saw you rest your ass across a table from the Chicago guy. If he hadn't recognized the dude from the bar, would you have even told me?"

"Probably not," she said honestly. "This has nothing to do with club business, *Luke*," she stressed his given name. "I have a student who's struggling, and I was meeting with his guardian in a public place for coffee and a discussion. If it were anything to do with the club, I might have told you, but because it's work, I would not have thought it worth a mention. It's no big deal. It's just work—my work, part of my job."

"Eddie, Eddie, Eddie," he said, scorn heavy in his voice, making tutting noises with his tongue. His hands clenched into tight fists, pressed into the tops of his thighs. "You fucking know better. A patched member is *always* club, regardless of where they are or if they're wearing their colors. Same thing with you, dammit. *Everything you do* is

Outrider business. It wouldn't matter if you went grocery shopping with him; it would be club business, because of *who you are*."

"He doesn't *know* who I am, Luke...Judge," she corrected herself when he frowned and shook his head at her avoidance of his road name. "He knows me as Eddie, the advocate assigned to a boy for whom he has responsibility. He also knows me as Willa's friend from the bar. But, that's it. Those two things...nothing more, nothing less."

She didn't want to mention their glancing meetings over the years, the way they seemed drawn to each other. She didn't want to share that, not yet, and certainly not when Judge was acting like a jackhole. Noticing the music had changed, she thumbed the volume higher, and Miranda Lambert's *Gunpowder & Lead* flooded the car. She thought this was the perfect woman-power anthem to be playing during this argument.

"And when Shooter gets here tomorrow, what then? Will you sit and have tea and crumpets with a Rebel member again, knowing what Shooter will do if he finds out?" He sneered and shook his head. "Eddie. Come on, you know better. I'm tryin' to help you out here. Rules are rules, and any club that's not support or affiliate is dangerous—off limits. I know the Rebels and Riders have a good relationship, but between Outriders and Rebels? Not so much, except for Tugboat. Relations aren't bad," he shrugged, "but they're not something we've ever worked on. Being not bad, sis...that still puts them off limits."

Her heart fell in her chest and she focused on what he'd said about their dad. "*Fuucck*," she leaned her head back, rolling her eyes and then closing them, "are you kidding me? He's here tomorrow? Please tell me he's staying at the clubhouse with you." Twisting her head, she opened her eyes and looked at him. "*Dammit*. When were you going to warn me? After he was already in town?"

Sarcastically, he said, "Oh, hey, Eddie, it nearly slipped my mind. Daddy's coming to visit, but since you didn't tell me about meeting with a Rebel, I couldn't be bothered to give you more notice, so here's your twenty-four hour warning that our father will be in town soon for a visit. And, sweet sister, he's staying at your apartment, not the Riders' clubhouse. Don't wanna give people the wrong idea. He ain't takin' over; he's only here to see you." The corners of Judge's eyes creased as he grinned coldly. "There you go. You've been informed."

Without warning, his head rocked backward and he groaned, "What the *fuck* you are listening to? Jesus Christ. Your list is like country, country—opera? What the fuck, Eddie?"

She brushed her fingertips across her eyelids, careful of displacing her contacts and ignoring his segue. "My apartment? *Fuucck*." She ran her tongue along the edge of her top teeth, biting down on it for a second to clear her mind. "I hate you." She blew out a hard breath. "Have you spoken to Tug? You said he's Rebel now, so is he based here in the Fort, or in Chicago? I'd like to see him too. It's been a...a long time." She listened to the music for a second and then laughed. "It's from *Buffy*."

"What?" he barked, holding his palms up and looking confused.

"The song, it's from *Buffy the Vampire Slayer*. You know, the TV show? There was one episode that was a musical. This song is from that show, *Walk Through The Fire*." She smiled, deliberately trying to lose the edge of her anger, purposely softening her frown into a neutral expression.

Judge looked attentively at her, considering the emotions he saw on her face. She knew she'd been able to force casual well enough when he leaned his head back, saying, "Huh. Loved that show. Naw, haven't talked to Tugboat for a couple of weeks. He's out of Chicago, so he's only here once in a while. I have to go through channels and shit. I'll go ahead and call Bingo tonight, get him to pass an invite to Mason and Tug for Friday night."

"What's happening Friday night?" she asked, and then rolled her eyes at the mocking smile that crossed his lips. "Never mind, it's a clubhouse party I'm sure. I won't be present, in that case. You can just tell Tug I said hello."

"Aww, Eddie. You know Shooter will be pissed if you don't show. You can leave before it gets crazy. Bring Willa; she can finally meet more of the brothers." He grinned at her. "She'll have a good time, and you'll stay busy keeping her out of trouble."

He started to get out of the car and paused, standing with his back to her. "Stay away from Bear, Eddie. I ain't fucking around and I don't want to have to tell you again. And Eddie, that hate goes both ways, sweet sister." He slammed the door closed and stalked away, straddling his bike and waiting pointedly for her to pull out of the lot so he could follow her.

She sighed in exasperation, thoughts of Bear pushed from her head as she considered Shooter's imminent arrival, making mental errands and grocery lists. "Fuucck," she repeated as she entered traffic, seeing first Judge pull out behind her, and then a second bike further back. Turning away from her rearview mirror, she concentrated on the cars in front of her on the way home.

26 - Mica

Mason sat on the back of a barstool, his feet on the seat, leaning his shoulders against the wall behind the bar. He often sat like this, because it gave him greater height and he could better see over the crowd. Tug sat on a stool at the bar in front of him, nursing a beer. He'd been back in town for a couple of weeks now, but it was nearly time to head back to Fort Wayne. In the past few years, Tug had spent as much time there as here, trying to keep everything on an even keel. Bingo made it hard. He'd been a good chapter president at first, but it was wearing on him, and they'd heard from more than one club over the years that he was making life difficult for everyone in the Fort.

They'd been moving Slate, Bear, and Tequila back and forth from city to city almost as much as Tug had been gone, trying to maintain a unified club. Everything was fucking hard now. Fucking work, and he was tired of almost everything in his life. He laughed at himself, thinking, *Goddamn, can't I get easy for once? Just once, I'd like sweet and easy.*

"What's going on with Mica?" Tug asked quietly. "Any idea why she dropped the hockey player like she did?" Mica Scott was Mason's neighbor, but had been known to the club long before she moved in next to him.

While still a teen, she'd been savaged by a boyfriend, and escaped him by banishing herself to Chicago, exiled far from friends and family in Texas. She'd lived there since, going to school and eventually opening her own business.

When that man's brother found out what had happened, he swore to keep her safe, and then when he joined the Rebels, it extended

Duck's vow to every brother in the club. Now, she was more than a friend to the club; she was their Princess, something to be cherished and protected, and every Rebel knew her name. Since her ex-boyfriend had recently become an active threat again, stalking her, they had organized a security detail for her, keeping her as safe as they could.

Her friend and employee Jessica Nalan was fostered in by default, and could be found at Jackson's most nights with her live-in girlfriend, innocently annoying the members, but always protective of Mica.

Adding to all of that was Mason's deep affection for the woman. It was clear to everyone that he loved her fiercely, but he'd long ago shifted himself to the side in an attempt to let her have a life that wasn't filled with the violence and turmoil that came with being in a club.

"She's trying real hard to not talk to me, but that shit ain't gonna fly. I know she loves Daniel, so there has to be a deeper reason behind her vacating on him like that. Not that I'm feelin' any sympathy for the asshole, since he stood back and let her walk away, but now she's fucking unhappy again, and *that* shit ain't gonna fly either," Mason growled, bending over and slapping his glass onto the bar top. His fist thumped his chest, and he heard Tug echo him as he said, "She's a fucking treasure."

Shaking his head, he told Tug, "She and Jess are thick as thieves, and you know when those two get together things are bound to go sideways. Why don't you head over to the office this afternoon and see if you can coax some info out of either of them?"

"Sure, Prez, will do. I'll wheedle." Tug nodded, picking up his mug and taking another slow drink.

***

"What the hell, Bear? I don't need this shit. What I need is for you to get your ass to Little Rock. I don't need you fucking arguing with me.

Seems to me like every time I ask you for something, you gotta fucking argue. I'm telling you this shit is gettin' old, man. Old and tired, so you need to goddamn well drop it. Take a brother with you if you want; fuck, take two if you need—but Slate's depending on us being present, ready, and having his back when he rolls into Texarkana. I wouldn't give a shit if you were laid up in a fucking body cast; this is non-negotiable." Mason was beyond annoyed, and his irritation came across the phone loud and clear.

Bear sighed in frustration. He was willing to go. It wasn't that. He just needed to finish working on the most recent round of bike orders. He opened his mouth to try to explain when Mason said the one thing guaranteed to kick any Rebel's ass into high gear: "Mica's cousin is with Slate. She's family, brother, a fucking treasure."

"You got it, Prez," he responded immediately, all thoughts of declining the trip pushed out of his head as he rolled upright, seated on the side of the bed. Mason ended the call and he tossed his phone towards the end of the bed. He reached down to adjust his erect cock, dream details teasing his mind with images of grey eyes looking up at him as her plump lips wrapped around—fuck, now he needed a shower. A cold one.

His apartment was one of four on the renovated upper floors of FWO2, and he heard the familiar sound of an engine revving in the shop below. Closing his eyes, he tilted his head to listen carefully and smiled at the ring of the pipes as the owner or mechanic torqued the throttle.

Dragging his ass through the shower, he dressed, and then packed a small bundle of clothes, rolling a single pair of jeans around a shirt and bandana. Ready to leave, he looked around the space and walked out of the apartment, pulling the door closed behind him.

As he moved down the hallway, he reached for his phone, dialed, and once the call connected, said, "Duck, we're riding. Slate needs us to meet him with a few brothers from our Little Rock chapter. He's down in Texarkana with Mica's cousin." He'd have to talk to him privately about Duck's blood brother's involvement. It wouldn't do for him to be blindsided when they got there, but he needed Duck to come with him. The man was the closest thing they had to an expert on Nelms.

Still on the phone, he clattered down the stairs, sweeping the garage with a searching gaze, and gave the members working on their bikes a sharp chin lift of approval at the tidy state of his domain. He'd been the garage manager for a while now, and they knew he'd hand 'em their asses if they left his shop a mess, something he liked to remind them about whenever he got a chance.

He responded to Duck's easy agreement with brief, terse instructions, "Meet me at Jackson's. Gimme thirty minutes."

He gave his bike a quick road check, placing his clothes in the saddlebags. Swinging a leg over the seat, he paused for a moment and looked down with a wistful smile. Tracing the faces painted on his tank with one fingertip, he spoke so softly even someone standing close would have been hard-pressed to hear him. "Miss you, angels. I'm takin' a run; you should come with." Patting the tank with the palm of his hand, he flipped the key and started the bike, balancing it between his thighs as he heeled the kickstand up and out of the way.

With a raised hand, he saluted his brothers as he rolled out of the shop and into the street.

A day later, he and Duck rode up to the fairgrounds in Texarkana, along with about thirty members from the Little Rock chapter of Rebels. Greeting Slate with a grin and a forearm grip, he assessed his friend's frame of mind while he asked for an update.

Slate angled a look over at Duck and said quietly, "He ain't gonna like this, brother."

Gauging the need, Bear correctly decided a distraction was in order, and yelled for Duck, "Why don't you find a cage? Go make a quick run and get food for everybody."

Slate nodded his approval, removing some money from his wallet and handing it to Duck. "I've got just me and Mica's cousin here, but it looks like you brought some appetites with you, so get plenty of groceries," he said with a small laugh. "We don't cook shit; we just eat it. Make sure you figure that out."

Off to one side, they waited patiently as the members slowly sorted themselves, finding places to wait comfortably for instructions. Slate and Bear stood in companionable silence for a few minutes, observing the coordinated chaos of the fairgrounds, where rodeo competitors, horses, trucks, and trailers milled across the lots. Eventually, Bear spoke, asking, "How's the trip been with the girl?"

Slate's bitter laughter surprised him, seemingly torn from the man without consent. He spoke in a painfully even tone. "It's been fucking torture, man. She's something else. Pretty, smart, talented, and fucking relentless."

"Huh. You bag that shit?" Bear asked jokingly. He wasn't prepared for the warring looks of anguish and desire that swept over his friend's face, and this time, the laughter was dragged out of *him*, his mouth open wide with amusement. "What the hell, man? You fucked Mica's cousin? Holy shit, Mason's gonna kill you. He's gonna skin you alive."

"I didn't fuck her. Not...I didn't." Slate pushed his hands into the front pockets of his jeans. "I wanted to, but stopped. And Mason already fucking knows and sentenced me to this trip anyway." He cut his gaze over to Bear. "No telling Mica, though. I don't want to give that woman any more reason to hate me. We're finally back on good terms after...after I failed her."

"Fuck, Slate. I heard about what went down, and that shit isn't on you, brother." Bear shook his head. Mica's ex-boyfriend had slipped into her house and beaten her severely months ago. Slate was on what they all called babysitting duty that night, and had stopped the attack. The fact he hadn't prevented it apparently still grieved him, but from what Bear heard, there was no reason for anyone to expect what had happened. It was typical of Slate to take on responsibility that wasn't destined for his shoulders. It was one of the things that made him a good brother and a great officer.

"So, with Nelms—tell me what's going down," Bear said, shifting so his back was against the side of the horse trailer.

Slate nodded and began talking, "His company is contracted to provide livestock for the rodeo, and those trucks should be getting in this afternoon. It's a big payday for him, so he's expected to be here in case anything needs attention. He shows up, he's ours. Brother, when we find him, we finish him." The last part came out flat and cold, and Bear's gaze swung to Slate's face to see an almost feral look, top lip lifted in a snarl.

He drew a pained breath when Slate continued, "Nelms drugged and raped Mica's baby sister nearly two months ago. Every single thing he's done to Mica isn't enough for him. All the scars on her body and her mind aren't enough; he had to figure out the one thing she's been afraid of for more than a decade. That's the main reason she left Texas, you know? She didn't want her shit leaking out onto her family, and look where we are now. After everything that woman's been through, everything she has given up—everything that's been taken from *Mason*—the fucker still makes a play like that."

Slate looked at Bear. "If I find the fucker—*when* I find him—he's going to ground. If you have a problem with that, I need to know now, brother."

"I got no difficulty with that. I got your back, as always, brother. Mica's a fucking treasure." He pounded his fist over his heart. "And she's one of us. She's a fucking Rebel, Slate. Rebel Wayfarers forever," he began the saying, and he and Slate finished it together, "forever Rebels."

But, for all their anxious preparation, Nelms hadn't shown. The stock trucks had rolled onto the fairgrounds without him, and no one, not even his employees, knew where he was. This absence made Bear skittish, because the man had proven relentless in his pursuit of Mica, and this was out of character. After his ruthless attack on her little sister, it seemed like he'd passed up a perfect shot to gain more leverage with a favorite cousin, and that just didn't track.

He and Slate had agreed Duck needed to know what his blood brother had done, but Bear wanted to control the situation and decided not to tell him until back at the chapter clubhouse in Little Rock. Setting off from Texarkana, they rolled onto the compound a couple hours later, and Bear motioned his friend over. "I need to tell you something, Duck. This is rotten shit, and I hate to even speak of it, because I know it's gonna stir shit up, but you gotta know."

He saw his brother flinch as he began with one word: "Nelms." He stopped and shook his head, starting over. "Nelms got to Mica's little sister, Molly. Happened a few weeks ago, Slate and Essa should be on the phone with Mica now, and it'll be the first she's known about it. Duck, there isn't an easy way to say this, man. He drugged and raped her, and left her with a little rider. In a few months, she's gonna have a kid because of him."

Duck recoiled and spun away, leaning over and retching noisily. It looked as if he was gagging on the evil his blood kept spreading. Bear had seen him deliver a retribution beating that broke bones; he'd been standing alongside him when they dealt in a terminal way with the punks that beat up Mica months ago, and Duck had shown little emotion with either. This reaction was bone-deep, because it was a betrayal by blood. This was why Duck had vowed to keep Mica safe, because he felt responsible for what his family had done.

"Get that shit out, brother," he urged him quietly. "We still have work to do here before we can head home. Mason's gonna want a report about the chapter, so we need to make sure we see it all. Good, bad, and indifferent, we gotta check it all. Straight and narrow according to Mason's rules, right?"

Duck unfolded, wiping his mouth with the back of his hand. Slapping his back, Bear offered him a bandana and continued, "So, the quicker we get back, the quicker I can work on the fucking bikes some more. It's the only thing I really want to do, man. Now come on and help me get home."

27 - It's a party

"But what do I wear?" Willa yelled up the apartment hallway from her position in front of her closet. "What do I wear to a biker party? I don't own leather!"

"Just jeans and a t-shirt. No leather, please, God, don't be so weird," Eddie called back to her as she poured them drinks in Willa's kitchen. "Got your Goldschlager, Wills," she called again, tipping her glass of tequila to her mouth and taking a long sip.

They were headed to the Riders' clubhouse in an hour, commanded by her father to appear this time. She'd ducked out on the last party, but Judge had contacted Willa directly this time and knew she didn't have any conflicts. *Damn the woman and that streak of honesty.* He'd also invited Willa, and nothing would do but they go together. She'd worked hard to keep this shit out of Willa's life, and Judge tore that fence down with one call.

Sliding wildly onto the tile flooring in the kitchen in her sock feet, Willa grabbed at the edge of the cabinet to keep her balance and stop the glide. With a wide smile, she picked up the glass of clear liquid on ice and looked into the depths of it, laughing. "Gotta love a liquor that sparkles." She giggled. "It at least pretends to be happy to see you," she said, taking a drink.

Eddie looked at her outfit and shook her head, groaning, "Uhhh huh. Wills, pretty sure I said *jeans*."

"And I heard *dress*." Willa gave her a small, sideways grin. "It lets me wear my kicky boots." She held out one foot and looked down at the sock covering it. "But I forgot to put them on. Be right back." She turned, fake skating away in her socks.

Tipping her glass up again, Eddie took another sip while she waited on Willa. It had been another exhausting week with Shooter staying at her apartment, his second visit in two months. He was there right now with Judge and a couple of club members, which was why she'd decided to come over here to get ready for the party. It was good to see her dad and catch up, but she was completely ready to get back to her routine and life.

After the meeting with Rob Crew, she'd been able to reassure her boss and keep everything in place for Rafe, continuing services as-is until his home life settled down. Visiting the new apartment and meeting his grandmother made her feel a lot more comfortable about her recommendations, and within days, his teachers had reported a positive difference in behaviors.

She and Shooter had been to Checkerz twice this visit, but hadn't encountered Rob, and she wondered if he'd been recalled to Chicago. From what she'd overheard during a conversation between Judge and their dad, it sounded as if he were a troubleshooter for the Rebels.

With or without Bear, Judge assured her Tug would be at the party tonight. He'd been a big part of her life growing up, had filled in for her family on more than one occasion, and she was excited to see him again. It had been too long since they had a chance to catch up, and she was looking forward to having a chat.

"How's this?" Willa asked, her short heels clipping briskly as she moved from the carpeted hallway to the tile kitchen floor.

"Looks great, Wills," Eddie told her with a smile; the woman really did look hot. The smile dropped from her face as she continued, "I'd be happier if you were in jeans, but it's your funeral. A gorgeous funeral, but still a funeral."

While Eddie had dressed for comfort in jeans and a short-sleeved t-shirt over a long-sleeved thermal, Willa had gone for casual dressy and had on a maxi jersey dress with three-quarter length sleeves. The dress left most of her shoulders bare, her hair swept up into a messy twist, held onto the back of her head with a clip. Eddie's own hair was plaited into two braids, and she'd put her glasses on tonight. There was dressing up, and then there was mousing down, and Eddie knew where she wanted to be right now.

"Let's get rolling," she said, pushing Willa's drink across the breakfast bar towards her and finishing off her tequila. Dragging her keys from the front pocket of her jeans, she twirled them noisily until Willa slammed her empty glass down, and then walked over and opened the door, headed out to her car.

At the clubhouse's main entrance, she was waved off, and a prospect told her that non-member cars had to be parked on the street. Making a face, she went up a few blocks and turned around, finally locating a space at the curb a couple blocks down. They gathered their things, preparing to go inside.

Turning in the seat to face her friend, she smoothed her features into a serious expression and said, "Okay. Two rules, Willa. One, you stay with me. We buddy up all the time, even to the bathrooms. No exceptions, no deviations. Two, you only take a drink from me or Judge. If you set your drink down and lose sight of it, you dump it. If you think anything is off with it, you dump it. If someone hands you something and that someone isn't me or Judge, you dump it. Got it?" She didn't want to frighten Willa, but she also didn't want anything to happen to her.

"You really think that's necessary, Pookie? Your dad and brother are here, and I've met a bunch of these guys. You think someone would spike my drink?" Willa scoffed, and Eddie reached across and grabbed her hand tightly.

"Yes, I think someone would spike your drink. Neither of us has property patches, and in some clubs when you're at a party, that means anything goes. I don't know about the Riders. I plan on being out of here before things get to the crazy stage, but I know from talking to Judge there are a lot of out-of-town guys here tonight. It's my experience that things can go from okie-dokie, straight off to LaLa land pretty fast at these parties, so we're both going to play it smart." Taking in a deep breath, she blew it out and looked over at Willa. "Are you ready, my favorite foolish woman?"

"As I'll ever be," Willa sang, opening the door on her side and climbing out. Eddie watched as the prospect got a glimpse of Willa, seeing his prominent Adam's apple bob in his throat when he swallowed, reaching to swing the gate open. Seeing his reaction underscored her feeling of unease, and she thought this would either be an interesting night, or go very, very wrong.

"I'm Eddie," she introduced herself to the prospect. "Shooter's daughter," she added when he didn't shift his gaze from Willa's breasts. That still didn't lift his eyes, so she continued flatly, "Judge's sister," feeling vindicated when he finally jerked his eyes to hers and she saw that Adam's apple bobbing in his throat again.

"I'm with her," Willa said with a laugh, sashaying past him and following Eddie towards the clubhouse door. "You made that poor boy sweat, Eddie." She laughed again as she caught up to Eddie just as the door swung open from the inside.

Eddie stopped in her tracks, her arm flying out to push Willa back in an effort to avoid colliding with the men flooding out through the doorway. A sea of curious faces were now focused on them, and she adjusted their position so their backs were partly shielded by the wall of the building, drawing frowns from some of the men.

"Is Shooter inside?" she asked calmly. It was always best to establish you were known and expected. One of the men cocked his head to one side and frowned at her. She recognized him from the bar the first night she'd seen Rob. He was the mustached man with longish white hair held back with a bandana. He was also grinning at her.

"Eddie?" he asked, stepping away from the group of men and towards her and Willa.

She nodded warily, keeping the rest of the bikers in sight while she looked at him. His eyes crinkled at the corners, and she caught her breath. "Tugboat?" she squealed loudly and threw herself at him when he gave her a confident chin lift. She slid her arms around him, underneath his leather cut, and nestled her cheek against his chest, drawing in a deep breath infused with the familiar smells of oil, leather, and musk. Feeling his arms settle around her shoulders, she laughed as she heard a loud lip smack on the side of her head.

She leaned back and looked up into the face of a man who at one time had known her better than her own father. When she was little, he'd been her babysitter for more hours than she wanted to admit. He'd cheerfully attended her elementary school dance and music recitals, held her as she cried when her goldfish died, helped with homework, and he and his old lady had taught her how to make chocolate chip cookies. Really good chocolate chip cookies. Stupendous chocolate chip cookies that she still made for her school kids as a treat.

Her smile faded a little as she recalled he was also the man who had stoically withstood her frantic, despairing blows to his defenseless back and body on one of the worst days of her life as she and her mother were retrieved, returned like errant children to the clubhouse in California.

She backed up a step, holding the smile on her face with some effort, remembering against her will how he'd beaten up a boy who had bragged about grabbing her ass on the school bus. The boy had been hospitalized for three days. They had only been fifteen, and the boy hadn't meant any harm by what he'd done. This was the world she'd tried to escape, what she had tried to distance herself from, and here she was, literally back in the embrace of the club.

"Good to see you, Eddie," he said, hands on her shoulders as he looked down at her warmly.

"You too, Tugboat," she responded with an outrush of breath, and then allowed herself to relax, remembering the affection he and Nytro had showered her with, and deciding to only consider good things tonight. "But I think we saw each other a while ago. I just didn't realize it was you!" He looked floored and tilted his head to one side. "God, how did I not recognize you? We were at Checkerz." She gestured behind her. "Willa and I were having a couple of drinks."

He tipped his head back, laughing loud and long. "You fell on your ass, girl. I won a bet on you. Thanks for the beer." There was a scuffling noise behind him and he whipped his head around, addressing the men with a growl. "Go to the bikes. I'll be there in a few." The group who'd been waiting on him faded into the darkness along the edge of the parking lot. Eddie watched them go, seeing their shadowed forms round the corner of the building and disappear.

"I did fall on my ass," she agreed with a wry smile and a laugh. "Hey, Tug, um...Bear was with you then. Is he...is he inside now?" She held her breath, tense and anxiously anticipating his answer. God, she wanted to see Bear again, touch him and see if that connection was still there.

"Naw, he has business to attend." Tug frowned at her, his thumbs rubbing small circles on the curve of her shoulders. She felt the tension leave her muscles in a rush of disappointment at his response. "How do you know Bear?" he asked, entirely too casually. *Something was up there for sure.*

"One of my kids is in the Rebel family—" she began explaining, and then saw the look of shock that crossed his face, his fingers tightening on her arms. "Tug," she laughed, "not *my* kid, but one that I teach. I don't have any kids. So, anyway, one of the kids I teach was having problems, and the dad's out of town, so I met with Bear and he helped make things right for the kid and his family."

"Good God, woman. You had me worried you hadn't told Shooter about something important, like bein' a grandpa." He snorted and shook his head. "I heard Bear was helping with Rabid's kid. It's good you are involved in that. Gives me confidence it'll be done right. Hey, I gotta go, Eddie doll. We're after some supplies and...other things. I'll be back soon though, so I hope to see you later tonight, or tomorrow." He pulled her in for another hug, kissing the side of her head again. "Love you, girl."

"Love you, too, Tugboat," she murmured against his chest.

She and Willa watched him retrace the steps of the group, following them around the corner of the building. Within a few seconds, the roar of bikes filled the air and the women saw a string of lights pulling out of the side lot and onto the street. With an unseen signal, all the bikes dramatically picked up speed and were out of sight within moments.

"So that was Tugboat?" Willa asked, still peering into the darkness along the edge of the building.

With a fond smile, Eddie answered as she pulled the clubhouse door open. "Yeah, that's Tugboat. Come on. Let's go find Shooter or Judge and let them know we're here."

***

Mason swayed back and forth from boot to boot, only just moving as he stretched his legs surreptitiously, hearing Bootleg spout on about the challenges of leading a club in Fort Wayne. It had been a while since he'd had time to travel any distance, and his muscles were complaining a little after the ride down. That was one of the tradeoffs of his position in the club; he didn't get to do as much riding as he'd like. Hell, he didn't get to do as much of *anything* as he'd like anymore.

That was about to change though, because he was flying to Texas tomorrow with the intention of riding back on a bike bought from a member down there. He planned on bringing Mica back too. She needed shaking up to get her out of her rut, hiding out down in the Lone Star state. *Fuck*, he thought to himself, *I'm glad I went ahead and picked up that other bike for her to ride back with me. It's past time for her to learn she's capable of anything. The promise of me teaching her to ride alone should be the incentive she needs to get off her ass.*

Swapping his beer bottle to his other hand, he brought himself back into the present and sidelined his thoughts for now as he reached out to shake hands with yet another River Rider club member introduced by Bootleg.

Some of these guys wanted to believe they were real hard asses, seeming determined to try their hand at intimidating him with a rigid grip or by posturing like a fucking rooster. Fucktards were always in for a surprise, because he didn't back down for anyone, much less a bunch of piss-ant lower-level club members. How the hell did they think he'd managed to hold the position he did in a national club? *Stupid asshats.*

This guy was named Baker and seemed easygoing, but even as he responded to the greeting with something safely noncommittal, Mason's gaze caught on Shooter, where he stood across the room with his son, Judge. Seeing them together made him miss his own boy, Chase. He needed to take a run down to Kentucky soon, see the boy, make sure his ex-wife was doing right by him. One day, he hoped to bring Chase into the club, have him around like Judge was there for Shooter. His ex had almost fucked everything up, keeping Chase's existence secret from him until a couple years ago. He'd have to get that rolling before long; his boy was already fifteen, and you couldn't start too soon.

Because he was already watching Shooter, he saw a change in the man's face and posture before it even registered with him that the door had opened for the first time since Tug left to pick up some supplies for the party tonight. Shooter's features softened almost imperceptibly, and lines formed at the corners of his eyes as his cheeks lifted slightly. Whoever it was, he was pleased to see them.

Mason twisted to look at the door in time to see two dark-haired women come into the room. The first one looked so much like Shooter she couldn't be anyone except his daughter Edith. He'd heard she was called Eddie around the club. She moved into the room guardedly, scanning the faces and clearly mapping the exits along the way. Her posture visibly relaxed when she found both Shooter and Judge already walking towards her.

The woman behind her was different; apparently a citizen, she was put together like this was a fucking dance club, wearing a long, casual dress that clung to her legs as she walked across the room. She was stunning, and given the vibes coming off Eddie, he was surprised she wasn't nervous, but she didn't seem to be at all. Her gaze was skimming across the interior of the room like it was the first time she'd seen it, and her open appraisal of the men scattered around the room amused him for some reason.

Her eyes paused on him, looking leisurely up and down his frame, lingering for a long time on his crotch. He captured and held her gaze, raising his beer bottle towards her in a mocking salute. Eyes widening as she realized she'd been caught, a visible blush worked its way up her neck and across her face as she dropped her chin, breaking eye contact with him.

Taking another drink from his beer, Mason padded across the room to where Shooter and Judge had met the women. It didn't register until he was halfway there that he'd left Bootleg and Baker standing and talking to the air, but that shit didn't matter anyway. Everyone in the room knew who held the power in this club, and he felt like he'd already given Bootleg more than his due.

Stopping next to Shooter, he looked at the woman in the dress, speaking without shifting his eyes. "Eddie, I'm Mason, President of the Rebel Wayfarers."

She looked at him bewildered, and glanced at the other woman, saying with a nervous grin, "I'm not Eddie." She made a hand gesture over to Shooter's daughter.

He nodded, and still looking at her, asked, "Judge, you got any kind of claim?"

Eddie stepped between them, and he glanced down at her face and then back up at the woman, dismissing her interference, even as she said, "She's my friend and guest; she's not on the menu, Mason."

He heard a laugh as Judge told him, "Naw. No claim, Mason. That's Willa. She's a creature of her own control."

"Good enough," he responded, deftly sidestepping Eddie, moving closer to Willa. She looked up into his face with curiosity, the corners of her mouth tipping up, stretching her lips in an indulgent smile that transformed her, bringing a sparkle to her eyes and softening her face. She was more beautiful than he'd realized, and he found himself smiling down at her. He heard Judge bark out another laugh and turned his head to see what was funny, realizing he was also looking at Willa. "Got something to say, Judge?" he asked, quirking one eyebrow up in a question.

"Naw," Judge snorted, "but I've never seen Willa without words. It's kinda refreshing."

Her gaze cut over his shoulder to Judge and she frowned prettily, saying, "Your asshole is showing, Judge. You should get that looked at."

Mason tipped his head back and roared with laughter; she was a little mouthy, and he liked a woman who wasn't afraid to give it back like that. His gaze caressed the lines of her shoulders, which were left nearly bare by the material of her dress that was stretched tightly across her tits. It fit snug down around her body, and from her hips, the fabric hung loose to the floor, draping over the curve of her ass. She was softly rounded and wouldn't break under him. She'd be able to take anything he gave her, and he imagined her hips begging for his hands to pull her back onto his cock. *Fuck*.

Shooter shook his head, one arm reaching out to lay across his daughter's shoulders as he tucked her close into his side, pulling her away from Mason and Willa. "Doll baby, glad you could finally make it." He leaned down and kissed the top of her head, but his eyes never stopped scanning the room, something Mason noted since it proved Shooter wasn't as comfortable in this clubhouse as he'd prefer.

"We'd have been here fifteen minutes ago, but the prospect outside wouldn't let me park in the lot. So I had to go down the street and turn around, and then find parking," she complained, then giggled. "He looked like he was going to have a heart attack when I told him I was Judge's sister."

Mason deliberately tore his gaze from the woman, and felt an unmistakable need to have his eyes on her again that was nearly impossible to ignore. More than that, he wanted to know what it would feel like to hold her next to him, tucked into his side, in his arms...under him. He wanted to strip her naked, play with her tits, suck the tight buds of her nipples into his mouth, go down on her, and eat her pussy until she quivered under his hands and mouth. He wanted to undress her slow then fuck her hard, watch her face as she came with him buried balls-deep inside her...

Holy fuck. He took a step back, shaking his head, glancing up to see a quick look of frustration flash across her face before she locked it down into impassivity. Goddammit, he didn't need this, especially with another citizen; he had all he could handle on that front with Mica right now.

Distracted, he watched as Judge tipped his bottle to his mouth, letting a wash of beer pass over his lips and down his throat as he swallowed. Tossing the now-empty bottle into a nearby trashcan, he turned to Mason and asked, "Heard you had some shit go down in Texas. Anything the Riders need to worry about?"

Mason and Shooter made nearly identical noises of disapproval and disappointment as they both looked at the man. The shit that went down in Texas was an attack on Mica by her ex, and ended with him sending that same ex on a trip with a final destination. He sure as fuck wasn't going to share *that* with Shooter's boy.

Shooter motioned with one hand for Mason to proceed, and smirked a little when Judge realized what he'd done. "Aw fuck, never mind, Mason. Sorry, man. Respect. Wasn't thinkin'," embarrassed, he apologized before shouting across the room at a prospect for another beer.

"Like I'd fucking tell you anything about my club's business, Judge, much less with the present company. What the hell are you up to?" Mason growled at him, and it was interesting to see that the younger man didn't back down. If anything, he settled a little deeper into his relaxed but ready stance as his eyes narrowed on Mason. Shooter's boy was good.

He heard a noise beside him and glanced down, surprised to find Willa's eyes moving between him and Judge. She was pressing her lips into a tight line and seemed to have found a brand of nervous that didn't set well on her. She must have forgotten her hair was up, because she ran her fingers through it, fluffing it, and when she encountered the clip, she absently removed it. This allowed her chestnut hair to flow down and cover her shoulders, and even though her hair was beautiful, Mason straight away missed the sight of her skin and curves.

"Put it back up," he muttered, stepping closer to her, watching as her body jerked in reaction to both his softly-voiced order and the desire rolling off him. He wanted her on display again, wanted his eyes on her, wanted it *right fucking now*.

Gathering the waves of hair in both hands, she quickly bundled it up, and raising her arms, used the clip to pin it to the back of her head again. Her movements set her breasts shifting in the dress, lifting them and arching her back. He watched with attentive focus and could almost imagine what they would feel like in his hands…in his mouth. *Fuck,* now he was hard.

She looked up at him, clearly confused by their interaction, and he gave her a one-sided smile as he tossed his bottle away, folding his arms across his chest. "That's better," he praised her, letting her know he approved. He watched as her mouth opened with a soft gasp while she shivered, goose bumps rising on her arms below the sleeves of her dress, her nipples hardening into peaks underneath the material. *Goddammit. I don't need this. So responsive, and I haven't even touched her yet,* he thought, feeling his cock thicken, pulsing with his arousal, and then—the moment was suspended, interrupted by sounds coming from outside the clubhouse.

All three men turned, instinctively moving to place themselves between the doorway and the women. The coordinated wall of muscle and leather they created stepped towards the door in a concerted movement when it crashed open.

Mason took in the scene in front of him and barked out an order for Judge to get the girls to safety as he dropped to one knee, making himself a smaller target while pulling his handgun from the back waistband of his pants. With competent skill, he aimed it at the two disheveled men entering the room, holding a senseless Riders' prospect in front of them. They looked strung out, their clothes as unkempt as their bodies, waving handguns, yet neither of them appeared overly accomplished with the firearms. Mason knew from experience that you didn't stop respecting a gun simply because it was in amateur hands; often a gun was far more dangerous when held by a novice.

He clocked Judge's movement and heard a scrape of retreating footfalls behind them, confident Judge was handling the women. Glancing over at Shooter, he saw the man had taken a stance behind a pillar and was looking over at Bootleg, shaking his head, waiting impatiently on the club president to call for defense.

The bangers were shouting, and Mason watched with cool amusement as the ungainly weight of the motionless man pulled their arms down, allowing him to slip limply to the floor. With their human shield gone, the men were unprotected, and members of the River Riders closed in, immobilizing and disarming the intruders within moments. Once secured, they dragged the men through a door and down a staircase to the basement level.

The entire conflict had taken less than sixty seconds to play out and there had been no shots fired, thankfully, but *Jesus,* this emphasized the shit security his club had here in Fort Wayne. He could easily imagine this happening to his own clubhouse, and it pissed him right the fuck off.

Climbing to his feet, Mason slipped his handgun back into its holster at the small of his back, flipping the magnetic strap closed with his thumb. He pulled out his phone and tapped a quick message to Tug, letting him know what had gone down and to come back sooner rather than later.

Willa, he thought, wondering if she had been frightened. He looked around and didn't see Judge, but caught sight of Shooter as he jogged up the stairs, taking them two and three at a time, and assumed that was where the women had been taken. His phone rang and he answered when he saw Slate's name on the screen.

"Yeah?" he said curtly, eyes restlessly sweeping the now unthreatened room.

"All okay, Prez?" Slate asked tensely. Seemed news had traveled fast.

"Ah yeah, Riders are taking care of their shit right now," he said, rolling his neck as he heard the first screams from the basement. "I'll be on the road back in a couple hours. This shit's handled. Drives home what you told me about the security for us here in the Fort though, so I think we're gonna want you to deal with that soon."

"Whatever you need, Prez. Glad things sorted okay," Slate said.

Mason sighed, and said, "Brother, I've heard shit-all from Daniel after our talk, so I got with Denzie down in Texas. He's still got that Sportster. Gonna have both bikes delivered to the ranch tomorrow afternoon, couple hours after I'm supposed to get in. You sure you don't want to go down with me? He's still got that Fatboy too. Would be a good bike for Jase. We could bring it back." Jason Spencer was a friend of the club. Not quite a hangaround, he was one of Daniel's hockey players who'd decided a few weeks ago he wanted to buy a bike.

"Naw," Slate drawled, "Jase's gonna buy Road Runner's old bike. Road's ready to get rid of it soon as he picks his new Bobber up from FWO in a couple of weeks. You don't need me along for this run anyway. It's not like you're planning any drop-in chapter visits along the way. I've got your flight info. Hang on, lemme dig it up."

There was silence on the line for a second, then Slate continued in a quieter voice, "I got a question though, Prez. If you can get her to ride with you—to come home—how long do you think it will be before you make it back to Chicago? I was thinking we might want to throw Mica a party, if you can get her to ride back."

"I'm gonna do my damnedest; that's for sure, brother," Mason clipped. "We fucking need her there. *I* need her there. Even if Mica's not with me, if she's home, at least I know I can keep her safe. Tired of using your contacts down there to watch her back." He felt a presence behind him and turned, seeing Shooter, Judge, and the women standing right behind him.

Catching another flicker of emotion on Willa's face, he thought this one looked like disappointment or regret. He wasn't sure what to make of that, and turned his attention back to the phone, confirming the flight details that Slate read off. "I'll see you tonight. We can go over the shit I need you to take care of while I'm on this run. Soon as Tug gets back from wherever the fuck he went, we'll head back to the clubhouse here, then I'll be on my merry fucking way."

Ending the call, he slid the phone into his jeans front pocket. Shooter asked, "Did Bootleg come over and explain what the fuck that was about?" At the same time, Judge asked, "Going on a run?"

Mason shook his head, deciding to only respond to Shooter. "He hasn't said squat to me, man." Mason rubbed both hands over his scalp, rasping against his short hair. He pulled a beanie out of his back pocket and slipped it on when he heard the sound of bikes from outside. "That'll be my men. I'll cut them off in the lot. Riders don't need any additional shit from them about this going down with me in here."

He stuck out his arm, saying, "Shooter, man, it's been a pleasure, as always. It's good to see you, brother. Don't be such a stranger. Give me a call sometime; I miss talking to you." Grasping each other's wrists, they pulled in and bumped shoulders, thumping solidly against the other's back with their fists.

"Phones go both fucking ways, brother. We could both be better at bridging that gap," Shooter said as they pulled away.

Nodding as he turned to the younger man, Mason repeated the gesture, saying, "Judge, you do your old man proud, son. Proud. Watch his back for me, would ya?"

Receiving a brief, "You got it," in response, he nodded sharply at Judge.

Mason inclined his head at Eddie and Willa, his gaze traveling down, and then back up the dress, coming to rest on her face with those wide, trusting, hazel eyes. "Ladies," he said as he turned around to leave. There was the briefest brush against his hand and he broke stride for a second, looking down to see a piece of paper nestled in his palm. He crumpled it tightly and thrust it deep within his front pocket before walking towards the door.

***

Eddie saw Willa shiver for the umpteenth time tonight as they watched the Rebel Wayfarers' President leave, walking steadily out of the clubhouse, the door closing quietly behind him. She didn't think the shivering was due to a chill in the air, or even from adrenaline at what had happened. She was pretty sure it was a physical reaction to the man, someone Willa should never have met.

She should not have been here tonight. This was why Eddie had tried to leave this life behind, to keep the people she loved safe. Her dad coming into town had complicated things so that now she'd put her best friend into a dangerous situation—and then the bangers had barged in waving guns, escalating things.

She reached out and grabbed Willa's hand, threading their fingers together. Tugging to get her attention, she asked, "Are you okay, Wills?"

Receiving a silent nod in reply, she was going to say more, when Shooter intruded, "Time to go home, doll baby. Judge will drive you." Opening her mouth again to argue, he cut her off. "Nope. No mouth. Don't you give me any fucking shit, Edith. Not a healthy goddamn thing to risk right fucking now." She shut her mouth with a snap, frowning at him.

He turned to her friend, his gaze examining their joined hands and saw Willa's eyes were still on the now-closed door. "Willa, I'll only say this once. You don't know me, but if you are important to my girl, then you are important to me. This is notice you're on radar. That means you're gonna be protected. By my boys, my brothers, my son—but not by, or from, Mason."

He reached out, seizing her chin, turning her head and forcing her to look at him. "Hear me, gal. I can't make you do shit, but you gotta know Mason is not someone to fuck with, even for someone in the life, and surely not for a gal as sweet as you. He's family, but he's got shit—in his past, both long ago and recent, and most likely in his future. Right now, he's hung up on a fucking princess that has drilled his ass into the ground. This is a hard life, baby, and it makes the men who live it hard too. You should look elsewhere, darlin', and save your sweet for someone who can return it in kind. You got me?"

Eddie saw Willa's eyes had grown large in her face. She looked shaken as she listened to Shooter. Nodding wordlessly at him in response, he held her gaze until he was evidently convinced she'd heard him. Giving her a chin lift in return, he released her face from his grip.

Turning to Judge, he said, "Get the keys, get some brothers, and get these gals home safe." Receiving an affirming nod from his son, he reached out and wrapped his arms around Eddie's shoulders. "Tell me now, doll baby. I got shit to do," he murmured, kissing the top of her head softly.

"Love you, Daddy," she whispered as she wrapped her arms around him, still holding onto Willa's hand.

"Love you more, baby girl," he returned firmly. "I'll talk to you soon." He backed up a step, shouting as he turned away, shouldering past Riders members, headed for the club president. "Bootleg, you got some shit to answer for, mother*fucker*. My goddamn daughter was..."

28 - Fort Wayne bound

Bear's chest heaved as he dragged in a harsh breath, his shoulders screaming from the strain of supporting his body. The chains binding his wrists were looped around a hook in the ceiling, secured over his head, suspending him. He could barely feel his hands anymore, but knew they were badly swollen. The plastic sheeting that covered the floor was splashed and dotted with blood, the toes of his boots making complex, abstract designs as they trailed across from side-to-side, again and again, following his body as it was punched and pummeled, swaying with each hit and shove.

They'd been going at him, taking runs at him by turns as they exhausted themselves with their efforts. Panting with his exertions, his current tormenter paused and grabbed Bear's hair, lifting his head to look into his face. "Fuck, he's not with us again," he said, letting go and stepping away.

Eyes closed, Bear let his head fall back between his arms, taking advantage of this brief break in the action as the four men in the room gathered in a knot near the door, bunching together as they talked. His head snapped up, eyes wide when the unmistakable sound of gunfire came from just outside the room. The sudden movement sent his body rotating lazily, and he twisted his head desperately from side to side, craning his neck in an attempt to see and track the movements in the room as the door burst open.

Rebels swarmed inside, guns and chains in hand, and he saw one of the men who'd been working him over fall to his knees, stretching his hands into the air in an unconscious parody of Bear's position. He heard a shot as he continued revolving, dangling from the hook, and the next rotation afforded him a view of the man's body, now sprawled on the floor, a bloody chaos where his face had been.

It was over within seconds, and the next revolution showed the other three men restrained near the wall, a dozen of his brothers towering over them. He groaned and jerked as arms wrapped around him from behind, grinding his punished ribs together. The arms lifted him as a set of hands pulled the hook from between his wrists. He recognized Slate's voice in his ear, telling him to keep his arms up, and he laughed through a throat raw from screaming. After hanging like he had been, his shoulders were locked in place, there was no way he could bring his arms down, even if he wanted to.

They laid him on the floor atop the plastic sheeting, and Bear felt the late afternoon sun slanting in the windows washing over him, warming his face as he heard movement around him, the plastic crackling as someone got on the ground near his hip.

"Goddammit, Bear. What in fucking hell were you thinking, coming in here by yourself? You looking to get fucked over, maybe dead? Is this your way of taking care of the shit that blisters your fingers and kills the life in your eyes? You selfish bastard. Goddamn fucking *selfish* bastard. You think this is fun for me to watch? For your brothers to see? Fucking *shit*. This is a goddamn *fucking* cluster...Charlie-*fucking*-foxtrot...FU-*fucking*-BAR," Mason was yelling, his voice rapidly gaining in volume as he approached their position, coming in from the side of the room.

Goose's face swam into view above him, and Bear saw his mouth moving, but could only hear Mason's words. "You better be o-fucking-kay, Bear, 'cause I'm gonna wanna kick your goddamn ass into next week for pulling this shit. You don't put us through this shit, and you better listen to your goddamn President. You will not check out on my fucking watch, brother. *Not on my watch.*"

Bear grinned, tasting sharp copper in his mouth as his swollen lips stretched and split painfully across his teeth. Mason was pissed—he could hear that clearly—but he was *here*. Slate was *here*. His brothers. They'd come for him. *Saved me. Do anything for them. My brothers...my family.*

He heard Slate murmur something and felt fingers brushing over his shoulders and wrists as the restraints were removed, but he didn't bother to look, instead keeping his gaze on Goose, seeing the man flinch and wince as he inventoried injuries. Bear knew he was fucked up; the men had been on him ungently for hours. Goose was their resident medic, and Bear was glad to see him, but surprised. He was normally in Fort Wayne, and they were a long ways west of that town now.

Bear's thoughts flickered back to yesterday morning, when he'd been sitting in Des Moines for the third day in a row, waiting to see if the rogue members from that town's chapter would finally show their hand.

Bear tiredly scrubbed his palms across his jaw, dragging his fingers through his short beard, running them across his scalp. He tugged on his hair gently as he stretched his neck, rolling his head. Mason's campaign to keep him busy had worked; he hadn't been able to wrench on one of his bikes in a long while. He missed it, but less now than a month ago, and far less than a year past. Since they'd begun expanding the club again, it seemed like he was traveling all the time. Bouncing around from chapter to chapter, hanging out and visiting, just like he was doing here in Des Moines.

Hell, for the past year, he'd only seen the inside of his apartment twice, and one visit had been short, barely a half-day, until he was called out again. Even with that, he was feeling better than he had in a long time, more grounded and steady, oddly enough, given he was playing the part of a nomad.

After being Slate's understudy for years, working side-by-side and observing him in action, Bear had long since gotten the hang of sliding into a chapter and sitting, waiting...watching. He'd be quiet and still until he'd get a glimpse past the veneer and gloss, deep into the corners, in the shadows some members would rather no one know about.

Rebels had three hard and fast rules. Those rules, laid down by Mason, were sacrosanct, the core of their club, and easy to understand: no hard drugs, no military grade weapons, and no whores. Finding any of the three being run out of a chapter was damning, and every member knew it.

Right now, he was sitting in a shithole of a diner, waiting. The shit going on in this chapter was bad, and he was waiting on the scales to tip to bring in Slate. Unfortunately, it would be enough to close the chapter, which he hated, because that kind of shit uprooted families and closed businesses.

He and Slate spoke several times a week, and when Bear uncovered shit, they worked closely together. Along with Mason, they'd coordinate the best way to manage fallout while taking action against transgressing members or officers. The severity of the offense was considered when the method of correction was decided, and final call was always Mason's.

That call came into play when any of the three rules were being broken, either at the member level, which was easiest to deal with, or across a chapter, which could be fucking hard to root out. The chapter level was also goddamn dangerous, because those traitors liked life the way they had it, no changes wanted, and they'd do anything to keep things status quo.

Most times, Mason's censure ran the gamut from fines, loss of rank, to loss of membership. At times, the reprimands brought violence, and if they were left with no other options, they took care of business any way needed. Slate's responsibility was getting Bear's backup in the right place, at the right time, once they knew what was going down.

A couple months back, Slate had made him an offer to move to Fort Wayne permanently. Tired as he was, he was wishing he'd taken him up on it. Mason would have backed the move, because of anyone in the club, Mason understood the toll this kind of work took on a man. He was tired of the routine of wake up, fuck somebody up, go home alone...rinse and repeat. He decided to call Slate tomorrow, see if the offer was still open. Eddie was in Fort Wayne, which was an excellent incentive to finish things up here and head out, sooner rather than later.

Over the months, through the miles, he'd found himself thinking about her all the time, and his desire had not faded with time and distance; if anything, his need for her had grown more powerful. He woke from dreams about her far more often than his nightmares now. Regularly speaking to Tug, he'd been able to keep up with her life from a distance.

When he'd walked out of the restaurant that day, he didn't get far. There was a bike in the lot and he recognized Bulldog sitting on it and knew the man had clocked him leaving the place. As pissed as he'd been at himself, he needed to make sure she'd be okay and had ridden his bike across the street, parking in the shadows.

Sitting there, he watched and waited for Eddie to leave, seeing a second bike roll in and park on the other side of the building. Bulldog pulled out and left a couple minutes later. It had taken a while; he thought she must have stayed to drink her tea. His breath stopped in his chest when she finally walked out. She affected him like that, the need for her strong and fierce, even from a distance. As she climbed into her car, his whole body tensed when he saw a shadow separate itself from the darkness near the front wall of the restaurant, stalking towards the passenger side of her car.

He'd been a heartbeat away from starting the bike to tear across the street, when he recognized Judge. He got into the car for a few minutes, then climbed back out, following Eddie out of the parking lot on his bike. Bear trailed after the two of them, then stayed to watch as Judge hung out in the parking lot of her apartment building until another Rider came to relieve him, noting he didn't go inside.

He thought back to the first time he'd seen her up close, that day in the bar, remembering how angry Judge had been about her backdoor escape from his control. He'd wondered what place Judge had in her life. What if they are involved, *he thought, despairingly.*

The thought infuriated him, and after some consideration, he realized it was because he knew Judge would be going back to Cali sooner or later. As Shooter's son, he'd be pulled back eventually. If she was Judge's—if they were together—she'd go home to Cali, leave Fort Wayne...leave him alone again without even the glimpse of her to quieten him.

He'd questioned Tug, knowing he had a history with Shooter and Judge, and breathed a deep sigh of relief when through their conversations, he realized she was Shooter's daughter, which made her Judge's sister. It explained so much, and he felt an enormous weight lift off his chest at Tug's words.

He'd heard through casual exchanges in clubhouses about an incident that had gone down at the River Riders clubhouse. Eddie and Mason were both present, which made the whole situation more delicate, but Shooter handled it well. He took over the club that night, then four months later, closed it down for good with no bloodshed.

That was not long after Bear had left Fort Wayne at Mason's request, and he'd carried some worry about Eddie when he heard that Judge had eventually followed Shooter back out west, but Tug assured him she was staying put. Knowing she was still in town meant he could dream of seeing her again, fantasize about holding her, having her. After the diner, he hadn't been surprised how thinking of her could make him want her. The mere thought of her. He needed to see her, wanted to see her, wanted to know if that spark remained.

Shaking himself, he pulled his thoughts back to the present, focusing on the current sticky situation of a club he now had proof was dealing in prostitution, and drugs that came along for the ride. The door to the diner swung open, and he saw three mid-ranking members saunter in, not even bothering to scope out who else might be there. They took a booth not too far from him, and he watched their reflections in the window as they leaned over the table, their heads tilted together conspiratorially.

Concentrating on watching the men, he'd been surprised when a handgun appeared beside his cheek, the cold metal roughly tapping the side of his face. Held in the hand of a man he would have normally called brother, the gun turned on him, and his only regret in the moment was losing his chance with Eddie. His stomach turned at the thought, followed swiftly by anger acknowledging this would happen at the hands of a man wearing a Rebel Wayfarers' patch on his cut. Betrayed. *"Come on, Bear. Get the fuck up and walk outside, nice and easy," the member said in a muffled voice.*

"What about his stuff?" he heard someone question, looking up to find the other three men walking over.

"We takin' him to the warehouse?" another of the men asked. He was cuffed in the side of the head by the pistol-wielding member.

"Shut the fuck up. Don't talk about shit," the gunman said, "and you, get the fuck up." This last was accompanied by another ungentle prod of the gun against his head. Bear climbed out of the booth, walking outside only to be hit hard on the head and shoved roughly through the side door of a waiting van, dazed and bleeding.

Lying on the warehouse floor, Bear briefly wondered how Mason and Slate had found him. Stiffening from pain as one of his arms was gradually and gently brought down by his side, he rolled his head to see Mason squatting nearby, his expression grim while he watched Goose work. "Prez," he gritted through clenched teeth, and Mason's gaze flicked to his face, waiting patiently as if he had all the time in the world, the flare of his nostrils the only indication of his rage. Mason could have a singular focus, making you feel you were the most important thing he had to deal with. Bear thought, *I like that about him.*

Swallowing, he groaned, "Huh. Uh. Prez." Feeling one of the splits in his lip with the tip of his tongue, he continued, "Got a memory stick in my pocket." His tongue pushed at one of his loosened molars. "Mason."

He felt a sting in his shoulder and turned to see Goose removing a syringe from his arm, tucking it back into a small toolbox he had open on the floor beside him. Swallowing again, he tipped his head back to Mason, trying once more, "I got it. I...all, Prez. I got it. Everything you need, brother. You needa geddit to Myron. This shit goes deep here. I godit."

He felt the pain from his busted ribs recede, the cement floor oddly softening beneath him as the drug began to take effect. Taking in a deep breath, he felt the broken bones in his chest grate together, and laughed soundlessly at the wonderfully painless yet peculiar feeling. "Hmm. Oh, goddamn, that's better. It was hurtin' like fuck. Goddamn Goose is a miracle worker." He tried to focus, beginning to slur his words. "Mason. *My brother.* Save my life 'gain. Rebel Wayfarers forevah," he began, and quietly slipped below waves of peace and silence as from a distance, he heard Mason finish, "forever Rebels."

***

Mason watched as Bear succumbed to the drugs, thankful he'd finally passed the fuck out. *Goddamn,* it hurt to look at him so bloody and swollen. When the man had grinned up at him, it was a grotesque rictus of blood-smeared teeth from the raw splits in his lips. There were few spots on his body that weren't purpling from bruising; even his jeans were saturated with blood.

"Goose?" The single word asking volumes, he turned his head to look at the three men on their knees across the room, watched over by people they had once called brothers. These were men Bear had trusted, men who had almost killed him trying to find out how much of their treachery he'd uncovered. Mason was far beyond angry; he was deep into fucking rage territory, furious at their betrayal of his family.

"I hope it looks worse than it is, Prez," Goose told him. "I count at least four fractured ribs, and he's got torn muscles in his left shoulder. Dunno about surgery. Head wound and lacerations from being pistol-whipped. It looks like mostly soft tissue damage. He's gonna need some time and space to heal after I get him stitched up and wrapped tight. I knocked him out good, so he should be out for a while. I wanna get him transported while he's still unconscious, help keep his pain to a minimum."

Mason nodded, yelling across the room, "Deke, get the van these motherfuckers used to bring him here. Let's get our brother loaded up and out of this fucking shithole."

He stood, gaze sweeping the men in the room. "I'm resolved, brothers. This shit ends here. Devil needs his demons. If you feel different, get the fuck outta here." He pointed down at Bear, lying still and limp on the bloody plastic at his feet. "This is my brother. He's bled for me. His last words before Goose knocked him the fuck out were 'Rebel Wayfarers forever'." Mason's heart swelled as he heard the quiet chorus from across the room finish the phrase, "Forever Rebels."

Crouching back down to one knee, he dug into Bear's front pocket, pulling out the memory stick the man had been so worried about. Holding it up, he shook it once and then looked from the tech in his hand to the men across the room, his face twisted with anger. "This is what they were after. Bear said it has final proof of their betrayal on it. Any man here feel you need to see what he found?" He pointed down at Bear, asking, "Do you need more proof than your brother lying in his own blood here in front of you?"

The men stood stoically, some of them shaking their heads but their bodies and feet did not shift. "Alrighty then, we're in agreement." He swung his gaze to the three men who knelt on the floor. "God forgives;

Rebels don't," he said as he pulled his gun from the holster in the back waistband of his pants, walking across the floor towards them, Slate at his back.

***

"I still don't fucking like it," Mason said, scowling at Tug. The man was seriously pissing him off.

"You don't have to like it. You just have to agree," Tug responded. "I'm getting tired, Mason. It's time I slowed down, enjoyed the wind more. You already have a good officer in Slate, and he's a brother, a true brother for you. I want to go to a chapter with little drama and hide out for a while. Means you need to have somebody else you can depend on, someone you can trust. I believe in my heart that person is Slate, but only if you get him better support."

"Dammit. He's so fucking messed up about Bear. He feels responsible, since he's the one who convinced me Bear'd be a good candidate to sort our shit out." Mason scrubbed one hand across his jaw, picking up his mug of coffee with the other one.

He was fucking tired. He'd been up since yesterday morning, because there'd been another conflict between Dominos and Disciples. He was getting fed up with Hawk and Mange not being able to clear their own shit. Fucking women.

"That's a no-shitter. Slate always wants to think he's responsible for bad happening, Mason." Tug scoffed. "Boy needs his head smacked a little, get those ideas out. Your new president is running himself to the ground in Fort Wayne, trying to sort the rest of Bingo's shit out. True, he's about got everything back under control, except that one banger drug dealer, but fuck. We all know we have a long-term fight with the bangers and gangs in just about every city. The Fort ain't no different."

Shaking his head, he continued, "So we give him someone he can trust, someone to lean on who has already proven their loyalty to the colors, a brother who believes in him. Bear is every bit of that, so let's give him to the boy to lean on. Slate's done good incorporating the right Fort members into his ranks, but there's a difference between *having* to trust someone, and trusting them voluntarily. We give him that, Mason. We give him Bear. Remind him why we're in the life and what's important. Goose said Bear's healed enough to ride comfortably," Tug persisted, "and if you let me go, I'll be there with them."

"Goddammit, Tug, I know all that. But, fuck, I made Bear leave the bikes once, and look at the shit that turned into. He nearly fucking died, brother. He's healing physically, and even mentally he's better now, but he still gets elbow deep and goes blank-minded every chance he gets." Mason sighed. "We can't force our brothers to be whole again, can we? Tell you what...if he's willing, I'll be good with it."

He paused. "Fort Wayne's a different town since Shooter folded the Riders chapter there. You heard from him or Judge lately? I keep hopin' he'll call and say they got their SoCal shit sorted enough for Judge to come back. I want Chase to meet him, now that my boy is with me."

There was a knock at the door, and Red stuck his head in, glancing around the room nervously. He tucked the tip of his tongue into his cheek, and then, blowing out a rush of air, said, "Prez, you need to come see this." Ducking back out, he shut the door behind him as Mason and Tug looked at each other wearily.

"Guess I better go see." Mason sighed, standing and walking to the door. "Shit never fucking ends." He followed Red upstairs to one of the unassigned rooms, where Red pointed at the door and then turned to walk away. "Hey," he called, stopping Red's retreat. Tipping his head towards the door, he asked, "What the hell am I walking into?"

"You need to see," was all the answer he received.

Mason opened the door and stood, feet spread wide, black leather boots firmly grounded. He braced his hands on the top of the doorframe and sighed heavily. Hearing footsteps behind him, he glanced over his shoulder to see Tug coming up the hallway. "Tug, pack up; you get your way. You're going to Fort Wayne today."

Peering into the room around Mason's frame, Tug chuckled once, and then quieted when he saw the look on Mason's face. "Ain't the worst thing he could have done." He walked away to go to his room and put together a kit to take on the bike, knowing he'd have a rider behind him on the way to the Fort.

"Stupid shithead," Mason muttered and looked into the room again, his gaze skimming over the faces and bodies lying across either end of the bed. His gaze settled on the youthful frame in the middle, Chase, his boy, lying on his side, naked with a whiskey bottle cradled in one arm. His other hand was tucked between his knees as he curled on top of the covers.

Not a used condom in sight, Mason thought, *fuck*. The boy had been here for a couple of months, since his mother dropped him off. Mason had only known about the boy for a couple of years. They were still getting to know each other, and in a move that could have proven disastrous, his fucking ex-wife had thrown them together without warning.

He walked over and gently nudged the girls awake, helping them gather their clothes as he ran them out of the room. Untucking the blanket and sheet from the foot of the bed, he dragged the covers up over Chase, taking a moment to run his hand tenderly through the boy's dark hair, so like his own. It had grown until it was long enough to flop over his eyes in the most annoying way. A soft half-smile on his face, Mason walked to the door, glancing back as he closed the door.

Pulling his phone from his pocket, he dialed a number from memory, saying briefly, "Sending Chase to you for a couple weeks." He hung up, stalking up the hallway towards his own room, which he knew would be thank-fuck empty. The girls knew better than to hit him up. He sighed, wishing he could leave it alone, but as they often did, thoughts of Mica crept into his mind and he shook them off, reminding himself she was safe, she was loved, and she was still untouched by the life...just like he'd wanted. "Yeah, but I'm one *stupid* motherfucker for giving her up," he growled at himself, cutting off as his phone rang.

Slate still had sleep thick in his voice as he asked, "Prez...what the fuck is going on?"

Mason gritted his teeth, "He's needing a change in scenery for a while, maybe more than a couple weeks. Found him drunk, sleeping between two club whores a little bit ago. He'll be riding down with Tug, so you should expect them both for breakfast."

"All right, Mason," Slate said patiently. "I'll take him on and see what's up. How long do I get Tug?"

"He's Chase's ride, so you get Tug until my son comes home," Mason responded. "Let me know if you run into issues, or if he gives you any fucking shit. Boy's sixteen going on dead if he can't monitor his mouth."

"Yeah, boss." Slate yawned and Mason disconnected the call. He'd send Bear down next week. Tug was right; Slate's eagerness for Tug's presence revealed he wanted familiar people around him. Bear would do well there, since he was known to the members from his trips with Tug, and it would give him a chance to finish healing, maybe more than just physically.

29 - Surprise

Bear looked around the apartment, taking in the sterile décor, so similar to the one he'd had in Chicago. Slate had hooked him up with a place to live, and now they were neighbors, since he and Melanie had moved into the same building not long ago. Slate had renamed the woman Ruby when he claimed her as his own. Bear laughed to himself. Mel's hair had always been one of her most striking features. Trust Slate to take the less traveled road for her nickname.

The doorbell rang and he started, frowning hard. He wasn't expecting any visitors; the members knew he'd be back at the clubhouse for church later, and it wasn't like he knew anybody else in town. Walking over to the door, he squinted through the peephole and jerked back in disbelief, grabbing the doorknob and twisting it forcefully to pull the door open wide. "Mom!" he cried in surprise, a grin plastered on his face.

He reached out to wrap his arms around his mother's shoulders and hugged her tightly. He felt a tension he didn't even know he was carrying relax and loosen as he leaned the side of his head against hers, taking in a big, shaky breath.

"Robby," she laughed, "ease up, son. You're squishing me."

"Where did you come from?" He released her to grab her suitcase, gesturing with his other hand as he ushered her inside the apartment.

"Well, first I came from Painted Post, where my parents settled long before I was born." She swatted his shoulder with the palm of her hand, still laughing.

"Oh, my God, Mom," he grinned, "you know what I mean. When did you get into town? How long can you stay?"

She reached up, cupping his jaw with one palm. She said softly, "As long as you'll have me." Wrinkling her nose at him with an unsure look, she said, "I kinda sold the house."

Eyes wide, he snorted a laugh of surprise. "Kinda? How do you 'kinda' sell a house you've owned for decades? It sorta snuck itself onto the market and accepted offers on its own? What the hell?"

"Are you mad at me?" She pulled a grimace. "It'd been so long since you'd been back I didn't think you'd mind. I decided it was way too big for me. A nice family with two young boys bought it. Can you believe the first thing they want to do is renovate that old treehouse? It made me happy to hear laughter in that backyard again." She was looking at him and waiting nervously for a reaction.

"Woman, I'd never be mad at you. Are you crazy? Good God, have you met my mom? She'd smack me if I got in her business." He softened, a small smile curving his lips. "Hey. Seriously, Mom. I'm glad if you're glad. I think it's cool they want to fix up the treehouse. Andrea, Joel, and I spent a lot of hours out there." He offered her a one-sided smile, faintly surprised there was no pain associated with the memories of those long-ago summers; there was a fondness mixed with sadness at the loss, but it was no longer overwhelming.

"You'll stay here as long as you want, then. Lemme show you the spare bedroom and we'll stow your bag. I'll have to run out and get some food though. I didn't move in very long ago, and I've just been eating out a lot. Lemme make a call, beg off an obligation for tonight. Then we can cook and play conversation catch-up." Carrying her bag, he walked down the hallway to the last door.

She followed him and leaned in, hummed quietly as she looked around, and then glanced back down the hallway. She asked, "Son, exactly how long have you lived here?"

"Just a couple of weeks. Hey, how'd you get the address? How the heck did you even know to come here instead of Chicago? I don't think

I've talked to you since I moved. I was waiting for things to settle down." He was puzzled, a frown creasing his forehead.

She ducked her head, again apparently unsure of his response. "Well, I called your cell and you didn't pick up, so I called the shop where you were working. FWO2? The man who answered the phone told me you'd moved. I asked him to where, and he gave me this address." Tilting her head, she continued, "One flight later, here I am. Voila! You never seemed to want me to visit, so I decided I wasn't going to give you a chance to tell me no." She cocked her head the other direction, lifting her shoulders in a small, sheepish shrug.

"Do you know who you talked to?" He scowled, pissed off. What if the call had been a ruse to get at him? There were still plenty of ex-members around who had a hard-on for him, and this might have turned out very differently if it had been one of those men who instigated the call. He waited for her answer, ready to tear someone a new asshole for giving out his information like that.

"Davis Mason," she smiled, "nicest man, very polite. Said he was a good friend of yours."

Staggered, he thought, *What the hell*? *What is Prez up to now?*

"I'm here now." She yawned, covering her mouth with one hand and looking into the bedroom again. "That bed looks pretty comfy. Why don't you go do your thing tonight? I'm beat, Robby. I'll nap, and then get to bed early. We can catch-up tomorrow. I didn't realize I was so tired. I'm sorry."

"Sure thing, Mom." He nodded and wrapped her into another tight hug, kissing the side of her head with a sigh. "It's no big deal. You rest, and I'll run pick up some food, grab dinner for you. I'll be back late from my meeting, but we'll sit and visit tomorrow."

***

Bear looked around the room at the Fort Wayne members gathered for church. Since Slate took over as chapter president, this was a regular, much needed event. Bingo had slacked on meetings for a while, which had allowed the membership to fragment.

"I'm telling you I don't trust that fucker," Deke growled, swinging his head to look around the table filled with members sitting for church. "Manzino waltzes into one of our businesses and basically hands himself over to us, then after a beatdown, with no further argument, the motherfucker agrees we're right and he needs to move on?" Shaking his head, he added, "I don't buy it. He's stalling for someone, or something."

"I agree he's not to be trusted. But, we can't find anything that indicates he was other than truthful." Slate pointed at Bear. "You still got nothing in your net about the man?"

"Nothing, Prez. I got nada." He ground the words out, wishing he could provide a different answer. A local drug dealer that had given them months of pain and grief, Manzino had done as Deke outlined, and then had ghosted right after Slate and Hoss turned his ass loose. Since then, the entire club had been unsuccessful finding him.

Slate spread his hands, speaking to the entire group. "If you get solid word, bring it to me. I will land on that motherfucker with both feet. But, I can't deal with what we can't find. We're off lockdown as of now, unless something happens. We all know Rabid's still in the wind, too, so watch for him or word of him."

Rabid's time as a Rebel had been cut short when Slate had discovered he and Ramone, another member, had been stealing from the club. Ramone had been dealt with, but Rabid had pulled a runner to try and escape the retribution the officers and members would rain down on him, and hadn't been seen since.

"All right, brothers." Slate picked up the gavel beside him and pounded it on the scarred table one time. "We're done here."

Bear looked across at Tug, seeing him stroke his mustache thoughtfully, and grinned to himself; that man was planning something, plain as day. Tug glanced over as a prospect came through the now-open door, pressing against the tide of full-patch members leaving. He looked anxiously around the room until he found Bear, then rushed over. Leaning close, he said quietly, "There's a woman here asking after Rob Crew."

"What woman?" he asked, standing and following the prospect into the main room, Tug hard at his heels.

Pointing across the room towards the pool tables, the prospect wordlessly indicated the woman standing with her back to him, and his breath hitched in his throat as she slowly turned and her grey eyes locked on his face. He'd begun moving forward when he heard Tug take in a ragged breath and felt a hand on his elbow, slowing and turning him.

"Brother," Tug said gruffly, "remember, man. In here, she's not just Eddie. She's Shooter's girl and Judge's sister. Tread lightly."

Bear nodded once in acknowledgement, then pulled his arm free from Tug's grip and turned again to face the woman who'd been occupying his dreams for so long. The room seemed to stretch around them as he took the last dozen strides to her, each step feeling as if it took five minutes to complete. He felt the weight of his brothers' gazes on his back as he stood between them and her, his eyes focused on her face.

Stopping directly in front of her, he crowded her space, her head tilting back to look up at him. She smiled uncertainly, her features taut with nervousness as she chewed on the inside of her lip. He reached out a hand, gently tucking a strand of hair behind her ear, tracing one fingertip along the edge, his touch causing her to gasp and release her lip from its captivity. That tingle...God, the spark was there. Had always been there. The feel of her under just that light stroke of his finger made his cock stand at attention, his muscles tightening as arousal curled low in his belly.

"Eddie." His voice was raspy, deep with desire, barely recognizable to himself. At her name, he saw her shiver, bright circles of color blooming in her cheeks. He lowered his head towards hers, placing his lips near her ear, speaking softly. "Whatcha doin' here?"

He heard her tongue sweep across her lips and felt the puffs from her breath stir the air alongside his neck as she spoke. "I heard you were back in town. I...uh, I wanted to see you." She said the last in a rush and his heart beat faster at her answer, an involuntary smile lifting the corners of his mouth.

"I wanted to see you, too," he confessed to her, still speaking softly, his body protectively curled around hers without touching. "Let's get something to eat. I haven't had supper yet."

There was a quick intake of breath and she responded quickly, her words broken into choppy sentences. "Dinner, yeah. I'd like that. With you."

He straightened, looking down into her face, seeing some of the tautness had fled now that she was more sure of her welcome. He asked, "Did you drive?" She shook her head in response and his smile broadened. "You'll ride with me." More of a demand than a question, she still nodded, and a smile broke across her face too.

He cupped his hand around her upper arm, curling his fingers as he slid them down until her hand was captured in his, then he was pulling her towards the outside door. It was quiet in the main room of the clubhouse, and he saw Slate eyeing them from the doorway to his office, Tug leaning against the wall nearby, his eyes narrowed in silent warning to Bear.

Outside, he stood next to his bike and frowned at Eddie. "I don't have a lid for you. I never have a need, never have a rider."

She shrugged, casually pulling her hair into a ponytail, then she swiftly braided that, securing it with a second hair tie. He was drawn to her, that easy competency, even with something as small as her getting ready to ride on his bike behind him. *God,* he thought with a thrill, *she's gonna be wrapped around me.*

"It's okay. I'm not worried." She spoke few words, but her smile told him the things she hadn't said, that she trusted him enough to keep her safe, and he felt a warmth spread throughout his chest.

Straddling his bike and starting it, he flipped the passenger pegs down and then held out his hand. She grasped it, skin-to-skin, and he gasped, feeling that welcome vibration throughout his body. Settling onto the seat behind him, her thighs were snugged tightly around him, hands clasped across his stomach.

Looking down at the tank, he traced the lines of his angels, then turned so he could see Eddie's face. "Ready to go?" She nodded, tightening her grip as he rolled them carefully out of the lot and into the street, heading north at the first crossroad.

Pulling into the parking lot, he felt her shift against his back. Parking in the line of bikes there, he looked back, seeing a tight look on her face. "Eddie, what's wrong? Would you rather go somewhere else?"

"No, the food here is always good," she said. "Steve and Michael are excellent in the kitchen." She sighed as she looked around. "But here at Checkerz, I can't be just Eddie." She shrugged. Stepping off the bike, she squared her shoulders and reached up to remove the ties holding her hair into the braided ponytail.

He sat for a moment, then said, "Get back on. I know a different place." She tipped her head to the side, looking into his face. "Trust me, Eddie." This drew a smile from her, and he watched her redo her hair. Clasping the hand he offered, she shivered when their skin touched as she reversed the process, climbing back onto the bike. They left the bar, going south and then west.

About thirty minutes later, he pulled into the parking lot of a small Mexican restaurant in Huntington, west of Fort Wayne. She leaned on his shoulders to swing her leg across the bike, rubbing her ass with both hands once she was on the ground.

"Don't ride much?" He towered over her, smiling, in her space again like he was at the clubhouse, his body curving around hers possessively. Even without touching her, he could feel the electricity in the air between them.

"Nope," she said. "I haven't voluntarily ridden in years." Still rubbing her ass, she looked at the front of the building and then back up at him, observing with a wry smile, "Hope the food inside tastes better than the outside looks."

"Oh, it does." He paused, looking down at her, reaching out and caressing her cheek with the backs of his knuckles, and she stilled under his touch. "The best part? They have more than thirty different kinds of premium tequila. If I remember correctly, you happen to like tequila a little bit." Her face lit up, and she gave him her widest smile and an eager nod of agreement.

Laughing, he opened the door, following her inside.

***

Four hours later, they were still sitting in the restaurant, occasionally eating chips and salsa, sometimes taking a drink, but always, constantly talking. Sometimes their words would walk over the other's in their eagerness to hear and be heard, to share. Their quest for knowledge about each other had been nonstop, and they'd offered up stories both funny and embarrassing about their childhoods and adult lives.

Eddie had never felt so comfortable with a man so quickly. She loved seeing his green eyes light up with amusement at her stories of college and work. His face was transparent and easy to read, transforming with every emotion, and she loved that he was having as good a time as she was. She was glad she'd taken a risk tonight, seeking him out at the clubhouse.

She reached out, taking the last unbroken chip from the basket before offering it to Bear as he sat in the booth across from her. He shook his head. "No, thanks. I'm stuffed. I don't think I could eat anything else. At least not tonight, but maybe not ever." He groaned dramatically, rolling his eyes, and she laughed aloud. She'd been doing a lot of that tonight and it felt good.

"Lightweight," she scorned him with a giggle, dragging the chip through the salsa and popping it into her mouth. She picked up her glass, looking at the remaining tequila, ice gradually melting into the liquor and took a sip. He'd switched to water early on and was now working on a cup of coffee. She liked that he was playing it safe, being careful, knowing it was because she was with him.

"How did you find this place?" she asked, reaching out to stroke one fingertip across the back of his hand. They had shared these kinds of casual caresses frequently throughout the night, nothing pushy, each simply wanting to feel that electric connection between them again. "I've lived here for years and never heard of it. And I *love* tequila!"

He smiled indulgently. "You're still working with Rafe, right?" She nodded and he continued, "He has an older sister, Lucia. She'd dropped out of school, never got her diploma. With their family life, she never saw it as a possibility. I convinced her otherwise and got her hooked up with a tutor. She studied and worked hard, got herself ready, so I brought her over here to do the GED testing. It was supposed to take more than four hours for the whole test, so I had to find something to fill the time. The guy proctoring the test recommended this place for food and I found it to be excellent."

She tilted her head, looking at him, asking, "How'd she do?"

Proudly, he said, "Aced it in one. She's going to Ivy Tech now, getting some of her basic credits out of the way, then we'll see where she wants to go. She's still wrapping her mind around the idea of having options." He shook his head in what looked like disgust. "Over the years, Rabid fucked his family...hard."

"Where is he? Rafe told me he's been out of town for a couple months. He seems nonchalant about it, but I can tell he's anxious." She toyed with her napkin, folding and unfolding one corner in on itself and then back out.

"Eddie," his voice cautioned, "that's club business. I can tell you that right now he's in the wind, but that's it. I'm not looking for him to come back. Don't worry. I still have power of attorney, so I can keep things going for the kiddos. My man Rafe is something special, and he's done well these past couple of years. He's so smart at things like math and science it blows my mind. Between him and Lucia, they are a force to be reckoned with. Throw in Miguel and Roderigo? Man, that house is full of an amazing energy and life." He had an awed look on his face, and she could see he was genuinely invested in those kids.

"Rafe's the one who told me you were back in town," she confessed, ducking her head. She reached out a finger and pushed the remaining chip fragments around in the basket. "He said you asked about me."

He agreed softly, "I did."

She looked up and their gazes met and locked, the attraction ever a palpable thing between them. He reached across, gently covering and cupping her hand with his palm. They sat for a minute, him stroking her skin with his thumb, when they were startled by someone noisily clearing their throat nearby.

The waitress held up a pitcher of water apologetically, asking, "You folks need anything else?"

Bear pulled back, taking a bill from his wallet and handing it to her on an outrush of breath. "Naw. We're good. This should cover us, darlin'. Keep the change."

Eddie saw the waitress' eyes grow big at the hundred-dollar bill he'd given her, and then felt Bear grasp her hand again, tugging and pulling her from the booth. Outside, he stood close to her and she shivered.

He reached up, his palms delicately cupping her jaw on either side of her face as he looked down at her. *Kiss me*, she thought, and then grabbed her bottom lip hard between her teeth to help steady her breathing.

Lowering his mouth towards hers, he hesitated before touching her, hovering there for seconds. *Dammit, kiss me*, she thought wildly, and then impulsively rose on her toes to press her lips to his, closing the distance between them.

His reaction was delayed, but prompted by her actions, his mouth began moving over hers, lips softly working against her as he deepened the kiss leisurely. Dragging his tongue across her lips, he groaned into her mouth when she opened to him, stroking into his mouth with her own tongue, letting it dance with his. *God he tasted good.*

His hands held her face tenderly, but she could feel the trembling in his arms as he strove to retain control. Reveling in the knowledge he was as moved as she was by the kiss, she unhurriedly lowered from her toes and smiled against his mouth as he pursued her down, not letting their connection break.

He was kissing her as if his life depended on the next movement of their lips, the next lick of their tongues, on the very contact with her mouth. Savoring every part of her, his tongue flicked and flattened against her teeth, then her palate, traced the shape and softness of her lips, devouring her with every movement. His thumbs traced across her cheekbones, stroking in time with the efforts of his tongue as it became a synchronized assault of her nerve endings, his every touch heightening the sensation.

She felt his pelvis pressed against her stomach, backing her ass into the seat of the bike. His hips thrust against her deliberately, rhythmically, the erection outlined in his tight jeans pressing against her core, every drive timed with his attack on her mouth, with his touches on her cheeks, the leather of his cut brushing against her arms. Where he wasn't touching her skin, she felt the stroke of the air on her, those portions of her body feeling bereft and abandoned even as she became conscious of the layers of clothes separating their skin. She wanted to feel him everywhere, around her, inside her. He was making love to her mouth, and she felt responsive echoes clenching deep inside.

She had no idea how long they had been standing in the parking lot, immersed in each other. Nothing mattered except the next rushed gasp of breath, the moans that came from deep in his throat and vibrated down into her lower belly, the evidence of his arousal hard against her stomach. Growing need and desire filled her; she was drowning in him, in the sensations he provoked with his touch, his kiss. When he slowed and stilled, panting hard, she unwillingly surfaced, his lips still covering hers, their huffs of breath mixing in their joined mouths.

Pulling back gradually, their lips parted grudgingly, unwillingly. She felt him rest his forehead against hers and smiled when he lovingly brushed their noses together. The skin around her mouth gently burned with the abrasion from his short beard, and her lips felt tender and swollen.

"Damn," he said quietly, but with emphasis. She stood immobile in his embrace as he softly dragged his lips across her cheek to the shell of her ear, using the tip of his tongue to trace the edges, barely breathing against her skin. He slid one hand gently down her neck and across her collarbone, cupping her shoulder, then trailing fingertips down her arm to her hand. Raising it to his lips, he held her fingers captive in his hand as he folded it across his own cheek.

"Damn," she agreed, looking into his green eyes, seeing his dark pupils were widely dilated with desire. "It's been a long time coming," she murmured.

"Yeah," he breathed, and they stood that way for long minutes, the thrill and crackle still in evidence everywhere their skin touched. Finally, Bear moved, tucking her into the front of his body and carefully wrapping his arms back around her like he was afraid she would shatter beneath his touch. She heard him murmur her name against the side of her head and made a quizzical noise in acknowledgment.

Her hands were pressed against his back and she felt him tense, then he said her name again, like a benediction. "Eddie," he said one more time on an outrushing breath, his voice a little stronger.

"Mmm?" she hummed in reply, not wanting to lift her head from where it rested against the hard planes of his chest.

"Let me get you home. You work tomorrow. Like the way you look rested," he spoke indistinctly and she pulled back, looking up into his face. His pupils were still dilated, proof his desire hadn't faded.

"You like the way I look rested?" she asked.

"Eddie," he said softly, "I've watched you for years. I've seen you rested, seen you tired, watched you drag yourself to work sick, watched over you out dancing with Willa and your girls. Seen you tipsy, angry, happy, and calm. I like you rested."

She hummed again, leaning in and rubbing her cheek against his chest, the smooth fabric of his shirt separating her skin from his. "Okay," she agreed finally, pulling her hands around to his front, pressing her palms flat against him, her thumbs rubbing small circles.

"I'd like to see you again," he said, gazing down at her. "I want to see you." It felt like he could see into her, see the uncertainty she had because he continued on a rush, "I *need* to see you. I gotta know where this goes, Eddie. I've...it's been forever since I've had anything like tonight. I've waited for this, and *God,* I'd give a lot to kiss you like that again." He had a small smile on his face. "That was just...*damn*."

She knew she should be glad he didn't assume he'd be invited inside when they got to her apartment. But a small part of her wanted him to push the issue, wanted his desire for her to be so extreme that in an effort to be with her tonight, like her, he'd risk rejection.

Again, as if he could read her mind, he leaned forward, softly kissing one corner of her mouth. "I want to...mmm...stay with you." Moving to the other corner of her mouth, he kissed her there too. "Want to be with you. In you. Want to fuck you, Eddie. Bury myself inside you. We belong. You're where I belong. Want you. I *know* you feel it too."

"Bear," she whispered, "I do."

He slanted his mouth across hers hungrily, kissing her fiercely, their tongues fighting against each other for a moment before he pulled back, panting. His hands slid down her back, cupping her ass, pulling her against him, pressing his hard cock into her belly while he searched her face. "Want you," he said, and then closed his eyes. "Want it to be right, for both of us. We fit, Eddie, we belong." He dragged in a hard breath, kissing her lightly, even as she felt him tremble under her hands. "Want so much for this to be right."

Without giving her a chance to respond, he took in another deep breath and stepped back, pulling her away from the bike as he straddled and started it. Wordlessly, she settled herself on the seat behind him, wrapping her arms around him and resting her cheek against his back.

She kept her eyes closed on the ride home, concentrating on the feel of him under her hands, the smell that surrounded her, the knowledge he wanted her. It wasn't until they pulled up in front of her apartment that she thought to wonder how he knew where she lived, and then laughed silently at herself. Since Shooter folded the chapter here, the Rebels had taken on the imagined chore of keeping her safe, making sure she knew she wasn't alone. Of course he knew where she lived.

Feeling Bear's muscles tense and bunch, she lifted her head to see a bike parked nearby, with an occupant still astride the seat. Squinting, she stared for a moment, then grabbed his shoulders to balance herself as she got off the bike. She'd barely taken two steps before she felt an arm circle her waist, pulling her back and setting her behind him as Bear put himself between her and the biker across the lot.

There was a low laugh, then a sneering voice drifted across to them, "Eddie, tell your boy to shut it down."

"Judge," she scolded, "get out here in the light where we can see you." Her palms flattened against Bear's back. She felt the muscles underneath her hands ease to some extent, but his fingers kept their hold on her hip, his thumb and palm spreading across her lower belly possessively. She wasn't about to test his patience by trying to push past him. She suspected he'd like that about as much as he liked finding someone waiting in front of her apartment in the first place, even if it was her brother.

Judge dismounted the bike in an unhurried fashion and strolled across to where they stood. Stalking over in front of Bear, the two men stood chest-to-chest, silently posturing. She covered Bear's hand with her own, wrapping her fingers around his palm, holding onto him tightly as he slowly relinquished his tight grip on her hip.

"Judge," came the gruff greeting. She felt his chest rumble with it where her breasts were pressed hard against him.

"Bear," was Judge's terse response, his eyes cutting over the man's shoulder to meet her gaze. "Gonna crash here tonight, Eddie. I'll wait inside."

"You still have your key, so why the hell are you out here?" She was annoyed, frowning at her brother.

His eyes cut back over to Bear as he smiled slyly. "Heard you might have company. Wanted to see you home safe."

Bear's muscles strained and grew rigid again, and he made a noise that sounded suspiciously like a growl, leaning forward as Judge returned the gesture. They were now inches from each other, and Eddie was beginning to get irritated at them both. "She's safe with me," he said, and Judge laughed rudely.

"Luke," she barked out his name, using her imitation of Shooter's voice to pull his frown back to her. "Get into the house. I'll be there in a minute." He didn't move, his eyes flicking back to the man in front of her and she blew out an exasperated breath, huffing tendrils of her hair out of her face.

"Bear." Tugging on his hand, she half-turned to face him as she spoke quietly, "Hey, you. Rob." He ignored her, staring fixedly at Judge. "Goddammit," she muttered. She had to defuse this somehow.

Knowing he wouldn't be able to, she gave Judge her back, twisting to put herself between the two men, placing her hands flat on Bear's chest. "Hey, I had a good time tonight." Without tilting his head, he glanced down into her eyes and she felt Judge backing away, then heard him moving slowly around them towards the front door.

Turning them gradually so her back continued to be towards Judge, she kept talking, "I'd like it if you wanted to see me again, Bear," she laughed. "Did that sound needy?" She heard the door close and prayed Judge had been on the other side of that noise, knowing she was right when she felt Bear relax slightly underneath her palms.

"Not as needy as I feel," he responded in a voice suddenly gravelly with desire. "I like that you want me to want you. It tells me this is going both ways between us. We've been dancing around for years, and now I feel like I've missed too much. We've wasted entirely too much time."

He cupped his hands around her face, closing his eyes and tracing her features with his fingertips blindly, slowly questing and stroking across her forehead, down her nose, along her jaw, and up along her hairline, smiling the entire time. "What are you doing?" she laughed.

"Memorizing you," he murmured, not opening his eyes. "Keeping you in my mind for later." At her gasp, he looked at her, smiling confidently. "I can't come in with him there, so...yeah, I'm going to use you later," he confessed softly, dragging his thumb smoothly across her bottom lip, levering her mouth open and dipping it inside, tracing across her tongue with the tip. "It's going to be so much better this time, because I've had your mouth, got your taste." He leaned in to replace his thumb with his tongue, kissing her leisurely. "That okay with you?"

"Yeah," she breathed her response out when he broke the kiss, his green eyes staring into her grey ones. "That's...hot."

He pulled her in, embracing her tightly, and then firmly set her back and away, settling himself on the bike. "Gimme your phone," he said, and she pulled it out of her pocket, handing it over in response to his clear demand. He punched in a number and she heard his phone ringing in his pocket before he disconnected the call, giving it back to her. "Call me if you need anything, Eddie. Leave a message if I don't answer, or I'll come find you and make sure you're okay." He smiled, admitting, "I'm a worrier."

She looked at him; he hadn't asked her to call to talk, just to call if she needed something. "Okay," she said slowly. "Call me if you wan— if you need anything too." Her insecurity surfaced and she stumbled over her words.

He sat still on his bike until she reached her apartment, starting the engine when she waved before closing the door. She stood inside, leaning against the entry wall, listening to the roar of his bike as it dwindled to silence in the distance.

Her head went up, her spine straightening as she drew in a breath and turned, yelling. "Judge, what the *fuck* was that?"

30 - Trouble

He lifted his head, blearily looking at the phone screen before he answered, recognizing the ID indicated Hoss, Slate's second. "Get down here, into the parking garage," he heard, and the call was disconnected before he could respond.

Bear swung his legs tiredly from the bed. He hadn't been home long. He'd gone on an extended ride after leaving Eddie at her apartment last night, trying to clear his head, getting back home just before noon. He'd been stunned with the intensity of his instinctive reaction to her brother, but it was because he felt in his gut that Judge somehow brought danger to Eddie just by being around. Shaking his head, he stomped into his boots and grabbed his cut, running for the elevator, surprised to see three club members already in the car headed down.

"What's up?" he asked, and drew in a harsh breath when the terse reply was, "Ruby's been taken."

The elevator dinged, reaching the parking level, and he exited the car, standing for a moment to take in the chaos there. Strewn across the area were about thirty bikes, parked without regard to defined spaces or lines. Just as spread out were the men, all Rebels, standing in close groups or alone, each clearly struggling with their current powerlessness.

Bear saw Hoss about five feet away; he was squatting down talking to someone on the floor of the garage. Goose was there, and there was a significant amount of blood, both on the concrete and on his clothes, as well as on the clothes of...Slate. Bear suddenly realized it was Slate on the floor and knew the member who'd spoken on the elevator had to be right when he said Ruby was in trouble. He could see that truth by the devastation written on the face of his friend.

"What can I do?" he asked, watching as Slate violently vomited, all efforts at communication halting. Hoss looked up at him, his palm up in a 'wait' signal as he turned back to Slate, listening as Goose spoke to them. A few minutes later, his name was snarled, and he looked up from dialing Ruby's number again, knowing it would go straight through to voicemail again.

"There are cameras in the garage. Find the footage and get it to Myron," Hoss ordered, helping Slate stay on his feet as he threw up again.

Finally, something concrete he could do. Turning, he stepped into the elevator, impatiently riding it to the main floor and heading to the security offices at a run. He'd felt so useless downstairs, not knowing how to help. USB drive with a copy of all available camera angles for the garage in hand, he quickly took it up to his apartment, plugging it into the laptop while he called Myron.

Slate stumbled into the apartment, and without a word, he pulled the phone from his hand and talked to Myron, then watched Bear upload the footage to the club's local server. He let Myron know when the transfer was complete and hung up. Bear watched him punch in Ruby's number with shaking fingers, shouting an anguished, *"Fuucck,"* when it again went straight to voicemail.

"Slate, her phone must be turned off," he offered, knowing it was not news.

"They took her right from me, Bear." He handed the phone back. "Get to the clubhouse, now." Staggering a little, he walked out of the apartment, right past Bear's confused mother, who was on her way inside.

"Robby, who was that?" she whispered, watching Slate as he continued towards the elevator, taking in his bloody clothes and the wound on the back of his head.

Bear shook his head; now wasn't the time to try to explain the club to his mom. "A friend. He's a friend. He and his girlfriend were attacked, and we're trying to find the girlfriend now." He kissed his mom's cheek. "I'll call you later, let you know how things shake out. I'll be back."

He made his way towards the door, wincing at the bloody handprints on the wall from where Slate had balanced himself.

***

Hours later, he and several others were drawn into an intense discussion with Slate. Security footage had shown the Devil's Sins, a rival club, had snatched Ruby, using something to knock Slate out quickly and without undue violence, the split in his scalp caused by his head smashing into the concrete on the way down.

There was reason to believe she was being held in town at a location the Sins had used as a clubhouse in the past. Handpicking members to go on the raid, they divided those men into groups to enter both the front and back of the building at the same time, in a coordinated effort to get her back safely.

Mason had authorized any force necessary, and Bear knew from experience that anyone present in the building where Ruby was being held—from the Devil's Sins or otherwise—would be considered complicit in whatever was going on. You don't hang around with shit like that going on and not have a clue. People were going to die tonight, he knew, desperately hoping it wouldn't be Ruby.

Thirty minutes later, they were moving on the Sins' clubhouse, the men silently heading towards their assigned entry points, then in position and ready. Bear saw the display of his phone light up with a message from Slate, ***Going in,*** and he called out to his group, "Go. Go in now."

Deke kicked in the door, splintering the frame and driving the man standing behind it to the floor. Bear heard men enter through the backdoor on the same level, and then the sound of gunfire came from the basement. He split his men, sending half up to the second floor to search, sweeping the main floor with the rest of them.

He found Tequila in the kitchen at the back of the house, three strangers in Sins' cuts out cold on the floor. He was holding his gun loosely in his hand, standing over them. The men upstairs were shouting, "Clear!" as they moved through the rooms, then he heard the scuff of leather soles and rapid footsteps running from the front of the house towards where they stood, between the backdoor and whoever was coming their way.

Two Sins members barreled into the room, one of them attempting to reverse direction, scrambling towards the basement stairs while the other reached into his armpit, pulling out a small handgun. Bear and Tequila fired, their bullets twisting the man from side to side before he fell on the floor with a thump. The second man stopped moving and settled to his knees, lifting his hands into the air as Deke came into the room.

Casually clocking the kneeling man in the head with the butt of his pistol, Deke wordlessly continued to the basement stairs, and Bear realized he could hear sirens approaching. Several Rebels came into the room, their eyes sweeping side-to-side, silently taking in the four men on the floor, as well as the body with the spreading pool of blood.

Gunny slipped up the stairs, pausing briefly to tell them, "EMTs are on the way. She's alive, I think. Need a blanket." He shook his head, saying cryptically, "Fucking Rabid." He left the room, coming back with a brightly colored comforter he carried down the stairs as the sirens came to a halt in front of the house.

Bear looked around and took a deep breath, needing to calm the commotion surrounding him, as well as inside. He took in another breath, choking on the smell of blood and death in the room. "Brothers, she's in the basement. Slate's got her. Let's get these motherfuckers out of the way before we get too much company. Find a cage, a van, something. Remember, there are no innocents here except Ruby." Seeing nods from around the room, he was ready when the EMTs swept around the corner and into the room, stumbling to a halt at the sight of all the downed bodies.

"Downstairs," he yelled. "Get downstairs and take care of her." That got their boots moving again, and he snapped at Deke, "Go with them. Make sure they stay on fucking target."

With a sharp nod, Deke threw a set of keys at him, saying tersely, "The van Goose brought is in the back. Ruby don't need it." He followed the EMTs down the stairs.

They'd gotten three of the breathing bodies out before he heard a yell from downstairs and recognized Deke's voice. Sweeping the room again, his eyes settled on the face of the man who had been surrendering, shocked to realize it was the man from the security footage, the one who had touched Ruby. This was Demon, president of the Devil's Sins, and the goddamn reason they were here.

Tug came upstairs, looking around and nodded to Bear. "Rabid's downstairs," he said and shook his head at Bear's groan. "I know. Mother*fucker* signed his own warrant in this, man. Fucking shit, I don't know if she's gonna make it. I think she is..." He stuttered to a stop and smoothed his mustache down agitatedly. "But I don't...I don't know. Shit goes south fast, man, we gotta have Slate's back."

"Ruby?" Bear asked, pressuring Tug to give him the answer he wanted, anguished because he was not reassured by the look on his brother's face. *What if it was Eddie?*

"Like I said—not sure, man. It's bad. They're working on her now." His voice was unsteady, harsh with anger. "Let's take the trash out, secure them back at the clubhouse. Mason's on his way now that he knows she's been found. Slate will go to the hospital with her, and Goose is riding along in the bus too." He shook his head. "They fucking electrocuted her. Rabid did it. I've seen his work before."

Closing his eyes, Tug took in a breath, punching the wall. "*Goddammit*. Slate just got her, barely managed to find peace, and this shit rains all over everything. Man was a fucking brother; that's a betrayal that can't be forgiven."

Bear looked in his face as he opened his eyes and nodded, knowing exactly what Tug meant. He'd been betrayed before too. "God forgives; Rebels don't."

***

He watched Mason tiredly scrub his face with his palms, scratching his fingernails roughly through the short beard along his jaw. "Dirty work tonight," he said, turning exhausted eyes towards Bear. "Y'all did good though. Fucking took care of business. Saved a brother's life."

Bear looked at him with a question on his face and Mason made a harsh noise. "Man looked for that woman all his life. You think he could endure losing her? Keep living?" Shaking his head, he slapped a big hand down on Bear's shoulder. "He wouldn't. I know what it's like to need someone sharing your air just so you can keep breathing in and out. If she hadn't made it—and according to Goose, it was not fucking likely for a while—if she'd died, Slate wouldn't be long behind her."

Narrowing his eyes, Bear hissed, "It *can* be survived. *Fuck*. I'm living proof of that, Prez."

"Bear—brother," Mason said with compassion, eyes fixed on his face. "You've not been living. You survived, yeah. I see that. Hard as fuck losing your family the way you did, and you survived, yeah...but you stopped living. From that moment on, you've just existed. You turned something off like a switch...and existed. Nearly the whole time I've known you, you've only *lived* when pushed out of your zone."

He reached out a hand, squeezing the back of Bear's neck tightly and held him at arm's length, staring at him intently. "Slate doesn't have that switch, man. You hear me? He wouldn't live long if he lost Ruby." Still looking attentively into Bear's face, Mason's expression changed and he nodded slowly. "And I'm thinking you might be losing your tight hold on that same switch. Keep coming at it, man. You're making headway, brother. Progress, yeah?"

Dropping his arm, Mason turned away, then looked back. "Ride with me to Chicago in the morning. I need you there for something. We'll talk to Myron about the family. Rabid's fucking woman overdosed and died years ago, and those kids are alone except for the grandmother. Gonna take care of them, no matter what."

The rest of the night was spent doing damage control. Bear worked to smooth things over with the local cops, dealing directly with Deke's brother for the most part. When Bear looked a question at him after finding out his brother was a cop, Deke shrugged. "I'm the black sheep, he's the white hat, man. Comes in handy though."

Bear was about to head out of the clubhouse and home to pack a bag when they got word Ruby was going to make it. It seemed the entire membership pulled in a deep sigh of relief at the welcome news.

Dragging into the apartment, he was surprised to find his mother awake. Sitting on the couch, she was curled into a blanket near one end, with a cup of hot tea on the table at her elbow. *Shit*. He'd forgotten she was even here; he'd hardly been home since she'd shown up. "What are you doing up, Mom?" he asked, dropping his shoulders and rolling his neck. *Fuck*, he was tired. He'd been up going on three days now.

"Robby, you look beat. Been a busy night?" she asked, then paused, but not long enough for him to respond. "Honey, who were those men in the garage when I got home? They knew me, called me 'Mrs. Crew'. How do they know me? And your friend, the one who was leaving as I came home, he looked hurt. Is he okay?" she asked him directly, never one to beat around the bush.

Yawning, Bear selectively answered her as he walked towards his bedroom. "Yeah, was a busy night. We found the girlfriend, so everything's going to be okay." He stepped inside, closing his door and taking off his cut.

Reaching back, he'd grabbed the neck of his t-shirt to pull it over his head when his door opened, his mother belatedly knocking. "You didn't answer me, Robby."

His back to her, he stood for a moment, thinking about what he could say and how much he really wanted her to know. She'd only been here a couple of days, so this seemed to be an awful lot to drop on her at once. Deciding to wing it, he turned and spread his hands, asking, "What do you want to know?"

"Who were the men in the garage?" she asked.

"Slate, the man who was here, he and his girlfriend live in the building. They were headed home after lunch and were attacked in the garage. When word spread about what happened, all our friends came over to see if there was anything they could do to help." He was pleased with his carefully worded response. It was entirely true, but limited in details.

"Is he okay? You said you found his girlfriend. Is she okay?" His mother pressed for information, but these were easy questions to answer, since things had turned out well.

"Yeah, he's good. Got a split in his head from falling down, but good. Ruby, the girlfriend, she's okay too. Gonna be in the hospital for a couple of days, but she'll be fine and out before she knows it." He waited patiently, knowing she had more to ask.

"How did your friends know who I was? I walked through to the elevator, and one of the men called me by name." She arched an eyebrow at him, waiting.

"I don't know, Mom. I have pictures of you here, so maybe he recognized you from those." That was true; he had a picture of himself with Andrea and Ashley in his bedroom, but the main room had a picture of his mom and dad on the wall, alongside one of him, Andrea, and Joel. "What did he look like?"

"Nice looking. White hair, he had on a bandana. Do all your friends ride motorcycles?" She took another few steps into the room, sitting down on the edge of his bed.

He settled down beside her, toeing off his boots. "Yeah. Most of us work at the shop too. That sounds like Tug, Mike LeRoy. I trained his nephew in the Navy. In fact, his nephew became my replacement when I wanted to separate. Tug's a good friend; I've known him for years." Twisting his neck, he looked at her with a grin. "Nice looking?"

Laughing, she playfully patted his shoulder as she rose to walk out. "Stop it, silly. I'll let you rest. I'm glad everything worked out okay. What a terrible thing to happen to your friend. What did the police say?" She paused in the doorway, waiting on his answer.

"Cops said they're going to look into it. I think they're waiting until they can talk to Ruby." He hedged his answer, because what the cops actually said was they didn't appreciate the Rebels taking care of their own business, but at the end of the day had no evidence of anything happening and nowhere to go with their displeasure.

"Mom, I gotta go back to Chicago for a few days. I'll leave my checkbook here and have my finance guy get you on the account so you can get groceries and stuff. I'll be back soon as I can."

She frowned, but said, "Okay, son. I'll be here when you get back."

Within four hours, he and Mason were sitting at Jackson's, the club's main bar in Chicago. Myron was coming over to meet with them here, but right now, all Bear could think about was the bedroom in the back of the bar where he was going to crash soon. He had a sudden thought and looked over at Mason with a question. "How'd you know for sure it was my mom when she called looking for me? It pissed me off at first, knowing someone had handed out my address, but then she said it was you. Her exact words were, 'Nicest man, very polite'. How'd you know it wasn't a play?"

Mason barked out a harsh laugh. "Shit, man, she offered up way too much information for it *not* to be your mom. She sounded pretty down, said you hadn't called in a while and wasn't answering your cell so she was worried." He shrugged, picking up his beer bottle and taking a drink. "First, I thought she wanted to visit, but then she told me she'd up and sold her house, didn't have anywhere else to go. Right thing to do, man, sending her to you."

Rolling the bottle between his hands, Mason looked down for a moment and then up into Bear's face. "You got family like that, you need to keep them close. Most of the boys would give their right arm to have a mom like that. I know my boy would." He shook his head. "I would've."

Standing as Myron came in through the door, Mason said, "Let's go to the office, and talk about Rabid's kids."

31 - Falling for her

He'd only been gone a couple of weeks and thought about Eddie constantly, but they'd been so busy he'd only been able find a few stolen minutes to call or text. The kisses they'd shared had imprinted on him, and he wanted her near him with a ferocity that frightened him. He imagined he saw her everywhere he looked, only to find it was a poor replica, an illusion. Now that he was back in Fort Wayne, he couldn't get her out of his head. He wanted her near, needed to see her—to touch her. Now.

He spoke to the members who'd been watching out for her, finding she'd kept to her normal routine, which didn't often alter. She went to work, saw her friends, went out to dinner on Thursday nights at Marie's, every so often saw a movie Saturday morning, and sometimes went to Checkerz on Saturday or Sunday.

Sitting in a chair in the main room of the clubhouse, he looked across at Gunny as he told Bear thoughtfully that he'd never seen her with anyone, and Bear knew Gunny understood his questioning was more than casual.

"I don't know what it is about her, man," Bear said. "I haven't been able to get my head straight since I first saw her."

"Fuck it out," came the crude comeback, and they both laughed. Gunny slapped his shoulder. "Honestly, man, the best way to get over someone is to get someone else under you. Fuck it out; get your head straight. I know from Mason that you've had an unfair ration of shit. Don't let a bitch fuck with your head."

Bear looked at him from under his brows, frowning. "She's not like that, brother. She's more like Ruby or Mica than any of the bitches around the club."

"Fucking Ruby," Gunny swore. "I can't get the sight of that fucking bedframe out of my head. Rabid was my brother, man. He was *our* brother. How the hell did he go so far off the fucking reservation?"

"Same kinda shit I found in chapters everywhere," Bear told him. "People make bad decisions, and then they have to justify them. They sort their lives out how they like them, and want to keep things settled out that way...so fuck the world, ya know? They'll do whatever they have to in order to keep things like they have them."

He shook his head. "And then someone like me or Slate comes along, turns over their monkey cart and they don't know what to do. So they panic and do the first thing that comes into their mind. Not making excuses, not at all. Fuck no. What they did to me? Did to Mica? To Ruby? Shit like that doesn't come with an excuse label. But it's human nature, man. We keep what we want, throw the rest of the shit at the people in our way."

"So, how you gonna get her out of your head?" Gunny asked, stretching his feet out and crossing his boots at the ankle.

"I dunno," he said truthfully. "Maybe the first step is to figure out what it is about her that's got me so twisted up on myself." He shrugged. "Maybe I don't want her outta my head."

"It's Thursday, ya know," Gunny said with a grin. "That means it's tacos and tequila night at Marie's."

Bear sat up, tipping his head to the side. "You hungry? I think I am. Yep, I'm kinda hungry for tacos. You happen to know somewhere that has tacos tonight?" He laughed as Gunny moved, getting his feet under him, standing and looking down at Bear.

"Ready when you are, brother." Laughing, he reached down, locking wrists with Bear and pulling him to his feet. "Come on, slacker. Let's ride."

***

"She sits at a booth on this side with Willa. Always," Gunny told him as they watched the crowd in the bar mirror. "Should be coming in any time now."

Even before he saw her, Bear knew the moment she walked in the door, because the hair on his arms lifted as if with a static charge. He remembered the shock he'd felt when they touched, the explosion when they kissed, and wondered what it would be like to hold her, stroke her, lift her so she could wrap her legs around his waist. His musings were cut short by a thud on his shoulder.

"There. Told you. Like clockwork. Her and Willa," Gunny said in a low tone, indicating with his head the reflections in the mirror.

***

Eddie stumbled as they walked across the threshold and Willa steadied her, asking, "Drunk by osmosis now?" They laughed, continuing towards their favorite booth, waving at the waitress on their way past.

"Do you feel that?" She stroked her hands up and down her arms. Shivering faintly, she scooted into the booth, smiling and thanking the waitress as she delivered their unspoken drink order. "Thanks, Marnie. I'll have two soft tacos, beef, with sour cream," she said, nodding towards the special board that listed one-dollar tacos.

Willa leaned back, taking a smacking drink from her weak margarita. "Feel what? Hey, Marns, I'll have the same, but with chicken, and no sour cream. And a hard shell."

Eddie sipped her tequila as she looked casually around the bar. "It's freezing in here. Why do you do that? Why do you say your order is the same, then change everyth—" She froze, looking at the bar. He was here. Here. She very slowly and deliberately set her glass back onto the table, lifting her eyes to her friend. "Wills, we need to go. Now."

"We just got here," Willa cried, picking up her drink again. "I don't wanna go yet."

"Wills, *he's* here." Her chest was tight. She found she couldn't take in a deep breath, and she desperately *needed* to take in a deep breath. "I need to get out of here." Sweat popped up on her forehead and she swiped across it with the back of her wrist. Her reaction was quickly ramping up into a panic attack and she couldn't control it. Bear was here. *Here*. They'd barely spoken after he dropped her at her place and nearly got into it with Judge. She thought they'd connected, thought she'd found her sweet, but then he hardly called, and when he did, they barely talked before he was hanging up. Pair that with his walking out of the diner before, and she felt she was headed for heartache if she saw him again.

"'Zoid is here?" Beginning to slide to the edge of the booth, Willa looked around the bar and spotted Bear sitting at the counter with another biker. "I'm just gonna go have a little, bitty, twist-his-titty chat with the ginormous asshat."

"No," Eddie said sharply, tossing some money onto the table. "I'm leaving. If you want to stay, fine, but I'm leaving. Don't talk to him, please. I can't, Wills. I can't do this. So just don't, okay?"

Looking into her friend's face, Eddie willed her to understand how humiliated she would be if he found out the effect he'd had on her. She'd wanted him, so she'd taken on her family over him. She'd fought with her brother, fought with her father for the right to see him, and then he hadn't even been around.

Like Shooter had told Willa, a woman needed to have a care who she gave her sweet to, and it clearly wasn't Bear who deserved her sweet. Not once had she seen him since that night. In two weeks, he'd only called twice, and those conversations had been stilted and brief. All her efforts and arguments with her family hadn't mattered in the end, because he just wasn't that interested. She was ashamed she'd misread things with him so badly.

The skin on her arms raised into gooseflesh, her nipples pebbled, peaks hardening into tight buds, and she felt a taut clenching in her groin. Closing her eyes, she groaned, "He's on his way over, isn't he?"

"Yup," Willa said. "Want me to cut him off? I'll cut a bitch, woman. For you, I'll cut a bitch."

Before she could respond, his low, husky voice came from beside her and she felt the cushion of the bench dip as he sat. "Eddie." Using the strength of his body to slide her over into the booth, he pressed his leg and hip tightly into her. A strong arm circled her shoulders, bringing warmth and that delicious, inescapable electric charge with it. She could feel him pressed all along her body now, every cell attuned to him. Her lips were desperately dry. Licking across them without opening her eyes, she heard him draw in a quick breath and knew he was looking at her mouth. *Sweet. He could have been her sweet.*

"'Zoid," began Willa in an aggravated tone of voice, and then she squealed, "No, thank you. No. Nope, I said no. Hey, this is my—" She cut off in mid-sentence and Eddie looked up to see the other biker sliding into the booth next to Willa, pushing her over much as Bear had done with Eddie.

She dropped her eyes to the tabletop, reaching out with a shaking hand to pick up her tequila glass, bringing it up to take a long, slow drink. She was pleased to see she'd steadied remarkably as she set it down, and emboldened, she turned in the seat to look at him, sliding out from under his arm as she did so.

"Bear," she acknowledged casually. "Hi. We were about to leave. Sorry we can't stay."

He frowned as he shook his head at her, not quite calling her on her lie. "You just got here."

"And now we're leaving, 'Zoid," Willa spoke up from across the table.

Ignoring her, Bear continued to look down at Eddie, his gaze moving between her eyes and her mouth, then skimming down her body and back up to her eyes. He leaned in, reaching out with his arm again and pulling her into an embrace. "I missed you," he whispered, his breath stirring the hair on the side of her head.

She sat stiffly in his arms, turning her head away from where it wanted to nestle into the crook of his neck. He smelled so much like...home. Leather, oil, and his own musky, male scent. The creaking of his leather cut called to her. She wanted to run her hands across his chest and back beneath the vest. Heat blazed across her skin everywhere they touched; he was scorching her, burning away her resistance, and she was losing the fight to hold herself at a distance from him. "Oh, please, you hardly know me to miss me," she scoffed with a scorn she didn't feel. "And I strongly doubt you missed me at all."

"Eddie," he breathed her name, his tone chastising her. "Missed you. I missed you, so much." He scrubbed his cheek against hers, the scruff rough against her skin. His arms tightened around her and her traitorous hands slid up his back, holding onto him against all her best intentions. She laid her head on his shoulder, breathing deeply and leaning into him. "Come with me," he urged. "Let's go where we can talk. We had some shit go down and I need to explain."

"Here you go, girls, tacos." The voice came from beside the table, accompanied by the sound of plates sliding into place in front of the two women. "You boys want some food?"

Eddie pulled back, Bear's arms tensing around her and then loosening bit by bit, letting her move away slightly. He kept an arm around her shoulders as she turned, tugging her into his side, and she laid her head against his chest for a moment, then straightened.

"I'd take a taco or two," said the biker next to Willa. He reached out, gathering up the money from the table, straightening it into a neat pile that he set next to Eddie's plate. He and Willa were sitting with about two feet of space between them, as far apart as possible on the small bench seat. He had a beer in front of him and had placed a bottle in front of Bear too.

"Eddie?" Willa's simple question encompassed a world of concern and support. If she decided it was time to leave, they'd walk out together. The problem was that she didn't want to leave now. Now that she'd touched him, that he was holding her, she was intoxicated by Bear, drowning in him again. His touch, his scent, his voice—everything conspired to keep her here, beside him.

She reached a hand out to pick up her glass, sipping deliberately at the tequila, shaking her head at Willa, and receiving a nod in response. She sat the glass down and closed her eyes, breathing in deeply and blowing the air back out slowly. Raising her eyes to meet his green ones, she traced his features with her gaze, only realizing she'd brought her hand up when he leaned his cheek into her palm. "I need to explain," he told her again, and this time, she nodded. Nuzzling his face into her hand, he licked and nibbled from her palm to the pad of her thumb, drawing it in between his teeth and shaking it with a soft growl.

She hummed in pleasure, her mouth opening in a silent gasp. He smiled and reached up, covering her hand with his own before threading his fingers around hers, drawing their joined hands down to his hard, muscular thigh. "Do you want to eat before we go?" He looked at her plate as he asked and she nodded again, bemused, incapable of speech at the moment.

Turning to the waitress, he ordered food for himself and another round of drinks for the table. "I hope you can eat with your left hand," he said with a small grin. "I'm not willing to give this up." He pulled their clasped hands to his mouth, kissing the back of her hand gently, rubbing his thumb over her knuckles. *Sweet.*

"Yeah," she spoke on an outrush of breath and raised her eyes to see Willa and the biker watching them attentively. Humming again, she opened her mouth, and then closed it as Bear tucked their hands back into his lap and the backs of her fingers grazed his erection through his jeans. Blowing out a huff of air, she looked at the other man and said, "I'm Eddie."

The biker threw his head back, laughing hard, and she saw Willa look sideways at him. "Yeah, and this is Willa. That's Bear. Ha," he chortled and continued to chuckle for a minute. "I'm Gunny." He shook his head. "Introductions concluded. Debriefing complete. Now can we have a fucking drink?"

***

Bear waited impatiently, sitting beside Eddie, watching her every move. Devouring her with his eyes, he hadn't realized how much he'd missed seeing her face while he was away. It was hell being so close to her, but having to limit himself to innocent contact: his thigh pressing against hers, his arm wrapped across her shoulders and draping down along her ribs, his cheek laid on top of her head, his nose buried in her hair. *Thank God, she's letting me back in.*

He looked down at her plate, watching her sift through the remains of her tacos with the fingertips of one hand, the other one trapped in his and held firmly against the top of his thigh. His throat felt raw, unused, his voice sounding filled with gravel as he asked, "Ready to go?" She didn't look up at him, simply nodding in agreement.

Willa spoke up from across the table. "You drove, Pookie. Don't strand me."

Eddie leaned back, pressing her shoulder blades into his arm, and dug her keys from her front jeans pocket. She went to slide them towards Willa, then paused. "Hold up." She pulled the keys back, separating a small grouping of keys and keeping that in her hand, sliding the main ring of keys across. He looked a question at her and she responded, "My house key."

Bear stood, drawing Eddie up with their joined hands. He settled her on her feet, tipping his head to check if she was too tipsy to ride. Satisfied, he smiled down at her and pulled some bills from his wallet, handing them to Gunny then reached over, picking up the pile from beside her plate and tucking it into her back pocket.

Willa gave him a look meant to wither, then cut her eyes over to Eddie. "Call me, Pookie. Sooner rather than later. I need to know you're okay, girl." Eddie nodded at her, and he felt her fingers tighten around his hand.

Flashing a reassuring smile at Willa, he told her, "See ya, sweetheart," as he tugged Eddie towards the door.

Outside, he smoothed his hands down her arms. "Do you have a jacket?" His hands refused to let her go and he pulled her into his chest, wrapping himself around her. He heard her murmur something, but couldn't make it out, asking, "Hmm? What was that?"

She shook her head, scrubbing her face across his shoulder. "No, Eddie, you said something. What was it?" he pressed her, wanting to know what had distracted her.

"You've got too many clothes on," she reproached in a rough, hoarse voice, and he cupped the back of her head, drawing her face into his neck and pressing her body into his.

"God. Ditto," he said softly. "Here," he dug in his saddlebag for a moment, coming out with his jacket and a helmet, "put these on, Eddie."

She cocked her head. "You bought a helmet?"

"Yeah." It had bothered him that she hadn't worn a lid last time. He wanted to keep her safe; it was his privilege, his responsibility, but he didn't know how to tell her that without sounding like a control freak, so he simply said, "I want you safe."

Pulling it on, she smiled at him. "With you, I *am* safe." Shrugging into the oversize leather jacket, she grinned at him, holding her arms down at her sides so the cuffs hung inches off her hands.

Reaching down, he grabbed the empty sleeves, pushing them gently up her arms until he uncovered her hands. Wrapping his fingers around hers, he lifted both hands to his mouth, kissing the backs of her fingers. "You gonna be warm enough?" he asked, and she nodded.

As they mounted the bike, he realized he couldn't take her to his apartment; it was filled to overflowing with people right now, not the least of which was his mother. She settled in behind him, wrapping her legs tightly around his hips and he closed his eyes, absorbing the electric thrill of having her so close to him. "Eddie, is your place okay?" If she said no, they'd head to a hotel; there was no way he'd be taking her to the clubhouse.

"Yes," she said firmly. He turned his head and captured her mouth in what was meant to be a brief kiss. His lips quested after hers and he twisted around to wrap his arm around her neck, groaning when he felt her fingers sliding through his hair, tugging him closer to her. Swear to God, this woman tore away all his restraint. He pulled back, because if he didn't stop now, he'd be taking her over the tank of his bike in a few minutes and not caring who saw. She was breathing hard, her breasts pressed against him and he felt her heartbeat thudding in her chest.

"Okay then," he rasped, releasing her and turning back to the bike, starting and revving the engine a couple of times. "I remember the way," he said with a small laugh, and then groaned again when she wrapped her arms around his waist, one hand resting low on his belly.

Parking in front of her apartment, he felt her small hands grip his shoulders, balancing herself as she climbed off the bike. She handed him the helmet, but wrapped her arms around the jacket, looking up at him with that damn lip caught between her teeth. He reached out, gathering her to his chest, and held her tightly for a moment. "Inviting me inside this time?" He'd made no move to dismount the bike, wanting to make it clear this was her decision to make.

"If you don't come inside, I'll be disappointed." She spoke the words softly, looking up at him.

"Never been one to let people I care about down." He shifted and stood while keeping his arms loosely around her shoulders. "Wouldn't want to begin with you."

Inside, he looked around curiously, seeing the décor was warm and inviting. There were primitive paintings alongside what looked like stitched wall hangings, and her furniture was a mix of new and old, with the two constants being natural wood and beauty. Tugging at their still joined hands, she drew his attention back to her. Smiling up at him, she started backing down the hallway, pulling at his hand again.

The hallway walls caught his attention. He saw framed pictures of all different sizes, crammed edge-to-edge in the available space. Every picture had someone in it; there were no empty, scenic views. Pictures of her and Willa, Judge and Shooter, a woman who looked so much like her it had to be her mother. Pictures of a young Eddie and Shooter. Pictures of a dozen different kids surrounding one of Tug sitting on an older bike. Posed portraits butted up against candid and action shots, and he saw two photos of what looked like kindergarten classes. There was a picture of Ruby and Lockee that caught at his breath. He'd forgotten how sweet those two were together before everything happened. There was a picture of...him.

He paused, looking at the picture, which had to have been taken several years ago in Checkerz. Right after he'd been patched in, it was the night he'd first seen her up close. Glancing down, he saw the blush rising in her cheeks and knew she didn't want him to see this. Near the picture of him was one of Rafe, as well as his sister and two brothers. Bear focused in on those instead. "You have pictures of Rafe and his family?"

She nodded, stepping back towards him. "I have pictures of lots of my kids." She pointed to clusters of pictures, usually near a central image, like the one of Tug. "I try to hook them up with mentors, people who have more weight than I do in terms of giving advice. These kids hear it all the time from me, but somehow, it means more coming from someone who's not being paid to help take care of them. Tug is amazing with kids." She smiled fondly. "He's always been like that. He was a rock when I was growing up. I don't know what Luke and I would've done without him."

Tracing her fingers across the frame around the picture of him, she said, "And Rafe has you. He's got lots of stories about how good you are to him, and his brothers and sister."

He felt that touch as if she was trailing her fingertips down his naked chest instead of a picture. Tugging sharply at their joined hands, he pulled her into his arms, dropping his mouth onto hers in a desperate kiss. Sliding his hands down and cupping her ass, he pressed against her, hearing the gasp of breath as she moaned into his mouth.

Bending his knees, he slipped his hands down past her ass and wrapped his fingers around her thighs. He straightened, lifting her, bringing her legs up and around his hips. Running one hand up the back of her thigh, he pushed around and underneath, stroking her through the fabric of her jeans. His touch brought another moan to her lips and he ate it down, still slanting his mouth over hers again and again, fucking her with his tongue.

She wrapped her arms around his neck, holding on tightly as he began walking up the hallway. Pulling back, she gasped, "Second door on the left," and then pressed her mouth back to his, sucking and biting at his tongue.

He opened the door, glad there was enough illumination from the hallway to see a clear pathway to the bed. There was no need for lights, no chance for her to withdraw, no hesitancy...he wanted her like she was right now, giving as good as she got, kissing him like he was necessary for her heart to keep beating.

He rested his head against hers as he looked down, seeing the buttons on her shirt, and murmured, "I can manage these." Starting with the top button, he made quick work of them, pushing her shirt open, treating himself to the sight of light green lace barely covering her breasts.

He moved one hand back underneath her, stroking with long, firm touches of his finger, front to back, then forward again. Feeling the heat from her core through the fabric of her pants, he knew she'd feel even better wrapped around his cock. His other hand slipped up her side to her breast, using a finger to pull the cup of her bra down, exposing her hard, pointed nipple. Dropping his head, he stroked it with the flat of his tongue, rolling it into his mouth and sucking gently.

Feeling a moan rattle through her body, he absorbed the vibrations with his mouth, taking even more of her breast in before letting it slip out tenderly. He caught her nipple between his teeth and nibbled gently, then kissed and licked the sting away, leaving only the pleasure.

Moving to her other breast, he licked and sucked it through the lacy material. He tugged with his teeth and pulled the fabric away from her body, hearing her gasp abruptly as he released her. Her arms loosened and he braced one arm across her back under the jacket, continuing to stroke her core firmly with his other hand. Her hands slipped restlessly down over his shoulders and across the leather vest towards the waistband of his pants and he held his breath, waiting to see what she would do.

"You have too many clothes on," she murmured, repeating her words from earlier. He released her deliberately, letting her body slide down the front of his, descending a torturous route across his erection. "Let me help you with that," she said. Kissing his chest, she unfastened the buckle of his belt. Dragging it from the loops, she dropped it on the floor and reached for him again, unbuttoning the fly of his jeans.

He stopped her with one hand covering hers. "Slow," he instructed, waiting until he saw acknowledgement in her eyes before releasing her. He reached out, unfastening the front clasp of that lovely green lace and covered her breasts with his palms as she continued unbuttoning his jeans. The lacy fabric pulled back to the sides under her shirt, leaving her naked and framed by his jacket, the dark leather a pleasing contrast against her creamy skin.

He groaned aloud when the backs of her fingers ran across the swollen head of his cock, setting it throbbing and jerking in his pants. If he wasn't careful, he'd come in his jeans like a teenager. "Slow," he growled again, and she nodded without raising her head.

Seeing her like this, bare to him but covered in his leathers, made him feel more possessive than he'd ever imagined. Gripping the hair at the back of her head, he tugged, raising her face to his for a fierce kiss. "Want you," he groaned against her mouth, raking her bottom lip between his teeth. "We belong." She made a noise in her throat, but that wasn't enough; he needed her to say it back to him. *She was his, dammit.*

He looked into her dark grey eyes, which were clouded with heated desire. Tracing her jaw with the tip of his nose, he tugged at her hair again and kissed her thoroughly, telling her, "Mine. You are mine. You belong to me. Tell me you understand, Eddie." He reached between them, unfastening her pants with one hand and jerking them open enough to slip into her panties, cupping her mound possessively, claiming her. He slid his fingers through her folds, feeling the slippery wetness there. "Wet for me. God, you're drenched.

"Tell me," he said, pushing a finger deep inside her and feeling her hips reflexively lunge against him, taking his finger deeper with every thrust. "This is *mine*." Kissing her, he punctuated every word with a thrust of his wrist, *"You. Are. Mine."*

"Yes," came the word on an outrush of breath. "Yours, Bear."

He gasped with the thrill of her acknowledgement of this thing that had been simmering between them for years. "I need to see you, Eddie, all of you. Need to touch you." He started slipping the jacket and her shirt off her shoulders, taking the bra with them, and then paused. "But I want you wrapped in my leathers. Just my leathers."

Pushing his jeans down mid-thigh, he removed his boots and socks, then let the pants puddle on the floor. He bent down, grabbing at his wallet and pulled a condom from inside, tossing it onto the bed. Taking off his cut, he folded and laid it across the back of a nearby chair, and tugged his t-shirt and thermal over his head, standing unselfconsciously naked while he helped her finish removing her clothes. He reached over, picking the jacket up from the bed where it had fallen, and held it behind her so she could slip her arms back into the sleeves. "I want you like this."

Kissing her again, he pushed his hips into her, shuddering at the sensuous feel of her soft skin against his hardness, the gentle give of her flesh to his insistent thrusts. Dipping down, he bent his knees and slipped his cock between her legs, rubbing the hard length along the lips of her pussy, coating himself in her wetness.

He stroked into her mouth with his tongue using the same rhythm, his cock throbbing as the head swelled with the rush of blood, the skin growing taut as he hardened. The sound of their mouths moving against each other filled the room, as did the rush and brush of his skin against hers as he fucked her thighs, pressing his pelvis against her clit with every push.

Sliding his hands down and across her back, he kneaded her ass firmly with both hands. He pushed his fingers around and down, feeling the wetness spread liberally around by his cock. "God." He breathed into her mouth, stopping mid-stroke, nearly pushed over the edge by the feel of her skin on his, his abdominal muscles clenching and jerking as he strained not to come.

Her mouth made a greedy sound against his neck, and she pushed against him...once, twice...before he sank to his knees in front of her. Using his thumbs to spread her wide, he said in a voice filled with passion, "Stand for me, Eddie. Stand still." Pressing his mouth against her, he nuzzled his nose into her curls and breathed deeply before he delicately flicked her clit with his tongue.

"Ah," she gasped, and he looked up to find her eyes fixed on him, her mouth open. He smiled against her, gently nipping at her clit, then releasing and rolling it with his tongue. Circling the nub with his fingertip, he pushed down her slippery folds to her entrance, levering his finger deeply inside and then retreating, advancing again with two fingers, spreading and stretching her.

Pulling back, he slid in a single digit, and then back to two, alternating the number of fingers inside her with every slow, deep stroke. His tongue continued its assault on her clit, over and over, tirelessly lapping and licking her as he fucked her with his fingers. He pulled her clit into his mouth, rolling the bundle of nerves again.

He heard her intake of breath and heard her say, "Bear," and knew she was close. He felt her stiffen, pushing against him, grinding into his face as she came, her walls clenching down on his fingers tightly, relaxing to clench again as she groaned and sighed, her head sagging backward.

Gently kissing the inside of her thigh, he rubbed his nose up and down her lower lips, drinking in her scent while she came down from her climax. "I can't wait to feel you come like that underneath me, around my cock," he murmured, looking up and locking his eyes on hers, and he smiled to see the flush that accompanied the darkening of her eyes.

"Yeah, you want that too. Don't you, Eddie?" he asked, feeling her fingers tug the hair at the back of his head, trying to pull him away. She was trembling, shaking from the aftermath of her orgasm, struggling to remain standing and still as he'd demanded. Ignoring the sting from her fingers tugging, he pushed his mouth against her, gently drawing her clit into his mouth, rolling it with his tongue again and again, and smiling as he was rewarded with another sharp yank at his hair, this time pulling his face into her.

"Lover," she said, and he thrilled at her use of the pet name. "I can't...my legs won't..." He felt her quivering and raised up to a crouch, kissing along her thighs to her hip and belly. Slowly standing, he slipped his hands below the leather, cupping the sides of her breasts and pressing them together, moving his mouth from one peak to the other, nibbling softly. Rising to his full height, he slid his hands over her ass and lifted her, bringing her with him onto the bed, draping them across the mattress and pillows, dropping down beside her.

"I need to be inside you." He nuzzled the side of her face and captured her lips in a kiss. Moving to his knees, he sat back on his heels as he opened the condom, rolling it down the length of his cock. He grinned with secret knowledge. The condom was new. He'd gone for years without carrying one because he had no need, but once he was certain he was coming back to Fort Wayne, he'd visited a pharmacy and made a purchase.

Moving between her open thighs, he reached down and dragged his fingers along her center, stroking and opening her as he moved his cock to her entrance. He kept his eyes locked on her face, not wanting to miss a moment of having her for the first time as he slowly pushed into her.

***

Moving her hips to meet his slow advance, she used her heels for leverage against the mattress as her thighs spread wider, gasping as he slid in inch by inch, seating himself deep inside with one long, slow stroke. She flexed, straining up against him again, feeling the ridge of his pelvic bone as it pressed firmly into her clit.

"Go slow. Slow. Eddie, slow down. I don't know how long I can last." He exhaled hard. "It's been a long time." He moved deliberately, thrusting in and then pulling out to the edge before gliding in again, setting himself deep every stroke.

She rocked her hips up to meet his next drive, hearing his breathing change again. "I know," she said softly. "It's been a while for me, too. We can go slow, lover. Take your time; I'm not going anywhere."

He stilled and she ran her hands up his biceps to his shoulders, then back down his arms to his hands, threading her fingers between his. He slid her hands up the bed, above her head, stretching full length over her, giving her his weight as he pushed into her again, his knees and thighs pressing her legs apart as she cradled him with her hips.

He released his grip on her hands and lifted onto his elbows, framing her face with his hands. She tipped her head up to kiss him gently. He'd been so possessive earlier, and his greedy desire to have her had ratcheted her need up to match his. Now he was being tender and she smiled against his mouth, this man—her man—seemed to be a contradiction of emotions where she was concerned.

"I won't break," she teased him, clenching her inner walls around his cock. He gasped and his eyes closed, his hips giving an involuntary plunge that she rewarded with another hard clench.

"Mmmmm," he groaned, muscles in his jaw popping as he clenched his teeth. His eyes opened, sweeping her face as he pressed his mouth to hers for a hungry kiss, his tongue demanding she open for him, stroking the inside of her mouth, possessing her. After a moment, he pulled away, resting his forehead against hers while he tried to get his breathing under control. She felt him twitch and jerk inside her, and her breath caught in her chest. “I’m not…experienced, Eddie. I don’t…I’ve not been with…” he trailed off. “I’m not experienced,” he repeated.

“You could have fooled me.” Smiling, she bantered, but then felt him sag, motionless against her. Something was off, his face was a study in stoicism, but the lip clenched between his teeth told a different story. “Lover, it’s been a while for me too,” she repeated herself, reassuring him as she tugged his lip from between his teeth with her own. “More than seven years,” she murmured, kissing along his jawline. She tensed, hoping he wouldn’t make the connection between the time they first saw each other and what she’d inadvertently revealed.

“Eleven for me,” he told her quietly, and she froze. It felt as if her heart were faltering in her chest. From their conversation a few weeks ago, she knew his wife had been dead for eleven years. Did that mean he hadn’t slept with anyone since she died? He pressed his face into the crook of her neck, murmuring, “I’m afraid I won’t make it good for you.”

This wasn’t the right time for that conversation, so she shook her head slowly, murmuring against his neck. “Just love me, Bear. It’s already good; can’t you tell? Baby, if it’s good for you, it will be good for me, and this is sooo good. Tell me what you want.” She moved under him, kissing along his neck and shoulder, running her hands up his biceps and across his back, down to his ass, pulling and tugging him deeper inside her.

He began moving again, picking up the pace, and she felt a sheen of sweat on his body as her hands continued to roam across his skin. He lifted himself onto one elbow, cupping her jaw in his palm and turning her face towards his. “I want to see you,” he said hoarsely, and she felt another orgasm beginning to coil inside, lifting her higher.

They were fucking hard now, the bed shaking and shifting with their movements. His body was moving over hers masterfully, his hips rotating with every down thrust. Her breathing became erratic, her mouth open, gasping for air. He ran his nose along her cheek, breathing his words into her ear. "I want to *see* you." He held her gaze with his, watching as she shattered beneath him, his mouth covering hers as she called his name.

She regained her senses gradually, feeling the clasp of his arms around her, the hard surface of his chest against her breasts, his welcome weight anchoring her to the bed. She felt him inside her, still hard, his cock twitching and jerking with every harsh breath he took. "Baby," she asked, moving her head so she could see his face. "Why didn't you finish?"

He shook his head, closing his eyes, refusing to look at her. *Oh, no you don't,* she thought. *You don't get to shut me out after that.* Still sensitive, she shivered and clenched her inner walls down on him firmly, holding him with little pulses and then releasing deliberately when he groaned, but remained unmoving. She questioned herself, *I'm not that bad in bed, am I?* Feeling uncertainty and fear creeping around the corners of her mind, she quivered beneath him.

"Make it good for me," she pleaded, and that shocked his eyes open, looking straight into hers. "Show me you want me."

***

He'd held back, paying attention to her, reveling in her responsiveness to him, drawing out her reaction to his touch and their lovemaking. When she'd come around him, he'd watched her face, seeing the raw emotion, knowing he'd given it to her, brought her to it. What he hadn't expected to see was the love that shone from her eyes. Seeing her so open and vulnerable, wrapped in his arms, in his leathers, covered by him...she was his, and he was hers. He'd buried his face in the pillow beside her head, listening to her as she came, feeling her shaking and shivering as her orgasm rolled across and through her.

What he'd felt in response scared the shit out of him. They connected on a level far deeper than physical. Every time they met, every encounter—that electrified reaction they'd had to the other should have been his warning, a heads-up that what they would have was soul deep and lasting. He was afraid to expose himself again. He couldn't do that, because he'd lose her. People died and it sucked so bad, made life so fucking hard...and he knew he'd lose her. Eventually, he'd lose her, and he could not go through that. Not again. Thoughts of Andrea and Ashley, Slate and Ruby, flickered through his mind, and he knew he wouldn't survive again. He didn't care what Mason said; he couldn't do that.

She trembled, moved gently against him, and he heard her questioning. He knew she was aware he'd held back, hadn't crested with her, even though it would have been so easy to let go. She tightened around him, holding his still-hard cock inside her. He kept his eyes closed, irrationally thinking, *If I don't see her, I can't love her*. It could still be okay.

The pain in her voice finally registered, tearing his reasoning apart, and he opened his eyes to find her beautiful grey eyes inches away, filling with tears. He saw uncertainty in her gaze and knew she was questioning herself—questioning them. *She's mine,* flew through his mind, and his hips uncontrollably bucked against her as he spoke the word, "Mine." He saw her lips quiver and then curl at the corners as she offered him that damn trusting half-smile, her chin tilting up in a pleasured response, even as a tear trailed down the side of her face.

Pushing into her, he felt her hand slip up his neck to cup the side of his face, the coolness of the leather sleeve pressing against his shoulder. Rearing up, he looked down her body, seeing her pale perfection surrounded with the black leather of his jacket, and he crashed his mouth into hers, the rawness of his emotions stripping him of any finesse. He needed to be as close to her as he could get. Deeper inside her, with her.

"Lover," she named him, murmuring against his lips, her hips moving with and against him. She accepted the punishing pace he set, their bodies slapping into each other hard and fast, slick skin sliding deliciously as they moved together in their passion.

"Eddie," he groaned, and she grabbed at him, pulling him deep as she rocked up to meet him again and again. Clenching around him, he wasn't sure if she was once again close, but he couldn't slow down, couldn't stop the train that was rushing down the tracks towards him. "Fuck," he ground the word out between gritted teeth, arms tightening around her, holding her to him as he jerked and came. His cock buried deep inside her, then he thrust erratically with short strokes.

She tensed and he was afraid he'd hurt her, then heard her reverent, hushed gasp of "Lover" as he felt her climax, triggering more than a few additional plunges of his hips. Slowing, he drew in a hard breath, pulling in their combined scent, sweet, musky, and...her. *Eddie*.

The sound of their wildly erratic breathing filled the room. Outside, he could hear the click and whir of her refrigerator as it kicked on, the sound of far-off traffic, and the roar of motorcycles leaving the parking lot.

The beating of her heart was audible as it thudded against her chest wall; he could feel it where their bodies were connected. It resonated in the center of his chest, underneath his sternum, and he recognized with a shock that it was the same rhythm he'd kept so many nights, tapping with his fingers to that phantom beat.

When he could move again, he shifted to one side, pulling her close for a kiss, exploring her lips with his, gently nibbling and dragging his tongue along the seam where hers were pressed closed, drawing her out and gaining entrance. Licking and stroking softly, leisurely, he worked his mouth across hers, lavishing her with attention, worshiping her with love before easing and slowing.

"Bathroom?" He pressed his forehead against her shoulder, stroking unhurriedly down the center of her chest with his fingertips, feeling her shiver in response.

"Next door," she responded quietly, moving to get up, and he pushed her down with a gentle hand on her shoulder.

"It's okay. I'll be right back." He nuzzled along her jaw, dropping kisses down the column of her neck. Rising from the bed, he pulled off the condom, staring down at her. She was a portrait in sensuality, posed with her hips tilted to one side, one foot casually tucked behind her other knee, his jacket gaping open and exposing both breasts, her nipples rouged and relaxed, her dark hair tumbled around her softly smiling face, her grey eyes hooded with satisfaction. He dipped down for a kiss, telling her, "You are so beautiful."

Coming back with a warm, wet washcloth, he tossed himself onto the bed beside her, bouncing her around a little and earning a laugh. First, he wiped her face ear-to-ear. Seeing the puzzled look on her features, he explained. "I know I was rough." He took in a deep breath. "I want to make sure you are okay. I need to know I didn't hurt you."

She smiled at him. "I'm better than okay, Lover."

He made an agreeable noise, telling her, "Yes, you are."

Washing her breasts carefully, he examined them closely for bruising, seeing nothing except the rosy pebbling of her areolas as her nipples reacted to the coolness of the air after being dampened by the warm cloth. He kissed them, gently kneading with one hand, watching her response to his attention, seeing her face ease and relax even more.

He moved to his knees beside the bed, tugging her hips towards him, pulling her legs and bending them, setting her heels into place on the edge of the bed. He tipped her knees outward, opening her to his examination as he used the still warm cloth to gently clean her most private area, working it in between her folds and carefully around her clit, knowing she was sensitive and taking care not to stimulate too much.

This was something Andrea had always loved, him tending to her after they had sex. He was glad to see Eddie enjoyed it after making love too. That thought made him pause. Why would he think of what he'd done with Andrea as sex, but with Eddie as love? He had loved Drea.

Shaking his head, he stood, gently shifting her into the middle of the bed, and tugged the covers up and over her, still wrapped in his leathers. Depositing the cloth in the bathroom, he came back, crawling into bed and wrapping his arms around her. He tucked her into his chest, holding her as he fell asleep, whispering her name.

32 - Nice jacket

Eddie stretched as she woke, jerking when her hands encountered a hard body in the bed beside her. Her eyes flashed open to find amused green ones looking down at her. “Hi,” she whispered, her gaze traveling across his face, smiling and open as he leaned over her.

“Hi back atcha,” he responded, dropping down to place a chaste kiss on her lips.

She turned her head, gauging the time as mid-morning from the light seeping in around the window curtains. “Hungry?” she asked, moving to roll out of bed, finding herself trapped by his body as he angled across her, holding her in place.

“Starving,” he said, rolling his hips into hers, pressing his erect cock against her, sliding it over and across her clit, drawing a gasp from her as her inner muscles tightened involuntarily. “I find myself extremely,” he thrust his hips again, “hungry this morning.” He lowered his head, capturing her mouth in a hard kiss, pulling back to nibble his way along her jaw, nuzzling into her neck below her ear and nibbling her skin softly. “Eddie,” he growled, “I want you.”

Biting down on her bottom lip, Eddie moved her legs, spreading to accept his width and weight, cradling him. She was already wet and ready for him, aroused by his words and desire for her, and with one slow stroke, he thrust inside as she gripped his arms, fingers tightening convulsively around his muscles. He slid one hand down her ribs and across to her ass, tugging at her leg, bringing it up to rest against his hip as he drove deeper, pulling another gasp from her.

"Eddie," he groaned, lips questing for hers, and he slid his tongue deep into her mouth, stroking hers with the same intensity he was using to fuck her. "God," he ground out. "You are so hot." He pulled his head back, looking at her. "You belong to me." He made it a statement, a declaration, as he had last night, and she shuddered underneath him, his possessive words evoking a primitive reaction and her orgasm slammed through her.

He abruptly pulled out, dropping his cock onto her stomach and ejaculating on her skin there. She felt him jerk and twitch, hot liquid pooling on her belly. "God, Eddie," he groaned. Sliding off her to one side, his hand moved up her body to her breasts, moving the jacket to the sides so he had a clear view. Trailing his fingers through the thick liquid, he smeared it up, massaging it into her skin. Bringing his hand down, he pushed his fingers inside her, drawing out her wetness, mixing and spreading it with his semen. He brought a finger tentatively up towards her lips, and she heard his gasp of pleasure as she greedily pulled it into her mouth, sucking and licking it clean.

"That's so hot, Eddie. Holy...why is that so hot?" he asked with a gasp, and she felt his cock twitch where it rested against her side and hip.

She pursed her lips, running her tongue deliberately over them, taking in every iota of flavor. Smiling at him, she quietly said, "More," and opened her mouth, waiting.

"Fuck," he ground out, leaning over and kissing her hard, his hand swiping across her belly and bringing more to her lips as requested. He kissed her around his fingers, their tongues swirling and clashing, sharing as they devoured each other.

Long minutes later, he rested his head on her shoulder, her fingers trailing through his hair while his hand played across the sticky mess on her skin. "Because you marked me," she said. She smiled as she felt him jerk; he'd been a million miles away and seemed to have forgotten he'd asked a question. He tipped his head up and she laughed. "It's hot, because you marked me and I loved it."

"Mmmm," he murmured in agreement. "Hot."

"It was," she agreed and laughed again, "and now it's not, because it's sticky." She raised on her elbows to look down her body, watching as his hand traced designs across her skin. "I'm going to grab a quick shower."

"Okay if I start some coffee?" he asked tentatively, looking unsure.

"Lover," she leaned down, resting her lips on his, "anything you want to do is okay. In my house, with my body...anything." Kissing him hard, she didn't give him a chance to respond before she jumped from the bed, grudgingly removing the jacket for the first time since he'd put it on her naked form last night. "I might be in love with that jacket," she said teasingly. She shivered, missing the warmth of the leather, but the humor fell from her face as he whipped his head around to look at her.

Trying to recover the easy feeling, she joked, "What? It's a nice jacket." Turning for the hallway, she walked steadily out, intensely conscious of her nudity, but unwilling to admit it by grabbing her robe from the back of the door.

Resting her head against the inside of the bathroom door, she rolled it back and forth against the hard wood, chastising herself. "What the hell are you doing, Eddie?" She whispered, "This can't be anything more than what it is. You don't do bikers, woman."

Startled by a soft tapping on the surface at her back, she quickly moved as the knob turned and the door was pushed open. "What's your stance on global warming?" He walked in and closed the door behind him, standing naked, carefully watching her reflection in the mirror.

"Global warming?" She was confused, tilting her head with her question.

"Yeah, global warming. Is it a thing, or not?" He leaned into the shower enclosure, turning on the water and testing with his hand, adjusting until satisfied, and then tugging on the lever that turned the showerhead on.

"Uh...it's a thing, I think." She was still unsure what he was doing.

"Okay then, good thing I decided to conserve water and shower with you." He turned to her, wrapping his hands around her hips, pulling her into him. "Since it's a thing and all."

She lowered her eyes and he lifted her chin with his hand, cupping his fingers around her jaw. "I made you self-conscious back there. I didn't mean to. It caught me off guard; that's all. What you said." Leaning in to kiss her, he said, "I'm sorry." Looking into her face, he continued, "Sorry I was an ass, Eddie. Not sorry you might love that jacket."

She offered him a halfhearted grin and a shrug. "It is a nice jacket."

"It is," he agreed solemnly, "and it looks good on you. That jacket that you might love, it looks really good on you. You look exquisite in it. Totally hot." He smoothed a hand up her side, cupping and lifting her breast as he bent down to take the tip into his mouth.

Smiling widely now, she responded more confidently, cradling his head to her chest. "It does look hot on me."

He picked her up, stepping into the shower with her pressed against his body, pushing her up against the tile wall, warm from the flow of water. He gripped behind her knee, picking her leg up, and his cock stroked deep inside her on a slow thrust. "I look hot on you," he spoke, with his mouth against her neck. Bending his knees and lifting her again, he settled them against the wall. Her legs wrapped around him as he pounded into her, hard and fast, the steam swirling around them.

***

They spent the day in careless relaxation, effortlessly picking up where their conversation had left off weeks before. Lying on the couch together, her head was on his shoulder as she looked up at him, the TV on as background noise. "Are you more like your road name, or your given name?" She watched with apparent avid interest as he thought about her question.

"My road name means more to me," he told her. "It was given to me by Mason, my president. Actually, a good man said it first, but he's no longer with us. You knew Lockee. It was her dad, Winger. It seemed silly at first; I wasn't even in the club at the time, just loved working on my bikes. I've...grown into the name."

"Fair enough." She nodded, agreeing, rubbing her cheek against his bare chest. "I was almost afraid you'd be all burly and furry when I got your shirt off," she laughed, trailing her fingers across his nearly hairless chest, tracing downward to where the slim trail of dark, curly hair led off his abdominals and into the waistband of his pants. He sucked in a quick breath, trapping her hand with one of his and holding it tightly against his chest.

After a moment, he chuckled, registering what she'd said. "Never thought of it that way." Snorting, he said, "When Winger said it, he was upset, because DeeDee had walked into the room where I was sleeping and found me naked. He yelled at her and ran her out, then told her to keep the girls away from the guy who was 'big as a fucking bear'. Mason picked up on it, and I was so named."

Drawing lines with her fingertip, she followed the dips and planes across his chest. Smiling, she kissed his pectoral, darting her tongue out to lick across the flat, brown nipple. He drew in a breath, gasping, and she giggled at his reaction, nestling down beside him. He loved hearing her like that; she sounded relaxed and happy. Her next question brought him back into focus. "You don't call me by any pet names. Why is that?"

"Ummm." He took in a deep, satisfied breath, pressing his lips to the top of her head. *I could kiss her forever*, he thought. "For now, you are Eddie to me. That name encompasses everything you are. I don't want to minimize my feelings by substituting a name for yours. I don't need to distract myself from who you are. You are Eddie. Wonderful advocate for kids who desperately need your help. Eddie, who looks delicious wet in the shower. Totally fuckable when dressed only in my jacket. Yeah, that's Eddie too."

Tilting her head, she looked up at him with a frown. "Is that what pet names mean to you? A way to minimize feelings? Does it bother you when I call you 'lover' or 'baby'?"

He drew in another breath, tensing his arms around her as he shook his head. He needed to explain, make her understand. "Nope. Doesn't bother me at all. I think it's endearing. I don't have anything against pet names, but I don't have an appropriate one for you yet that means as much to me as your name does." He smiled down at her. "Call me anything you want. I'm okay." He frowned. "Well, except for one thing."

"What don't you want me to call you?" she asked, surprised.

"Just the one thing." He paused, waiting until her eyes found his to sell the joke. "Don't call me Pookie. I've seen your brother's face when that happens. It's not pretty."

She laughed. "Lukie Pookie. Willa's a goofball."

"Why does she call you Pookie?" His thumb stroked in small circles on her hip, gently caressing her through the long t-shirt she wore.

"I wouldn't let her call me Pooh." She grinned, moving her hand across his chest again.

"She wanted to call you poo? Like shit?" He made a face and shook his head. "That's messed up."

Laughing, she corrected him, "No. Not poo, Pooh, with an 'h'. Like Winnie the Pooh."

"So Pooh became Pookie?" He kissed the top of her head again. "That's still messed up."

"I guess you had to be there," she said, moving against him restlessly.

"Oh, yeah? I think I'd rather be here," he said quietly, tipping her chin up with a finger and kissing her softly. He rolled her to her back and covered her with his body. "Or here. I'd rather be here," he repeated, rubbing his hardening cock against her silky panties. Reaching down, he slid the crotch to the side and used his fingers to open her, pushing gradually inside. "Mmmm. Wet for me. I'd much rather be here," he whispered, thrusting deep and holding. His eyes closed as he tightened, moving against her by minute amounts, surrounded by her heat. She moaned and he savored her clearly growing desire.

"Here is my favorite place. Definitely here," he murmured against the side of her head, making slow love to her, stroking her body with his cock and hands. He was licking and nibbling on her earlobe, her neck, dipping his head down across her chest to her breast, drawing it into his mouth.

She arched under him, gripped with a gentle orgasm, her mouth open and gasping softly for breath. He slowed and stilled, waiting for her eyes to open and come to his. He needed to ask this question, but required her full attention. "Eddie," he said when she looked at him at last. She made an inquisitive noise in acknowledgment, and he laughed once, and then again when her eyes opened wide at his cock jerking inside her.

"Eddie," he began again, and sobered. "Are you on birth control?"

She closed her eyes, tipping her face to the side, saying quietly, "No."

Dammit, he thought. Saying aloud, "Fuck, Eddie, this is the third time I've been inside you without protection." He thrust deeply, groaning. "You feel so good," he said, moving reluctantly to pull out. She surprised him, locking her ankles around his ass, not letting him leave her body.

"I know it's not foolproof, but it's the safest part of my cycle," she said. Lifting her eyes to meet his again. "Pull out only if you want to." She relaxed her legs back down, her knees tucked tight around his hips.

"My job to keep you safe," he whispered to her, rolling off her and striding into the bedroom, coming back out tearing a condom wrapper with his teeth. Making quick work of rolling it down his length, he stretched out on top of her again.

"My job to make it good." Grasping her clit between his fingers and thumb, he pulled and rolled, covering her mouth with his as she gasped. He slid his cock between the folds of her pussy, lubricating the condom before he stroked deep into her with a single, driving thrust.

33 - Take the ride

"Sugar." Waking, she heard the deep rumble of his pleased, satisfied voice through the wall of his chest, where her ear was pressed against it. Smiling because he'd picked out a pet name for her, she lifted her head to find him still asleep, but shifting in the bed beside her, his rest uneasy.

"Sugar and sweetness," he murmured, his face soft and relaxed as he dreamed. "My angels."

She pulled back when he moved and thrashed a little. "No." This pain-filled sound was drawn out and low. A muscle ticked in his jaw as his teeth audibly ground together. He wasn't dreaming about her. "Run, sweetness," he sighed deeply, taking in a swelling breath as his face twisted, his movements becoming more agitated, panting and repeating, "Run, sweetness. Ash."

He jerked awake, and she barely had time to register his wide, unfocused eyes before he was off the bed, his steps erratic as he walked to the wall, doubling over to lean his forehead against the plaster. Trembling, his hands clenched into fists over and over, the pattern of tighten and release, tighten and release exhausting to watch.

"Bear?" She spoke his name into the still air of the room and saw him lurch upright like she'd lashed him. Turning around to face the bed, his gaze darted over her and away, as if he couldn't stand to look at her. Maybe he couldn't stomach the sight of her in the bed before him. He seemed to take in the darkened room, one hand rising, fingers thumping against his chest in an irregular rhythm. His other hand reached up to cover the bottom portion of his face, thumb and fingers touching opposite cheekbones, his mouth entirely covered by his palm as if fearing what would escape if he didn't physically control himself.

He stood like that for what seemed like hours, eyes roaming the room, corner to corner, his body frozen in place. Deliberately pulling his hand away from his face, he kept the fingers of his other hand tapping out that uneven beat on his sternum.

"Eddie," he spoke flatly, his voice emotionless, and her heart sank, because with that one word, she knew he was leaving. He'd already pulled back from her, and there was an almost tangible absence in the room, as if he was already gone, even as he still stood before her not ten feet away. He would leave and there was nothing she could do to hold onto him.

Dammit, she'd looked for him, wanted this for so long, and wanted him. She wasn't going to give up without a fight. Part of a line from the movie *Fear and Loathing in Las Vegas* ricocheted through her brain, *'Buy the ticket, take the ride'*, right?

She thought about the picture painted on his tank, the angels who looked up at him every time he straddled the bike. The ones he touched so tenderly when he rode, before he got on the road, stroking the paint with a slow fingertip, sometimes without even realizing he was doing so. His angels. His wife and daughter. "You're still in love with your wife." She meant it as a statement, and he took it that way, simply nodding in answer. "There's no room for three of us in the bed, Bear." His eyes settled on her for a moment, and she saw tear tracks on his cheeks. "Not enough room, baby." He looked at her, into her...and shook his head. He'd only spoken the single word since awakening, only her name, nothing else.

"You said I belonged to you," she reminded him composedly, thinking of how intense he'd been when he said it earlier, when he called out 'mine' as he touched her, convincing her it was truth. "You said we belonged." She shifted, sitting cross-legged on the bed, beginning to silently weep with the sheet pooled around her waist.

She watched as his eyes slowly cleared and the thumping of his fingers at last gained rhythm, his breathing easing as some of the tightness left his shoulders and arms.

"Mine," he breathed, walking back towards the bed, gathering her into his arms as he stretched out beside her, laying his head on her shoulder and closing his eyes with a sigh. His fingers transferred to her chest, resting for a moment on her breastbone, and then he tapped out a rhythm in time with her heartbeat. He was still gently tapping when she finally dozed off, unable to keep herself awake, but no longer afraid he'd be gone when she awoke.

***

He felt the soft brush of hair against his back, recognizing the weight of an arm where it lay wrapped around his waist. Slowly surfacing from sleep, he found his hand wrapped around Eddie's much smaller one, holding it tightly to his hip. Lying there, he stretched, finding his muscles used, but not quite sore from the activities of the night...and day...and night before. It felt good. He felt alive.

Turning onto his back, he twisted in her embrace, slipping his arm under her head and cradling her into his side. He settled her on his shoulder so he could stroke up and down her bare back. Her skin felt so silky under his fingers. Seeing goose bumps on her skin, he tugged the sheet up to cover her, sliding his arm underneath, maintaining constant contact with her oh-so-addictive skin.

He tipped his head down, looking into her face, and stilled when he saw distinct evidence of tears there. Had he hurt her last night? He'd been careful, holding himself in check, and had looked her over more than once to make sure his greedy hunger for her hadn't resulted in injury. Cupping her head in his palm, he gently rocked her in the bed, humming a nonsense tune until he remembered, and the song abruptly dried up in his chest.

He had hurt her, but not physically. He'd dreamed. In the bed beside her, he'd dreamed of his angels. She'd seen the aftermath of the nightmare, seen him destroyed.

He'd been set to run, do what he did best and go somewhere to get out of his head, but she'd stopped him. *How?* How'd she talked him down, gotten him back into bed? Gotten him to go back to sleep, that place that held so much fear for him?

Closing his eyes, he again saw her sitting in the middle of the mattress, surrounded by white sheets and pillows, her dark hair tumbling around her shoulders. She'd said something. What was it? Frustrated, he blew out a harsh breath between his teeth, and sleep disturbed, she rolled away from him, turning onto her back.

He snuggled down in beside her, resting his head on her pillow, lifting the sheet enough to get his arm around her body, cupping one breast in his palm. He calmed and moved his hand, releasing her breast and resting his fingertips in the center of her chest. Eyes closed, with a shiver of terror, he heard her voice telling him there wasn't room in her bed for him. *No, that's not what she'd said. There wasn't room for three.* He shook his head faintly, moving so his ear was flat against her chest.

His hand moved, fingers lightly tapping out a rhythm between her breasts, keeping time with the heartbeat beneath his head, echoing in his ear. *You said I belonged to you.* She'd thrown that out like a challenge. Why? Because she'd seen he was about to run?

He sighed, his mouth moving against her soft skin. Moving his hand, he cupped her breast, tipping it up towards his mouth, capturing the nipple between his lips and stroking it leisurely with his tongue. "Mine," he murmured. "Forever mine. You've always belonged to me. Mine."

He felt her fingers sifting through his hair gently, softly massaging and relaxing him. "Yours," her sleepy voice agreed with him once again, tracing his cheekbone with the pad of her thumb. "Bear?" Sounding more awake, her lifting tone indicating it was a question.

"Hmmm?" He kissed her skin gently, cupping her breast again, rolling her nipple between his fingers.

"Tell me about them," she said, and this wasn't framed as a question, but it was. It was an invitation to bring them out. This was her asking him to trust her with his stories, his past—with his angels. An appeal for him to let her in, show her who he was before they were gone, and afterwards.

He made a noise and felt her fingers tighten in his hair, just short of painful. He'd welcome some pain right about now, embracing anything that would occupy his mind and relieve him of the responsibility to tell the stories right, take away the fear he could never do them justice. There was an obligation to make her understand how he still loved them, but differently from when they were here beside him. He still loved them, but because the pain of losing them never got better, never went away, the heart covered it with distance. Overlaying it with a measure of space, of grace, blunting the pain, and along the way, gaining a different love.

He still loved them, but it was a shadow, a distant cousin to what he'd once felt. And what he now felt for Eddie was so much more powerful and present. Their connection was so compelling and potent there was no way to consider it a betrayal of his past loves. She was addicting, arousing, and through everything, he needed her. She had staying power. He smiled, knowing she didn't yet understand, and he moved up past her shoulder, resting on the pillow near her head.

She looked at him as he began, "When I was thirteen, we moved to Bayonne, and our house was next door to the one Andrea and Joel lived in..."

34 - Quiet changes

It had been almost two months. Standing in the kitchen, he looked around the apartment, seeing the changes his mother had made. It looked homey, as if someone lived here now, even if that someone wasn't him. He spent far fewer nights here and was splitting his time away between Eddie's apartment and the Foscan household. Rubbing one hand along his jaw, he smiled to see his mom sitting on the couch, Miguel tucked in alongside her as she read aloud to him.

None of the apartments were big enough for their whole clan, but Myron was on the lookout for something that would work to house all of them. Eddie had a friend watching the listings too, but they needed a big house. A *big* house, one with at least seven bedrooms, unless he wanted the boys to bunk up, and he didn't, because they each needed their own space. Fortunately, he had a healthy bank account, money he'd never touched due to the source. He couldn't think of a better use of it than making a home for kids who hadn't had one before.

Movement across the room caught his eye, and he saw Lucia walking up the hallway, looking back over her shoulder at Eddie. She was laughing at something Eddie had said, and his chest clenched painfully and then swelled with joy at their easy affection and warmth. Eddie didn't treat Luce like a kid, which made her a good ally for the girl. Add to that her comfortable way with Rafe and the boys, and it was a nearly-perfect fit all around. *How the hell did I get so lucky?*

When Mason first suggested he adopt the kids, he'd balked outright. There was no way it was a good idea, not with everything rolling through the club at the time. The kids didn't need reminders of their dad, and Bear would be that, every time they laid eyes on him. He argued they had their grandmother, Rabid's mom, and had only known him a few years.

He and Mason had been holed up in Chicago dealing with all the shit coming about from Devil's Sins and Ruby's abduction, and he couldn't see his way past the next day, much less promise the rest of his fucking life. Mason now claimed it was his stubborn refusal that was the reason they'd had to be gone so long.

The paperwork would be final in another month, and their merged family already felt effortlessly comfortable. His smile faded around the edges, this...the kids were one of the best parts in his life right now. But, unless he was with Eddie, he hadn't slept well in weeks, dreams filled with dark pathways where he could see bare feet running, flying along in front of him, sometimes catching a glimpse of white-gold hair tossed over a slim shoulder.

He shook the worn memories away, eyes fixed on the sway of Eddie's hips as she walked towards him. She *was* the best part of his life, the place where the most good happened. He'd never get tired of this woman and was amazed every day that she was interested in him, wanted him, and wanted to be his. Pulling his gaze to her face as she neared, he caught her amused but patient grin when he lifted lips in a definite demand, quickly met as she leaned down, kissing him.

"Rafe and Roderigo will be back soon and we can leave," she said, seating herself across his lap, wrapping her arms around his neck.

"Leave?" he asked, kissing her again.

"You are at the kids' apartment tonight," she reminded him. "School day tomorrow. I need to sleep at home. Willa is coming over later; we've got a grant to write for technology aids for some of our kids."

He frowned. "I want to sleep with you." It seemed a reasonable request to him, but then again, he wanted to spend every second with her, which she seemed to think was a bit unreasonable.

Leaning the side of her head against his, she watched his mom with Miguel. "Maggie's good for him," she whispered. "His *abuela* doesn't read English. He'll be effortlessly bilingual with two doting grandmothers."

He jerked in surprise and she looked at him. After a moment, she shook her head in amusement and rested it against his shoulder. He looked at his mother with opened eyes. She'd taken on the role of a grandmother once and had it brutally ripped away. Now it seemed she was again offered the opportunity. He hadn't thought of it that way, but sure as anything, here she'd gone from having none, to having four grandchildren. His heart stuttered. He'd been a dad. Closing his eyes, he thought, *"Ashley"* only becoming aware he'd spoken aloud when Eddie stiffened in his arms.

He kissed the top of her head, murmuring so only she could hear him, "I just realized I'm gonna be a dad."

Stirring on his lap, she looked up at him with a perplexed look on her face. "You never stopped being a dad."

Or a husband, he thought, settling her back against his chest.

***

"I'm not really okay with you getting your license," he said, watching Lucia's face for a clue about her thoughts.

She lowered her head and he was surprised, thinking that would be it, but then she straightened and looked him in the face. "There are more than five million registered drivers in Indiana. Most of them go their whole lives without being in a wreck. The likelihood of my being involved in an accident, let alone a serious one, is small. I am nearly as likely to be in a wreck riding the city bus."

He didn't know if she was making this up, but it got his attention.

"I know Andrea and Ashley died in a car crash. Eddie's friend Lockee died too. That doesn't mean I will," she said. "If I get my license, I could help with the boys more, and it would make getting to classes much easier for me. I would like to take the test, and if I pass, then I can practice driving with you. If you believe I am not good enough, then I will drop it, but I would at least like the option of trying."

She'd lived too long without options for him to tell her no on this one. Her arguments were reasonable, after all. "Okay," he said with a shrug, and she grinned at him.

"Okay?" came her question, and he nodded. "Okay," she repeated more firmly.

"If you do well, you get to teach Rafe," he said, turning to walk quickly out of the room.

"Hey!" her surprised shout sounded behind him. "Not fair!"

***

Six months, and he was still comfortable. Myron had found them a home. It was huge, with five bedrooms upstairs and two down, as well as a finished basement. On Wayne Street, it was in the historical district, near Marie's. They'd moved in quickly. The kids were excited to have so much room in the house, as well as their own bedrooms, something they'd never had before.

His mother decided not to move, surprising him. She wanted to stay in the downtown apartment by herself. She'd settled in, taking a part-time job at a law firm, and she seemed to be enjoying herself. Tug had been a frequent visitor for the past few weeks, after his mom had been formally introduced to him at a family barbeque. His mom had taken the news of him being in a club much better than he'd expected, which made life a lot easier to explain.

Eddie was at the new house a lot, but not as much as he'd like; her job kept her busy, helping her kids. His cock thickened, throbbing as he remembered last night here at her house. He had to admit there were special benefits to having privacy. He'd made love to her in the kitchen, setting her ass on the edge of the countertop and plunging into her hard and fast as her fingers wrapped around the edge, holding herself in place against his frenzied thrusts.

He'd pulled up a chair and eaten his fill too, glad they were past condoms, because he could not get enough of seeing his semen mixed with her cream, smeared over her belly and thighs as she begged him to lick her, suck her, love her.

Seated at her desk, he reached down and adjusted himself, shaking his head. Idly wondering what her schedule was today, he tugged her calendar towards him. He stared at the date for a full minute, his head bowing under the weight as awareness crashed down on him. Yesterday had been the anniversary. He hadn't even thought about his angels. It used to be a date he was conscious of for weeks, sometimes months in advance, and it had slipped by unnoted. *How was that possible?* How had he forgotten about...it?

His phone rang and he absently pulled it from his pocket, answering without looking at the screen. "Is this Rob Crew?" The question came over the line, and he pulled the phone away, looking to see it was a local number.

"Yeah," he responded. "Who's this?"

"Mr. Crew, this is Cathy Hunt, ER coordinator at Lutheran Hospital," he heard, and his breath froze in his chest. "I'm afraid there's been an accident."

35 - New beginnings

Mason pulled his wallet from his pocket, twisting the chain that held it to his belt familiarly out of the way as he pulled the small piece of paper out. Smoothing it carefully on his desk, he looked at the numbers written there, along with a name, and picked up his phone. His gaze drifted up to the wall, going to the picture of Mica hanging there. She sat on her bike, generous lips smiling widely as she laughed at something Slate had said, hand to the back of her head, smoothing down her pigtails from where her helmet had rucked them up.

As he'd done at least once a week in the months since it had been tucked into his hand, he dialed the numbers and then sat there, looking down at the phone before hitting the cancel button on the screen. He smoothed the paper again, trailing one fingertip along the writing, and this time, his eyes didn't drift as he punched them in. Without hesitation, he hit the call button and sat waiting for it to connect.

"Hey," her voice said brightly, followed by a second or two of silence, then, "Gotcha. I'm not able to take the call right now, but leave...well, you know what to do. Ciao!" The message tone sounded and he sat for a moment too long, trying to think of what he could say. Hearing the tone indicating time was up, he threw the phone on the desk and ground out, "*Fuucck.* What the *fuck* are you doing, Davis Mason?"

Hearing a far off, "Hello? Hellllooo?" he looked down to see the call hadn't disconnected. Picking up the device gingerly, he lifted it to his ear, hearing her voice moving away from the speaker, saying, "I thought I heard someone, but now there's nothing."

"Willa?" he asked, and heard an indrawn breath on the other end of the line.

"Yes," she answered, and then said his name softly, questioningly, "Mason?"

He smiled involuntarily. *She recognized my voice*. After meeting him once, months ago, she recognized him. He knew he'd have been able to pick her out of a crowd with his eyes closed, but she had *known him*. Shaking his head, he asked gruffly, "Are you going to the wedding this weekend?"

"Yeah," she hummed, and then cleared her throat. "I mean, yes?" She sighed, saying the words more forcefully, "*Yes*, I'm going to the weeding. I mean the wedding. Yes. I'm going." She cleared her throat again and fell silent.

"You need a ride?" he asked.

She squeaked, "With you?"

"Yeah. With me. That's what I'm asking." He smiled; she was kinda kooky.

He heard a huff of air, and then she said firmly, "Yes." She cleared her throat again. "Yes, I would like to ride with you."

"All right. I'll pick you up Friday night. We're staying at the inn overnight. Pack a bag, small, mind you. Wear jeans for the ride up." He paused, waiting for her to respond, but when she didn't say anything, he finished with, "I'm real ready to see your face. Glad you said yes." He disconnected the call and raised his eyes, but this time, he didn't pause on the picture on the wall, instead seeing chestnut hair, hazel eyes, and an amused half-smile. He was taking slightly-kooky Willa to Slate and Ruby's wedding, and he was nervous for the first time since he could remember. He laughed and thought, *Fucking A*.

***

Eddie looked at her friend in astonishment. "Did you just make a *date* with Davis Mason? The same Davis Mason who Daddy and I both warned you off? *That* Davis Mason?"

Willa glanced over at her, but from her wide eyes, it was clear nothing was sinking in right now. Eddie shook her head and reached back from her stool at the breakfast bar to pull open the freezer and grab out the Goldschlager. Twisting the other way, she took a glass from the cabinet. Setting both in front of her, she looked at Willa again, a question on her face. At her friend's silent, slow, sober nod, she poured a generous amount into the glass and made a motion to push it over in front of her, but stopped when Willa shook her head. "More?" she asked, and got a frantic, fast nod in response.

Splashing another measure of liquor into the glass, she glanced up at Willa, who nodded again and reached out for the glass. Taking one small sip, she resumed looking into the space above Eddie's head, then took a larger gulp from the glass.

"Yes," she said, taking another drink before pulling up a stool facing Eddie.

"You did," Eddie agreed, bringing a bottle of tequila from the freezer before grabbing herself a glass. "You fucking did. You made a date—*a fucking date*—with the President of the Rebel Wayfarers club. A fucking bike club president. *National* president. Wills, they don't make dates. Presidents like him don't make dates...they just...I dunno, look at what Daddy did with Judge's mom. They just fuck, I guess. I know Bear thinks the world of him, and so does Slate, but still—men like him don't date." She poured herself a half-glass of tequila, picking it up before she even set down the bottle, taking a long drink.

"We're going to the wedding," Willa said, finishing off her schnapps and setting her glass down in front of Eddie for a refill. "He's picking me up Friday. I'm supposed to wear jeans," she giggled.

"Friday? What the hell? The wedding isn't until Saturday. Why is he picking you up Friday?" Eddie frowned, thinking she wasn't going to like the answer to this question.

"Friday," Willa confirmed. "We're staying at the inn the night before," she giggled again, her voice rising on the last few words as if it were a question.

Eddie's mouth fell open and she snorted a laugh. Pinching her thumb and finger together, she used them to point at Willa for emphasis. "What. The. Fuck. Booty call...you get a booty call and you agree—with no argument, mind you—to spend the night with a man you met for twenty minutes, once...nearly a year ago."

She tipped more liquor into Willa's glass and shook her head. "What am I going to do with you, Wills?" Sliding the glass back over to her friend, she lifted her own and clinked the rim against Willa's, snorting her laughter. "Here's to hoping he's worth the effort in bed. A fucking booty call. At least it's not a date!"

***

Bear rose from the couch in reaction to the furious, persistent knocking at the front door, shifting a sleeping Miguel off his lap. "Hold on; I'm coming," he called, striding across the room. Flinging the door open, he leaned against the frame with one arm, surprised at his visitor. "Tug, man," he said with a grin, "didn't know you were coming over. Come on in. Want a beer?" Stepping back, he opened the door farther, walking away towards the kitchen.

"Yeah, beer'd be good," came in response and he heard the door close. "How's the boy?"

"He's good. Doc said it was a clean break; he'll be healed in a couple of weeks. Goose looked him over too, said his arm was looking all right. Fucking kids." He shook his head, setting two bottles on the countertop, pushing one across to where Tug was standing. "What brings you by, brother?"

Tug had a pensive look on his face, and he glanced around the apartment. "Maggie around?" he asked casually, picking up his bottle.

"Nope, she's shopping with DeeDee and Ruby, picking up some last minute things for the wedding." He cocked one eyebrow and asked, "Whatcha need, Tug?"

"So she's going to the wedding? She's already planning on being there?" Tug wriggled his mustache back and forth, then reached up to stroke it smooth.

"Yeah, I think so." Taking a drink from his beer, he asked, "Why ya askin', Tug?" He was pulling the old man's leg. He already knew there was potential for something between his mom and his friend. "Wonder who she's going with?" he mused.

Tug bristled, taking a long drink from his bottle. "You think she's going with someone?" He put down the bottle and unbuttoned the cuffs of his shirt, distractedly folding them up his forearms. "Goddammit," he muttered, then lifted his head. "Don't tell her I came by," he warned, turning to walk towards the door.

"Tug...brother," Bear laughed, "I'm fucking with ya. She's going, but with me and Eddie; she isn't with anyone. Stick around. She'll be back in thirty or so. I think she'd be glad to see you here," he grinned. "Not giving you my blessing, mind. That'd be fucked up."

He sobered, continuing, "Brother, I need you to hear me. Need you to listen to me. I'm gonna tell you here and now—don't fuck with her. Do not fuck with her. You got me? If you screw with her and she gets hurt, brothers or not, I'll fucking kill you."

Pulling the corners of his mouth down, Tug scowled at Bear for a moment, and then they both heard the sound of a key in the front door and turned that direction. Bear laughed soundlessly at the look of fear and anxiety that swept over Tug's face before the man could smooth it away.

"Robby," his mother sang from the hallway, "can you come help me with these bags?"

He made a mocking bow to Tug, watching as his friend moved towards the door. Tug paused for a second, looking back at him. He nodded, telling Bear, "Good man. I got ya. I'd expect nothing less, brother."

Bear caught a glimpse of his mother's face when she recognized Tug, and he saw wonder and pleasure there. "Mike," she said, "I didn't expect to find you here. What a nice surprise."

"Let me get those for you, Maggie," Tug said gruffly, quickly moving to take the bags from her hands, then stooping to scoop up the ones from the floor. "Did ya buy the store out, woman?" He pretended to stagger beneath the weight, drawing a laugh from her as she gently slapped his shoulder.

Bear bit his lip, holding back a smile, and decided to leave them to get to know each other better. "Mom, Miguel's asleep on the couch. His pills are in the kitchen and he could have another one any time, if he's in pain. I'm headed over to Eddie's for a bit," he said, grabbing his jacket. "I think Tug wanted to know your plans for the wedding. I'll be back about eight to grab the boy. See ya." He scooted around them, turning his face away and smirking at the wide-eyed look of panic on Tug's face.

"Okay, Robby. Tell Eddie hello from me," she said, turning back to Tug. "I'm going to the wedding, if that's your question, Mike," he heard his mom say as he closed the door on Tug's reply.

36 - Exes and ohs

Bear looked around at the crowd milling across the fields of the campground. Standing around one of the fire pits with a dozen Rebels, he tried identifying the various other patches on Slate and Ruby's wedding guests, giving up when he didn't recognize some of the ones from the far western states. Hundreds of people, bikers and citizens, had shown for the party, and he knew Slate had been humbled by the turnout. He and Ruby were on the road now, heading to an island off the Georgia coast for their honeymoon.

"Rob," he heard a familiar voice call. Turning to see who it was, he feigned surprise, clutching his chest in astonishment.

"Fucking Baugh brothers." He grinned widely, striding towards them with his arms outstretched. In the first years after Donny had closed the taxi and bike businesses, he'd gotten back to Norfolk at least once a year to see them, typically on his east coast run to visit his mom and Andrea's family. In the past couple years, he'd not made the trip, and now realized how much he'd missed seeing his friends.

Greeting them with forearm clasps, he drew each into a one-armed hug, thumping their backs soundly with his fist. "Dennis," he slung an arm around his shoulders. "How's it going? Still rehabbing hard?"

Dennis made a wagging motion with his hand, fingers spread. He reached out and thumped Bear's chest with the backs of his knuckles, pointing with a sweeping motion at the people in the field.

"Yeah, Slate has a shitload of brothers. Everybody wanted to see the fairytale play out, man. He looked for his woman for a long time, finally found her, and then nearly lost her. If anyone deserves the fairytale ending, it's him." Bear accepted a beer from Donny, stepping backward to sit on one of the log sections arranged around the fire pit as seats.

Dennis frowned at him, sighing hard before he said, "You. More."

At a loss, Bear looked at Donny to interpret, but he shook his head. "No idea." He turned to his brother, asking, "Denny, you want to see Bear more often?"

Shaking his head, Dennis squatted down in front of Bear, thumping his chest again, repeating, "More. You. More." Nodding his head, he ruffled Bear's hair, and then reached out to tap a finger against Bear's ring finger. "Eddie. You."

Bear ducked his head, hiding a grin. "I deserve my own fairytale ending with Eddie?" He knew he'd finally understood when Dennis hooted, laughing and slapped his shoulder. "She's something else, man. Keeps me guessing. Love that woman." He reached out and tapped Dennis' chest. "She's my more, man. You got that shit right." He smiled when he remembered the musical cryptogram Dennis had written out for his birthday years ago. The deciphered message had simply said, *Always Want More.*

"Saw your mom. She's looking good. Who's that guy with his hand on her ass?" Donny asked, cutting his eyes towards Bear, gauging his reaction.

"Fucking Tug, man. You don't remember him? He was part of the crew that came to Norfolk for the first order of bikes. He's also the uncle of that Navy guy I trained. His old lady's been gone for a long time, so he's alone, like Mom. I dunno what I think about it, but as long as she's smiling, I'm staying out of it," he said with a laugh.

"She said you adopted some kids?" Donny's surprise was clear in his voice and on his face, and Dennis turned to follow their conversation. "How's it feel to be an instant dad? Eddie and now kids, you're filling the holes in your life all at once. That's great."

"I didn't have holes, Donny," he said heatedly. "Kids needed stability, and I'd been working with them for a while. Their dad gave me power of attorney years ago because he was traveling. When he died, it seemed right to step up."

"Just seems sudden, you going from no kids to four kids. No woman for years to a steady girlfriend. It looks good on you. I gotta say you are looking the best and most rested I think I've ever seen you." Donny drank from his beer, his gaze on the crowd, which was settling into knots of friends and extended families, the sound of guitars and harmonicas beginning to flow through the air.

"Eddie's good to me," he said agreeably, turning to Dennis. "You bring your flattop?" With a nod, Dennis pointed to him. "Uh huh, mine's in the tent. I'll grab it; you go get yours. We'll play a bit, yeah?" He waited, watching Dennis rise and walk towards the inn and the parking lot.

Turning to Donny, he spoke to his friend in a bitterly pained voice. "Not sure where you're trying to go with this, Donny. Not certain why you aren't easy with the changes in my life, but I won't stand for you trying to convince me I'm making a mistake. You haven't been around much, but I'm present in my life every single fucking day. Eddie and the kids make my life better. More. I'm good with them. I love them."

Donny held up his palms in a warding off gesture. "Whoa. Easy, man. I didn't mean anything. I, for one, am glad to see you're finally moving on. In this case, I think forgetting is a gift, Rob. Getting past the loss couldn't have been easy, knowing how you struggled for years."

Bear was suddenly sick to his stomach. He hadn't forgotten Andrea. Or Ashley. They were in his thoughts every day. In his heart. He loved them. He'd made room for Eddie and the kids in his heart too. Loved them too, not more...not instead of. He hadn't forgotten his life with his angels.

Hanging his head, he groaned. Except he had forgotten the anniversary of the day they died. Hadn't remembered it until he was sitting in Eddie's house with a hard-on, thinking about her. Not his angels. Then the ER called, and he raced over there, finding Miguel had broken his arm on the playground at school. He'd gone home that night, wrapped up in the kids and Eddie, and hadn't thought about his angels a second time until now, three weeks later. Twenty-three days. *They did not suffer.* Fuck. He *had* forgotten them. *Fuck.*

"Bear." He heard her soft voice call his name and looked up in shock. She stood there with his PRS in her hand, as if he'd conjured her with his thoughts. She was making him forget. He was sure she didn't mean to, but she was making him forget his angels. "I ran into Dennis. He told me to get your guitar."

Donny laughed. "He told you?"

Grinning, she said, "Yeah. He said, 'Bear', and then did this." She handed over the guitar, and he accepted it automatically as she moved her hands as if still holding it across her body and strummed the air. "I understood it to be 'Bear needs his guitar'."

She walked over, hugging Donny, and said, "Good to finally meet the both of you." She backed up, taking a seat in the grass near Bear's feet, leaning her shoulder against his leg. "Whatcha gonna play?" Her face was tipped up to look into his, and he smiled down at her.

"Whatever Dennis wants, sugar," he responded, reaching a hand down to cup her chin. "Love you, Drea," he said, and then realized what he'd said when he saw the shock on her face. "Fuck. Eddie, wait," he said reaching out to hold her as she rose to her feet.

She shook her head, chewing on the inside of her lip as she unwrapped his fingers from her arm. "It's okay, Bear," she said carefully, and paused before continuing, "Love you too. I need to check on DeeDee, see if there's anything she needs help with. I'll find you later, baby."

He watched her walk away, headed into the twilight falling on the field, her form becoming indistinct as she moved away from him.

Donny was blessedly silent for once, only moving to hand Bear another beer.

***

He rolled over quietly, sliding away from Eddie's back, tucking the sleeping bag tightly around her when she sleepily complained about the loss of his heat. He propped up on one elbow, smiling and gently tracing her features with his fingertips. He thought about the night of their first kiss, when he'd brazenly told her he wanted to remember exactly what she looked like so he could picture her later when he jacked off. He snorted. *She'd thought it was hot.*

Standing, he slipped into his jeans, and with bare chest and feet, he unzipped the flap on the tent, stepping outside into the chill of the night. A few fires still dotted the campground, and he heard the murmuring of conversations from across the field. He stretched and looked at his phone to see the time, wondering what the hell he was doing awake at four in the morning.

He and Dennis had played songs for hours, their audience growing large by the time he looked up to see Eddie threading her way back to him. Smiling up at her as he sang, he silently asked her to forgive him. They were playing Saving Abel's Addicted*, and laughing, she mouthed the words back to him about being addicted to the things he did between the sheets. He nodded his enthusiastic approval to the amusement of the people watching, keeping his eyes on her face as he and Dennis finished the song.*

Reaching up, he tugged at her hand, pulling her down onto his lap where he buried his face in her neck, breathing deeply. "I love you, Eddie," he whispered, and she turned in his arms, wrapping her hands behind his neck.

"I love you too. My man." She kissed him chastely, and he growled, deepening the kiss, sweeping her mouth with his tongue, claiming her for all to see.

Slipping the phone into the front pocket of his jeans, he tucked his thumbs into his belt loops and leaned back, looking up at the night sky. Twice during his career in the Navy, he'd had the opportunity to go on deck when the sub had surfaced in the middle of the ocean. Both times, he'd been awed by the magnitude and brilliance of the stars in the night sky. The view that stretched above him here reminded him of that feeling; it looked as if he could reach up and touch the glowing diamonds. Smiling when he sighted a shooting star, he watched it cross the visible sky, disappearing behind the canopy of treetops surrounding the field.

He heard footsteps heading his way, leaves crunching underneath leather-soled boots. "Bear," came a softly spoken greeting, and he swung his gaze down, recognizing Judge's voice and matching it with the shadowy form in front of him.

They'd seen each other several times since the nearly disastrous confrontation in front of Eddie's apartment, and had come to an uneasy truce. She'd reminded Bear more than once that them not getting along because of her didn't make sense because her brother was no competition for her affection. He'd finally decided he simply didn't like Judge, but couldn't put his finger on the reason.

How had the asshole known he'd be up, or was it coincidence he was walking past just as Bear stepped out of the tent? Shaking his head, he gruffly responded to the man with a terse, "Hey."

"Was a good weekend, wasn't it? Fucked a bunch of gash. Goddamn, Slate looked pussy-whipped carrying the redhead outta here. I'm surprised the Rebels are gonna keep him on as an officer." There was a slight slur in his voice, and Bear chalked his stupidity up to being drunk.

"Judge, you need to mind your mouth, motherfucker. Slate's a brother, man." That was the only warning he'd give the asshole, and part of him hoped he'd keep disrespecting so there'd be a reason to deliver the beatdown the man had needed for so long.

"Sorry, sorry. Respect. My sister's man." He laughed condescendingly, but his words were the right ones, backing Bear off the balls of his feet as he relaxed a little. He didn't respond, and they stood in silence for a few minutes, Judge shifting back and forth, feet stirring and crushing the dry leaves into dust on the ground.

"Eddie sleepin'?" The question was abrupt, and he tilted his head at Judge, still unsure what the man wanted.

"Yeah. We're headed back home in the morning. She helped Ruby and DeeDee a lot this weekend." He smiled; she'd been almost as excited about the wedding as Ruby. "She's exhausted."

"Saw Mason with Willa. That's an odd pairing." Judge shifted on his feet again. "They look good together, though. Pretty evenly matched. He'll take good care of her. He's a good motherfucker." Again, Bear chose silence, not responding to the puzzling statement.

"Fucking tent. You didn't even get my sister a bed to sleep on. No fucking wonder she's exhausted. Wonder how long Eddie'll be happy to live like this, man. You think she likes taking care of those kids for you? They aren't even your kids, man. How long is she gonna play with you?" He laughed, swaying on his feet.

"She could have her pick of club and chapter presidents out west. Shooter gets a half-dozen offers a month for her; she's considered a goddamn prize. Any one of them and she'd be living in the lap of luxury, never have to work again. She'd be evenly matched with a brother like that. She'd have her own fucking kids, not sleeping in a tent with a glorified mechanic. Fuck, she's got no sense." Even if he couldn't see the man's face, the scorn came through Judge's tone clearly.

Fists clenched as he struggled with control and he leaned forward. "Judge, you need to stop talking. You're drunk and you're embarrassing yourself. Fuck, man, you're embarrassing Shooter. Shut up and go sleep it off." Turning, he ducked back inside the tent, dropping his jeans to the ground before climbing back into the bag with Eddie, curling himself around her.

***

They were headed home the next morning, and Bear was tired. He hadn't been able to go back to sleep after the exchange with Judge, and was ready to be home. He smiled; this morning as they cooked breakfast, Eddie had been full of stories about the weekend. She was proud everything had gone off with hardly a hitch, making the day memorable for Ruby and Slate.

As they approached Fort Wayne, he leaned back slightly, easing off on the throttle, waiting for her to put her face beside his so he could ask her a question. "Apartment or house?" He saw her wrinkle her nose, knowing before she said anything what her response would be.

"Apartment," she told him, and he made a face but nodded, turning the bike towards the apartment where she still lived. If he had his way, she'd move in with him and the kids, but he hesitated to push her.

Backing into a space near her door, he inclined his head back, waiting with closed eyes and a smile until she leaned up and grazed her lips across his. She made a hungry noise, gripping his bottom lip between her teeth, then running her tongue along the indentions left behind. "Love you," she whispered, and he smiled against her mouth.

"Love you, too," he said, twisting to grip her waist, pulling her off the bike and around onto his lap with a smooth movement. He took off her helmet as she giggled and then tipped her head up, giving him access to her neck, where he spent a considerable amount of time nibbling and kissing from her shoulder up to her ear, and then back down again.

He stood, picking her up as he swung his leg over the seat of the bike, drawing her close to his chest. "I need you, Eddie." He kissed along her jawline. He didn't want to let her go, couldn't make himself release her, so he held her in his arms through the doorway, kicking the door closed behind them. Pacing up the hallway to her bedroom, he kept up a constant stream of gentle kisses, licks, and tickling nibbles, pulling sighs and giggles from her.

Sitting on the edge of the bed, he laid her back across his lap and removed her boots, and then his, dropping them on the floor. Unfastening the buttons on her jeans, he gripped the waistband in both hands, smiling at her as she arched her ass up, wriggling her way out of the tight fabric. Repeating the motion with her panties, he gently stroked up the inside of her thighs, shifting so he could rest her legs on the mattress. Propping on his elbows between her knees, he looked up her body, watching her stomach hitch and jerk with every soft touch.

He reached up with one hand, beginning with the bottom button on her shirt and unfastening them partway, leaving the top two still buttoned. He kissed her hip softly, unfastening her bra, pushing it to the side, leaving her breasts bare except for the soft cotton shirt that covered the top curves. Kissing and licking across the top of her bikini line, he rolled her nipples between his fingers, drawing a quick moan from her.

Cupping her breasts in his palms, he rolled and kneaded them for a moment, then dragged his fingertips over her ribs. He prolonged the sliding touch down her sides, curling his hands around her hips as he held her to the mattress. Licking his lips, he looked into her eyes, seeing his own lust and passion reflected there. Dipping his head, he held her still as he ran his tongue slowly and steadily upward along the crease where her leg joined the rest of her body, gently nibbling across her soft skin.

He heard her gasp and held her gaze as he moved his face center between her thighs, rubbing his nose and lips against her clit and labia, slipping his tongue along her folds, using it to open her for his exploration. He nuzzled into her, letting his teeth graze across her clit, drawing another sudden gasp from her throat. Wanting their encounter to be soft and slow, he smiled when she tried to buck her hips up and he held her down effortlessly, forcing her to accept the tender touches he was willing to provide.

Her legs were moving restlessly and he shifted his grip, trapping them under his arms, holding her lower body immobile as he ran his tongue down from her clit to her opening and back up. Again and again, he teased her gently, giving her brief, fleeting touches from his teeth or the tip of his tongue, followed by comforting strokes using the flat of his tongue, eating at her until her arousal was peaking towards frustration.

Releasing her hips, he slipped one hand back up to her breast, rolling the nipple again, stroking the curve along her side, lifting and cupping her breast. His other hand moved between her legs, and he slid two fingers deep inside her, persistently pushing them in and out as he gently sucked her clit into his mouth then rapidly flicked his tongue over it side-to-side.

She arched up, pressing against his mouth, her knees parting to give him more room. He thrust his fingers into her, feeling her begin to tense and tighten inside. “Bear,” she said in a husky voice. “I’m close, baby.” He pushed his fingers deep, rolling and twisting them inside her as he massaged her clit roughly with his thumb, kissing the inside of her thigh when she climaxed, her inner walls clamping down on his fingers.

He watched her face, her lips open and panting, eyes tightly closed as she arched her neck, pressing her chin into one shoulder. Easing her down with gentle licks and touches, he slipped up into the bed beside her, kissing his way up along her hip and side, over her breasts, taking first one and then the other into his mouth, and sucking deeply. He continued his journey, mouthing his way over her shoulders and up her neck, nibbling on her earlobe gently.

"Love you," he whispered, and she twisted in his arms to face him, kissing his lips.

"Love you, too," she responded, laying her head on his arm.

He hadn't meant to doze off, but the lack of sleep the night before finally caught up with him, and he toppled off the edge, coasting underneath the smothering dark cloak of sleep. He felt Eddie's fingers dragging through his hair, smoothing and restlessly combing it across his temples. *Andrea's hands cupped the sides of his face, drawing his mouth down to hers.*

"I don't blame you, baby," she said to him, pulling back so he could see her eyes, and he frowned. One was a brilliant blue, and one a smoky grey. She kissed him again, and her hair wavered between the white-gold he remembered, and a dark brunette that looked familiar.

Kissing him again, she repeated her words, "I don't blame you, baby." He heard the sound of the surf in her voice, and turning, he saw a beach stretching out in front of him. Looking back, he didn't see her, but there were footprints in the sand beside him and he grinned. Those had to belong to Miguel. They were too small for anyone other than Ashley.

"Daddy! Daddy!" He heard an excited voice in the distance, seeing an umbrella shading a cluster of chairs halfway down the beach. Thrilled at the eagerness in her voice, he set off jogging towards the sound, smiling at the ringing laughter as she called him again. "I won! I won! I beat you, Daddy! I'm waiting! We're all gonna be just fine."

Darkness descended on the beach, and he saw the flicker of flames reflecting from leaves crunching underfoot. He walked towards the collection of logs under the umbrella, seeing Drea waiting for him beside the fire. "Be kind to yourself, baby. You can do this standing on your head. I don't blame you," she said, and he frowned.

"Blame me for what, sugar?" he asked her, reaching out to stroke a fingertip down the side of her face. Where he touched, a stark, shadowy

mark marred her features, but she was oblivious to the creeping corruption, still smiling at him, even as it spread, leaving a dark hole where she had been.

"Daddy!" He heard Ashley seconds before she ran into his leg. He reached down reflexively to steady her, and was horrified to find the same dark stain spreading out from where his fingers touched her shoulders and arms. "I love you, Ash," he said desperately. "Sweetness, I love you." He fell to his knees as he removed his hands, urgently needing her to hear him and know before she was gone too.

"I know, Daddy. I love you, too. Exes and ohs," he heard her say, and then she was gone, a darker shadow in the night.

"We love you, Daddy!" He heard a call, and turned his head to see Miguel and Roderigo standing nearby, their dark hair replaced with white blonde.

He woke, covered in a cold sweat, his hair drenched, chills shaking his frame. Reflexively jerking upright and out of the bed, he heard Eddie's sleepy murmur behind him and saw her reaching out, patting the warm space he had so recently occupied. "Baby?" she questioned, lifting her head to look at him.

Climbing back into bed, he crawled up beside her, not noticing when she frowned and moved away from his clammy frame. "Eddie," he whispered, pausing to wait for her grey eyes to swing and focus on his face. "Sugar," he began and cut himself off with a grimace. "Eddie, did you ever think about having kids? Is that something you want?"

She reached up to push his hair back away from his temples. "Maybe someday. Not right now, but it would be...I dunno." Her face dropped into a half smile. "It would be nice, I guess. Is everything alright, baby?"

He leaned in, lightly kissing her lips. "You'll be a good mother." He trailed a fingertip down the curve of her cheek, shivering when a chill moved down his spine, suffusing him with a feeling of dread. He moved up in the bed, leaning his back against the headboard, levering her up alongside him, her head in his lap. He held her as she slept, with the material of his shirt clinging to him as it gradually dried.

About half an hour before her alarm was due to go off, he eased out from under her and stood beside the bed, looking down, watching her sleep. He reached out his hand, but stopped short of touching her, looking curiously at his fingers trembling as if with palsy. Her iPod switched from *The Mirror* by Black Water Rising, and he heard the first strains of the anthem guitar licks of The Veer Union's *Bitter End*, his lips rising in a contortion of pain matching the lyrics of the song.

He had a duffle stored in her closet; sighing, he retrieved it, quietly and methodically packing the few things he had in her apartment. By the time her alarm went off and she stirred in the bed, stretching, he'd set a kettle of water on the stovetop, heating it for her early morning tea and was waiting in the living room, seated on the edge of the couch.

He stood when she walked into the room, picking up his bag and turning to face her. He saw the look of confusion on her face, closely followed by a wounded one, and he dropped his gaze, staring at the floor between them. Shaking his head mutely, he moved towards the door and was pulling it open as her hand hit it. She was frantically pushing to close it, her fingers pressing on the wood so hard her knuckles were white.

He turned and opened his mouth, but in the end, he just stood there futilely. He couldn't find the words to explain what was in his head: his horror at losing himself so deeply in her that he forgot his family, his fear that he was holding Eddie back from things she wanted, maybe needed. Donny and Judge were right; he'd been going about this all wrong, and she'd gotten hurt in the process.

***

"Don't say anything," she begged him, petrified, because she could see in his eyes he was leaving. "Just...don't say it." She closed her eyes, pressing her trembling lips into a thin line and trying to control her breathing.

"Eddie," he began, and she shocked them both by raising her fist and thumping it hard against his chest, startling him into silence. She pressed her knuckles against her mouth, her fingers worrying her bottom lip furiously as her mind raced into overdrive. He was packed and leaving. He'd prepared for this while she lay sleeping in the bed they'd shared, and now he was going to leave.

"I'm not stupid, Bear." Her breath hitched and caught as she fought back tears, her throat tight. "I know what you want to say, but I don't want to hear it. If you think you're saying it for me, you're wrong. You feel the need to explain yourself, and I don't want to hear it." She knew what it looked like when love was gone; she'd seen that same look on Shooter's face when he'd admitted Luke was his. She was just like her mother after all.

She tried and failed to catch her breath, biting the inside of her lips hard, the metallic taste of blood flooding her mouth. Her voice broke as she said, "If you need to go, I'll be fine, Bear. I can see you're already gone in all the ways that matter. Daylight's wasting, so you better get in the wind. I'm fine. I'll be fine," she whispered the lie, looking away from him and turning to grip the edge of the door, pulling it wide and preparing to close it behind him. Close the door on everything she loved.

He hesitated, clearly wanting to say something else, but she wouldn't give him an opening. Eyes firmly on the angle where the wall joined the ceiling, she refused to look at him. She didn't understand, but if he was going to do this to them, to her, then she wouldn't make it any easier. This was what she'd expected all along. Why would he want her?

He halted in front of her and her traitorous gaze fell to his. She saw raw pain and exposed emotion moments before he dropped his mouth onto hers, capturing her lips. He cupped the back of her neck with one hand, holding her secure against him as he stole her breath with the fierceness of his kiss.

It felt like both a farewell and a promise, but one she couldn't bear to think about so she gave herself into the goodbye. Pressing back and stroking her tongue into his mouth when he would have pulled away, drawing him into her until they ended with slow, soft kisses, lips pulling and pressing together between her sobbing gasps.

He rested his forehead against hers, eyes closed tightly. "Say goodbye for me?" he asked with a voice husky from emotion. "Say goodbye?"

"Goodbye, Bear," she whispered to him, and he nodded, their heads moving together. She didn't know if she could take the pain much longer and turned her face away, taking a step backward and breaking the grip of his hands.

"I tried to..." he said, and then stopped himself, turning to walk out the door without another word. She heard the scuff of his boots along the cement of the sidewalk, moving away from her apartment and out of her life.

She pushed the door closed with one shaky hand, sliding down the wall at her back and wrapping her arms around her knees. Leaning her forehead against her crossed arms, she stopped fighting to hold back the tears, her body shuddering with the force of her sobs.

37 - Lemongrass

"No, Willa, you're wrong. I couldn't make him stay. I can't compete with a ghost, and his wife still holds him. He still loves her," she spoke into the phone, walking from the kitchen into the living room. In the two weeks since Bear had left, she'd had a steady stream of calls and visitors, all checking to see how she was, how things were, if she needed anything. She was sick and tired of people walking on eggshells around her like this.

After spending the first night waterlogged in the tub, alternating between crying and adding hot water to her bath, she'd taken stock and decided she wasn't going to be *that* woman. She'd made herself get up the next morning as if nothing had happened. She'd called Maggie and told her about the kids' appointments, bowing out of their lives, figuring his leaving her was enough explanation.

Consciously and determinedly, she pushed her emotions down, tamping them into the deep, dark corners of her psyche. She hadn't stopped loving him, and suspected she'd never be able to, but she wasn't going to be her mother and let this...loss change her.

Thank God, her job was demanding, because it more than kept her occupied. Simply marking time and going through the motions at work wasn't an option; she had to be fully engaged and her kids needed every bit of her every day. Several nights, she'd scheduled home visits or meetings, which extended that busy refuge into the evenings, but she eventually had to go home. Alone.

Home, she scoffed to herself, because she hated going there now. It was too quiet, and memories of him were everywhere she looked. She'd taken to eating dinner standing in the kitchen, because that was the one room in which they spent the least amount of time, and even there she couldn't look at the countertop without tears.

Pulling her attention back to the phone, she couldn't remember the last thing she'd said, but Willa was still responding, so she couldn't have been zoned out for too long. "—Deke said."

"Hmmm?" she answered lightly, glad Willa couldn't see her face as she screwed her features into a wince, waiting on her friend to call her on her inattentiveness.

"I *said*," she scolded, "he left town the same day he walked out on you. Only his mom and the kids have heard from him. Deke said he didn't think *any* of the members had."

"I'm going to paint the living room," Eddie blurted out. "Tequila and painting, what can go wrong?"

"Focus, Eddie. Come on. Aren't you worried about him?" Willa was pushing her tonight. At least she hadn't tried to insist on coming over again. Eddie was running out of excuses to keep her away. Wovenwar was playing in the background, *Death To Rights* transitioning into a new song, *Father/Son.*

"Bear's a big boy," she whispered. "He can take care of himself, Wills. I'm tired of talking about my relationship. My failed relationship. I don't think I can say this any more clearly, but listen to me—Bear left, because he wanted to. No one made him, and just so you know, I *did* try to stop him, but he still left.

"Shit happens, Wills," her voice was high and broken, "and it sure happened here. I love him. I miss him." She took in a shaking breath. "But I'm not Andrea." With a laugh so full of sharp edges it cut to the quick, she said, "I'm about as far from what he had before as you can get. It shouldn't be a surprise to anybody I wasn't what he wanted."

"Eddie—" Willa whispered, but she cut her off.

"I'm tired of talking. See you tomorrow."

Disconnecting the call, she contemplated the walls of her living room, listening to *Freak Show* by SkyBurnsRed and looking over the color swatches she'd already painted on the walls with wide, hurried, careless sweeps of the paintbrush, saying to herself, "Lemongrass it is."

38 - Drowning sorrow

His expression sobered as he told her, "I'm not kidding about Bear, Eddie. He's a bad motherfucker. Mason uses him as chapter enforcer. He goes in, straightens shit out, and people are missing when he's done. You need to stay the fuck away from him." Judge scowled across the living room at her, apparently watching to see if she would take his warning to heart this time.

"Is that why you came back from Cali? So you could warn me off Bear all up close and personal? Have an in-my-face kind of conversation?" Furious, she stood from the couch, stalking into the kitchen, where she leaned against the breakfast bar, trying to control her anger.

It wasn't enough that her dad called every other day, telling her another crazy story about something Bear was supposed to have done, but now, Judge had ridden halfway across the country to try and put a stop to her relationship. She laughed once, the sound torn painfully from her, and then continued helplessly, because Judge didn't know he could stop talking, stop trying to convince her she and Bear weren't right for each other, because they were already over. He'd left her. He didn't love her.

"No, I was invited up to Pokagon," he said, a perplexed look on his face. It was hilarious he didn't know. She'd baffled him. Hilarious. He'd followed her into the kitchen and was helping himself to a beer. He pulled her tequila from the freezer, pouring a healthy amount into a glass and turning to slide it across the counter towards her.

She swung around, surprised, laughter dying as she asked, "To the wedding?" Thrown, she looked at him. "I didn't see you there. Huh, I didn't realize you and Slate were so tight." She picked up the glass and sipped, humming at the punishing burn. "If you've been in town that long, why haven't you been by before now?"

He sneered through a laugh, "Fuck, Eddie, we're not tight. It's about the club; it's *always* about the club. My whole life since I turned thirteen has been about the club. No college for me, fuck...no graduation, either. Always about the club. You know that. Shooter wanted a presence at the most important fucking gathering of the year, so he sent me. I feel like a goddamn politician sometimes, glad-handing my way through shit like that. I did come by here a couple of times, but you weren't home. Since I never connected with you, I've been staying at the Rebel's clubhouse."

He watched her closely, and she frowned at him. *Something is off with Luke.* "Why didn't you call me? Is something going down I need to know about?"

"I thought you'd want time with your boy," he said, tipping his head to one side, "but I get the distinct feeling he's moved on...as expected. He didn't stay long, did he?" He shook his head, reaching out a finger to tap the back of her hand.

"What does that mean?" she asked, taking another drink of her tequila and shifting a half-step away from Judge, drawing her hand back.

"I heard him and his friends talking after the wedding. You know, the brothers from Norfolk? He basically said he was marking time with you," Judge spoke evenly, seemingly unaware of the brutal nature of his words. "I talked to him the next morning, and he sounded worried you wanted kids and maybe something more." He tipped his head to one side again. "It appears he's cut you loose. You aren't together anymore, are you? Un-fucking-attached. Un-fucking-believable."

Eddie bit her lip hard, waiting for peace to flood through her with the sting of pain, but it never came, her mouth now as numb as the rest of her. She lifted her head, finishing off the glass of liquor, now seeking numbness of a different kind. "Nope. We aren't. Glad it made your day, brother. Thanks for the support." She looked away. "I need a shower. Wanna pour me another? I'll be right back out."

He smiled grimly at her, reaching out to open the freezer again. "Sure thing, sis. You got it," he said.

***

Eddie grabbed the sides of her head, groaning. This had to be the worst hangover in the history of boozing and hangover-ing. *Oh, God, let me die,* she thought, easing her grip as she tried in vain to control the dry heaves threatening to wrack her body.

"She's waking up." That was an unfamiliar voice close by, and hearing it speak so close to her head pulled her eyes open, squinting painfully against the weak light of a van's dashboard visible between the captain's chairs in the front.

"Give her another shot." That was a different voice, but one she knew. The vehicle bounced under her as she lay on the floor, rolling her around and causing another bout of heaves.

The first voice questioned the wisdom of doing something, but she wasn't quite sure what. "You sure she can take more?"

"Give it to me. I'll fucking do it." That second voice was angry. Really fucking angry.

Her head felt too large and top-heavy, her neck weak, allowing her enormous skull to loll back and forth against her shoulders while she tried futilely to gain control of her muscles. There were few things working just yet, but she remembered grabbing her head, so she used her semi-cooperating hands to scrub at her face. She decided that was a bad idea as she hissed with pain when her raw and smarting palms scraped across her face. Maybe the pain could be used to try and drive alertness into her system.

"Dun wan shot," she slurred, barely recognizing her own voice.

"Dun fucking care." That was a sarcastic rebuttal, and the identity of the voice was still dancing frustratingly out of reach in her mind when she felt the sting of an injection into her thigh, the muscles already taut with pain.

She used her tongue to swipe at the inside of her mouth. It was cottony and dry, her lips smacking loudly as the little bit of muscular coordination she'd regained slipped back out of her control. "Tirst," she cried, weak sobs breaking from her throat. "Tirsty."

A hand gripped her hair painfully, viciously holding her head upright, tension on her scalp pulling against the sway of the vehicle across highway lanes. A relentless pressure on her lower jaw caused her to open and wetness flooded the tissues of her mouth, the muscles in her throat working automatically to swallow the water being poured into her mouth.

She choked and coughed, her lips closing slowly of their own volition as the hand holding her jaw moved away. She felt herself separating from reality again, easing into the dark, where the madness waited for her. Her senses were wrapped in cotton, eyes fixed, unfocused on the ceiling of the van, and she watched the shine and flash of lights glancing across the expanse, the shifting angles and perspectives of the light creating chaos in her mind. It was pure relief when her eyes flickered and closed, releasing her into sleep again.

***

Surfacing, swimming up from unconsciousness yet again, her body was laid across hard bundles on the floor of the van. Listening closely, she barely made out the solo running commentary from the van's driver over the Occupy Yourself music playing from the speakers.

You know me best, and that's the worst. "If he gives her more, he's gonna kill her." *Come through the walls, in whispered sighs.* "I didn't sign on for this. We can't get out to the coast soon enough for me, but no speeding. Nope, nope, nope." *Pushed apart, families fight.* "Obey the laws, they said. It's a three-day drive, they said." *Is it the blood, we know to try?* "I didn't count on an asshat for a partner, clearly." *Blame yourself, you're not my face.*

It sounded as if only one of the men was awake. If she could gather enough control over her body, she could open the door and jump. Hell, the guy driving didn't seem too happy with what was going on here, whatever that was. He might even stop and let her out.

She didn't know how long it had been since her last memory of standing in her kitchen in Fort Wayne. She couldn't wrap her mind around what was happening. Why would someone kidnap her? She wondered if anyone knew she was missing, then thought about how reclusive she'd become since Bear left and knew it was unlikely. She'd effectively pushed everyone away, which meant no one would miss her anytime soon.

Searching her memories, the last concrete thought she had was of coming out of the shower, wrapped in her robe. *Judge had been standing in her kitchen.* She clenched her eyes closed tightly, hope washing through her. If Judge knew, he would rally help. He had to know what was happening. He might be following them right now, waiting for a chance at rescue.

She needed to remember what had happened. What if he'd been hurt? Her eyes flew open at the thought, and then she crashed them closed again, hissing as the pain in her head shattered her concentration. Carefully, she edged back into her memories in an attempt to keep them from dissolving, escaping from her.

"Go get dressed, sis," he told her.

Her mouth silently shaped her responses, echoing the words running through the memories in her mind. *"Why? I'm not going anywhere."*

She picked up the glass on the cabinet, taking a healthy drink before setting it down. "I plan on staying home. You hungry?" Taking another drink, she made a face and shook her head. She didn't remember picking the glass back up. Her thoughts were growing fuzzy around the edges.

"Let's get you dressed," he said, restating his initial demand. Drawing in a gasp, it had felt as if she was struggling to breathe in enough air to inflate her lungs.

*She'd watched in confusion as her hands stretched out, dropping the glass on the edge of the cabinet, where it shattered, splashing red liquid onto the floor. Gazing down, her eyes slid closed before she forced them open again, staring blankly at the freely-bleeding gash in her leg. "*Fuck,*" she heard as she crumpled to the floor, feeling the pressure as the broken glass sliced through the skin on her knees and the palms of her hands.*

More aware of her surroundings, she took inventory of her body's aches and injuries, feeling the sting and burn from the glass-inflicted cuts she now remembered receiving. Nothing seemed to have needed stitches, even though the wound on her thigh felt as if it were gaping widely, her fingertips drawing out harsh pain as they slipped inside the deep slash in her flesh. She was barefoot, but relieved to be clad in ripped sweatpants and a t-shirt, her hair loose and tangled around her head.

The van hit a series of bumps, causing her head to roll and repeatedly crack hard into something solid with rigid edges. She involuntarily cried out in pain, the throbbing already between her temples made worse with the blows she took. She felt blood flowing from her temple and was suddenly nauseous.

"Stay on the fucking road." The snarled comment came from the front seat and Eddie froze. She knew that voice, and with that recognition came stark fear. On the speakers, Occupy Yourself transitioned into a new song, *Born Into Trouble*, and the lyrics made her blood run cold. *Gone before I knew you, life was easier, made your case*. There would be no rescue; she knew that instinctively. *Love lost in your censure, hate growing, lodged in its place.* Judge spoke to the driver again, asking, "She wake up again?"

"No," was the clipped answer, and she heard Judge shift in his seat, turning to look back at her, where she lay in the floor of the van. "I'll shoot her up anyway." He sounded bored, saying in a lilting singsong, "Sleeping Beauty needs her rest." Feeling the needle slide into her thigh again, she opened her eyes, looking up into his face as he smiled down at her. "Ni-night, big sis," he chortled as her eyes fluttered closed, his cruel smile the last thing of which she was aware.

39 - Coming home

"Baugh, I don't give a fuck what you think he needs. You put the motherfucker on the goddamn fucking phone," Mason snarled, beyond tired of the runaround he'd been getting from the east coast for the past two days. He knew where Bear had run to when he left, and goddamn it, he'd given the man time and space, fucking ample of both, but this was too important to dance around his feelings.

He heard the opening strains of an acoustic performance in the background, and Donny's voice came back on the phone. "He's got three more songs. This is *Painkiller*, the only Three Days Grace song he does. He gets done, I'll give him your message and ask if he wants to call you back."

"Baugh, I'm telling you right now you don't fucking understand me. You will not give the man a fucking message; you will inform him he needs to call his goddamn fucking President right the fuck now. I'm fixin' to rain all over your motherfucking parade. There is shit, and then there is deep shit, and this is a fucking abyss." He disconnected the call, throwing the phone on his desk in disgust.

He'd let Bear run for too long and he knew it, but the man's pain was hard to deny. He was hurting now, but he'd be hurting so much worse if things shook out the way Mason was afraid they were headed. It could be too bad to heal at that point, and he wasn't going to let that happen if he could prevent it.

Twenty minutes later, his phone rang and he scooped it up, snarling, "Goddamn fucking shit," under his breath as he answered it without a hello. "Bear. I need you, brother." He heard the intake of breath from the line and waited for an argument that didn't come.

"Where at, Prez?" Bear's acceptance was clear in his tone, and if his enthusiasm was lacking, Mason knew that no matter what was asked, he'd do his dead-level best to get the job done.

"Back to Chicago first, man. I'll give you two days to get here. You need Myron to wire you cash?" Mason was hesitant to tell him over the phone. He needed to see the man's face when he learned what happened to his woman. *His woman*...Mason took in a breath, his mind moving to Willa. He hadn't seen her since dropping her off at her apartment after the weekend in Pokagon, but that didn't mean she was not on his mind.

"Nah, I'm good," came the response, and Mason had to remind himself what he'd asked. "Okay, man. Get in it soon as you can and call in the morning. Let me know where you are."

Disconnecting the call, he dropped his head into one hand, the other tapping out a restless rhythm on the desktop. Rubbing his temples with thumb and finger, he thought of Willa and her kooky-ass way of just...being. The tapping slowed and eventually stopped as he calmed, remembering how she'd fit behind him on the bike. It had startled him to think she was the only woman other than Mica he'd ever had ride tail. Willa was becoming persistently embedded in his mind, coming to the front at diverse times, like this, to soothe...or arouse him. He picked up the phone and tapped a speed dial number. "Tug, how's my boy doing? With this shit going on, I was thinking about coming down for a few days."

***

Bear pulled into the clubhouse parking in Fort Wayne. When talking to Mason this morning, he found plans had changed and they'd be meeting in the Fort instead of Chicago. Rolling to a stop, he saluted the prospect in the lot and parked, backing his pipes to the building before he unfolded himself listlessly from the bike. Stretching, he groaned as his muscles protested and pulled.

He heard a noise and turned to see Melanie standing on the far side of a car in the lot, her hands resting on the roof as she looked at him. Her face was somber and she waved somewhat uncertainly, then shook her head and got into the car without a word. He saw her beach ball-shaped belly as she struggled to slide behind the wheel and he smiled. It wouldn't be long now until she had that baby. He frowned, watching her drive away, thinking, *Ruby. I need to remember to call her Ruby now.*

Grabbing his bag, he walked into the building and found a full house of pissed off men. Still in the dark over what had happened, he tossed his bag down along the bottom of the wall and looked for Mason or Slate. Hell, Tug or Deke would do to find out what was going on.

"Bear." He heard a shout and turned towards the sound, seeing Mason's head sticking out of the office behind the bar. "Get your ass in here."

Stepping into the office, he found it packed with Rebels, Slate seated behind the desk. Turning his head, he saw Mason leaning against the inside wall and watched him reach out with one hand, pushing the door closed...hard.

The slap of the door into the frame had hardly died in the room before Mason began speaking, and as he did, it felt like all the oxygen was being slowly evacuated from the room. It had to be, because there wasn't anything to breathe and his voice sounded as if it were coming from a great distance. He'd started off with the name etched forever in Bear's heart, but what he said after that had disabled Bear. There was an eerie echo from the past, and he couldn't breathe, couldn't *fucking* breathe, couldn't move. Frozen in place, he looked at Mason, watching his face.

"Eddie's gone." *They're gone, Rob.* "It sounds like Shooter recalled her to Cali." *There was an accident.* "Judge was here until the day she went missing, and we think he was probably the repo man. Two days ago, the Malcontents, that Diego club Shooter's been having problems with, put out notice they are no longer having problems. Everything's hunky dory." *I'm so sorry.* "It's fucking odd this happens just as word is circulated that their President is about to have a new old lady." Mason paused, looking at him.

"Got anything to say, brother?" His president's question nearly went unheard, Bear's attention inwardly focused, listening to the racing of his heartbeat, the rush of breath in and out of his lungs in pained gasps. *How could Eddie be gone?*

"Bear." He heard the sharp, barked tone from Mason and was startled into raising his eyes, his gaze captured by the hard, grey eyes of his friend. "I need to know, brother. You want a response? We are here and ready, all your brothers willing to ride at your back if needed. Tell me what you want."

He said, "I don't want—" and was interrupted by a hissed *"Fuck"* from Slate. Holding up one hand, he shook his head and tried again. "I need—" He closed his eyes and swallowed hard, covering one side of his face with his palm, shaking his head. "She's gone?" His voice was cracked and quiet.

"Yeah, her apartment door was swinging in the wind when we went to check on her. She wasn't answering her phone, but that's been the norm for the past couple weeks. When she didn't show for work, Willa called me. We found the apartment unsecured, but the only thing out of place was a broken glass in the kitchen.

"There was some blood, but not much. It looked like someone had fallen on the glass. We asked around. Some of the neighbors saw a van, and one of them remembered seeing Judge." Mason was watching him closely.

"How long?" He had to force the words out. She'd been taken and he hadn't known. Off licking his wounds, playing as if he had no responsibilities or cares. He'd simply expected her to wait for him, to understand his goodbye wasn't forever. *I didn't know.*

"Four days." The terse reply came from Slate and he twisted to look at him. There was no softness in that face now, the angles of his cheekbones standing out in sharp relief, and Bear realized this had to be making him relive the nightmare of Ruby's kidnapping less than a year ago. It was a wonder he'd been able to allow her to leave his side, much less the clubhouse.

He realized what Slate had said and whirled to face Mason. "Four—*fuck*, Prez," he said, his voice low and hard. *She's been gone four days and I didn't know.* "We got no time for a run. I need out there today. Four goddamn *days*?" His voice rose in volume until he was roaring, bending forward at the waist, the wood of a chair back cracking between his fingers. "They can't have her. *She. Is. Mine*."

"Fucking A." He heard the fervent response and knew without turning it was Slate. He was watching Mason's face and saw a ripple of relief move across it, there and gone in a flash. He heard Slate speaking behind him again. "Dig, need six tickets to San Diego ASAP. One way. We'll need seven coming back, but don't know when yet. Call me when you have...okay, sec."

"Bear, who do you want with you, brother? Dig needs names." Slate paused, waiting.

He saw the slightest nod from Mason and drew in a relieved breath. He hadn't been sure of him until now. "Mason, me, Tug, Deke, Tequila, and Duck," he said, looking around the room and finding willingness in every face he saw there. Slate relayed the information and hung up on the call.

Mason looked him up and down. "Go clean up, we'll want to leave as soon as we have a flight." Bear nodded, turning to open the door when Mason's hand grasped his shoulder, stopping him. "You with us, brother?"

He knew what the real question was. He was being asked if he was too damaged to be counted on, if he was okay enough to have at their back. Nodding, he said, "Yeah. I'm with you." He took in a deep breath. "I'll be fine once we find her…once I know she's safe."

Tug stepped over, reaching out with a hand to halt Bear. "Brother," he said with anguish in his voice. "You had the right of it, man. I'd never have thought Judge could hurt her. And Shooter, fuck, I've known that man virtually all my life." He shot a glance at Mason, who shook his head. "I know he loves that girl. I can't—" His voice hoarsened and caught. Licking his lips, he began again, "I can't believe he'd hurt her."

Bear grabbed his hand, pulling him into a one-armed clinch, whispering harshly, "He needs to pray to God he doesn't. He's your friend, but she's my life."

Grabbing his bag, he took the stairs two at a time to the second floor, turning into the first empty room he found. He turned on the shower before moving back to the bedroom to pull off the clothes he'd been wearing since leaving Norfolk. His motions slowed and he closed his eyes. There was something nudging him, circling around, but he was not quite able to bring it into focus. Teasing him, it retreated farther every time he tried to reel it in. He shook his head, dismissing whatever it was. This was no time for confusion.

Stepping into the shower, he tipped his head back under the hot water, letting it run over his shoulders and chest as he washed his hair. Lifting his face, he scrubbed it with his hands, feeling the trails of heat the water made as it rinsed the soap from his skin.

He stilled, his brain finally granting him a full-on look at what it had been trying to tell him, and he quickly turned off the water, jumping from the shower and shoving still wet feet into a clean pair of jeans. Pulling a shirt on, it twisted and clung to his chest as he leaned down to grab his boots, forcing bare feet into them.

Running down the stairs, he started yelling halfway down, "Tug? God*dammit*, where's Tug?" One of the members wordlessly pointed towards the office as the door flew open and Mason stepped out.

"*What?*" Mason snarled out his question and Bear ignored him, pushing past him into the room.

"Tug," Bear said, breathing hard. "Where's LeRoy?"

A half-smile lifted the mustache at the corners of his mouth, and Tug said exactly what Bear had hoped to hear. "San Diego."

***

Petty Officer Carter LeRoy stood in front of the hanger on the private airfield in Potrero, California, watching as the small jet taxied towards him from the runway. For the past four years, he'd been assigned to a submarine allocated to SUBRON11, a fleet based out of San Diego. At the moment, his boat was in Arco, the floating dry-dock, so he'd had lots of spare time to spend ashore.

He'd been surprised by his uncle's phone call last night, but once he understood his old Petty Officer was involved, you couldn't have kept him away from whatever this was. He watched the ground crew handle the plane as it parked, securing the wheels before rolling a narrow set of stairs over to the forward cabin door, getting them in place as the door opened.

Crew was the first man down the stairs, followed quickly by his Uncle Mike, and then several additional men. Suppressing his initial reaction to salute, he reached out and grabbed his friend's hand for a quick shake before being enveloped in a hard hug from his uncle.

Walking backward, waving them forward, he led them into the darkened hangar, music blaring loud as they entered the enclosed space. LeRoy recognized the strident tones and driving beat of Otherwise's *Soldiers,* and felt a prickling of premonition drag through the air.

"I've got everything you asked for. Two vans, four bikes. I have a friend on standby." He thumbed back towards a man sitting at a folding table in the corner, waving a hand at the stereo and pausing until the volume of the music decreased. "That's Dave; he's an EMT. I had a conference call with your guy Myron earlier. We have the up-to-date SAT imagery he requested. He indicated you needed enough information to put together a SATKA. I believe we have sufficient data."

At a questioning glance from his uncle, he clarified, "SATKA is a surveillance, acquisition, tracking, and kill assessment. He read me in on what was going on, and I have an additional SITREP for you." Tug sighed, and he clarified again, "Sorry, SITREP is a situation report. I'll try to rein it in, Unc, but you were Navy, so you need to think back and remember the lingo. I know it was centuries ago, but come on," he teased, then quieted when no one reacted.

Drawing them across to another table along the wall, he pointed to printouts and maps. "Myron said you were going in with only six guys. No offense, but from what I can see, that's insane. The property is in a canyon and there are closed-feed cameras all along the way. The latest pass shows about forty-five vehicles onsite, including the van you wanted to know about. It hasn't moved from where it was first parked. Rob," he faltered, "we can pull in sailors. You know we can. You still have friends here, man."

His uncle reached out, wrapping his palm around the back of LeRoy's neck. "We have everything we need, kid. I have knowledge that's not going to show up on your printouts. I lived in that house for nearly fifteen years off and on. For every obvious way in, there are two more you'll never find."

LeRoy looked at him and frowned. "From back when you and Aunt Jilly lived out here?"

A pained look spread over Uncle Mike's face and he nodded. "Yeah, from living out here with Jillian." He straightened, looking around. "We have a plan, and it's shit, but it is *so* shit it should work." LeRoy saw the men nod with uniformly somber faces and his heart swelled. "Count me in. Whatever you need, Crew."

A little while later, he caught his uncle over by the coffee pot, and together, they leaned against the countertop, mugs in hand. He asked, "How'd you get ahold of a private jet on such short notice?"

Uncle Mike laughed sharply, saying, "Fucking hockey players. They play and fight like hell on the ice, but off it, they are all big kids with toys. More money than sense, most times. We've got a friend of the club who owns a team in Chicago; he arranged the plane. It's going to be waiting on us here for a week if we need it. Hope to fuck we get shit sorted before then, but it's good to know the right people, kid."

"How the hell did your guy get clearance to pull images from the satellite network?" LeRoy sipped at his coffee, cutting his eyes over to his uncle.

"Less you know, the better, kid." That was the only response he got before Uncle Mike straightened and moved back over to where the discussions were winding down between Crew and the tall, dark-haired man who seemed to be in charge.

"All right, Tug. I think we got it. Come tell us where we're fucking up," the man called across the room, and his uncle raised a hand, already on his way.

***

Bear looked around the group of men, etching their faces into his memory. They were each fully aware that any or all of them might not walk away from today's action. He'd picked men he trusted, but he'd also selected for the minimal ripple effect in case something went wrong. That's why he hadn't asked Slate, even though the man was the best brother and friend he'd ever had. He couldn't do that to Ruby, to their baby. He couldn't be the reason the child lost a parent before it was even born.

Tuning back into what Mason and Tug were discussing, he heard them settling on the final details. Tug had found few flaws in their plan, and his knowledge of the compound's layout was the most critical component, his involvement giving them the confidence to bet on their success.

Scuttlebutt had the transfer set to seal the newly-crafted arrangement between the Outriders and Malcontents was scheduled for right after nightfall, so they planned to time their approach for just before it happened. With their faces covered and on unremarkable bikes, they hoped to be mistaken for Malcontents members arriving early, which should gain them access to the compound.

More than a few of the Outriders had expressed their displeasure and unhappiness with what Shooter was doing, and from those loose lips, they had gained a significant amount of intel.

One member with a military medic background had groused about the situation for an hour in a bar last night. Eddie had still been so drugged upon arrival, she was unable to even walk or hold her head up. He said he'd had to counteract the drug used to keep her sedated for the long trip from Indiana to Cali, and was still worried about her. Something about a head injury that kept him from treating her with proper dosages. Bear's stomach churned at the thought, and a slow heat of anger built inside him again.

He looked around, seeing his brothers...his friends, and made a decision. This wasn't right. He couldn't do it. He wasn't willing to lead them into danger. It would be better if he slipped in and out alone—quickly and quietly—fast as can be.

He needed to have his hands on Eddie, to be able to judge for himself if she was okay. *Judge*, he thought with a burst of anger. The man wouldn't be the only one granting himself that title, and when he had that motherfucker in his hands, he would not go lightly on Eddie's brother. The cocksucker had taken her away, drugged her, and was willing to support their father's surrender of her to a man few people knew. Just give her away, hand her over to this Blue Line, the unknown factor in this mix, the reclusive president of the Malcontents.

Stepping out the backdoor, he looked the motorcycles over, selecting the most likely one for his use. Without giving himself time for second thoughts, he set about disabling the rest of the bikes, detaching the throttle control from the handlebar of each, knowing it would be a simple fix when it came time for LeRoy to turn the bikes back in where they'd been rented. He flipped up the kickstand for the bike he'd chosen and pushed it at a slow run up the road, into the darkness, until he was far enough away to risk starting it.

Once started, he straddled the bike and put on the helmet, pulling the dark visor down to hide his features. With the map to the Outriders' compound memorized, he rode quickly up the road towards it, swaying and leaning into the curves, heeling the bike over recklessly. He felt more than heard his phone go off, the vibration in his front pocket frequent and insistent. Ignoring it, he continued on, turning at the landmarks he'd learned, approaching the long drive to the compound after about thirty minutes of riding.

The gates were unmanned and opened wide, and he saw the goddamn van, exactly where the satellite pictures showed it to be parked. He rode on towards the back of the building, intending to park amongst the bikes there, and found an open spot on the edge, well away from the entrance.

He stood up off the bike, settling it over on the kickstand, leaving his jacket and helmet in place, hoping they would give him a few extra minutes of anonymity. Through the visor, he saw a figure approaching, and waited for the expected challenge. "Hey, you know where you are, man?" The words came from the opposite direction of the man he could see, and he swung his head around to find three more men flanking him. *Fuck*.

“Yeah,” he drawled. “Shooter sent for me.”

“Yeah.” He heard a laughing voice say, “I don’t think so.” He groaned silently as he saw Shooter step out from behind the men, his head cocked curiously to one side. “Who’s the asshole under the lid, boys. Let’s take a look—see who’s got the balls to roll up to our house uninvited.”

His arms were pinned behind his back and hands roughly removed the helmet. As soon as it was free of his head, he tried to whip his head back, intent on catching his captor by surprise in an attempt to free himself. Instead, a hand thrust roughly into his hair, the pull and tug on his scalp holding his head immobile and upright.

“Goddamn Bear.” He heard a voice he recognized, cutting his eyes to see Judge standing on the periphery of the group, face swollen and bruised. “Stupid motherfucker. You shoulda listened to me, man. Shoulda stayed gone.” He felt a sweep of wind, followed by a burst of light and pain, and then nothing as darkness swept over him, relieving him of being present.

***

Bear groaned, trying to pick his head up off the floor, and found himself entirely unsuccessful, so he rolled it side-to-side, opening his eyes a mere slit, attempting to take in the room. He first saw the black leather swimming into focus from the corner, where shadows had taken up residence. Groaning audibly, he saw a man step into view. “Not your best idea,” the man told him, squatting down nearby. His voice was familiar, almost tauntingly so.

“What were you trying to do?” the voice continued evenly, and he heard the man’s boots shifting on the concrete floor as he stepped closer. “Were you planning to stop me from taking Edith?”

“Fuck you,” he ground out between gritted teeth and heard the man laugh.

"Yeah, that's what I thought. They said you're the sad sack she's been fucking. Hmmm. I don't see the draw myself. To Edith, that is. She's nothing like your first wife. Now *that* woman was something else." Still laughing, the man settled onto his ass, comfortably leaning against the wall. "Andrea was unique, or so I've heard."

He took a deep breath and recognized the familiar scrape of ruined ribs as they rubbed against the wall of his chest. He lifted his head, staring through swollen eyes towards the man. He used his elbow to leverage himself towards the wall, scraping across the floor on his ass.

"You don't know fuck all about my family, then or now, motherfucker. Stay away from Eddie, goddammit. She's *mine,*" he roared the last word, his head blasting him with pain. He heard a raw laugh, and then got a good look at the man's face for the first time and catching his breath in shock.

"Jo—" he began, interrupted by the man's hand across his lower face, covering his mouth.

"*Blue Line,*" was growled across the space separating them. "Don't fucking forget that name, *Bear*. Blue Line."

He nodded, and Blue Line removed his hand from Bear's face, wiping it on his own jeans with distain before pulling a bandana from his pocket to continue the cleanup. "Fucking bleeding all over, man. Suck that shit in or something, I don't want no more blood on my hands." He looked hard at Bear as he said the last, and nodded once.

"What to do with you." He tapped his lips with two fingers, feigning perplexity. "Do I take care of you, or let the Outriders do that for me?" Looking down, he asked, "You got friends coming in anytime soon?"

"Yeah, motherfucker," Bear shot back. "Two hundred Rebels are about to descend on your ass. You're gonna need more than a tissue to clean up with after they are through with you."

"Probably more like five or six additional men, lightly armed against the fifty we have here, who are sporting an arsenal." Blue Line yawned, tipping his head against the wall at his back.

Bear nodded; he'd gotten the message. "Where the fuck is Eddie? I heard her asshole brother almost killed her to keep her quiet on the trip out here. Where is she, man?"

"She's in a private room in this facility," came the reply. "And her brother has been...severely chastised by daddy for his mistreatment of my property."

Bear came off the floor with a yell at those words, stopping when his forehead painfully ran into the muzzle of a gun. "You are just fulla bad fucking ideas, aren't you?" Sighing, Blue Line holstered the gun, pointing towards a door in the corner of the room. "Exit there, please."

In the hallway, Bear heard voices coming from the right, but Blue Line steered them the other direction. They walked further into the compound, the rooms off the hallway becoming progressively smaller, based on the increased frequency of closed doorways. Some of the doors had peepholes like a hotel, but from the outside in. Some had prison-like flaps in the door, where you could pass a tray of food through or shackle someone's wrists prior to removing them from the room.

Now that he was upright, the swelling in his face felt like it was gradually diminishing, and he stretched his eyes as wide as they would go, trying to take everything in. If he found Eddie, he would have to remember the way out in order to get her to safety.

"Here," Blue Line said, halting in front of an unremarkable door, to Bear's eyes indistinguishable from the dozens of others they'd passed. He stepped back, allowing Bear to reach the viewport, speaking in a hushed voice once Bear's inrush of breath told him he'd been able focus on the room's lone occupant.

"She's okay for now, Rob. I'm not the one who took her clothes, but because she's bare, you can see there are few bruises. You're in a lot worse shape than she is, because she's got value at the moment. She's been dozing in and out from the drugs still working their way out of her system. Judge nearly killed her somewhere in Nevada with a huge dose but *she's okay for now*." He stressed this repeated statement, and continued, "I can get her out of here, or I can get you out of here." He slapped the metal door beside Bear's head. "What I don't think I can do is get you both out, goddammit. What the fuck were you thinking coming in here alone?"

"Joel," Bear faced his brother-in-law. "Me? What are you doing in here? Jesus fuck, man, you're a biker? In a club...in the life? There are no words, man. What the fuck?"

"Things are not always as they seem." He shook his head at Joel's words and then froze when he heard Shooter's voice from across the hallway.

"No, they are not. Appearances can be deceiving. I've always told my boy that same thing."

He saw Joel stiffen in surprise, and they turned to see Shooter step out of the room alone, leaving the door open behind him. "You boys seem to have quickly found a common ground that surprises me, *Joel*," he sneered. "Makes me wonder how honest your offer for my daughter is, if you would think about rescuing the one man who can vie for her affections. Gives me pause to think maybe I should decline the offer now, take up the one from the Jackals instead. Hmmm?"

Without thinking, Bear reached out, pulling Shooter close to him by the throat, holding him tightly with both hands as the man struggled, trying to pry the choking fingers off his neck. Bear slammed the man against the wall, groaning against a sudden, sharp pain from his ribs as he lifted Eddie's father high, his feet dangling, kicking. Bear slammed him against the wall again and held him above the floor until the man slumped in his grip.

"You...we get her out now," he growled at Joel, groaning from the pain in his chest again as he shoved Shooter through the doorway, dumping the unconscious form onto the floor and pulling the door closed.

Wincing as he moved, he opened the door to the room where Eddie lay. Running his hands gently over her skin, her legs and arms, up her shoulders to turn her head to face him, he reassured himself she was unharmed, other than the obvious fact he couldn't wake her up.

He watched as Joel disconnected all the lines, waiting impatiently until he saw she was clear before gathering her to his chest, clutching her desperately, refusing help. Following Joel outside, they reached the drive as he heard motorcycles coming fast around the last corner, and looked up to see a van following the bikes closely. He stood there, legs firm as tree trunks as his brothers slid to a halt around him, seeing the side door on the van slide open, LeRoy's friend holding onto the overhead handle and a seatbelt to keep himself in the vehicle.

"Hand her in," he heard, and felt hands relieving him of Eddie's weight. He thought to himself, *She is so light, never a burden*.

"Keep her safe," he said, agonizingly short of breath as he turned to head back into the compound.

"Get in the fucking van, Bear," he heard Mason snarl at his back and saw the man's face contorted in rage. "We got this, Brother," Mason said, a little more controlled. "Let us help you, man."

There was an unsubtle push on his ass and he tumbled into the van beside Eddie's motionless body, groaning at the pain in his ribs, feeling liquid bubble up his throat with every breath. He felt a needle slide into his shoulder, looking over to see the medic and Joel focused on him instead of Eddie. He tried to complain, but then his thoughts were overtaken by blackness. He welcomed it, now knowing his dreams would be filled with her.

He woke once on the jet, hearing as well as feeling the vibration from the engines through his body. Looking around, he saw Joel seated nearby, facing him and watching an adjacent seat with intent. Joel looked up at him, seeing him awake, and nodded, whispering, "She's gonna be okay," as Bear slipped underneath the dark horizon again, headed into sleep.

40 - Back to love

"Why won't he wake up?" He heard her voice, seemingly coming from nearby, but muffled with dozens of layers of cotton gauze, giving it a far-away quality. "If he's so okay, why is he still asleep?"

There was a responsive mumble, but he couldn't make out the words from this male voice. She responded, her tone becoming shrill and worried. He hated making her worry. "But you fixed that. You said two days ago you'd fixed his lung. No more holes, yay. So why the *fuck* is he not waking up?"

Bear licked his lips, almost gagging at the pain in his throat from just that slight movement. Damn, his mouth was dry. "Eddie," he tried to whisper, still struggling to convince his eyelids it was past time to open wide. Fumbling, his hand crept across the covers, seeking something he knew had to be there; she wouldn't leave him alone. He needed to touch. "Eddie," he managed a breathy whisper this time, his questing fingers finding and rejecting a hard, plastic object, continuing on.

Exhausted, he tried to take in a deep breath, shocked at the pain that suffused his entire body, focused in his chest. *Goddamn fucking* shit *that hurt,* he thought, struggling against coughing, because he instinctively knew that would hurt so much worse if he succumbed to the urge. Humming in frustration, his fingers finally found what he'd known had to be there, wrapping themselves around her small hand, hearing her gasp of surprise. *Took you long enough, sweetheart.* He listened to the tone of her babble more than the words. *God,* he thought, relieved, *she still loves me.*

"Bear, baby. Oh, baby, love you. Open your eyes, baby. Come on. Open your eyes. Bear, open your eyes. Open *your eyes*, dammit." Why was she so pissed at him? Last he remembered, he'd been rescuing her ass. You'd think that would give him more than a day's worth of happy. Her fine ass. A smile quirked the corners of his lips as he remembered her voice in the bar that night, saying, *'My ass is fine', and he'd responded with, 'That ass* is *fine.'*

"Your ass is fine, Eddie," he whispered, and she laughed. *Oh, God, that laughter.* He'd never get tired of hearing that. She was hiccupping and crying though. He couldn't have that, wanted more of the laughter. "Eddie," he said, finally convincing his eyelids he meant business. They opened a fraction and her face slowly swam into focus.

Both of her hands were clutching at his one, and she raised it to her cheek, kissing it with her soft lips. She had dark, bruised-looking half-circles underneath her shadow-filled eyes. He didn't like her looking so worried and tired, and he frowned.

"Eddie," he repeated, tugging their joined hands towards his head. He wanted to get his mouth on her. He needed her. She made him… "Need you. Eddie. You make me whole. Never again. Never away again. Love you, Eddie. Mine." He slid down that damn steep hill, eyelids wavering closed as he told her again, "Love you, Eddie. My fine Eddie." Smiling, he fell asleep to the sound of her bright laughter.

The next time he awoke, he was successful in remaining alert for at least a little longer. He felt a familiar weight on his shoulder, and turning, saw tousled dark curls captured into a ponytail. He smiled and kissed her head. She'd tucked herself into his side, and his arm was curved around her waist, holding her there, even in his sleep. He shifted in the bed, the pain much less intense this time, and he wondered how long he'd been out.

Looking around, he recognized they were in his bedroom in Fort Wayne. He heard the door open gently, and he shushed whoever it was coming in, seeing Lucia's face peeking around the frame. He smiled, waving her forward with his free hand, and she crept in, settling on the edge of the bed near his hip. "Hey, Luce," he whispered, feeling Eddie beginning to stir.

Her eyes were fixed on his face and he wasn't sure what emotion he saw there. He waited for her to speak, seeing her eyes dart between Eddie's face and his own. He reached out his hand and grabbed hers from where it was twisting around its companion in her lap. "Lucia," he whispered, "it's okay, punkin. I'm not going away again."

There was a noise from the doorway, and he looked up to see Rafe and the two boys standing there. "Come on in, guys," he said. "Keep it to a mild roar, yeah?" Miguel and Roderigo moved quickly towards the bed, but pulled to an uncertain stop behind their sister. Rafe followed at a more deliberate pace, but the anxiety in his eyes belied his calm appearance.

"I'm not going away again," he reassured all of them, realizing what he was promising. "This is my family, the six of us. You are my family. We're all here for the long haul, okay? I love you, guys," he whispered, one hand stroking down Eddie's back while the other brushed across Lucia's hand.

He felt the change in her breathing as she woke in a rush, tipping her head up to look into his face. "Bear," she breathed, stretching up to feather kisses along his jaw.

"Sweetheart," he murmured. "My heart. I love you, Eddie." He angled his head to capture her mouth with his, hearing giggling in the room at their display of affection. "My heart," he said again with a smile.

"Luce," he rolled his head to look at her and the boys, "punkin, I'm starving." Making piteous eyes at her, he stuck out his bottom lip. "Is there food in the house?" She stared into his face for a long minute, apparently satisfied with what she found there, because she nodded at him once, with a decisive movement that told of much more than mere agreement with his question.

His arm tightened around Eddie when she would have moved, holding her close to his side as his daughter stood, smiling down at them. “I can make soup. How does that sound?” she asked him, stepping backward and using her hands to usher the youngest boys ahead of her towards the door.

“Sounds great, punkin,” he responded with a smile, turning his eyes to Rafe, who remained in the room, shifting uncomfortably from foot to foot, looking anywhere but at the two people lying on the bed. “Rafe,” he started, but the boy interrupted him.

“You don’t get to do that again. They worry. *We* worry. We need you. This is our family too. No more leaving.” Rafe nodded once, and having said what he intended, turned towards the door.

Bear struggled up onto one elbow, calling after him, “Rafe?” He stopped, facing the door, but clearly listening. Bear remembered the advice from the boy’s counselor to be direct and to the point. Subtle emotions were not recognized. Nuance be damned, he needed him to understand. “Raphael, you are my son. I will never leave you again. I love you. I’m sorry I went away. You are *very important* to me.”

Rafe looked back, giving him a single, tense nod before he smiled, joy lighting up his face in the most perfect way. “That makes you my dad,” he said with wonder in his voice. “Can I call you Dad?”

“Absolutely, son,” he responded without hesitation, and felt Eddie’s breath catch in her chest. “I’d like that a lot.”

Looking down into Eddie’s face, he heard the door click as Rafe pulled it closed behind him. “My heart,” he whispered, softly kissing her forehead, feeling it wrinkle into a frown beneath his lips.

“Bear?” She was apparently asking permission to ask a question, and he found that funny, laughing soundlessly, pleased there was little pain.

“Yeah, sweetheart?” he prompted, kissing her forehead again.

"We're okay?" This was whispered, and he heard the unspoken questions pushing at her, stealing her self-confidence.

"Better than okay, sweetheart. I love you so much, Eddie. I'm so sorry." He shifted so he could see her face. "I am so, so sorry," he repeated. "You are my heart, my life. I fucked up big time. I hope you can forgive me, sweetheart. When Mason told me you were gone, it felt like someone had ripped my heart out of my chest. Then, when I saw you lying there on that bed and couldn't wake you...my God, I thought I was going to lose it. All I could think was that I'd failed you. If I hadn't freaked out and walked away—if I'd been there, you wouldn't have had to deal with all that shit. I'll make it up to you. The rest of my life, I'll work to make it up to you. Just...stay. Please? Stay? I love you."

His voice broke and he buried his face into her neck, clutching her to his chest as desperately as he had when he carried her from her father's compound. Muffled by the kisses he was pressing against her skin, he said, "I love you so damn much, Eddie."

"I love you, too," she whispered, her hands smoothing his hair back from his face, stroking his shoulders and sides leisurely.

"Soup's ready," Lucia sang from the hallway outside the bedroom door, and Bear's stomach growled.

"How long have I been out?" He struggled up onto one elbow again, looking down into Eddie's face.

"Six days in the hospital." She shrugged at the face he made. "We brought you home this morning."

"Are you okay?" He caressed her cheeks, stroking the backs of his knuckles up her jawline. "Last I knew, you were still out from the drugs. We got you in the van, and then they kinda threw me in too. You were still unconscious on the plane, I think."

She nodded, cupping one hand over his, holding it against the side of her face. "I'm okay."

"Just okay?" he pressed, not sure what he was asking, but it felt important.

She sighed heavily, her eyes darting over his shoulder and around the room, not seeming to see what was in front of her. "Yeah, just okay, for now. It's hard to get my head around everything. All of it, you know? My da— Shooter was willing to basically sell me. Never mind it was a bogus deal; he didn't know that. Judge...that hurts almost as badly. I never knew he hated me. Never knew. Not a clue. All my life, and not a single clue."

There was a commotion at the front of the house, and he tensed as he heard yelling voices advancing on the bedroom. Moving to cover Eddie's body with his own, he twisted to look at the doorway as it burst open, the door slamming in against the wall, bouncing back and hitting Willa as she barreled through. "Oww! Mother*fucker*, that hurts. Hey, guys." She waved, rubbing her elbow with her other hand.

"Uncle Joel called, said you were awake," she said, frowning at the bed. "Why are you...oh, God. I interrupted, didn't I? I didn't expect you'd have so much stamina so fast. Go Team Bear. I'm going. I'll go. I'll just..." She backed out of the room, pulling the door closed. It immediately opened again, and she stuck her head back into the room with a brilliant smile in place. "Soup is ready. I was told to remind you. Now I'll go. Carry on what you were doing. Carry on. Yay, Team Bear."

He groaned and leaned his head onto Eddie's chest, feeling it rise and fall with her barely-controlled laughter. "Y'all are a package deal, right?" he asked, smiling as he gently nipped at her breast through her clothes, drawing a gasp from her.

"Yeah," she breathed. "Wills and I are a package deal."

"No problem. I have a bigger package," he said, and she burst into laughter. He ran his words back through his head and laughed along with her.

"I have no complaints about the size of your package, baby," she whispered into his ear, tracing his earlobe with the tip of her tongue.

"I meant the kids and I are a package deal too. But it's a much larger..." He stopped, looking down at her as she closed her eyes, laughing hard. "It's...we're...aww fuck." He grinned down at her.

"I like that package too," she said, her eyes crinkling at the corners with her amusement.

Something Willa had said was teasing at the edges of his mind, and his eyes widened, looking down at her. "Uncle Joel?" She nodded, a comfortable grin on her face.

"He's been staying here since we all got back from California." She offered up this tidbit, and then said, "Joel is a nice guy. He thinks a lot of you."

"Yeah. Shit, I wasn't sure if I'd dreamed him or not. He was really there? He's here? Okay. Soup. Joel. Sleep." He nodded. "In that order."

Pulling himself with some effort to the edge of the bed, he stood slowly, the weakness in his muscles conspiring with gravity against him. He felt a tugging on the skin along his side and dragging the hem of his shirt up, he found a gauze bandage taped to his ribs. He felt around his back, where there was additional tugging, and found a tube and a bag taped to his skin.

"Sweetheart?" He said, swaying a little on his feet, and heard her call loudly for Joel. Sitting down hard on the edge of the bed as his legs gave way beneath him, he saw her feet on the floor beside his. *They are so tiny*, he thought, slumping forward and then gasped as wide hands and muscled forearms came into view, gripping his biceps and hauling him upright.

"Rob," a gruff, deep voice said, and he tilted his head up to see a worried look on Joel's face.

"Just stood too fast, 's all," he murmured. "Dizzied a little. Gotta pee. Then soup. Then Joel. Then sleep. Adjusting schedules for the reality of life." Joel's hard arms helped him up, steadying him as he staggered towards the bathroom. "So fuckin' weak," he complained, putting a hand on the wall to help support his frame. "'Fraid I gotta sit to pee," he said, laughing.

"Yeah, best to be safe. I'm not holding your dick, man." Joel laughed. "Much as I love you, got no interest in handling your junk."

Sitting at the table, he spooned soup as he listened to a sanitized version of events around the house since they'd all returned home. He was pleased everyone was restraining themselves, because there was no reason for the kids to worry or wonder about the coulda, woulda, shouldas, but he was still sad when the clock chimed nine, sending the kids to bed. Lucia volunteered to help with baths, and it broke his heart that she'd fallen back into the caregiver role so quickly, because of him. Because he'd selfishly bailed on them and left.

Once the little ears were gone, however, the conversation quickly turned to filling in the gaps in his memories, along with an explanation of how Joel came to be president of a California motorcycle club.

Joel was still in the Navy, now part of an anti-terrorist effort whose focus was on homegrown radicals. The Outriders club had gained attention a few years ago, when Shooter entered into a public war with a rival Oregon club. In response, the Navy sent Joel into the life undercover, patching into a military-based club in southern California that was known for being anti-crime, rejecting any criminal aspects of the more typical biker's life.

He'd managed to get close to Shooter, and had been making life hard for him over the last year, pushing him to ever more dangerous efforts to regain control over SoCal.

He'd heard passing comments about Rob joining a club, but the two men hadn't stayed in touch over the past several years. Without keeping up, he hadn't been aware of Rob's move from Chicago to Fort Wayne, never considering the woman he'd been offered as recompense for a botched deal might be connected to his former brother-in-law.

He'd been shocked to recognize Rob lying unconscious on the floor of the compound. Afraid to break his cover, he was forced to stand and watch for several minutes as Judge and other members continued to work Bear over with their fists and feet. It was only when one of them mentioned he was Eddie's boyfriend that he had a reason to stop them, able to claim the right to be the one to end him based on the past relationship with his soon-to-be old lady. Convoluted reasoning, but it made sense in the testosterone-laden world of the Outriders club.

Bear's eyes were drooping, but he needed to know. "What happened with Shooter and Judge?"

"Shooter is in custody; he'll likely spend a bit of time in the system. The local authorities were happy to accept custody of him and the evidence collected by my team in exchange for no charges against your guys. We'd gathered enough about his drug and gun business, even before he tried to branch off into kidnapping." Joel glanced at Eddie, his gaze falling to the floor.

"And Judge?" Bear shook his head, trying to clear the cobwebs creeping back. He was so tired.

"In the wind," Joel growled. "He got out before we locked things down, after we evacuated you and Eddie. We're watching for him. If he raises his head, we'll know it." He paused, then sighed, "Let's get you back to bed, man. I think you need some rest before you have to face your mom and Mason tomorrow."

"Fuck," he groaned, slinging an arm over Joel's shoulder.

"Let me get your pain meds," Eddie said, turning away before he stopped her with a gentle hand on her wrist.

"It's not bad," he said with a smile, "but I suspect I'll need them tomorrow after Mason gets done with me."

She laughed at him, coming up on the opposite side from Joel, wrapping her arm around his waist. "And Maggie, and Tug, and Slate, and Ruby…" she trailed off and gasped. "You don't know! Ruby had the babies," she whispered, her face changing.

At her tone, he was filled with fear, asking cautiously, "Everyone okay?"

"Yeah, they are great." She was chewing on the inside of her lip again.

"They?" he asked, then it hit him. "Wait, babies?"

"Yeah, Allen Martin and Danielle Susan are both doing fine, as is Ruby," she giggled.

He stopped, dragging them to a halt beside him. "Twins? She was pregnant with twins and didn't know it?"

"Apparently, she knew, but didn't want Slate to worry. He was furious for about a minute, and now, he's silly in love with them." She tugged at his waist gently, pulling him towards the bedroom.

***

"You are one of the stupidest motherfuckers I have ever had the misfortune to know in my life. Goddamn, but you piss me off, Bear." Shadows from the blinds slashing across his face, Mason was leaning against the wall in his bedroom, his posture deceptively relaxed when compared to his tone and language. This was pure Mason on a rant and

Bear had not been looking forward to this chat. "On my fucking watch, you try that shit. Stupidest motherfucker I know.

"You figured I couldn't fix the bikes? Think I didn't see you sneak out the fucking door? What were you thinking? What was your plan? Did you even have a plan? I gotta tell ya, man, if your plan was to get yourself put under wraps and get the shit beaten out of you, then I'd say you accomplished exactly what you were after. Have a fucking cookie.

"Go ahead, tell me what the plan was, because I'd really like to know. I'd like a fucking clue of what goes on in that shit-for-brains head of yours. I don't understand why I ever thought you were a smart man, because you clearly are one of the stupidest motherfuckers I've ever known. I told you once before, and you better listen to me this time. You don't die on my fucking watch," he snarled, baring his teeth at Bear in a terrible grimace.

Silence rang in the room for a few seconds, and then Mason said, "Well?"

"I didn't want anyone dead because of me." Bear closed his eyes as he spoke, his voice stark and raw. "I looked at the numbers, ran the plan in my head, didn't see a way to come out with everyone. I'd rather die than betray a brother, and having you follow me into that compound felt worse than a betrayal."

"You thick motherfucker," Mason roared, throwing up his hands. "I need you to track this. You listening? If that was Ruby, would you have gone in there at Slate's back?"

"In a heartbeat," Bear said quickly.

"If Slate had gone in alone and died, you doin' nothing to help, would you have been able to look his woman in the face?" This was asked more quietly, the words hanging in the air between them as if visible.

"No," he responded carefully, shaking his head and drawing the word out on an exhale.

"And if Slate and Ruby died, and you could have been but weren't there to help out your brother, your family...would you have been able to live with that?" Mason pressed, arms crossed tightly across his chest, beanie pulled down over his head.

"No," Bear whispered.

Mason's voice softened, "Then why would you believe less of your brothers, expect less from us than from yourself? This isn't a goddamn party, man. We don't hang out only to ride, to fucking drink and shit—this club is our family. You are our blood, and we need you among us. If you died, if you and Eddie went to ground, you'd leave a fuckton of hurt behind, brother. You tracking?"

Bear nodded from where he lay in the bed, and said, "Yeah, I'm tracking, Prez."

"We fucking need you among us, Bear. Your family—blood, club, kids, woman—need you among us. You got me?" Mason uncrossed his arms, tucking his thumbs into his belt.

"I got you, Prez. I'm tracking." Bear's eyes flicked to the door as it pushed open, revealing his mother's worried face, followed by a familiar, mustached Tug.

His mom came over to sit on the edge of the bed, reaching out a hand to stroke down his face. "Oh, son. It's good to see you awake, finally." She smiled, her lips quivering as she leaned in, laying her head on his chest for a moment. "I'm so glad you're okay, Robby."

She sat up as Tug stepped over, putting a hand on her shoulder and supporting her as she casually leaned into him. He gently stroked up and down her back, her face gradually losing the tense and fearful look it had carried upon entering the room. She turned her head and saw

Mason. With a smile, she greeted him. “Mason, good to see you. Even if it is under trying circumstances.”

“Maggie,” Mason responded, the corners of his mouth tipping up in a small grin. “Your boy is looking better. I think he’s finally getting a clue too.”

Tug snorted and laughed. “About damn time.”

***

He carefully walked up the hallway towards the kitchen; Bear refused to admit it was more of a shuffle than a stroll, but he was at least motoring under his own control today. He stopped short, staring at the walls. Looking back and forth, side to side, he marveled at the difference the pictures made in how the space felt. For the first time, this felt like home to him. Eddie had covered the walls with duplicates of the pictures in her house, creating constellations of mentors and kids, where smiles and nervous looks sat side-by-side.

He found many faces he knew: Tug, of course, with the doubled circles of older pictures from California, as well as the ones more recent, from their new hometown. Bingo and the many nephews and nieces he’d taken on after his sister lost her fight with cancer. Slate and Chase, himself, and his kids. *His kids.* That thought still took his breath away.

“Hey, baby,” he heard as her arm slipped around his waist. “Is it okay?” She sounded unsure of herself, as if she was afraid she’d taken liberties he’d not expected.

“Better than okay,” he murmured, kissing the side of her head. “I love it. This is perfect, our kids on the walls of our home.”

He felt her beginning to pull away, saying, “About that—“ and he interrupted her with a kiss, capturing her lips with his, gently and thoroughly exploring her mouth, nipping at her lips with his teeth.

"Move in with us," he whispered, his lips still touching hers, a reminder of their first kiss. "Move in with me. I love you, sweetheart. My heart. Eddie, marry me."

She drew in a breath, pulling air across his lips and into her mouth. He felt her smile against him and kissed her gently, his tongue sweeping and tangling with hers, the fierce yet soft touches dragging gasps from them both. Slowing, he nibbled at her lips, dragging the tip of his tongue across her lush bottom lip, now kiss-swollen and sensitive. Dropping soft kisses at the corners of her mouth, he asked her again, "Marry me, Eddie." She nodded, and he heard her swallow hard. "I need to hear you, sweetheart," he ground out, his throat choking his words as his arms tightened around her.

"I love you," she responded, and he clenched his eyes hard, waiting, but she stopped there. *Oh, God, she was done.* She was done. it shouldn't be a surprise she was done with him. He'd failed her, so she was done. He'd read her signals wrong or something, tried to push too fast, too far.

"My heart." He pressed a regretful kiss into the side of her head. "I wish I could turn back the clock. Take it back. Never leave, never walk away. I fucked us up, didn't I? Not a question, sweetheart. I'm so sorry."

Eyes still closed, he shifted, releasing her and allowing his arms to fall down by his sides. "If you need—" he started, but she interrupted him.

The anger in her voice shocked him, his eyes flying open wide. "No! You do not get to do that, Rob Crew. You don't get to push me away again, because of something you think or imagine. Look at me, Bear."

Her eyes met his and his heart clenched at the fierce love he saw in her face. "I said *I love you*, Bear. I didn't say 'if', or 'but', or 'and', because that's all I need. Your love. You. I need you. I love you; *yes I'll move in*. I love you; *yes, I'll marry you*. I love you; *yes to anything, baby*. I love you."

He reached out, gently wrapping his arms around her again, tugging and pulling her into him tightly, no space between them. Bending down, he rested his forehead against her shoulder, feeling her small hands stroking up and down his back, gentling him. He didn't even know when he started crying, but he heard the concern in her voice when she asked him, "Baby, are you okay?"

Shuddering and shaking with the wave of emotions that swept across him, he nodded, keeping his face pressed into the crook where her neck met her shoulder, hiding his face from the world. They stood that way for a long time, minutes passing, and still her hands and arms tirelessly soothed him, accepting his pain and giving him back love and comfort.

Finally, his hoarse sobs eased and he felt her hands on his head, her fingers stroking through his hair, keeping him anchored, tucked into her. Humming a wordless tune, she gently kissed his shoulder and neck, softly calling his name.

He moved his head, lifting and resting his cheek on top of her head, shifting his hold on her body. She let him guide their separation, letting go of him seemingly fingertip by grudging fingertip. He felt relieved by the release of emotion...freed, somehow.

She cupped his face in her hands. "You ready to eat, baby?" she asked him, and the corners of his mouth tipped up, amused at her selection of words.

"Always, sweetheart. Always hungry for you," he murmured to her, and softly kissed her lips.

"You know what I mean, Bear," she chided him with a grin.

"I know what I mean." He looked at her slyly. "And I mean what I say."

"So…moving in?" she asked him, and his breathing stopped for a second until he remembered how to pull air in and out of his lungs.

"Today," he stated, threatening to overwhelm her if she didn't accede to his demand. "We get your things today, sweetheart."

"Okay," was all she said, tugging him forward with their linked hands.

41 - Moving forward

He looked across the living room, enjoying the sense of peace that pervaded his house. His family sat around as they did most nights, Lucia studying for one of her classes, Rafe playing a video game, the two younger boys arguing over whose turn it was to take out the trash, and Eddie working on her laptop. Bear turned back to his screen, looking over the custom paint job he was sketching out.

Done in light, bright colors, it depicted a brilliant sunrise in a candy land, the sun huge, covering over half the tank. Silhouetted against the sun, figures stood facing the sunrise, arms interlocked. Two adults bracketed four stair-stepped kids, keeping their family safe between them. Their shadows stretching out behind them were cavorting and dancing independently of the figures, anchored to their paired silhouette by their feet. In the sun itself, darker strokes of color hinted at two figures, one larger than the other, watching over the family in the foreground.

Pieces of heart-shaped candies littered the ground near the family, and trailed onto the back fairing, where they would be large enough to see words and names etched on them. Sugar, Love, Sweetness, Faith, Punkin, Kiss Me, Sweetheart, My Heart, and My Son were a few of the phrases he'd completed so far. Those would be sprinkled in between six bearing their names. The front fairing would have swirling clouds and eight dandelion seeds drifting in the air.

He was happy with it so far. There were additional details he wanted to add, but he thought it was going to be perfect. It would kill him to cover his existing paint job, but he knew it was time to move forward. "Eddie," he called, waiting for her to glance his way, "come look when you get to a stopping point."

She surprised him by hopping up right away, setting aside her laptop and sauntering over towards him. He pulled her into his lap, sighing when she covered his hands with hers, where they wrapped around her stomach. She stared at his screen for a moment, then reached out a fingertip to trace the figures embedded in the sunrise. "Andrea and Ashley?" she asked.

He put his head alongside hers and nodded, asking, "Yeah, is it okay?"

"Oh, baby, this is so beautiful." She turned her head, softly kissing his cheek. "I love everything you create, but this feels like coming full circle," she sighed, reaching out to run her finger along the silhouettes, whispering, "Our family."

He turned his head, nuzzling into her hair. "My heart. Eddie, there's room to add another, if you still want. I found out not long ago that families aren't determined by size, that love is elastic—it stretches to cover as needed. So if you want to add, there's always going to be room."

She'd grown still as he spoke, and he pulled back, watching as a smile settled on her face. "Okay," she said, and he left it at that.

***

"Bear," he heard called across the garage and looked up from his workbench, where he was prepping for the paint job. He saw Red walking towards him with a box in his arms. "Mason wants you to call him."

Setting the box down near Bear's feet, Red walked back towards the office. Frowning, Bear pulled out his phone and dialed Mason while he used his pocket knife to slice through the tape holding the box closed. "Open the fucking box," he heard over the phone and grinned. Prez was always brief and to the point.

"On it, boss," he responded, and then frowned. There was a tank and fairing set in the box, primed and ready to paint. "Got a job for me?" he questioned, pulling them out and noting casually they were the same model his bike used.

"Don't paint over your angels, Bear," Mason said, and his breath caught in his chest. He couldn't respond and his friend seemed to know that. "Use the blanks, man. Eddie's got a plan. Give your angels to her; you got me?"

"I got you," he choked out and looked at the tank still resting on the bike as Mason disconnected the call.

***

"Would you come down here already?" Eddie was impatient as she called up to the second floor, and her tone indicated it. Bear strolled down the staircase, his sock feet making no noise as he snuck up behind her where she was facing into the living room. So intent was he on Eddie that he didn't see the other people in the room until after he'd goosed her in the ribs, making her jump and yelp, scolding him with a high-pitched, "Bear, knock it off!" Pulling her into his arms, her back to his chest, he looked around the room, seeing they had a number of guests.

Slate, Tug, his mother, Mason, and Duck were standing around the edges of the room, grinning at their antics. Releasing his hold on her, he made the rounds, slapping backs with the men and gently hugging his mom. Turning back to Eddie, his eyes looked up, his gaze fixing on the wall behind her and he froze in place.

His gaze swept to Eddie, noting the nervous look on her face before he returned to staring at the wall. *My angels*, he thought, and the corners of his mouth turned up into a small smile. Eddie had mounted his old tank on the wall, bracketed by the fairings. It was positioned over the arched entry to the room, prominently displayed.

He felt a hand on his arm, turning to see his mother's eyes welling with tears. Patting her hand silently, he looked back up at Eddie and sighed. That woman was going to chew a hole in her lip if she didn't stop it. He strode across the room, sweeping her into his arms and kissing her deeply, infusing his feelings of joy, need, and love into the movement of his lips on hers.

When they separated, she smiled up at him, asking, "So it's okay?"

"Better than okay. It's perfect, sweetheart," he replied, kissing her again.

42 - From here

Bear strode into the clubhouse, looking around at the familiar faces he saw in the main room. Walking over to the bar, he asked the prospect behind it where Slate was, and was pointed towards the office. Knocking on the door, he waited for a response before opening it and stepping inside.

Slate stood, walking around the desk to grab his wrist, pulling him into a one-armed hug. "Bear," he said, pleased surprise evident in his voice. "What brings you in?"

He took a deep breath, releasing his grip and sitting heavily in the chair facing the desk. "Do you remember the day we left Norfolk, headed this way?"

Slate sat, his brows furrowing into a frown. "Which one? As I recall, there were two different departures. We had that first run up here, your introduction to the road and the club. Then we had moving day."

"Moving day," he agreed, nodding.

"Yeah, I remember it. What's up?" Slate still looked puzzled.

"I told you about the tape. My daughter's dance recital? When we got to Chicago, you told me give it to Myron, and I did." He took in another deep breath.

"Yeah?" Slate cocked his head. "Did he hook you up?"

"I don't know. I told him I'd ask for it when I was ready, but the timing never seemed right...so I never asked." Bear wiped sweat off his forehead with the back of his hand, suddenly nervous.

Looking at him with dawning understanding, Slate traced the insides of his front teeth with his tongue, then asked, "You ready?"

"Yeah," he blew out a hard breath, "I think I am."

After making a quick call, Slate worked on the computer for a minute, then handed a thumb drive to Bear. "Click on that file, and you'll be able to view the video on any computer. Myron doesn't mess around," he chuckled. Sobering, he evidently noted Bear's shaking hands, because he asked, "You want somebody with you? Want me to call Eddie?"

"I'll call her," he responded quickly, then paused. "But...can we watch it here? Would you...I mean, would you want—"

Slate interrupted him, his voice warm with affection. "I'd be fucking honored, brother. Get Eddie over here. I can't wait to see your girl."

Twenty minutes later, Eddie swept into the office, focusing on Bear where he sat in the chair behind the desk. Slate stood at his back, and they were both looking at the screen. She came around the desk and looked mystified when she saw only an opened window on the computer.

Bear explained, "I wanted to wait for you, sweetheart." Reaching out to her, he grasped her hand, pulling her onto his lap. "I'm ready," he said, closing his eyes.

He heard white noise from the computer speakers, and then Andrea's voice as she whispered a quiet 'Thank you' to someone sitting close to her. His eyes opened and he focused on the screen, which was slowly scanning along a line of little girls dressed in pink and purple tutus over black leotards. There was one little girl in the middle of the line wearing a white tutu over a pink and black leotard. The camera stopped on her, focusing in, bringing her little face into sharp relief on the screen.

Her mouth was moving; she was talking to the instructor, who walked across the stage, bringing her a microphone. There was a burst of static, then her voice boomed from the speakers in the theater, making her cringe and blush, her eyes wide in her face. At an encouraging movement from the instructor, she lifted the microphone back to her mouth.

"I'm Ash Crew, and my daddy is in the Navy," she began, stopping in surprise when the audience broke out into loud applause. The grin on her face grew and she lifted the microphone back up, saying, "I know! I'm so proud of him too."

The applause died down and silence filled the speakers. He thought for a minute the sound system had failed on the computer, but then her voice swelled again and he focused on the screen, not wanting to miss a moment. "He's never gotten to see me dance, so Mommy is sending him a tape of tonight. I wanted him to see my wings." She turned around and he saw a small pair of wire and gossamer wings attached to the back of her costume. "Daddy, they're sparkly too," she whispered, looking over her shoulder at the camera, awe evident in her voice.

Turning back, she settled into her place again. "I wanted to tell him I love him. Exes and ohs, Daddy, big juicy ones. Think of me when you sleep. We're all gonna be just fine, Daddy. We love you, and Mommy said to tell you that you can do this standing on your head." She grinned, looking up at the instructor. "He's real smart," she said, proudly. "He'll figure it out."

Eddie's fingers were clenching his tightly, and he felt Slate's hand resting on his shoulder. As Ash handed the microphone off, there was a noise in the room, and he glanced over to see his mom and Tug standing near the door.

Music flooded the speakers, and he looked back to the screen in time to see his daughter standing in the middle of the stage. Still and quiet, she faced the camera confidently, her head up, back arched, hands curled in the air above her head. Before her cue sounded, releasing her into the dance, he saw her mouth move and read the words on her lips. "We got this, Daddy. Staying power. For always." She smiled, then her features smoothed, becoming impassive. She moved elegantly across the stage, her grace and talent so vastly exceeding the other seven-year-old girls that even if he hadn't been her father, he could have looked at no one except her.

The music came to an end, and her figure was poised in the middle of the stage again. She had returned to where the dance had begun, coming full circle. The camera jiggled as it moved up, rising with the rest of the audience as they applauded the dancers. It stayed on her until, after an unmeasured period of time, she broke character, once again becoming a bubbly seven-year-old girl, giddy with her first solo dance at a recital, hugging her friends and lining up with them to take their bow. As the line swept down and then up, acknowledging the acclaim of the audience, the camera focused in on her face again, capturing her looking directly at the camera, eyes sparkling, nose wrinkled, joy evident on her face before the picture jerked, shifting to show Andrea's face as she held the camera at arm's length. "Isn't she fabulous, Rob? We love you, baby. You be safe, and we'll see you."

He vaguely heard his mother crying, but his eyes were focused on the screen where Andrea was in the forefront, and Ash could still be seen on the stage behind her. He felt a hand on his face and swung his head to smile at Eddie. Slate's tightly closed fist pounded his shoulder twice and withdrew. He heard the office door close and assumed his friend had left them in discretion.

Eddie was looking in his face with a worried expression, and he laughed, hugging her tightly. "What's wrong, sweetheart?"

"Are you okay? That had to be hard to watch, ba—Bear." She caught herself before she called him the same thing Andrea had on the tape, and he could see her struggling with some internal emotion.

"Yeah, I'm okay. She was wonderful, wasn't she? So good. I wish I could have told her how good she was," he said, hugging Eddie around the waist, resting his head on her shoulder.

"She was. That speech before, that was so sweet. 'Exes and ohs' must have been a thing with you guys?" Eddie asked, resting her cheek on top of his head.

"Yeah," he said fondly. "She liked to give me big, juicy ones, the more spit, the better." He laughed a little. "She was something else." He reached up, cupping the back of Eddie's head, pulling her in for a soft kiss. "I'm glad you were here. I love you, Eddie."

He felt familiar arms surrounding him, and his mother's head rested on his other shoulder. She squeezed tightly, and he saw her hand clutching at Eddie's, connecting them all with her love. "Robby," she whispered, "how wonderful you have this beautiful memory. Thank you for sharing it with us, honey. Love you."

He tipped his head, resting it against hers, saying, "Me too, Mom. Love you, too."

***

"Jase," called DeeDee, "Ruby left a bag. Can you bring it to me?"

He walked into the room carrying a large diaper bag and set it down on the couch next to her, where she had one baby cradled on her lap. The other infant, dressed in pink, was lying on the floor on a blanket, and he settled his length down next to her. "Hey there, Danielle. Little Dani, Jase's Dani. Whatcha doin', pretty princess?" he crooned down to her, and she gazed up at him with an absorbed, serious look on her face. "Look at how smart she is," he told DeeDee proudly. "She knows exactly what I'm saying to her."

DeeDee laughed, teasing Allen's mouth with the pacifier she'd found in the bag. Drawing a smile out of the baby boy, she pretended to put the pacifier in her own mouth, then when he frowned, threatening to cry, she quickly presented it to him again. "Sorry to disappoint, but she's reacting to the tone of voice, not what you're saying."

He scoffed, shaking his head down at the little girl, telling her, "Don't you listen to GeeGee. She doesn't know you like I do. She's jealous of your highly superior intellect, your smarts," he sniffed the air, "your farts. She's just plain jealous. Jealous GeeGee."

Bringing Allen to her shoulder, DeeDee softly stroked his back, bouncing him slowly and gently in her arms. She loved babysitting the twins, and Jason seemed to enjoy it as well, volunteering to sit with her every time. Watching him with little Dani, she smiled sadly. He was so good with the babies, never afraid of handling them, and didn't balk at a messy diaper either. He should have kids of his own to dandle and play with. She knew he'd argue with her about it like he always did, but she wondered again if she should put a stop to whatever this was they were doing...had been doing, and let him find someone more suited.

He looked up at her, his eyes shining as he reached out for Dani, gathering the little girl to his chest and mimicking her movements with Allen. "After we get the kiddos to sleep, it's playtime for the adults," he promised her, a lustful smile on his face. "I think I missed an inch of your body last night, so I'll have to cover everything again, make sure I don't leave anything untouched this time. It's very important I cover everything...with me. I might even say it's critical."

She smiled at him, rocking the baby, her heart beating faster as she anticipated playtime with him.

***

Ben Jones shook his head. "No. Watch my fingers. You can do this, Chase," Slate's little brother said, demonstrating the chord one more time. Chase attempted the combination again and Ben was more approving. "Yeah, yeah. That's much better. Do that again, okay? You got this." Ben was an accomplished musician and lyricist, having been front man for a band for several years before drug and alcohol abuse sidelined his career.

Bear watched them from across the main room of the clubhouse. He'd loaned Chase an older Fender he had. The kid was treating it with a great deal of respect, struggling to learn enough in a day so he could keep up with Ben when he played in the bar at Marie's tonight. He had to hand it to Mason's son; the kid was seriously stubborn. Snorting a laugh, he thought to himself, *Much like his old man. That apple didn't fall far from the tree, for sure.*

Ben hummed and then sang to the accompaniment of the two guitars, the one unsteadily playing a simple tune, while the other ripped through several melody changes, anchoring the song. Bear pulled his Angelus from behind the bar, walking over to sit near the boys. He listened to the song, not recognizing it, but learning the chords and intervals needed to support the lead and rhythm. Closing his eyes, he put his fingers to the strings and frets, tentatively strumming, sliding into the song behind Ben, supporting and backing up his playing.

Once through the stanzas and chorus, he became more confident, competing with Ben's guitar for the lead part. They ended that song, and before he could say anything, Ben swung into Vanessa Carleton's *Unsung*, a fast paced song with sarcasm-laced lyrics. Chase followed them as best he could, focusing on Ben's hands as he shifted into the rhythm guitar role. Once done with that song, Ben started with a more complicated Radical Face song, *Winter is Coming*, and Bear laughed aloud.

He'd learned this one with Dennis, now playing it with Ben and Chase he easily provided the rhythm guitar part as he pounded on the box of his guitar, building and holding the song together while Ben's clear voice sang them through the middle eight. Winding down into the outro, he caught Ben's eyes and grinned, realizing he'd really missed performing with another musician like this, playing on their individual strengths to build something larger than they could create alone.

The song finished and he saw Chase shaking his hands out, rubbing the tips of his fingers. "Stick with it and you'll build calluses soon," he told him, and Chase nodded at him. Turning to Ben, he asked, "When are you and Occupy Yourself going back on tour?"

"Soon," was all the answer he got, but he saw the frustrated look on the young man's face. He and the band had been off the road for a long time now, but Slate was still unwilling to risk his brother's hard-won sobriety to support something that was sure to be full of relapse triggers. Without Slate's backing, Ben couldn't afford to get the band back playing anywhere but local venues. At least they had a stage as often as they wanted at Marie's, where the patrons were enthusiastic fans.

Impulsively, he asked, "Mind if I sit in on a couple of songs tonight?" Ben had offered many times, but Bear had always turned him down. Tonight, it felt right for some reason, and he waited anxiously for the reply.

"Fucking A, man. That would be awesome," came the response, along with the boy's patented full-on, rock star smile.

"All right," he said, standing with the guitar in his hand. "I'll see you there."

***

Mason looked down at his little namesake, a content expression on his face. He lifted his gaze from where he sat in the window seat, staring out across the yard towards his house. He'd seen Mica sitting here so often over the years, in good times and bad. Startled by a touch on his shoulder, he looked up into a face similar to hers, but with its own brand of obstinate willfulness blazing in her brown eyes. Reaching back with one hand, he patted her on the leg, smiling.

"Hey, Molly," he said. "How you settlin' in, sweetie?" He looked past her towards the door. "Where's Tomas?"

Mica's little sister ran her hand over his short hair, leaning down to kiss the top of his head, and then peered over his shoulder at the boy he was holding, Jonathan Mason Rupert. "J.J. is on his way in, and Tomas is getting a ride with him," she said fondly, her Texas drawl clearly identifiable. "That man spoils the stuffin' out of the boy."

"That boy is worth spoiling," Mason said, cupping the back of Jon's head as he moved him, settling the sprawled limbs more comfortably across his lap. "Mica and Daniel won't be back until late. I told her it would be easier on everyone if Jon spent the night with you. Hope you don't mind."

"Nope, I don't mind. It actually is easier than trying to move these deadweights at night. I swear the boys triple in weight when they sleep." She laughed, turning as they heard a noise in the kitchen.

"Fas...fas," crowed the little boy perched on the legs of the man maneuvering the wheelchair into the room.

"Yeah, Tomas, we're going fast," J.J. Rupert said, with an ear-to-ear smile for Molly. "Baby," he breathed. "I missed you."

"Silly man," she told him. "We were in the same car for three hours. I've been out of your sight for less than five minutes. You can't have missed me that much."

"Five minutes too long, baby," he said, pulling to a stop beside her, wrapping one gloved hand possessively around her leg. "Mason," he greeted his friend. "Jon behaving today?" He lifted Tomas from his lap, holding him by the hand until he was sure the boy was stable, grinning at his disappointment voiced at being placed on the floor.

"No moah fas?" Tomas' bottom lip pouted until he saw a large, brightly wrapped package on the floor nearby. "Oh...pwitty," he crooned, walking towards it.

Mason said, "All for you, Tomas, my man. Can you open it?" The adults laughed as he plopped down next to the package, which was nearly as big as he was.

"Mason," Molly scolded, "you have got to stop bringing him presents every time you come visit. You live next door, for God's sake. You'll go broke in months if you keep this up." She walked over and squatted down next to her son, unobtrusively helping him unwrap the gift, opening the box to slide out something that looked like a turtle shell.

J.J. laughed. "Mason, man, you know the turtle thing is only a TV show, right?"

"It's a bilibo. Won't turn him into a ninja, I promise." Mason laughed. "Website said it's good for creative play, and I saw kids playing with them at the store. There's no wrong way to do it. Look at him; he's got the idea." They watched the little boy playing with the toy for a few minutes, first turning it into a stool to sit on, then a basket to gather toys with, finally a bowl to sit inside, rocking wildly back and forth.

On his lap, Jon was restlessly squirming, scrunching his face up as he stretched his limbs out. Molly reached out for him, and Mason handed him up reluctantly. He didn't get as much time with the boy as he'd like. He'd missed out on Chase's entire childhood, and as a result, he was loving seeing Tomas and Jon as they grew, fascinated by watching them as they reached milestone after milestone.

Molly stood, bouncing the boy gently, humming a wordless song. "I'm going to lay him down; he needs a longer nap." She leaned over, kissing the top of first Mason's head, then J.J.'s. "Love all my boys," she whispered, squatting down next to Tomas and kissing the top of his head too.

Mason watched her walk away, and the smile slowly faded from his face. He looked around at the home, which was gradually losing Mica's touch and personality. He'd spent countless hours here over the years, talking to her, teasing her, comforting her. When J.J. spoke, it almost made him jump, so lost was he in memory.

"I don't think I ever thanked you," Daniel's brother said, fingers fiddling nervously with the wheel grips on his chair. "Danny is the richer for your sacrifice, Mason."

Mason scoffed. "Ain't no sacrifice to do the right thing. She loves him, man. I'd be a shit friend if I got in the way of that."

"Whatever," J.J. said. "She's good for him."

"He's good for her," Mason argued, grinning.

"Who was that pretty gal I saw you with at Slate's wedding? I haven't seen you to talk to since then, but meant to ask." J.J. moved his chair near where Tomas was playing, reaching down to tousle the boy's hair.

"Willa," Mason said quietly.

"Mica said she liked her," J.J. offered, looking up at Mason with a sly grin. "Said she might be a keeper."

Smiling wryly, Mason stood, crossing his arms across his chest and looking outside for a long minute. "Might be," he finally agreed. "Hey, I gotta scoot, man. Tell Molly bye for me."

Walking into his house, just across the alleyway from where Molly was living in Mica's home, he went into the living room and settled on one of the couches there, tipping his head back to stare at the ceiling. He'd seen Mica talking to Willa at the wedding, and positioned himself close enough to overhear a portion of their conversation. He smiled, remembering how Mica had unsubtly interrogated the woman he'd brought to the event.

"You're from Fort Wayne?" Mica asked, sipping from the open bottle of water in her hand.

"Yes, I've lived here most of my life," Willa answered. "I work in the school system here."

"Are you a teacher?" Mica looked out across the field, eyes searching until she found Daniel standing in a group and she smiled at him.

"Not a chance." Willa laughed. "Kids are mostly terrors. I do IT for the district. Maintain the existing infrastructure, influence new purchases, investigate adaptive technology aids for special needs kids, wheel the A/V cart down the hall...all the fun stuff. I sit at the cool kids table at lunch too."

Mica smiled at her. "I do programming. PHP, HTML, a little JavaScript, some jQuery." She pointed at a small, blonde woman standing nearby holding the hand of a much taller, dark-skinned woman. "Me and Jess have worked together since college. She's the wiz kid. I've never been able to throw a development project at her that she couldn't figure out." Jess daubed something that looked like jelly on the woman's nose, laughing and rising on her toes to lick it off. "She might not look like it right now, but she's hella smart." They both laughed.

Mica nodded towards her youngest brother-in-law running in circles and swoops across the field. "See the crazy man running? He's my husband's brother Dickie. That's my nephew Tomas on his shoulders." Looking across again, she pointed. "The man yelling at Dickie from over there, getting his hair pulled by the little one? That's my husband Daniel." She laughed. "Looks like Jon's having a good time."

"Jon?" Willa questioned, tipping her head to one side.

"Jonathan Mason," Mica turned to face her, "my son."

Willa breathed, "Mason."

"Yeah. That man is something special to me. He's special to a whole bunch of people, but I claim first place in the line. I've known him for a lot of years; there is no better man. He and my husband are the two

most important men in my life. I love him." Mica was staring into Willa's face, and the fierce look on her features took Mason's breath away. "And I would kill anyone who hurt him. He deserves to find happiness. He's always the one showing up for other people, fixing their messes, healing their wounds. He very much deserves to have someone to do that for him."

"He's a nice guy," Willa agreed. "I was surprised when he called me and asked me to ride up with him. We'd only met the once, months ago, then when he didn't call, I'd kinda given up on hearing from him." She shrugged, looking embarrassed. "I thought it was meant to be a booty call, but then I found out he booked us into separate rooms. I would've—" Her eyes dropped to the ground and a blush found its way to her face as she stopped talking.

"Willa, his invite means something. But you need to remember—I. Would. Kill. Anyone. Who. Hurt. Him," Mica repeated herself, enunciating each word carefully and with emphasis. "He doesn't date, so the fact you're here with him means something. He invited you here to be with him at an event where he would be surrounded by his friends. People he considers his family. It means something. Him giving you space...that means something too."

Willa's chin tipped up, and she nervously pressed her lips into a thin line. "I hope so," she said.

Mica reached out, gripping her hand and shaking it gently. "It does."

Mason opened his eyes, smiling.

***

She stood quietly, looking at herself in the bathroom mirror. Her eyes took in her wild hair, pinned carelessly on top of her head, tendrils loose around her face, and her grey eyes partially hidden by the glasses perched on her nose. She reached up, cupping her breasts through her shirt with a considering look on her face.

Wrapping her arms around her stomach, she smiled softly and inched up her shirt hem with her fingers. Exposing her belly, she dragged fingertips across it, side-to-side and back again. The door opened behind her, the entryway filled with an anxious male presence.

“Well?” he demanded.

Her eyes met his in the mirror, and she smiled.

THE END (of this story)

THANK YOU FOR READING *Bear*!

This is Book #3 in a series. *Bear* is the result of a chance meeting with a Navy man (/wave Rob) on the Appalachian Trail in Georgia, along with a single image burned into my brain of a man looking down at the tank of his bike with a wistful expression on his face. This story is the blending of those two elements, and I fell in love with the characters as they danced their way through my dreams. You can learn more about Mason, Jase, and DeeDee's stories in Book #4 of the Rebel Wayfarers MC book series, *Jase*, available May 2015.

If you enjoyed this book, please leave a review on Amazon or Goodreads.

Goodreads.com/book/show/23293333-bear

If you didn't enjoy it, please let me know! How, you ask? Website...social – I'm easily found!

MLdeMora.com
Facebook.com/mldemora
Twitter.com/MariaLisadeMora
Pinterest.com/mldemora/

REBEL WAYFARERS MC BOOK SERIES

While these books are all intended to be readable as standalone stories, there is a sequence if you are reading the series:

Mica – Book #1: Amazon.com/dp/B00L7H0W9O/
Slate – Book #2: Amazon.com/dp/B00M4TEDCQ/
Bear – Book #3: Amazon.com/dp/B00O3X2OFE/
Jase – Book #4: (May 2015)
Mason – Book #5: (December 2015)

BEAR PLAYLISTS

I put together YouTube playlists of music both mentioned in the book, and used during writing and editing. Want a peek into the mind of me? Be sure of your decision, it's not always normal here!

Bear's playlist: bit.ly/bear-playlist
Eddie's playlist: bit.ly/bear-eddie-playlist

ABOUT THE AUTHOR

Raised in the south, MariaLisa deMora learned about the magic of books at an early age. Every summer, she would spend hours in the Upshur County library, devouring stacks of books in every genre. She still reads voraciously, and always has a few books going in paperback, hardback, on devices! On music, she says, "I love music of nearly any kind—jazz, country, rock, alt rock, metal, classical, bluegrass, rap, gangstergrass, hip hop—you name the type, I probably listen to it.

"I can often be seen dancing through the house in the early mornings. But what I really, REALLY love is live music. My favorite way to experience live music is seeing bands in small, dive bars [read: small, intimate venues]. If said bar [venue] has a good selection of premium tequila, then that's a definite plus! Oh, and since I'm a hand gal, drummers are my thing—yeah, Paul and Alex—you know who you are!"

Made in the USA
San Bernardino, CA
14 July 2017